Lead Me
Knot

Copyright © 2025 by S.L. Scott

All Rights Reserved. Except as permitted under the U.S. Copyright Act of 1976, no part of this publication may be reproduced, distributed or transmitted in any form or by any means, or stored in a database or retrieval system, without the written permission of the author. This is a work of fiction. Names, characters, places, and incidents are either a product of the author's imagination or are used fictitiously. Any resemblance to actual people living or dead, events or locales is entirely coincidental. Published in the United States of America. ISBN: 978-1-962626-44-6

IT IS AGAINST THE LAW AND COPYRIGHT TO USE ANY PART OF THIS BOOK TO TRAIN AI OR TO UPLOAD TO AI SYSTEMS OR SOFTWARE.

FOLLOW ME

To keep up to date with her writing and more, visit S.L. Scott's website: **www.slscottauthor.com**

To receive the newsletter about all of her publishing adventures, free books, giveaways, steals and more:

https://geni.us/SLScottNL

Follow me on TikTok: https://geni.us/SLTikTok
Follow on IG: https://geni.us/IGSLS
Follow on Bookbub: https://geni.us/SLScottBB

ALSO BY S.L. SCOTT

To keep up to date with her writing and more, visit her website: www.slscottauthor.com

To receive the scoop about all of her publishing adventures, free books, giveaways, steals and more:

Visit www.slscottauthor.com

Join S.L.'s Facebook group: S.L. Scott Books

Read the Bestselling Book that's been called **"The Most Romantic Book Ever"** by readers and have them raving. We Were Once is now available and FREE in Kindle Unlimited.

We Were Once

You do not want to miss the international sensation, **Best I Ever Had**. This book has won readers over with its emotion and soul deep love. **Best I Ever Had** is now available in ebook, audio, and paperback, and is Free in Kindle Unlimited.

Best I Ever Had

Audiobooks on Audible - CLICK HERE

Peachtree Pass Series (Stand-alones)

Long Time Coming

Lead Me Knot

Small Town Frenzy

The Westcott Series (Stand-alones)

Swear on My Life

Never Saw You Coming

<u>Forgot to Say Goodbye</u>

<u>When I Had You</u>

Never Have I Ever - Faris Family Series

Speak of the Devil - Faris Family Series

Hard to Resist Series (Stand-Alones)

<u>The Resistance</u>

<u>The Reckoning</u>

<u>The Redemption</u>

<u>The Revolution</u>

<u>The Rebellion</u>

The Crow Brothers (Stand-Alones)

Spark

Tulsa

Rivers

Ridge

The Crow Brothers Box Set

DARE - A Rock Star Hero (Stand-Alone)

New York Love Stories (Stand-Alones)

Never Got Over You

The One I Want

Crazy in Love

Head Over Feels

It Started with a Kiss

The Everest Brothers (Stand-Alones)

Everest - Ethan Everest

Bad Reputation - Hutton Everest

Force of Nature - Bennett Everest

The Everest Brothers Box Set

The Kingwood Series

SAVAGE

SAVIOR

SACRED

FINDING SOLACE

The Kingwood Series Box Set

Playboy in Paradise Series

Falling for the Playboy

Redeeming the Playboy

Loving the Playboy

Playboy in Paradise Box Set

Stand-Alone Books

Best I Ever Had

We Were Once

Along Came Charlie

Missing Grace

Finding Solace

Until I Met You

Drunk on Love

Lost in Translation

Sleeping with Mr. Sexy

Morning Glory

LEAD ME KNOT

S.L. SCOTT

1

Baylor Greene

"THERE ARE WORSE PLACES to be stuck in than in Dallas." I walk the length of the windows lining gate 16. "The storm will pass. It's only a delay."

I can hear a heavy sigh leave my sister's mouth on the other end of the call. "It's a delay that has you arriving in the middle of the night, Baylor," she says. "And if it's still storming when you land, driving out to Peachtree Pass won't be safe."

"An hour and a half."

"On a day with perfect weather. Two, even three hours on a bad night."

"Look, you might still see me as your brother, Pri—*Christine* . . ." Some habits die hard. I'm not sure I'll ever get used to calling her by the name my mom gave her instead of the nickname I've taunted her with her whole life. But I promised her and my best friend—my traitorous best friend who fell on his ass in love with my little sister—I'd give it the ole college try. "I'm a thirty-three-year-old man who takes care of himself all on his own in New York. I'll be fine driving in a little rain." I stop and stare at the jetway jutting from the building, not tethered to a plane.

She laughs. It's light but good to hear over the concern in her tone a minute prior. "I know you can take care of yourself. I'm used to worrying."

"Take the night off, sis, and get some rest since I don't know how long I'll be delayed. I can even sleep over at Dad's house instead. That way, I won't bother you and the kids or Tagger when I'm sneaking in."

"Dad needs his rest to recover from the knee surgery. And knowing him, he'll hear a sound and be jumping out of bed to investigate the situation."

Rubbing my temple, I lower my head. "Yeah, you're right. There's no sneaking around with those creaky floors. I'm not sure how to solve the issue."

Another sigh follows a pause in her words, but then she says, "You're only here until Monday, and you promised Beckett and Daisy you'd be here by morning—"

I start pacing again. She's right. I promised my nephew and niece I'd be there before they opened their eyes. "The Pass needs to get with the times. We need some modern conveniences like a hotel or, hell, even a room to rent out, but I promise I'll be there, even if I have to sleep on the front porch swing—"

"That's it." Excitement streams through her tone.

"What's it? The porch swing? I was kind of kidding." Remembering a certain hideaway my sister once made, I laugh. "There's always the barn—"

"No. And no to the barn. But there is Lauralee."

Although her best friend's name conjures a few good shared memories like my sister's wedding reception, I have no idea where she's going with this. "I'm going to need more, Chris. When you say there is Lauralee—?"

"She just finished the apartment above Peaches Sundries." She takes a breath, and then the words rush out. "She hasn't listed it for rent or on any short-term sites, but I know it's ready to be listed. You could stay there tonight and come out to the ranch in the morning." She tacks on, "Early."

It's not a bad idea. No tiptoeing around my sister and best friend's house trying not to wake up the littles, or ending up at the barrel end of my dad's rifle from sneaking into the house I grew up in. Both sound like good scenarios to avoid. "She won't mind? I can pay like any other renter."

"You know she won't let you, but you can offer if you want."

"Should I text her?"

"No, it's already late. I know she won't mind. Just go around to the back of the shop and take the stairs to the second floor. She's just pulled it together, so don't make a mess."

The rain hasn't let up, prompting me to glance and confirm that the flight or gate information hasn't been changed or canceled altogether for the night. Austin is still prominently displayed as if hope still rests in the sign, and there's still a chance we'll get out of Dallas at some point tonight. "How will I get inside?"

"The key is under the pot at the top of the steps."

We don't have much crime in Peachtree Pass, but thinking about that key giving any ole stranger passing through town free entrance to the apartment, or worse, to Lauralee, doesn't sit right with me. "It's great she's being safe," I reply sarcastically.

My sister laughs again. "You can mention it the next

time you see her." As the laughter dies down, she adds, "Be safe, okay, big brother?"

It wasn't storming the night our mom died, but an accident is always on the edge of my thoughts. I assume it is for my brother and sister as well. "I will be. I'll see you in the morning, okay?"

"I look forward to it."

When we hang up, the weight of all this travel drags my eyelids south, eliciting a yawn and exhaustion I can't shake. I head for the caffeine stand for a coffee and snack run, hoping to muster enough energy for the journey ahead.

I PULL up to the back of the shop downtown just before three in the morning and park near the base of the metal staircase leading to the apartment. The rain hasn't lessened, and lightning has given me a show in the distance. Thunder rattled the rental car a handful of times, causing me to slow down and drive with my hazards on a few occasions. Now, looking up at the apartment that I didn't know existed, I spy a turquoise door through the pounding rain and windshield wipers. I eye the potted plant protectively tucked under the roof overhang next to the door, marking my target.

But I wait a minute, taking in the back of the small strip building. It's the back, but it needs some attention. For tourists during the Peach Festival, there's charm in a small town when buildings look aged. This isn't chosen charm. It's looking run-down, except for the apartment. That turquoise door shone like a beacon.

I grab my carry-on from the back seat and dart from the car, locking it as I dash up the stairs. The overhang covers the pot but not me, so I quickly tilt the pot to the side, spot the silver metal key, and snatch it up.

I'm grateful at the moment, but it's fucking ridiculous she's left the place so accessible.

The door opens without a squeal, and I'm hit with the faintest scent of something good, like muffins that just came out of the oven or waking up on Sundays to the smell of pancakes and bacon. My stomach growls as I close the door and lock up behind me.

Despite knowing Lauralee most of her life, I don't know her well. She sure was pretty the last time I saw her, grown out of the awkward teenage years she had before I left for college. I once heard my mom mention she won Queen of the Peach Festival, as if that would matter to me for some reason.

Being here has me thinking about Lauralee Knot for the first time in years, probably since my best friend married my little sister. I have plenty of women to occupy my thoughts in New York and even more to bury my past in what's beneath me on any chosen night of the week. No expectations. No obligations. I have the freedom to do as I please at any time, which is more often than I should be proud to admit.

I open my case on the living room floor and grab my toiletry bag before finding the bathroom tucked inside the bedroom and to the left. I close the door but laugh, wondering why. *Habit?* Although I'm alone, I guess it's because I'm in unfamiliar territory.

I want to shower after I brush my teeth and strip off my clothes, but I'm too tired to go through the rigmarole of it. I decide that sleep is a better use of my time.

The room is too dark to find my way, so I use my phone to guide me, then set it on the nightstand. *Fucking exhausted.*

I drop onto the soft mattress, knowing I'll pass out in point two seconds after hitting the bed.

A loud clunk and someone gasping has me sitting upright. "Hello?"

There's no response, but the whoosh of air next to my head leads to something squishy knocking me sideways. "What the hell?" A feather from the pillow clings to the tip of my nose. I groan before the heel of a foot slams against my chest, sending me off the bed. My head meets the corner of the nightstand just as my ass lands on the rug. "Fuck!"

Bed springs creaking under pressure forewarns me of the impending shadow of a body ready to land wrestling-style on top of me. Lightning cracks, and the room brightens for a flash of a second, but it's enough to catch a glimpse of her staring. "Lauralee!"

Everything stills, and the silence in the room becomes deafening, but it might be the blood rushing in my ears. "Baylor?"

With my arms still up and ready to block her next stunt, the words leave my mouth in a fight against time. "It's me."

The sound of her landing on the hardwood floors is met with a rapid succession of footsteps across the room. She flips the light on, and my eyes clamp shut as I turn to the side.

"Oh my God." She asks, "Baylor, are you okay?"

"Not really," I reply, pushing up to sit. Touching the side of my head, I grumble, "That's gonna leave a mark."

"You didn't hit your eye, did you?"

"Barely missed. Fuck," I moan, a throb already taking over.

Her fingers are cool against the heat of my head, and as her body blocks the light, I finally open my eyes and look up at her. With her dark hair twisted on top of her head and held by a bright pink wrap, I get a full view of her face, causing my breath to choke in my chest. Not a lick of makeup hides her natural beauty, although concern rankles through her forehead.

Dropping to her knees in front of me, she rubs her fingers gently over the pulsing injury while her eyes stay fixed on it. When her gaze slides down to mine, she says, "I'm sorry. I thought you were an intruder."

"Guess I know why you leave the key out front. No one stands a chance against you."

Her hands fall to her lap as she rests back on her legs. "What are you doing here?" There's no anger in her tone, only curiosity, the lines of worry finally smoothing.

"Long story."

"I think we have time." She stands and offers me a hand. "But we need to get ice on your head." I don't need the help, but I accept the offer anyway so it's not wasted. She gasps, covering her mouth. "You're naked!" Oh . . . *right*. Her eyes fix on my lower half before she turns her back to me. Visoring her eyes, she squeaks, "Why are you naked?"

Naked is the least of my worries right now, not that she has much room to talk. Judging by the buds poking against her oversized T-shirt, I assume she doesn't have much on underneath either. Though I wouldn't swear an oath on it. I'd need a closer inspection for that . . . *fuck*.

What am I doing?

It's Lauralee. Not some woman coming on to me.

Maybe I have a concussion? That would explain having these thoughts about my little sister's best friend. Though there's no hiding that she's all grown, especially with that cotton fabric swinging lightly around her hips as she heads for the living room.

"I didn't know anyone would be here."

"Do you always sleep naked?" she asks, her voice traveling from the other room.

When I get up, I hit the nightstand with the bottom of my fist like it offended my family's name. "Are you taking notes or just curious?" I hear a scoff that makes me laugh as I spy my suitcase through the door. Shit. I walk to the door. I'm not shy about my body. I work hard enough on it, but I'm not looking to make this more awkward than it already is. "My clothes are in there with you."

"I'll turn around."

I stroll out of the bedroom to see her twisting a tray to crack free the ice. Bending down, I grab a clean pair of boxer briefs and slip them on. "All good," I announce. She didn't seem too bothered to see my bare body, but it's best if the entertainment ends the show on a high note.

She slowly turns around with her hands over her eyes. I can see the brown of her eyes as she peeks through the cracks of her fingers. And then she releases a heavy breath as relief washes through her, and a smile graces her face. "Hi."

"Hi," I say, stepping closer to the peninsula of a counter separating us.

"I wasn't expecting someone to break in and enter tonight."

"No one ever does."

Her lips tighten as she looks down at a sandwich bag of ice. Wrapping a dish towel around it, she says, "I don't have food here, like peas or steak, to keep the swelling down. Only ice." She reaches over the counter to rest it gently on my head. "It's going to get cold."

"I can handle it." I cover her hand with mine, thinking I'm replacing it, but she doesn't pull away.

Her eyes fall to mine again, and I see the moment something snaps her to reality, causing her to blink twice. She pulls her hand back as she shakes her head. "I should get you ibuprofen."

She's gone before I can argue otherwise. When she dips to dig through her bag on the floor, the shirt rides up just slightly. I'm an asshole so I more than check out the smooth curve of her ass. There's more than a handful to nip if we ever happen to find ourselves in a compromising position. Not that we would... *It's Lauralee.*

And I know she wants nothing to do with me, or we would have made the move back at that reception. I bend my neck to the side but straighten my spine when she stands. Rattling the bottle in her hands, she grins. "Found them." Seemingly pleased with herself, she sets the small bottle in front of me, then swings around the counter into the kitchen again.

"Thanks."

"I think you should take two." She gets me a glass of water and sets it down for me. I pop the bottle open and toss two pills in my mouth before chasing them with water. She hands me the ice pack again in a silent command. "How are you feeling?"

Chuckling, I reply, "I've been better." I return the ice to my head again. "You don't have to take care of me. It's late, and I'm sure you're tired."

"It is late." She leans against the counter and tilts her head. "I'm not even sure what time it is, but I kind of do need to play nurse since I'm responsible for this mess." *The images that evoke...*

"You were released from blame when I broke into the place." She laughs. It's sweet but a bit shy as she looks down. I lower my voice. "Hey." When she looks up again, I say, "I'm sorry for scaring you. I didn't think you'd be here. Christine didn't know you'd be here."

"I haven't told her I've been staying here."

I lower the ice again. "Sounds like there's a story to tell."

She gives a quick shrug before coming around the island again. "Not tonight, there's not. I have to get up in three hours." She glances toward the window where the lightning is fighting outside to get in. "The storm sounds worse than ever. You can't drive in that." Heading for the bedroom, she stops in the doorway and looks back. "So you can sleep on the couch out here or take half the bed for yourself. What will it be?"

I'm not one to pass up an invitation from a beautiful woman, even if she is my sister's friend and a former annoying kid to my friends and me. I set the ice bag in the sink before hightailing it to follow her back to the bedroom. "The bed. Definitely the bed." But when she turns, the halt of her forward steps has me running into the back of her and grabbing her waist before I run her over. "What?" I look over her shoulder and into the room to see something pink on the bed.

I'm not sure why a wry grin slides over my face. I guess this is the first time I've allowed myself to consider that Lauralee is not that annoying little kid anymore. And now, she's definitely making me feel things I shouldn't consider. But if she wants to have some fun on her own, I'm all for it.

She slips from my grip, diving for the mattress. With the breeze of her escape pushing past me, I look up. She is, in fact, not wearing anything under her T-shirt.

Fuck me.

She's definitely not the same girl I once knew . . . Nope. Lauralee Knot is all grown up and more gorgeous than I have a right to notice.

CHAPTER 2

Lauralee Knot

"Don't look, okay?" I request in a panic. Besides the plastic painfully burrowing into my stomach, the cool air of the room blows over my ass, causing goose bumps to populate across my skin. I reach around my back and lower the hem of my T-shirt down to cover my bare butt. I don't think he can see anything else, but I have a feeling I'll never live this down.

"I'm not looking, Lauralee." Baylor Greene is back—in town, in my bed mostly naked, and now probably ogling my ass.

Now I'm left reeling that I've exposed even more due to the Olympic-worthy hurtling of my body across the room. I might have been successful in hiding the vibrator, but it makes it worse that I was busted and didn't even get off earlier.

I've lost inspiration. And I was too tired from the long day to chase it. I drop my forehead to the mattress and close my eyes, unsure how long I'll need to remain in this position. "Are you looking?" He chuckles. "This isn't funny, Baylor."

"It's kind of funny."

I slide my head to the side to see if he's looking. He's facing away from me, showing off the definition of his broad shoulders and back, and muscular ass and legs familiar with working out. He's a freaking Adonis standing there like it's no big deal that I, a mere mortal in his presence, am being granted permission to stare at a Roman god on earth.

I drop my head down again, needing to collect myself. The front never did disappoint. That rugged, hard jawline of his, and a perfect nose that still holds one of the things that makes him even more attractive—the slightest of dents near the bridge from a rodeo accident at thirteen. But it's the blue eyes that run in his family, competing with the Texas summer sky and always vying for attention.

I'd almost forgotten how potent even a glance from him could be. I foolishly thought we'd made the faintest connection at Chris's reception a few years back. Guess we didn't since nothing came of it afterward.

Baylor Greene made me feel special when I was caught in the headlights of his attention. But I wasn't, I suppose, or there would have been more to the story instead of him returning to his life in New York City and forgetting all about me.

I roll over and sit up on the edge of the bed, setting my vibrator in the top drawer of the nightstand and shutting it. I move to my overnight duffel on the floor and pull out a pair of boy-cut underwear and slip them on. No way am I sleeping in a bra just because he showed up. "Okay, you can look."

You would have thought I'd said you can fuck me with your eyes by how he turns around and takes me in from head to toe and back up again. I cross my arms over my chest to hide my peaked nipples and jut my hip out. "Were you going to tell me I was showing off everything when I landed on the bed or just stare?"

The tip of his tongue rolls over his bottom lip, and he smirks. "Figured all was fair since you got a good gander at me."

"Was this after I kicked your ass?"

He chuckles again. "I'm not upset that you know how to defend yourself. Though, check on me tomorrow. I have a feeling this will stick around a few days."

Thunder rolls over the top of the building, rattling the windows. I duck my head, knowing it won't save me from anything. Looking at him again, I say, "I'd almost forgotten it was storming."

"I can be distracting."

"Especially when you're breaking and entering."

"Yeah," he says on a heavy sigh, "I should have knocked. It was raining and—"

"It's okay. You didn't know anyone would be here." I shift, tugging on the hem of my shirt. It's not the sexiest outfit to be seen in by a long shot, but this is Christine's brother. Who needs to be sexy for him? "Morning is coming sooner than I like."

"Is that a hint?"

"Not so subtle, huh?" Swinging my hand toward the bed, I ask, "Should we try this again?"

Thumbing over his shoulder, he replies, "I can sleep out here if you want more alone time." His cheeks split open in a wide, devious grin.

I roll my eyes. "It's way too early for this, Greene."

"And here I was just getting started, Knot."

Marching toward him, I stop and stand toe-to-toe with the big guy. He's at least six-three to my five-five, judging by how I fit neatly under his chin. I hold his gaze for a few seconds, then grin while cocking my brow. "I have no problem keeping my own company." I poke him in the chest. "Unlike you."

I flip out the light and return to the other side of the bed. Sitting, I dip my legs under before flopping on my back and tugging the covers up to my chin. Baylor's silent, which must be new for him, I imagine. But then his steps cross the room. When he lies down like a log falling in the forest, I fall against his side.

His arm comes around me too quick for me to escape, and his chest vibrates under my cheek. "If you wanted to snuggle, you could have asked. I'm always happy to oblige a woman with desires that need to be met."

"Ick." I shove myself off his hard body. "Just . . . no. I had no option. You sucked me into your void." Anchoring the ball of my feet against his legs, I finally have the leverage to move back to the other side of the bed.

"Sucked you in, or did you gravitate into my rotation?"

I turn my back to him, rolling as far away as I can get. Balancing precariously on the edge of the bed, I shake my head. "For the tiniest moment in time, I almost forgot what a jerk you were. Thanks for the reminder." I close my eyes and settle in, hoping to get at least two more hours of sleep before I need to get up early to prepare for the Saturday morning crowd.

Lightning startles me, and my eyes fly open to catch the tail end of the window lit up from the outside before it goes dark again. I release a slow breath, and whisper, "I hate storms like this."

There's no reply or snappy comeback. I can just hear Baylor breathing before he says, "The offer still stands."

My heartbeat thumps heavier in my chest as the thought of being held in strong arms and falling asleep next to someone speaks to the loneliness I've been feeling so much more lately. But it's Baylor... *and he's annoying.*

I scooch backward just a bit, tired of using my core to hold me on the edge of the bed. "We're not sleeping together."

"Then come closer and let me hold you." I hate how tempting that particular offer is since I really do hate summer storms here in the Hill Country. "Nothing will happen, Lauralee. I promise." The mattress shifts under me, and his hands slip around my waist. And I don't stop him.

He stills, but the heat from his hands makes me tempted to squirm.

"Okay," I whisper. He pulls me against his chest, my back warming from the contact.

His breath caresses my neck, and he whispers against the shell of my ear, "Unless you want it to."

"I knew you couldn't resist saying that." I try to push out of his arms, but they're wrapped around my middle like an unbreakable lock.

He laughs. "I'm kidding. I mean, if you want to do something, I'm up for it, but I promise you're safe with me if you don't."

"I don't." *Firm. Clear. Decisive.*

"Then it's settled. Tonight, we'll stay platonic."

I hate how much I like the feel of him around me. *No giving in*, I silently remind myself. Baylor Greene is the last person in Peachtree Pass I should be having sex with. Even if there aren't currently many, *or any*, other options. Technically, he's from New York these days—*Ugh!* No. Before I can change my mind, I reply, "Perfect."

"Yeah," he adds as if he must get the last word in, "perfect."

"What do you mean tonight? That makes it sound like we might not stay platonic another night."

"Never say never."

I barely stop the small grin wanting to grow. Pursing my lips to the side, I say, "Never, Baylor."

He sighs, the laughter almost all gone. "Received loud and clear." But then he kisses the top of my head like we're more than just platonic friends cuddling together because a bad storm rages outside. What is more concerning is that I kind of like it. "Good night, Lauralee."

And that, too. Dammit.

Never. I remind myself again as if I have no self-control when bumped up against a hot guy's hard-as-steel and built-to-impress body. *Especially because it's Baylor Greene holding me.* Nothing good would come from us hooking up.

I've solidified my stance, but I remain right where I am. I can enjoy the creature comforts of his muscly arms latched around me like I'm his for the night without having to overthink it. I close my eyes, holding the covers to my chest, as his warmth blankets my body, and reply, "Good night."

It could be seconds passing, but the quiet in the room keeps me awake with so much running through my mind about the man behind me that there's no way to find sleep in these conditions, these blissfully snuggly conditions. Simply because Baylor isn't a one-night stand, which I'm not opposed to having.

My thoughts scramble, and my heart starts to race. I part

my lips to get more air into my lungs, but I know what the issue is. I just don't want to accept it.

I want him.

I want Baylor Greene.

God, I'm a terrible person. This is my best friend's brother. By that association alone, he's off-limits. But would it be so awful for her best friend and brother to be together? Sexually, of course, and only one time. She doesn't even need to know about it. Oh my God, am I talking myself into having sex with him?

Don't do it, Lauralee.

"Can't sleep?" Why does he have to sound so rugged and sexy?

"No," I reply, keeping my voice quieter between us. "You?"

"I was exhausted when I got here, but it seems I have a second wind blowing through my bones."

I shimmy back just a smidge, tucking myself deeper into his arms, but stop when I feel one of those bones against my backside. Knowing how well-endowed he is after seeing him . . . *it*, in the flesh, I take a deep breath and exhale even slower.

Would it be so awful?

The tip of his nose just barely glides along the side of my neck. I don't even think it's intentional, just him shifting, though I want it to be. "You're tense. What's on your mind?"

"Nothing." I lift my head and punch the pillow supporting it less than his bicep just to throw him off the scent of my discontent. "Sweet dreams."

"Sweet dreams."

I can tell by how his body stays firm that he's not falling asleep anytime soon either. I stare at the window, watching the flashes of lightning and listening to the rain, hoping to find enough tiredness in me to fade into my dreams.

But even with my eyes closed, I'm not getting sleepy, but the opposite. I find my inspiration. Dammit.

I squirm free from his arms and fly out of bed. "Water? I need water." I dash out of the bedroom and into the kitchen. After swinging the door to the freezer wide open, I put my face inside the empty cavern, close my eyes, and try to cool my heated thoughts. But they're not going away, so I close the door and turn around, only to have my face captured in his hands.

My breathing is jagged, my heart racing out of my chest. As I stare into his eyes, I know my mission out here is fruitless.

But his lips don't meet mine. I'm not suddenly pressed to the cold steel fridge and taken advantage of. No, disappointingly. Instead, he caresses my cheeks with his thumbs, and when his gaze drops to my mouth, he runs the pad of one over my bottom lip. "I lied," he says, his voice husky with need and his body pressing against mine.

"About?" I pant.

"Earlier," he says, his mouth gravitating toward mine. "I was totally looking."

I want to smile, but I restrain myself under my growing need for him. He may be charming, but I refuse to be like every other woman in his life. *What's the fun in that?* "Not every girl would find that charming."

"It only matters if you find it charming." *Fine . . .* he knows how to make me swoon. I'll give him that. What else I'll give him remains to be seen.

I slide my arms around his neck because it's fun to be in his spotlight. The man can have any woman he wants. That he's looking at me like I'm something special is quite the aphrodisiac.

My smile is easily coaxed despite wanting to feign I'm hard to get. *Who am I kidding?* I lost inspiration months ago. So when a ridiculously handsome man is delivered right to my bed, who am I to question fate?

All logic and excuses fly out the window. I take hold of his shoulders and press myself against him. Lifting on my toes, I'm just about to kiss him, but stop and whisper, "Hungry?"

CHAPTER 3

Baylor

"Not where I thought this was going," I say, sliding my hands down to the curve where her shoulders meet her neck. "But I can't lie. I could eat something."

I hear her swallow in the quiet room before she asks, "Are we still talking about food?"

Massaging her shoulders gently, I lean against the counter and bring her closer to stand between my legs. "I'm up for whatever suits your mood."

Her lips part, and she tugs the lower one under her top teeth. Her breath steadies as if she's caught herself. Wrapping her hands around my wrists, Lauralee replies, "We should get some food. I can go downstairs and make something—"

"You don't have to cook for me."

"It could be simple like a sandwich. Or ice cream."

Earlier tensions have disappeared, and our bodies have eased against each other. There's no rush to the bed or to make something happen. I like it, actually. She's comfortable to me. "Seems sleep is going to evade us. Let's go down together."

She slides out of my hold, though her hand drags lightly across my abs until her feet take her out of reach, and she heads for the door. Taking the key off the hook on the wall, she tugs on the hem of her T-shirt. "Should we bother getting dressed?"

"We'll be soaked before we get down the stairs." I come around the peninsula to stand next to her. "Nothing like an adventure at three in the morning."

Excitement widens her eyes as she grins like she's about to get into some good trouble. Opening the door, she looks back over her shoulder. "We'll make a run for it." There's no question, but I can see by her raised brows that she wants to hear my thoughts.

"I'm right behind you."

With a nod, she turns back to the pouring rain and dashes out the door. I stay close as she uses the rail to guide her down. Twirling around the pole to safe cover under the patio, she unlocks the door to the shop and shoulders it open.

Inside, we stand dripping on the hard floor. My eyes are drawn to a face I've not paid enough attention to—dark lashes wet from the rain, high cheekbones on either side of her straight nose, all highlighted by the heart shape.

I slide my gaze lower to the fabric clinging to her body. Her tits round, a good helping and a handful, her nipples hard and teasing. The shirt dips down the curve of her waist to the swell of her hips. I remember her having a rockin' body at the reception, and we even had a moment that felt like it could have led to more. But then my nephew jumped in excitement when he saw doodlebug on the side of the chicken coop, and we lost the opportunity that had been presented. I can't remember what happened after, but I know it involved a lot of shots and stumbling up to my room, alone, before passing out just before sunrise.

I catch her eyes returning after a quick once-over herself and biting that lip again. I'm tempted to bite it for her. She laughs as if I've called her out. I don't laugh, but a wry grin has solidified on my face.

"We're soaked." Her eyes glitter with mischief before she turns away from me. If I'm reading her right, which I rarely get women wrong, she's nervous. Which is surprising, but what I know about Lauralee Knot, which might be only a small fraction of who she is, she's not a shy woman. I've seen her dance at Whiskey's on a Thursday night like she doesn't have work the following morning. I've heard a few stories about her and my sister sneaking out back in high school and skinny-dipping down at the river with some assholes from Dover Country. And she held her own the night of the reception. I might have been stumbling upstairs, but she looked fine and dandy from what I recall. So her being nervous almost doesn't make sense. She's known me forever, so that's the last thing I want her to be with me. I reach out, capturing her by the elbow. "Hey—"

"I'll get some towels," she says with her gaze falling to the floor. Sticking to the mats covering the tile floor, she walks like the lava might get her if she steps off. She opens a large cabinet and pulls out a stack of dishcloths.

I chuckle. She rolls her eyes and grins. "You get what you get." A small pile of them hits my chest before she eyes me again. "Guess you're stuck in those wet underwear."

"Yeah," I say, holding the tiny towels and glancing at the soaked black cotton hugging my body. Peeking up at her, I smirk with a waggle of my brows. "I can always take them off."

"Don't get ahead of yourself there, Greene."

It's hard not to with her. Even drenched, this woman is fucking stunning. I'm kicking myself for not seeing her outside my sister's shadow. *What would I have done anyway?* Fucked her back then and ditched her for New York City. She was a girl.

She's not anymore.

With the cabinet door blocking my view of her, I start to dry my body while watching the shirt come over her and down her arms. Yeah, I'm shameless. No use pretending I'm a gentleman when she already knows I'm not.

When she pushes the cabinet closed, her bare torso sports a white apron with a red-trimmed ruffle around the edge, unfortunately hiding what I really wanted to see. I never had a kitchen fantasy, but one's in the making with her looking that fucking sexy.

"Eyes up here, Baylor."

I look up, grinning. "That's quite the outfit."

"Better than freezing and dripping everywhere in that shirt."

"I definitely approve." The ruffle doesn't hide the rounded side of her tit or the tattoo on her ribs.

"I bet you do." She walks to the large fridge to peek inside. "Are we thinking soup or sandwich or both?"

Neither but I keep what I'm really craving to myself, or I might get whacked over the head with a bag of flour this time. "Whatever is easiest." I come closer, and ask, "What does your tattoo say?"

Her hand covers the bare skin over her ribs. "Oh . . . nothing really. Just something . . . I'm thinking chicken salad on croissants."

"Sounds good." I study her expression and the way she

appears restrained in some ways she didn't prior. "Did I cross a boundary I didn't know existed? Or is it a secret?"

With a shrug of her shoulders, she dips into the fridge. "Kind of."

Not sure which question she's answering, though it may be both. "Now I'm more curious than before."

Laughter shakes her shoulders, but she doesn't give me the pleasure of seeing her smile since she's faced away from me. "Curiosity killed the cat."

"Yet I still want to know."

"Living on the edge?" When she turns around with a glass container, she carries on like we weren't talking about the tattoo at all. "I made this before I closed last night. I think it needs time for the flavors to marinate." She glances at me. "So if it's not as good as—"

"I'm sure it will be great."

As much as I want to push the topic, it's not my business. And the way I see things potentially headed with her, I'll see it for myself anyway. I ask, "What can I do?"

"Something you're great at." She raises a brow and smirks. "Stand there and look good."

Chuckling, I weave my fingers through my hair. "Easy enough." Too easy. I move to the stainless-steel island in the center of the room that shines under the lights and look around. "I thought it would be bigger."

"Do you hear that often?" She snorts with laughter as she pops the top off the container. My ego isn't so fragile that I can't find her utterly adorable.

"You're as quick with the quips as you are the punches."

"You know firsthand." My hand moves to my head automatically, but I see concern ripple through her expression when she looks at it as well. "Sorry about that. I should make another ice pack."

"It's fine. No need to fuss. But lesson learned. Don't sneak into bed with Lauralee Knot."

She laughs. This time, it's more genuine and softer, but then her hands still, and she asks, "Why is that disappointing?"

"Because it's three forty-five in the morning, and you're delirious." She has me questioning if she'd feel the same when she's not exhausted. I'm starting to think it's worth spending some time in Peaches Sundries & More while I'm here.

She crosses the room and opens a bin on the far counter. "I appreciate you giving me grace, but I'm responsible for my own actions no matter the hour. Trust me, I've done worse at this hour." She takes two croissants out and returns to the steel table, standing across from me.

"Color me intrigued and tell me more. Tell me all the bad things you've done."

While she cuts the bread lengthwise and starts to dress them, she continues smiling. "I think you were right. It's too early."

"Is that your way of wanting to change the subject? Seems you like to do that a lot."

"Not a lot. I just keep thinking how weird it is that my best friend's brother—who used to tell us to scram—is so interested in me now."

This time, I shrug. "Years pass. People change." She's changed alright. "We're both adults and can talk about these things." Her brown eyes are set on mine, but there's no anger or any sign of being upset that a memory came back. I still feel the need to say, "I'm sorry I was an asshole."

She returns to topping the sandwich, then cuts it in half. "As long as you're not an asshole now, we'll be good."

"No guarantees."

Her mouth twists to the side. I can tell something hangs on the tip of her tongue by how her gaze lands hard on mine. "You don't have to be like that with me, Baylor."

"What do you mean? Be like what?"

"Play the part of the hometown hero who has everyone falling at his feet, the smooth playboy I'm pretty certain you are in New York, or hold the expectations of the Pass on your shoulders anymore. You can be you with me. No mask. No facade. Just be real with me."

There's no venom to her words, no warning, not even a judgment placed on me or my behavior. She's just saying what's on her mind and allowing me to say what's on mine. I'm not sure I like being under her microscope, though.

"Who says I'm not?" Even I hear the defensive edge in my tone.

She takes a deep breath, then tightens her lips into a straight line. Pushing the sandwich over on a napkin, she says, "Enjoy."

I drop my guard. Lauralee's not calling me out. She doesn't know me well enough to do it anyway, so I let it roll off my back. But if she isn't, why do I feel seen? "I'm not hiding who I am."

"Okay." She nods with a gentle smile.

Throwing my arms out wide, I reply, "No, for real. What you see is what you get."

Her expression falters, but then she wrenches the corners of her mouth back into place. "You don't have to prove anything to me."

Then why do I feel like I do?

I take a bite of the sandwich, needing time to think about what's going on here. Is it the hour, the woman, or the accusation that struck a chord? Probably all three. And why is this sandwich the best thing I've ever had?

I take another bite, watching her eat across from me. After I swallow, I ask, "Why do you think I'm not being genuine?"

"I think you're genuine." She lowers the sandwich to the napkin. "When you held me earlier to protect me from the storm, that was genuine. When you kissed my head, I know that came from the heart. But it's the show you put on. It's worked for you for so long that I don't think you're even aware you're doing it anymore."

My heartbeats grow heavy under her words. I'm not bothered by much, but this does the trick. I stare at her as she continues, "It's late, or early, whatever you want to call this time of night or morning. I don't have the energy to impress you, and I don't want to. I just want you to see me as someone you don't have to impress either because that guy doesn't stand a chance of staying in my bed."

I'm not upset, but she's hit a nerve like no one else has bothered to try. If I take the words for how she means them, it's not discomforting. She's calling it like she sees me and is still standing on the other side of this table like she's rooting for me.

I may not have known her before, but she's giving me a good taste of who she is now, and I like it. I like that she's comfortable enough to tell me what's on her mind. No guessing. No playing games. A real straight shooter. I grin. "What about the other guy? What are his chances?"

This time, a smile blooms across her pretty face. Her eyes are bright as if the decision was already made, and she's excited. "That guy has a real good chance."

"I like those odds."

"Me too." She finishes half the sandwich, then asks, "What do you think?"

Her hair has started to dry, the strands forming soft curls around her shoulders. "I think you're a fascinating woman."

Her cheeks pinken under the bright lights of the kitchen, and she looks down with a smile that holds plenty of secrets. Angling to the side, she whispers, "I meant about the sandwich."

"Best I ever had." I catch her attention, and that smile grows as if I'm in on those secrets with her.

Wrapping the other half of the sandwich in the napkin, she sets it aside and starts to close the container. "I think I'm ready to go back upstairs." She puts it in the fridge and closes it behind her. "How do you feel?"

No way am I leaving food behind. I finish the sandwich, still thinking about what she said. Some of it's starting to make sense, which has me rethinking things. I push that aside, though. I don't want to waste this night stuck in my head when I have a much better offer at hand. I nod to the door. "Ready when you are."

CHAPTER 4

Lauralee

"Should we stay up or go to bed?" I ask as if we do this all the time, as if . . . we're a couple who's had dinner, watched TV, and hung out together like it's normal. We're not, but oddly, it feels comfortable in a similar way.

Not that I know firsthand.

I've had boyfriends, but nothing that got to the living together stage.

"Definitely bed." After releasing a big yawn, he rubs his eyes and towels off again. We're both in dry, cozy clothes—me in a cropped and fitted tank top that matches a pair of pajama shorts and him in another pair of boxer briefs. Charcoal gray this time. I can't imagine he brought many pairs since he's only visiting for the weekend.

I head into the bathroom to brush my teeth. I don't so much as get toothpaste on the bristles when another appears at my side, ready to be loaded. Yeah, this is feeling very couple-y all of a sudden. But it doesn't bother me.

Maybe because it's Baylor, and I've known him for so

long. But I didn't expect to go from barely acquaintances to brushing our teeth together. That's quite a leap.

The swoosh of bristles fills the void in conversation, and a shy smile crosses Baylor's lips when we accidentally make eye contact in the mirror. I smile, too, because this is weird and fun and kind of wonderful in its own way. Sure, he's got this whole player act down to a T, but sharing this with him, like the sandwich downstairs, and even when I held the ice pack to his head earlier, gives me glimpses of what's convinced me is the real him. Maybe he's found in the quieter moments versus the boisterous ones he's known for. There's an appeal to both sides, but I'm becoming partial to this one.

I rinse my mouth and step aside from the sink for him to do the same. Swiping a layer of balm over my lips, I watch this man, all fit and cut, hard and handsome, funny, and he knows how to charm. I know that much. Would I kiss him, though? It's not the worst thought in the world. I bet he's a great kisser and even better with his hands.

We silently move around each other as if the habits of our nighttime routine have already set in. He steps out for me to finish up, then we swap places. I twist my damp hair up in a scrunchie, already knowing it will be unruly in the morning. I'll deal with it then.

The lamp on the other nightstand provides an ambience that two friends wouldn't typically need when going to bed. It's noted he made an effort to turn off the harsh overhead light while I was in the bathroom.

I smile as I slip under the covers and lie back on my freshly fluffed pillow. If I didn't know better, I'd think he was trying to woo me. But I'm not falling into a trap of mushy feelings at this hour. I was lucky enough to get a few hours' sleep before he showed up, but that doesn't mean my heart and mind won't play tricks on me.

The door opens, and I look over.

I don't mean to stare, but damn. *I'm definitely inspired.* He makes it easy to forget my better senses. "Hi," I say for no other reason than to distract him from my gawking.

He slips into bed next to me and looks over. His smile is relaxed but genuine, his eyes showing signs of needing sleep by how the lids are starting to hang a bit, but something in the blues makes me feel like he's right where he wants to be. "Hi, how are you?"

My smile grows. He's always been handsome, but something about seeing him so relaxed and at ease in his skin is special. "I'm good. How about you, Greene?" I ask, not as tired as I thought I was now that he's here.

He hums and lies back, his eyes redirecting to the ceiling. "I'm . . . why does this feel like we do it all the time?"

It's got to be the hour. Who has the energy for pretenses at four o'clock? "Do what exactly?" Twisting my lips to the side, I try my best to restrain the smirk that wants to come out to play.

I sense he's on to me when he chuckles. "Do you always flirt with men who break into your apartment at ungodly hours and get in your bed, or am I the lucky guy?"

Am I flirting with him?

Maybe . . .

"What? I can't have some fun in this extremely awkward situation?"

"That's just it. This doesn't feel awkward at all to me." His smile doesn't fade but hangs on and grows wider. He even rolls to the side to face me as if a casual look out of the corners of his eyes wasn't enough.

Stop overthinking this. It's just fun among friends. That's all. I roll to my side to face him because caution was thrown out quite a while ago. "What does it feel like?" *Fine, I'm flirting.* Doesn't mean I'm going to sleep with the man.

"Natural."

I could read so much into that answer, but instead, I stare into his eyes, choosing to spend my time appreciating him. "For me, too," I whisper.

He reaches to run the back of his fingers over my cheek, causing my heart to skip a beat. When he pulls his hand back, he says, "I should have called you after the reception."

"Why is that?"

"Because there was something—a spark, a gut instinct, something firing between us that night, and I was too stupid to follow up on it."

"No following required." I slide my gaze down to his chest. This feels so intimate, more than seeing each other naked. "You didn't owe me anything."

"I know. I thought about you, though . . ." He tips his head down until he catches my eyes again. "When I was back in New York."

"What did you think?"

"I should have kissed you behind the barn." Not sure why that sounds so illicit and sexy, but we're both grinning. Keeping his voice low between us, he asks, "Do you believe in second chances, Lauralee?"

Although my heart stopped beating earlier, it now starts racing. My lips part, providing space for much-needed air in the moment. Before I reply, I think about tonight and the detours this journey between us has taken. Do I want a second chance with Baylor? To pick up where we left off more than two years earlier? "When you say second chance—"

"I want to kiss you."

Boom. He drops the truth like a bomb between us, and whatever I say is going to detonate one way or the other. It's all relying on whatever I want and what I say next. Who am I kidding? It's a kiss, not sex. "I'd be open to that."

His cheeks become uneven as one side rides higher, and he lifts onto his elbow. His palm returns this time, cupping my face and holding me still as I study everything about this man's face in the span of the two seconds it takes him to home in on me.

The dusting of scruff covering his chin.
The way his eyes fixate on my mouth.
And how the warmth of his hand is calming as he closes in.

He grazes his lips against mine before pulling back to look into my eyes once more, as if needing permission is all that's stopping him. Should I be kissing my best friend's brother? *Probably not.* Do I want to? *God yes.*

I slide my hand around his neck and whisper, "What are you waiting for, Greene?"

"I've wanted to do this all night." He smirks just before his mouth crashes into mine.

Throwing my arms around him, I hold him close, so close until the weight of his chest lands on mine. His lips caress mine as his hand still graces my face, then lowers to my neck. Gentle pressure at the base of my neck has me squirming in need of more body contact. I move my hips toward him, which encourages him to shift his over me.

His length is hard, pressed against my thigh as he starts to seek relief. Feeling him already turned on by me, by simply a kiss and then deepening it, has me needy for more.

A girl can change her mind, can't she?

Dipping his mouth to my shoulder, he kisses me there, and his nose follows, taking a deep breath of me. The gesture sends a wave of goose bumps down my arms. "You smell so good, baby."

Doesn't matter what comes next, I'm all in. I attack his neck with kisses and nips, which causes him to chuckle. One of his hands finds the hem of my tank as he toys with it. "You want to play?"

"I want to play."

He moves his hand over my stomach and takes hold of my breast. Kneading and squeezing, he watches me just as he pinches the tip, sending a flare of pleasure straight down between my legs, causing me to buck. I tip my head back, my mouth falls open, and my breath deepens, wanting more.

Kissing me, he swallows a moan before it reaches our ears and teases my other nipple. When his knee slips between my legs, I open for him, giving him all the access he craves because I need this just as much. Maybe more. He feels so good, the weight of his body, the intensity of his touch, the way he's looking at me like I'm the one who can save him tonight. The buildup is too much, the foreplay too long. I hold his face and encourage him to look up at me just after he starts to go down. "I want you."

"I want you, too." He continues down, hooking his fingers over my shorts and takes them with him. Quick to pause, he leans right and kisses my hip. "Are those strawberries?"

I forget about the three small tattoos on my hip. "It was on a whim in South Padre, spring break after senior year. Too much tequila ... you know the drill."

The smile that reaches his eyes is so sweet as he stares down at the little bunch and kisses it again. "A trail of strawberries." Glancing at me, he adds, "I like where these are leading."

I giggle. Yes, giggle like a schoolgirl under his admiring gaze. My cheeks are heating, and it feels so good to release the tension. "Glad you like."

"You know what I like better?" The shorts reach my thighs, and his gaze travels to the apex of my legs. It's not a lingering look, but it's potent in its powers, making me want to clench my thighs together and rub feverishly. He doesn't let me. His fingers drag down my legs, making claims that he doesn't verbalize.

I don't know how I thought this would play out, but I wasn't expecting a sweet seduction from him. It rouses my yearning for him, pulling it to the surface as if it's been waiting for the opportunity.

He gets off the bed, taking my pajama bottoms with him and dropping them to the floor. Standing at the end of the mattress, he explores my body slowly, leaving the cool air to brush over my skin. But it's not the temperature that makes me want to beg him to return. It's the way he's taking me in.

Desire.

Approval.

Need.

A delicious combination burns in his eyes as he licks his lips. His eyes reach mine again, and he says, "Take off your top for me, Lauralee." His voice is firm, a command not a request that I'm more than happy to oblige. Especially since he's already taking his briefs off in front of me.

All's fair.

I sit up and strip my shirt away and toss it at him. He catches it with a grin as I settle back on my elbows. "You going to stand there all night and stare?"

"It's not the worst idea." He kisses the inside of my left thigh, then makes sure the right one isn't left out. Looking back up at me, he says, "I can't wait to watch you come."

I'm left lifeless, dead to the world, seduced to death with that simple phrase.

He flattens his hand over my stomach and kisses closer to where I really want him but stops shy of the spot. Nudging under my leg, I lift. He settles in with it draped over his shoulder and takes a lick like he's been dying to his whole life—eyes closed, deep inhale, and savoring right after.

I fall flat on my back and lie there with my arms wide open as this man's hunger for me gets the better of him, and he starts devouring me like I'm his last meal. I grab the pillow above my head and smother my moans though I know there's no stopping my body from wriggling under his tongue and lips, his mouth as he latches onto my clit.

"Oh my God," I whimper, the intensity striking like the lightning outside. My body feels alive, electrified as his mouth takes me, teases me, fucks me, and tempts me toward the edge. My mind is nothing and everything at once. His tongue, the feel of his hair between my fingers as I tug, the scruff along the soft skin of my inner thighs and that look he gave right before diving in that told me to get ready to hold on tight.

When he hums against me, his fingers tease my entrance before he slips in. The pillow is discarded as my back arches and my thighs clamp together. "It's too much. Too much," I plead to myself.

"Do you want me to stop?"

I bolt my head upright. "God, no. Don't you dare." I push his head down, and he laughs but then circles my need until I can't take much more. "I can't hold on." I shake my head, wanting to let go and float to the beautiful abyss.

"Let go, baby. Just feel. Feel how good—"

His voice, the tone, him. He sends me spiraling toward my

release. I reach the peak, and my body tremors beneath his warmth and care, his slick mouth, and big hands. I bite my lip to stop the blissful moan that wants to escape.

And as soon as my body finds peace in the stillness, he kisses my lips and my forehead before he falls beside me to lie. I roll my head to the side, and when he looks my way, I say, "That was better than any electronic."

We both laugh, and he says, "Good to hear."

But when his hand finds mine, and he takes hold of it between our bodies, I catch the beat of an errant feeling entering my heart. One that is new to me. One that's blooming only for him.

The laughter stops, and I look up at the ceiling, finding it safer in this space than staring into his eyes. I'm not sure what to say while we lie together like this. He's just as quiet, seemingly with as much on his mind when I steal a glimpse of him staring at the same boring ceiling.

I roll over and kiss his chest. I want to break the ice, but more so, I want him to feel as good as he's made me feel. I rub over his hard abs and start going lower, but he catches my hand and brings it to his mouth. He places a kiss on it, and says, "I know we keep saying all's fair, but you don't owe me anything, Lauralee. I wanted to do that for you." Slipping his hand under my hip, he pulls me into his arms. "Let's get some sleep."

Arguing doesn't feel right, so I believe what he says and snuggle against him. When I close my eyes, he kisses my forehead and whispers, "You taste just like shortcake. I think that's what I'm going to call you from now on."

A few years ago, heck, even a few months ago, I would have laughed him out of the Pass. But lying in his arms that hold me like precious cargo, I smile instead.

CHAPTER 5

Baylor

My size overwhelms her body. There's not one part of me that can't wrap around her in some form in length or width. As I hold her from behind, she fits nicely under my arm, curled against me in peaceful sleep. Her waist is small, but she's full in the hips. Her legs are lean, but I left a little hickey on the inside of her thigh when they softly gripped the side of my head as she came.

The depth of her eyes still draws me in each time her gaze lands on mine. Her dark hair is a mass of unruly curls that I can tell drives her nuts. I love it. It's chaotic and less perfect. Different from what I'm used to in New York. It fits the varied landscape of Peachtree Pass and the way she totters between what she wants, speaking her mind, and what she seems to hold back sometimes when she goes quiet.

Taking a few deep breaths, I exhale slowly. It took me years to find a rhythm to help me fall asleep with the noise of the city. Here, the quiet keeps me awake, and maybe the woman in my arms, though I've been content listening to the melody of her soft breaths.

I clear my mind and focus on her and her breathing, feeling the pull to go to sleep harder to fight. *Finally, my thoughts fade...*

OPENING my eyes to the dim sunlight of early morning, I roll onto my back, squeezing them shut again, and scrub my hand over my face. A groan comes from exhaustion, but the scent of baked goods softens the blow.

The unfamiliar smells and the way the light threatens to intrude from the other side of the blinds can't be marked in my mind. I sit up and look around. Time is absent. My surroundings can't be placed. A turquoise vase with pink flowers on top of a walnut dresser. A framed photo of a blue sky with a cloud escaping in the corner. *Where am I?*

My eyes dart to the empty bed beside me, and the memories of last night come rushing back. "Lauralee?"

Not a sound is detected, so I swing the covers off and walk into the living room. The apartment looks completely different in daylight. Bright. Yellow throw pillows on a blue couch. A green bowl has fake peaches filling the inside. Free of most clutter, but a few touches that make it feel like a home. A framed poster from the Peach Festival, dated from when I was in college, hangs over the couch. It feels like Lauralee in here.

I think it's safe to assume the delicious scent is coming from Peaches downstairs. She's already started baking for the day. I find myself smiling as I work my way to the suitcase I left open on the floor. Grabbing clean clothes and my Dopp kit, I move into the bathroom to shower.

Judging by the sunlight not flooding the place, I can probably get out to the ranch before everyone gets going for the day. I clean up and wash my hair and get ready afterward. Slipping my watch on, I grab my phone that she plugged in for me. Another grin slips into place. I'm starting to think I was too bullheaded to look twice at my sister's friend to notice the woman she'd become. And since I'd threatened my best friend when we were younger not to look at my sister, it makes sense that I wasn't eyeing up her friend.

I make the bed for her, then pack up my suitcase. I lost some time in the past few minutes, and the sun has risen higher. I'm not looking to make an entrance, unlike my usual style. Questions will come, but it's probably best if Lauralee and I keep quiet about our night.

After packing the suitcase in the rental, I check the door to the shop. It's locked. Good girl. I knock and step back, tucking my hands in my pockets. She probably would have been fine if I'd gone on about my day and taken off for the ranch, but a knot in my chest told me to stop by before leaving.

When the door opens, she's already smiling as if she's been waiting for me. "Well, hello there, stranger." Her hair is pulled into a ponytail high on the back of her head, and flour dusts across the bridge of her nose. Her natural pale pink lips beckon me to her, and the prettiest light blue dress with tiny white flowers covers the body I was lucky enough to hold last night. She's morning sunshine in human form.

God, she's gorgeous. "Good morning." I cup her face and kiss her like we've turned time back to last night. Deep. Sensual. More than our tongues connecting, which suddenly feels dangerous in new ways. But I needed one more to get me by because if this is all we ever have, I want to give us a hell of an ending.

Her hands slide over my arms until she's holding my shoulders. When our lips part, she lowers to her heels, and her eyes slowly open. A sweet smile upturns the corners of her mouth, and she asks, "What brings you by?"

"I wanted to see you again. And I wanted to tell you how much I enjoyed last night."

After stepping back to the doorframe, she shifts her weight onto her hip. One arm falls to hang at her side, but the other hand slides into mine, keeping us joined together. "Me too."

I'm not sure why I feel the need to explain. This wasn't that serious, but I do anyway. "I'm only here for the weekend."

"I figured. You heading to Rollingwood Ranch?"

"Yeah, I was supposed to be there last night. The weather," I say as if she can fill in the rest.

"It was bad, but we have a beauty of a day today." Her eyes look past me and into the morning sunrise sky. When her eyes return to mine, she smiles. "We weathered the storm and came out the other side."

"We sure did." I take a step back, not wanting to but knowing I should. What am I going to do? Stand around here all day bugging her? Our hands release each other's, and I nod toward the car. "I'm going to head out. Thanks for last night. I'm happy to pay you."

Her head juts back on her neck, her smile wiped clear from her face. With her brows tipped together, she asks, "What are you talking about?" When her hands fly to her hips, I know I'm in trouble. "Is that what you do in New York?" Her head falls back. "Ew. I knew I couldn't trust you."

I stare at her, watch the dramatics, hear the disgust in her voice, and try not to laugh. *I fail.*

She says, "What? Why is this so funny to you?" Her hands anchor to my chest and push me back off the little concrete pad under the patio to the apartment. "You know what? I don't care." Her arm flies into the air, and she points to the middle of nowhere. "Go. Baylor. Just go." I catch her hand and bring it to me despite her trying to wriggle it free. "Let go."

"Listen to me, Shortcake." I kiss her balled-up fist. "You're getting all hot and bothered over nothing."

"It's not nothing. You're treating me like I'm a wanton—"

"Landlord." I try, unsuccessfully, to loosen her fingers. I mean, I could if I wanted, but she clearly needs to hang onto the anger a bit longer. "Chris told me you're going to rent the place out. I used it, so I offered to offset some costs. I wasn't offering you money to let me go down on you."

"Oh my God." Her cheeks flame, burning red. "Don't say that."

"Don't say landlord?" I'm whacked in the chest, making me chuckle. But I catch her other hand. "Don't be so feisty. The money was offered with good intentions. I don't think you're a wanton anything. Quite the opposite, in fact." The stiffness in her arms loosens, and her head tilts just enough for me to know she's open to hearing more.

Before I can say anything, she says, "I can be wanton, but I wasn't being that with you . . . I mean, I was, kind of, but—"

I kiss her, pulling her into my arms. She sinks against me, and our breaths become moans as our tongues tangle together. When I feel the tension leave her body, I kiss her long and slow, savoring the sweetness of her lips and the way she makes me wish we were still in bed.

She pulls back with her eyes still closed and licks her

lips under a contented hum. When I'm given the pleasure of her beautiful browns again, she smiles. But reality sneaks into her expression, pulling most of the joy from it. "Do you want me to pack up a cinnamon roll or something for the road?"

"No. I got all I need right here." That helps with her smile, but she looks down, seemingly unsure of what to say. Lifting her chin until her eyes rise to mine again, I ask, "What's going on in that pretty head of yours?"

Hesitating, she takes a breath, and says, "It was good seeing you again, Baylor."

This isn't supposed to be anything other than a strange turn of events that brought us together for a few hours. I can understand her need to protect herself, but I still feel the urge to say something. "I don't live here or—"

"I know. No explanation needed." Taking a deep breath, she steps into the kitchen, this time more than a foot separating us. It feels like a mile, but I think my mind is playing tricks on me. Or maybe it's my heart. Either way, I need to ignore it.

I dip my head and give her a smile that doesn't feel quite right. "See you around, Shortcake."

"See you around, Greene." She closes the door, but one of us had to do it, so there's no need to place blame.

Not sure why I'm still standing here like there could be a different outcome, but this is it. I need to look at this time with her as another experience and place it where it belongs in the one-time thing drawer.

I get in the car, wondering why this feels different. It shouldn't. I start the car and let it go because there's no use dwelling on happenstance.

Every time I drive over the cattle guard of the ranch, I'm instantly reminded I'm home. Though I can't say it feels much like home these days. Even my old room feels more foreign than familiar, the more I live in the Northeast. My feelings on the subject are complicated.

The ranch is my sister's, my dad's, even more my best friend's than mine these days in title and principle. Doesn't matter. I've built a life elsewhere. Not better, just different. And sometimes different will have to do until something better comes along.

I park the car in front of the main house and head toward the door to check in with my dad. The front door opens, and the screen door squeals as he steps onto the porch. He works a smile into place, though I can tell he's in pain. That's one of the reasons I wanted to come back for a visit.

"Welcome back to the ranch, son."

I step up onto the porch and shake his hand. "Good to be back." He pulls me in for a hug with a solid pat on the back.

He turns to return inside, and says, "I need my coffee to get the engine runnin' in the morning. Care for a cup?"

"I'll take one." I follow him inside, letting the screen door swing shut. That sound brings back memories of running in and out of the house during the summertime. Really, it was year-round, and my mom always reminded me not to let it slam closed. I can still hear her voice in my head, and I smile.

I miss her so damn much it hurts if I let myself think about it. So I don't let my mind go there often.

Sitting, I watch as he starts the coffee pot and then joins me across the table. He looks at me, and asks, "How long are you staying?"

"I leave Monday morning."

"You lost a night to the storm."

I wouldn't say I lost anything, considering the storm brought me to Lauralee's. "It was bad."

"It'll dry up quick out here. We've needed rain."

The sound of a UTV reaches us before the motor is cut outside, and the squawk of the kids comes closer. "Sounds like we've got company."

My dad gets up to check the coffee. "They keep me young."

"That's a good thing." I get up and rush onto the porch to greet them. As soon as my niece and nephew see me, I bend down and open my arms wide. "Get over here, you rascals."

Beckett runs into my arms with little Daisy teeter-totting up the porch steps. My sister is right behind her, glowing in the sunlight, and pregnant again. I give Daisy a big hug when she makes it up the steps. Standing with her in my arms, I whisper, "I missed you, Daisy girl."

Christine says, "She missed you. She wanted me to show her Bay Bay photos again."

I open an arm and bring my little sister in for a hug with us. "Did you miss me, sis?"

"I did. I'm glad you're here." She not-so-subtly checks her watch with a grin when stepping away. "Though you're a little late. These kids are going to keep you busy today. Hope you got some sleep."

I chuckle as I scrub a hand over my face. "Not much," I admit, "but I'll survive." I don't bother telling her that what I did get was even better and worth the lost sleep.

CHAPTER 6

Baylor

"Thought I'd catch you fucking off down at the river."

Tagger starts laughing before he turns to see me heading toward the equipment barn. "The prodigal son returns. It's been a few months." He comes toward me in a summer straw cowboy hat, looking more at peace in the shadow of it than he ever was when he was living in the city. Tucking a rag in his back pocket, he holds out his hand.

"I can't say I'm so golden anymore." I take it, but we always bring it in for a bump against the chest. "I think you might have stolen the title when you decided to start dating my sister."

His laughter gets deeper. Holding up his hand to show off his ring, he says, "I fell for her before I knew what hit me."

I punched him when I found out he broke his promise to me. I forgave him when I realized how much he loves her. Three years later, I like to give him shit over it any time I can. That's what friends are for, after all. "Is that how it happened?"

"Something like that." He thumbs over his shoulder. "I want to show you something."

"What is it?"

"Let's head to the old barn and I'll show you." We start walking, and he asks, "Business keeping you away?"

"It's booming. How about you? You still in the finance game?"

He waffles his head. "Dabbling online but mostly investing in the ranch these days."

"I saw the last statement. Profits are up." Grinning, I add, "I like to see it."

"I'm sure you do since you get a cut of it." He tucks his hands in his front pockets. "Your sister gets the credit. She runs this operation."

"When are you going to let her retire?"

He balks and heads back toward the barn. "I don't think Pris will ever be happy sitting still."

I walk next to him, looking at how much the ranch has grown in the six years my mom's been gone. She'd be proud of her daughter for what she's accomplished. It's obvious from the new equipment to the extra ranch hands she's hired that the farm and ranch have grown exponentially.

I'm proud of her for taking on what I couldn't back then.

We round the side of the newest warehouse, the equipment barn, and the original barn from generations past comes into view. I say, "That should have been torn down years ago." It's decrepit, and the walls are leaning. "It's barely standing."

He says, "I'm planning on it, but I found a few things that I need to get moved first."

"Like what?" I follow him inside, hoping the ceiling doesn't give while we're standing under it.

Under the eaves of a now nonexistent second floor, he pulls back a cover. It's not even revealed before my heart starts racing in my chest. I know what it is. "Wow," I say, stepping closer. "I didn't know we still had it."

"None of us did. Well, maybe your dad, but he hasn't talked about it."

"Sore subject." I grin, staring at the front of the car. "I haven't seen it since I was a kid." I run my fingers over the silver hood. "1972 Porsche 911T Coupe. Damn, she's fine."

"There's no engine."

I nod, knowing the backstory, though I'm not sure he does. "This was my mom's dream car. She saw it in a movie and fell in love."

Tagger pulls the cover off the rest of the sports car. "Your dad said he bought it for her."

"To fix up. That never happened." I bend down to look through the driver's window. "Ripped leather."

"The body is the only thing that's in great condition."

"The body is all that matters." I study the dashboard before stepping back to take it in again. "There was nothing practical about having this car in the country, but my mom would say what's the fun in practicality."

He steps back, letting me take this in. I cross my arms over my chest, wondering if I have any claims to it at all. My sister owns majority share of the property. I would assume this comes along with it. My gut twists. I don't have much of anything from my mom except memories.

I wonder if my mom would be proud of me as well. My dad says as much on occasion. She even told me once on a quick visit when I flew her to see the city for the first time. But I can't stop thinking about how she'd feel now.

She was too young to die, to leave us out in the world without her tether.

"Baylor?"

Pulled from my thoughts, I look over at him. "Yeah?"

He chuckles. "It's not even eight o'clock, and your mind is wandering."

"Not wandering but wondering." Eyeing him, I ask, "What are you doing with the car?"

"I'm going to move it to one of the other barns to figure out the next steps. It's not a project I'm wanting to take on—"

"I will."

His eyes level on me. "You're handy with tools, but this isn't a tune-up. This is a complete rebuild. A costly one at that."

"I have the money, and I want to do it for my mom."

He goes quiet. How can he argue with that? He can't. At least, I'm hoping he won't. I'm still unsure who has the rights to it, but he seems confident he does. Crossing his arms over his chest, he looks back at the vehicle. "It's not mine to decide. I think you should talk to Pris and your dad, but I'll put in a good word for you, brother." He flips the cover over it again.

It's gutting to see it hidden away again, but more so that I have no say in the matter of ownership. "Thanks."

I follow him back out, looking back once more before we head into the large equipment barn. I'm slow, my whole being protesting leaving that car behind.

"You're moving slow today. You need some coffee?" he asks. "Didn't get much sleep or what?"

In the rising sun of the new day, I reach over my shoulder and scratch the back of my neck, trying not to think about those strawberry tattoos on my Shortcake, the taste of her sweetness, and how she sounded like an angel when she came. That's not something I need to share with him. "No, not much."

"The storm was bad. I was up earlier than usual to do some cleanup around the place before starting the day. We had a few downed branches by the house and some on the other side of the field near the front rail."

I've known him most of my life, if not all of it, and never seen him look happier. This is despite waking up at some ungodly hour to clean up branches around the property. He probably did it with a smile as well. Tagger sure is in his element out here. "How'd you make the transition back to this life so easily?"

Climbing up on a tractor that looks brand new to me, he replies, "It's in our blood, brother. This is what we do."

"No, we're both in finance. Well, you used to be."

Chuckling, he settles in the seat. "This is more satisfying. Pris and our kids are a big part of that, too. I wouldn't be here if I hadn't fallen for her. My son is thriving here, and Pris took him under her wing like one of her own. She's the glue that made this life possible."

"I should be pissed that you broke your promise to me about not dating my sister, but you make it hard to be mad about when it turned out the best for both of ya."

He looks ready to get on with his day, but before he starts the engine, he says, "We got away from this town so fast, I never had time to look back to see what I left in the rearview mirror. And don't get me wrong, Baylor, I don't have many regrets. But when I came back, I was ready for a change from the life I created. I needed the change and so did my son. We don't all travel at the same pace, but if you slow down a bit, you might find that the life you were running away from might suit you best." He starts the tractor, then yells, "You're here now. Why don't you go spend some time with your dad and your niece and your nephew? I'll loop around for some beers and hoops later." Patting the steel body of the tractor, he laughs. "I've been dying to get this girl out of the barn since she got her new tires."

I walk to the side to get out of his way. This is a man who used to pay for bottle service on the regular when we first moved to Manhattan after college graduation and could drink me under the table before we turned twenty-one. I taught him the best plays on the football field. He taught me the best plays off the field. And now here he is, excited about new tires on a tractor.

I don't know whether to shake my head in disappointment or wonder if I'm missing out. He stops just ahead of me and looks back. "You want to take her for a spin?"

"I'm good." There's never time to waste on the ranch, though I have to say I miss the days we used to take the trucks out muddin' or were getting up to no good until the sun went down. "I'll see you later."

"Hoops."

"Beers."

He drives the tractor around the back heading toward one of the back fields. So I start back toward their house down near the woods by the river. I owe those kids some play time like the awesome uncle I am.

I look around the property as I make my way across the fields alongside a gravel driveway they had laid since the last time I was here. It's a nice house. Big, made for large families. It makes me curious how many kids they want. He's already at two with one on the way, and we're the same age.

We're sowing seeds in different ways these days. Settling down looks as pretty as a picture when my head is clear of the noise pollution of the city. I don't mind putting in a hard day's work out here, but it's not the life I want to live as a bachelor.

Would I choose this life otherwise?

That's not a thought I've given room to breathe since before my mom died. It's probably best if I don't do it right now either. What's the point?

I have a great career, an apartment with incredible views, endless options when I'm wanting company, and conveniences twenty-four seven. Peachtree Pass doesn't even have a food delivery. Heck, there are only a couple of places in the entire county and the one next to Greene County to get food after five o'clock.

That chicken salad sandwich pops to mind. Tasty, like the woman who made it. I need to wipe this damn grin off my face before Chris catches sight of me. I'll never hear the end of it. And she never needs to know what happened last night with her best friend. Was that a conversation we should have had? Maybe it was understood. I can't imagine Lauralee telling my sister what we did. There's nothing to gain from sharing that news with anyone, but boy would it cause a dustup in this town if news got out.

Beckett comes flying out the front door, then jumps off the porch. "Uncle Baylor, want me to show you the fort I built?"

"Heck yeah, I do."

Christine comes out holding Daisy's hand. "We just had breakfast. I saved you some."

I'd forgotten that it's three square meals to keep you going out here in the Hill Country. I rarely have time to eat breakfast when I'm in the city, and lunch, unless I'm doing business, isn't a priority beyond something grab and go to eat at my desk.

"I'll eat, but later. Beckett's going to show me his fort."

She smiles wide, an ease in her stance and contentment in her eyes. "So you're the lucky one. He won't show us." She dips to pick up Daisy and anchors her on her hip. "Not even this little one."

Reminding me of his dad at that age, I'm almost transported back to a different time and place, both feeling foreign to me these days. Beckett slows just as he reaches me. "It's for members only."

Ruffling his hair, I ask, "Am I a member?"

"Just us. And Macon from class."

We start walking toward the woods on the back side of the house. Before we pass the porch, Christine says, "You two have fun."

I give her a wave along with Beck. He's growing faster than a weed and is taller than I remember. I nudge him. "This other member, Macon, is he your buddy?"

"He's my best friend." The pride in his voice has me thinking about Tagger and me at his age. We were inseparable. He was usually dropped off when we were young, but I'd go over to his farm some days too. Our parents knew how to keep us busy and out of trouble . . . until we got our licenses. There was no stopping us then.

"You know your dad is my best friend."

"Yeah, he talks about you. He said he wishes you were closer. Miss Christine says the same." We cut across the back acre of the house and head to where the trees grow tall and thickest. We call them the woods because they always felt mysterious compared to the wide-open fields. I'm sure others who knew better would have mocked us for it.

I can see the same excitement in his eyes that I once had as we close in on the border between the known and what magic is hidden in the trees.

"I miss them." Reaching over, I tug him to my side by

the shoulders. "You, too, big man. You know I was there the day you were born in New York City. Your mom and dad were so proud of you. I got to hold you right there and then."

"My mom is having a baby with Marcel in France." This is news ... "Do you think she'll forget about me?"

"Impossible. She loves you too much. When was the last time you saw her?"

We step into the brushy needle bed covering the ground under the trees. I let him lead—in conversation and to the fort—giving him space to speak freely. He replies, "She came to Austin last month for spring break. I stayed with her at an apartment on the lake."

"Did you have fun?"

"There was a pool."

"A pool? Well, that answers my question." He nods as if it really does say all that needs to be said. "I always wanted a pool."

He keeps walking, then stops to look back. "I miss you, too," he says, picking up where we left off earlier in the conversation. I move in, pulling him to me and wrapping my arm around him. He wraps his arms around me and looks up. "Why can't you live here?"

We start walking again. "My life is in New York, buddy."

"Your life can be here. We'd have so much fun. I'll even share my bunk beds. You can pick the one you want, and I'll take the other, though I prefer the top."

"Why is that?"

"Because the light from my booklight can't be seen under the door."

"You're sneaking to read books at night?" This kid is better than I ever was.

"Yeah. When I'm on the bottom bed, Dad said he saw

the light shining under the door and I shouldn't be up that late."

I see a structure made of branches ahead, but don't say anything because I want him to be the one to show me, but there look to be some good architectural skills on display. "I got your back. You can have the top bunk."

"Here it is." He runs around a tree and then stands in what looks like the start of a horse stall. With his arms wide, he smiles with pride and then points up. "I want to build a treehouse up there." When he looks at me, he asks, "Will you help me?"

"This is impressive, Beckett. Have you drawn up plans?"

"This is homebase but up there will be for members only. It's all in my head."

I cross my arms over my chest and look up. "There are some good branches up there. We can test the weight load and put a plan together."

He crosses his arms over his chest, mimicking me. "That's what I was thinking."

Grinning, I hold out my palm to him. "You sketch out your ideas and I'm in."

When he slaps his hand down on mine, we shake on it. "Really?"

"Really."

"Does that mean you'll move here like Daddy and me did?"

I see what he did there. *Clever kid.* But I'm not sure how to answer that other than to reply, "I'm thinking it will take a few visits. Maybe three to get the job done. How's your schedule this summer?"

He laughs. "Wide open."

And just like that, this kid got me to commit to hanging around Peachtree Pass more often. That sends thoughts back to last night and how this morning feels a little empty without Lauralee around. That's a new feeling. Finding an excuse to see her again, I ask, "Hey, want to go into town this afternoon and get some ice cream?"

We start heading out of the woods. "Can I get bubble gum ice cream?"

"You can get two scoops if you want."

He takes off running with his arms out like an airplane, and yells, "Yes," into the wind.

I'm a fucker for finding a reason to see her. Guess I'm about to find out if she's happy to see me again, too.

CHAPTER 7

Lauralee

THE TIMER GOES OFF JUST as I start frosting a cupcake order for pickup in one hour. I set the piping bag down and grab the oven mitts on the way to the oven. The delicious smell of freshly baked cookies escapes the oven as soon as I open the door. I take a deep breath as I pull the tray out and set it on the counter, never tiring of my job.

I get to bake and create for a living. What more could a girl ask for?

I hear the bell chime over the front entrance. "Be right out," I call, hoping they can hear me. I'm quick to wipe my hands on my apron before pushing the door that leads to the front counter. Said door whacks my ass, scooting me forward when my feet failed to do the job.

Looking more ruggedly handsome than ever in his T-shirt and jeans, Baylor says, "We came for ice cream." The smirk on his face says a whole lot more than that, reminding me exactly where that mouth was last night, causing me to squirm in place.

My eyes dip to the familiar little tow-headed cutie holding his hand. It's quite the sight to see a man of his stature taking care of kids, especially as protectively as he's holding Daisy's hand. "I can help y'all with that." I come around the counter and dip down in front of her. I poke her playfully in the belly. "How are you, punkin'?"

She giggles, tossing her head back and holding her belly, her curls bouncing with every laugh. Throwing her arms around my neck, she rests her head on my shoulder. She's become one of my favorite people in the world. I'm just lucky that I also get to be her godmother. Rubbing her back, I ask, "You want your favorite?"

Nodding, she steps back and touches my cheek with her hand. "Nilla pease, Leelee."

"Vanilla coming right up." I tap her nose and stand up, my eyes landing on Baylor again. "She's a classic kind of girl." I set her on a counter stool and when I look his way again, he smiles, making my cheeks heat from the sincerity found tilted in the corners of his mouth. I look away and take a quick breath to keep my heart calm, knowing it wants to race away if I let it. It didn't take long for me to become utterly ridiculous around him. I bet he's used to that reaction, but I'm not. "You in charge for a while?" *Why'd I just bat my eyelashes?*

By his smirky expression, I take it he's catching everything I'm putting down, even though it's involuntary. Get a hold of yourself, Lauralee. "Thought Chris and Tag could use a break. He wasn't wasting time either. I saw him heading to the house with some hand tools like a man on a mission."

"Is that a euphemism?"

"What?" His head jerks back on his neck. Covering Daisy's ears, he says, "No. Gross. That's my sister."

I start to laugh and top it off with an eye roll. Eyeing Daisy's ears still covered, I ask, "What do you think she'd think about what happened last night?"

"I don't know. She's not going to find out from me." He releases his niece's ears when she gets wiggly and knocks his hand away. "I wanted to ask you about that."

"Ask if I'm going to tell her? No. I don't think one-time bears mentioning." I hate that it suddenly feels less than for us. Especially when I can still see passion as his gaze rakes down my body. Assessing. Sexy. I clear my throat and change the subject. "I sense a Beckett in the area."

As if cued, he comes running from the back of the store holding up a package of Big League Chewing Gum. "Can I get this, Uncle Baylor?"

"I think I basically stock that for him these days."

Baylor eyes the gum and chuckles. "I used to love that stuff when I was young. You can get it. You still want ice cream, right?"

"Bubble gum."

I stand and move behind the counter again to get the scooper. "I should have known. I remember the first time you came to the store with your dad. You got the same flavor."

"It's the best flavor."

Holding my hands in the air, I shrug. "I won't argue." I put a scoop of vanilla in a small cup for Daisy, just how she likes it, and then two scoops of Beckett's favorite on a chocolate-dipped cone. Daisy has made herself at home at the counter while Beckett eyes up what else he can talk his uncle into buying him.

I turn to Baylor and smile, amazed that it only took one night to change our relationship, to create from nothing like we had before. Good or bad remains to be seen, but it sure feels good to be caught in the gaze of his attention. I tap his chin, though that bottom lip is tempting me. "And what would you like?"

"Mmm." He comes closer to the counter and studies his options, but his eyes never leave me—my eyes, my mouth, my chest. Even with an apron on, the heat from his gaze warms me from within. It's not ice cream he seems to be craving. "What do I want?" he replies, dragging out each word with intention in his tone.

Plucking the front of the apron, I try to let air in by fanning my body.

"Nilla," Daisy replies.

We burst out laughing. It feels so good to release the tension that had been building. I swing my gaze to her, noting she could use a wipe around . . . well, her whole face. Glancing at Baylor, I say, "You think about it while I clean her up."

I grab a package of wet wipes from under the counter and walk to sit next to Daisy. Her eyes are so blue that I used to only see Chris, but now I see Baylor, too. I wipe up her face just as she finishes her ice cream. "Was it good?"

"Mm-hmm." She nods and holds her arms out. I bring her to my lap as she attaches to me with her arms around my neck. Rubbing her back, I ask, "You tired? Is your uncle Baylor keeping you busy?"

She nods again, this time relaxing against me. It's not busy this time of day; the hours after lunch and before late afternoon sets in. I kiss the side of her head, then look up to catch Baylor watching me.

He says, "On the drive over, she said she wanted curls like Leelee's. Dark with long hair."

Her hair is so fine and light in color with sweet little

pigtail curls. I rock back and forth just enough to encourage the nap she's decided she needs. "Growing up, I was always envious of Christine's hair. The color and it didn't matter how messed up it got, mine looked like a rat's nest compared to it."

Leaning against the ice cream case, he rests his elbows on the top, appearing to be staying a while. I wouldn't be upset if he did. I just know the kids aren't going to let him lounge around too long.

He says, "I like your hair."

Simple but direct and sweet. "Thank you." I'd noticed his, but it doesn't matter how many times he drags his fingers through it, he always looks freshly-rolled-out-of-bed-sex appealing. Men have it so easy.

"I think I've decided."

Resting my head against the top of Daisy's, I ask, "Decided?"

"I've decided what I want."

His grin isn't even naughty, but his eyes are by how every insinuation lies in the bluest parts of them as they intensify on me. I bite the side of my bottom lip, but then whisper, "What do you want, Baylor?"

"Shortcake." He gives me a wink. "It's my favorite."

My mouth falls open as I stare into devilishly sexy eyes. I take a breath and clamp it shut, knowing I'm going to hell for flirting with him while holding a child. And God, Chris better never find out.

But then it hits me. *We're flirting.* Baylor Greene is flirting with me, and I'm doing it right back. My throat has gone dry, my hands are sweating, and my tummy clenches from the look in his eyes. Oh, he's good. *Too good at this.*

Unsure what to do other than stand, I'm careful not to wake Daisy as I go to hand her to him. She settles on him, turning her head to the other side, but her eyes are still closed.

"You know we're going to hell for doing this in front of her, right?"

"What are we doing?" he asks, holding her like she's his own.

And there go my ovaries.

Dragging my palms down my apron, I grab a cup and fill it with water from a pitcher nearby. I down half before I dare turn back. It's tempting to just disappear into the kitchen and pretend this never happened. What are we doing anyway?

How did this escalate so quickly?

I know how. The man is hot. *Fantasy hot.* Inspiring me to invite him over again. *No.* That would be too forward.

Forward?

That's what I'm worried about. I roll my eyes at myself and shake my head. I should be more concerned that I want to have sex with my best friend's brother, Daisy and Beckett's uncle . . . *Oh my God.* I'm a horrible person. Have I become so desperate that I'm not just thinking about the hometown hero in a compromising position, but I can almost feel his mouth fucking me like he did last night.

Good lord, the man's practically an out-of-towner at this point. He leaves on Monday. Baylor Greene is the last person I should invest my heart or anything in.

"Hey there," he says, his voice bringing me back to what's happening right in front of me. He grins. "You disappeared on me."

"No," I lie. "I'm right here." I lean on the counter, trying to act nonchalant when I'm the most "chalant" I've ever been, wound up tighter than a knot that won't come undone. "I didn't make any shortcake today."

His expression relaxes, the lines easing at the corners of his eyes. "That's okay. You can make up for it later."

My entire body alerts. "Later?" *Please mean tonight.*

"Well, you know, another time."

"Right." I shake it off like I understood what he meant all along. "Another time."

Raising his free hand up in the air, he says, "I'm going to ask you about money, and that does not mean I think you're desperate or wanton or whatever your mind concocts at the moment."

I roll my eyes. So I went a little overboard this morning. It was early. I lacked sleep, but most of all, I was riding a high from our time together and didn't want it to end so awfully. "I won't attack." I flash a smile at him.

"How much do I owe you for the ice cream and gum?"

"May I have this apple juice?" Beckett asks, suddenly appearing out of nowhere.

Baylor looks down and ruffles his hair. "It's like you sensed my wallet coming out."

Beck laughs. "I promise this is it."

"You sure? You left candy on the shelves," Baylor says, teasing him. "Grab your gum and juice. I got you covered."

"Thanks, Uncle Bay."

"You're welcome." When Baylor turns back to me, he says, "It's not on the house either. I'm paying, so go ahead and ring us up."

"Since you insist." I tap on the register keys, then tell him the total. After swiping the card he already has waiting, I hand it back.

His hand covers mine, the tip of a finger running over the top of my hand. "I've been thinking about today."

"Hope they were good thoughts."

The way his eyes are set on mine has me thinking they

were not-safe-for-work thoughts. He licks his lips, then says, "I'll stop by again before I leave town."

I'm not sure what he means by that. Stop by and hook up. Stop by with the kids for ice cream. Stop by to say bye on his way to the airport on Monday. And I don't have time to ask before he turns to leave. "Have a good day. Bye, Beckett?"

He turns to wave, but I'm still stumped by his hot uncle and what stopping by before leaving town means to that man.

God, I hope it's what I think it is.

"DINNER, LAURALEE." My mom's voice carries from the kitchen at the front of the house to my bedroom in the back.

"Coming." I close my laptop and push off the bed. Padding down the hall in socks because she keeps it as cold as an igloo in here, I tuck my hands in the pockets of my sweatpants. Bundled in a sweatshirt I got from Colorado when visiting Chris at college years ago, I say, "It's so cold, Mom."

"I'm burning up, sweetie. Sorry."

"It's okay." I inspect the casserole on the stovetop. "King ranch chicken bake?"

Her shoulders slump forward in defeat. "I wasn't inspired."

"I know the feeling."

She scoops some into a bowl and hands it to me. "Did many customers come in today?" My mom opened the shop and bakery before I was in elementary school. I grew up in that place and learned to bake in the kitchen. She's been trying to step away and hand it over to me for quite a few years, but she's struggling. Like me, it's her baby.

"Actually, business was good. Saturdays always are with people passing through town or visiting the Hill Country." I set my bowl on the table and pour two glasses of water before sitting down.

She sits next to me at the table with a fork in her hand. "That's good. Anything eventful?"

"Baylor is back."

A smile comes naturally from the sound of his name. She always adored him even though she knew he would wreak havoc if you let him. We're all a sucker for a bad boy, I guess. "How long is he in town?"

"Quick weekend trip. He brought Beckett and Daisy to the shop to get ice cream."

As soon as she swallows a bite, she coos, "I bet that was adorable." And then right on time, she adds, "I always thought you and Chrissy would have kids at the same time."

I used to snap back at anyone who made a comment implying I had fallen behind in life or wasn't doing things on their expected timeline, or worse, treated me like a spinster at twenty-nine. I'm okay with the pace. I'm okay being me. "She met her soulmate." I take a bite.

"It doesn't have to be as glamorous as that."

Lowering my fork, I laugh. "Soulmates are now glamorous?"

"Well, my point is, reliability, someone who can take care of a family is not the worst thing you can find in life, Lauralee."

"And how did that work out for you?" I hate myself the moment the words leave my mouth. "I didn't mean that. I'm sorry."

"Your father . . . um." She takes a sip of water. When she

sets the glass on the table again, she continues, "I confused love for responsibility."

"Because you were pregnant with me."

"We did the best we could." She sets her fork down and looks at me. Her eyes are green instead of brown. Mine come from him, something I've always had to live with. My darker hair is from his side of the family. My height, my attitude. All from him. The man who had no interest in seeing this parenting thing through.

I reach over and cover her hand. "I know, but you're the hero of our story. He lost the role the day he walked out and never looked back. Who needs a man? Not us."

"That's not what I want you to take from my past and my relationship with your father." With her other hand, she covers mine. "You're right. Don't ever settle for less than your soulmate, sweetie. You have the shop. You have a life. You never accept less than you deserve. You deserve the world." Tears swim in the corners of my eyes unexpectedly, but she's holding me so tight that I won't pull away to wipe them. She asks, "Promise?"

I nod, feeling too choked up to respond. Getting up, she hugs my head to her body. "I love you, Lauralee."

Reaching up, I hold her. "I love you, too, Mom."

We finish dinner, and I volunteer to do the dishes. She stays close, drying each piece after I wash it. "When is the apartment being listed for short-term rentals?"

The apartment . . . my own place, space, and where I finally feel like an adult. Unlike my bedroom down the hall, which was still painted pink from when I went through a bubblegum-pink phase in seventh grade, "I think it's ready," I reply, lacking the excitement I once had for bringing in the extra income. I just want to stay there, even move there one day. But that's not the sensible thing to do. Bringing more people to Peachtree Pass, selling more in the shop, and making more money to start building my own bank accounts and investments are important.

I hand her the last one and dry my hands. "I think I'm going to work on it tonight. Get all the last details in place. I'll probably be late, so I'll just stay there."

"Okay. I'm tired, so I think I'll get in bed early with a new book I got and read."

I hug her. "Thanks for everything you've always done for us."

She cups my face, looks up—I've been taller than her since tenth grade—and smiles. "It was truly my pleasure. You are such a gift in my life."

"Aw." I tuck my head to her shoulder. "Love you so much."

"Love you."

I don't waste time packing my bag and throw it in the car. Not sure why I'm in such a hurry, but it feels freeing to call somewhere my own. I have my own life. My mom doesn't hold me back from living it. She's good about not judging ... most of the time and knows about almost everything in my life.

But it's not the same when you still lay your head down in your childhood bedroom, resting on the same mattress I've always had, and staring at the same alarm clock I got when I was ten years old.

I'm sentimental, so I keep so much the same, except for my new place. That's where I get to reinvent myself, where I get to be who I am now in the present and not stuck in the past. I open the windows and let the wind whip through the car, sending my hair flying about until I pull it back in a swift motion while still driving.

It doesn't take long before I catch the last of the sunset

and pull into the lot to park behind the building. Grabbing my stuff, I truck up the staircase and let myself in. As soon as I close the door, I feel like I can breathe easier. Not because of my mom. She's amazing. But I sure like feeling my age for once.

I uncork a bottle of red wine and pour a glass before getting into my pajamas and settling in on the couch to watch a series I've been bingeing. After snuggling with a blanket, a plate of deli ham, crackers, grapes, and slices of cheese, I'm ready to dive back into the show.

After the interesting night last night, the early morning, and the long day, I don't make it two episodes or finish the second glass of wine before I'm sprawled with my legs hanging over the arm of the couch. A knock on the door startles me.

Sitting up slowly, I plant my socked feet on the floor and stare at the door. No one should be knocking, especially at this hour. Do I ask who it is? Pretend no one is home? The knocking is louder with the second rap, causing me to jump.

But then I hear, "Lauralee? It's Baylor." My spine sags in relief, and I'm instantly grinning like a fool. "Lauralee, you home?"

"Coming." I stand quickly, tugging at my crop top and shorts until they're righted in place. I moisten my lips and unlock the door while patting my hair and hoping it's not too wild. As soon as I see his gorgeous face, I smile. "Hey there."

"Hey there," he says, smiling like I'm the first sunshine he's seen after a month of storms. With his hands tucked in his pockets, he rocks back on his heels.

I laugh lightly when it seems all he really needed was to see me. Tilting my head, I ask, "What are you doing here?"

"I needed to tell you something." His hands fall to his sides as a more serious side takes over his expression. Why am I suddenly so nervous?

Gripping the door tighter in one hand, I drag the palm of my other down the side of my hip. "What is it?" My smile falters along with his, unsure of what he'll say next. "What do you need to tell me?"

His breathing has deepened, and his eyes are laser-focused on mine. Taking a step forward, he cups my face. "This," he says before his lips crash into mine, and he walks me backward into the apartment.

It happens so fast that I grab his shirt to hold, pulling him as close as I can, and kiss him right back, never wanting anyone more than I do this man. As soon as we part to take a long-needed breath, I ask, "What took you so long?"

"Damn traffic." He kisses me again, and all else fades away.

CHAPTER 8

Baylor

WITH HER BACK against the doorframe to the bedroom, she tips her head while her fingers fist my shirt, holding me as close as she can. "What traffic?"

I chuckle. "There was no traffic, Shortcake. I came over as soon as I could slip away from the family."

"Oh." A smile grows wide across her pretty face. "So no one at the ranch knows you're gone?"

"No one." I run my hand over her cheek, but my skin is too rough against her softness, so I push my fingers into her hair. I release the strands from the wrap holding it on her head and watch it tumble over her shoulders and frame her sweet face.

"In that case, we have all night."

"No sense in wasting a minute." I kiss her again, but it's not me moving this time. It's her, tugging me into the bedroom and toward the mattress. We're not going to take this slow. There isn't going to be a warm-up to get either of us in the mood.

We're already there.

Her nipples push against the thin cotton of her short top. Her lips glisten after being freshly kissed. A fire ignites in her eyes that tells me she's ready to do more than a little foreplay.

I grab her hips to stop her from slipping out of my reach and lift her. Her legs come around my center as I get a good grip on her ass. Her hands hold my face, angling me up to look into her brown eyes just before she says, "I hope you brought protection."

With her anchored around my midsection, I reach around to my back pocket and pull out the packets. Holding it up, the packets unfurl in rapid succession. "I brought protection, alright."

She eyes the string of condoms and starts to laugh. "And apparently some high hopes. Twelve, Baylor?"

"Anything's possible with you looking so good, baby."

Tossing the packets on the bed, I adjust her and slide my hand under her T-shirt. I rub my fingers over her pert nipple and then move to the other before pinching to watch her reaction. She sucks in a breath, but her eyes stay locked on mine. I lick my lips, and whisper, "So fucking sexy."

I nose under her shirt to taste her, to feel those perfect nipples against my lips. Her hands hold the back of my head, keeping me right where she wants me, exactly where I want to be. I flick her nipple with my tongue and take it between my teeth.

Gentle.

Gentle.

I nip just enough to cause her back to arch against me.

Rubbing her body against my dick, I'm so ready to be inside this woman instead of having layers between us. A groan rumbles through me, and when I lift my head, I kiss her again, stealing her breath and swallowing it down.

She rubs against me, her own wants murmured into my ear until she bites my lobe and whispers, "I want you. Please."

Please is all I need.

I set her on the bed and tug my shirt off first. She follows, taking hers off and tossing it wildly. Looking at her bare tits, I want to memorize each curve of her perfect body and the pink of her tips as goose bumps scatter across her chest. "You're beautiful, you know that?"

Her head falls to the side with a sweeter smile crossing her lips. "No, tell me again."

Grinning, I reply, "You're so beautiful, Lauralee. It's almost too much to take in." I start on the belt, but her hands replace mine. I could fucking come right here and now when she looks up at me like she's waited her whole life for this. "*Fuck* me, babe." I don't even know what I'm saying. I just know I can't wait to feel her from the inside.

"I'm trying," she says, adding a teasing smirk and a quick lick of her lips. My gaze homes in on the shine that glistens for me and the plush of those lips, which has me imagining what my dick would look like sliding in and out from that mouth. "You're so hard for me."

She's going to be the fucking end of me.

I reach for the crook of her neck, massaging any built-up tension, and slide up the back of her head. "So fucking hard for you."

Wrapping her hand around the base of me, she takes the other and slides it over my abs. She doesn't disappoint when she closes her eyes and takes me into her mouth. Stopping as if it's too much, the intensity between us, the size, the need for another breath, and slide farther down until she reaches her hand and sucks.

"Uh," I breathe out, closing my eyes and letting my head swim in the heat of her mouth.

When she slides back, I force myself to take her in, catching her eyes beaming up at me in pure pleasure. The vixen. She just might be the devil in disguise. *Fucking hell.* I'm ready for the downfall.

Taking me in again, she moves quick after a flick of her tongue over my tip and grants me a savoring moan. And then I'm deep inside her mouth again, tapping against her throat and yanked from the bliss over and over again until I'm on the verge of losing everything.

As soon as she swallows around me, readying herself, I hold her there. Her eyes flash open and stare up at me with questions. Gathering myself together, I stand firm, keeping my voice steady, and say, "I want to look at you just like this. Remember this when I'm back in the city and get off to the memory." If I could take a picture, I'd frame it and hang it above my bed. She's fucking stunning wrapped around me like this.

I pull out slowly. Leaning down, I tilt her chin up and kiss her gorgeous, swollen lips. "As incredible as it would be to . . ." My eyes drop to her mouth again as I run the pad of my thumb over the cushion of her bottom lip. "Finish here." I drag my gaze to her eyes again. "I'm going to come with your body wrapped around mine and caught in the best orgasm you've ever had."

"The best I've ever had is a tall order."

"I'm up for the challenge."

She bites her lip, and says, "I don't doubt that for a second." She stands with a smirk and pushes down her little shorts. "I've been counting on it."

Damn. I slowly exhale, looking over her bare body as she stands before me, allowing me to indulge in more than a once-over. "So fucking sexy."

And time is of the essence. I toe off my shoes and tug my socks from my feet before stepping out of my jeans and boxer briefs. Now it's just the two of us with nothing to hide behind but our words. No masks and no clothes. All of us exposed.

She leans back on her elbows, her gaze taking the scenic route to my face. Smiling, she says, "And here I thought tonight would be boring."

"Nope." I climb on the bed next to her. "I'm here to entertain."

I love the sound of her laughter when it's louder and taking up space in the room. It's the sound of Lauralee being who she really is; the joy that sparks in her eyes when she's excited matches this exact pitch of her laughter.

We scoot higher on the bed. But before she tucks her legs under the covers, I reach over to stop her. "Don't hide. I like looking at you."

Her cheeks heat pink, and her body squirms. "I like the way you look at me."

"Good because I can't seem to take my eyes off you." I roll to my side and kiss her. I cover her with my body.

She widens her legs, welcoming me in to settle between them. Our bodies grazing, her softness against my hard, my muscles to hers as our tongues tangle along with our legs.

Our mouths part when I reach down for the packets on the lower half of the mattress. When I return to reclaim my position, she's smiling. The tips of her nails scrape gently across my hairline before adding more pressure and dipping into my hair.

I ask, "What has you smiling like that?"

"You. You're the one I never saw coming." My chest tightens from her words, that fire in her eyes softening to a flickering flame. But then she says, "Seems you got me right where you want me. Now what are you going to do?"

"I have a few ideas." I rip a packet from the fanfold and sit up on my knees to cover my length. I like how she watches me, how desire coats her gaze and burns through the wriggling of her hips. I like that she wants me as much as I do her.

Dropping back down into place, I plant my elbows on either side of her head and position my dick at her entrance. When she cups my face and lifts to kiss me, I push inside her, swallowing her gasp and tasting her moan.

The heat shoots through my veins.

The embrace that feels like it engulfs my entire being.

The passion I feel for this woman culminates, causing me to pause as soon as I'm buried to the hilt. I drop my head on the bed beside her. With my eyes closed, I take this in, overwhelmed by the sensation of being inside Lauralee.

I've had thoughts since the reception and again last night, which didn't lessen the drive building in me to taste the forbidden. But this is better. So much better than I imagined.

"Are you okay?" she asks, whispering against my neck and placing a kiss there. Her arms hold me as her hands rub my back.

I smile when I lift my head, angling toward her. "I'm better than okay."

She smiles with the slightest of nods.

Balancing on one arm, I reach down between us, hooking my arm under her right leg and lifting just as I pull out and thrust back in. "Oh yeah . . ." I groan, picking up pace. "Does that feel good?"

"So good." She closes her eyes and holds on as I fuck, hitting her in all the right ways, judging by how her mouth hangs open and her back arches, putting those beautiful tits in my face.

The slap of our skin, the sweat on our bodies, and the sound of our connection have me pumping harder to meet her thrust for thrust until I can see her beginning to unravel beneath me. Erratic jerks, the squeeze of her body on my dick, and her thrashing head as she begs for more and harder.

I give it. I give her everything she wants and more than she'll ever need. "You going to come for me, baby?"

"So soon. Don't stop. Don't stop," she pleads, angling her hips so I can hit deeper inside her.

I dip my hand between us and flick her clit before rubbing the begging bud. With each stroke, I can hear her breath get wilder. But when her nails dig into my shoulders and she lifts off the bed, her voice goes ragged. "Oh God, yes, Baylor. Yes. Yes."

Little earthquakes radiate through her body, the tight embrace around me, dragging me with her. I fuck. I fuck. I fuck and then crash into the wave overcoming me. I float in the abyss, searching for the light. When I latch onto a star in the distance, I feel the peace that comes in the aftermath and give in.

It's only a whisper, but I hear the sweet melody of her words when she says, "Come back to me."

Pulled into her here and now, I smile against her skin. "I'm here. Right here with you, Shortcake."

I can feel the pull of her smile against my temple. She plants a kiss there before adding, "Roll over, big boy. You're smothering me."

Chuckling, I roll to the side and open my eyes to see hers

already on me. "That was . . . you're amazing, you know that?"

"No. Tell me again."

I grin wider and kiss her shoulder. "You are amazing, Lauralee Knot. How's that?"

"It'll do for now, but I might need to hear it again in the morning."

I dig my elbow into the mattress and lean over her to kiss her. "I can do that." When I fall flat on my back, though, I feel the exhaustion from the day catching up to me. "Tonight, I just want to hold you."

She doesn't have to be asked. She's already sliding up to my side and snuggling against me. "I can do that."

I kiss the top of her head and scrub a hand over my face. I'm not sure what kind of mess I just got myself into by coming over here, but I'm not too broken up about the repercussions that will rise with the sun come tomorrow. There's too much to enjoy in the present to worry about the future. "I sure am glad you answered that door."

"About that? Next time, give a girl some warning. I would have dressed a little differently."

"If I warn you, I don't want you dressed at all."

"That could be an option for next time, too."

I kiss her before lying back. "I like the sound of there being a next time."

"Next time you're in town?"

Rolling onto my side, I face her. "Next time, as of right now."

"I really like the sound of that." Kissing me, she uses her body to roll me onto my back. "But this time, I'm on top."

I was worried about hell, but I've died and definitely gone to heaven.

CHAPTER 9

Lauralee

What just happened?

Well, I had sex with Baylor Greene *multiple times* after he showed up like a man on a mission to see me and charmed me right into bed. And by charmed, I mean he kissed me like he couldn't survive another second on earth if he didn't.

I practically swooned to death right there under his passionate lips, his strong hold on me, and the intensity that we both totally understood where this was heading . . . to bed.

Lying with my head tucked into the nook where his shoulder meets his neck, I've slept very little, too busy staring at the ceiling and thinking about how much I like the feel of him in my bed, against my body, and how comforting his presence is.

Unexpected.

Unexplainable.

Unfortunate since he leaves in twenty-four hours.

He stirs and places a gentle kiss on the top of my head.

"Have you slept at all?" he asks, his rugged voice groggy from exhaustion yet still so sexy.

"A little," I lie, but maybe I dozed off a few times over the past few hours. I don't feel tired at all.

"What's on your mind?"

The slightest of laughs escapes me. "It might be easier to talk about what's not on my mind."

"Okay." I hear the lightness in his tone like a smile has taken hold. I bet it's a great smile, but I'm too comfy to move to see it in the dark. "What's not on your mind?"

"The Dow Jones and what makes the Curaçao liquor blue."

There's a pause in his breathing, but then he chuckles. "Being in finance, the Dow Jones is always on my mind. As for the drink, isn't it just blue dye?"

"I don't know. I've not been thinking about it, but I guess I'll add it to the long list of other things on my mind now."

"There's no need to concern yourself with things that can wait until daylight." His finger finds the base of my chin and lifts until our eyes find each other in the dim light of early morning that dares to sneak in through the crosshairs of the blinds. "What's got your mind all tangled, Shortcake?"

"Everything," I whisper, knowing full well that's a cop-out.

His left cheek lifts so slightly, but it's so comforting to see him relaxed and dare I say, happy. "This. You've been here for two days, and it already feels like you've unpacked and taken up your own corner of my thoughts."

"Oh yeah? Is that good or bad?"

I laugh, tempted to hide my eyes from him because I know they give so much away. I don't, though. I hold the contact and reply, "Too good if that makes sense."

"It does." Baylor slides his hand across my collarbone to

my back and then brings me in closer. "We struck like lightning. Out of the blue."

I nod. "With daylight coming, it's starting to feel like the end is near."

He kisses my forehead. "I don't have anywhere to be."

"Until the farm comes to life and your family starts looking for you again."

This time, I feel him nod against the top of my head. "Why don't you come out for lunch? Chris is planning a big meal to send me back to the city stuffed with some of my favorite foods. I think it's a ploy to get me to come back more often."

"I wouldn't be so upset if it worked." Why hold back? There's nothing to lose at this hour by saying what's hanging on my heart. The sun will rise, and we'll return to being the casual friends we've always been.

"Guess we'll see." Rolling to his back, he lies with his arm over his head as if the weight of something came over him. Maybe I said too much? Perhaps my being sentimental with a man I just had sex with is too soon? Maybe this is a lot for both of us to process? "Stop overthinking it."

"What?" I reply defensively because I was in so deep with my thoughts that I've looped back around to the top to start overthinking from the beginning again.

Turning to look at me, he asks, "Do you regret what we did?"

"No." I won't lie about that. "I liked it too much." I grin like a fool for this man.

Best part? He grins right back at me. "Me too, so how about we take one step at a time? Come for lunch at the ranch."

"And eat corn on the cob like I didn't have the best sex of my life just hours prior with the man sitting across from me while my best friend talks about her favorite potato salad recipe?"

"Yes." His hand finds mine. He brings it to his mouth and kisses my palm. "And tell me again about that best sex part."

I giggle. "How about you tell me about it?"

"Best sex ever," he whispers, shifting to his side to face me. He kisses my shoulder. My neck. That spot behind the ear that gets me worked up every time. The scruff from the shadow of his beard scrapes against my jaw, and then my lips are met by the pressure of his. He deepens the kiss as his knee spreads my legs apart for his body to take possession of the space.

I welcome him into me in all ways, this time taking the time to memorize the weight of his body on mine, the way his tongue twists with mine in a slow, calculated dance that has me humming in response. But it's his fingers dipping between my legs, the way he takes control of my orgasm, bringing me to the edge and then slipping on a condom to finish the job inside me that makes me miss him before he's even left the bed, much less Peachtree Pass.

I let go of my thoughts and the tension that uncoils from my body, releasing the worries I usually carry and embracing the release. He finishes just as I land back in reality. I hold him, needing to feel the erratic movements, the groan, the satisfaction as it rips through him like it did me. I need this to hold me when he's gone.

He exhales as he falls to his back on the mattress beside me. His hand takes mine with him as he holds it to his chest. "I think we should keep us under wraps at lunch."

I hadn't been thinking about lunch or that I was probably on the same page as Baylor when it comes to outing us. But hearing him say it as if I weren't . . . as if I'm now a lovesick teenager drooling over him changes things, and offense sets in.

Pushing up on my arm, I rest my weight on my hand and stare down at him. "Did you think I was going to waltz onto the ranch and announce we're sleeping together?"

He rubs my waist like he's trying to coax me back into his arms. "No, that's not what I thought. I just wanted us on the same page."

"That page being a dirty secret we're keeping?" I turn away, slipping off the bed.

"Come on, don't take it the wrong way."

"Is there another way to take it?" I snap.

"Yeah, how it's meant. It's too soon—"

"Please don't." I throw my hand up between us, hoping to stop him from saying more because if I let him continue, I'll feel the need to say something I might regret. So it's best to stop this conversation before it gets us both in trouble.

I grab a previously tossed shirt only to realize it's cropped as soon as I slip it over my head. With the lower part of my body fully exposed, I should probably be more concerned by how ridiculous I must look. Anger fuels a different energy, so I don't care one iota about my bare ass as I walk into the bathroom and shut the door.

I'm not sure what to do other than pace the tiny space, but taking two steps in one direction and three in the other isn't enough to burn off steam.

A soft knock on the door has me standing still. "Don't hide from me, Lauralee. Let's talk about this."

I hate miscommunication, but this doesn't feel like something that will work itself out through words. His words cut like a knife after what we just did. I move closer to the door. "Baylor, I don't want to argue—"

"Neither do I. Come back out here. We'll get some rest and see how things are in the morning."

I can be mad all I want, but he's being reasonable. I'm sure he's right. It's the late hour, a lack of sleep, but it was also expectations that had no right to grow into something of substance. I open the door to see him dressed in his boxer briefs, a small smile weighing on his cheeks that leans more toward sympathy than charming, but when I look in his eyes, I'm not sure how to read the emotions inside.

Taking me by the upper arms, he holds me with care as if I'm on the verge of breaking. "We're tired. Messages get mixed in the late hours. It doesn't have to be like that, though."

I slide my fingers across my forehead, wondering how I got here with him. It's not like me to invest in something not real, but I did with him. Embarrassment slips through my veins. With few options to get out of this unscathed, I say, "I haven't slept much."

With the minutest nod, he says, "Let's change that."

I'm better than the weakness I feel. I lean against him, hoping to hide what's on my mind and deal with this in the daylight. "Yeah, we should sleep."

When he walks to the bed, I detour to grab my pajama shorts and pull them on. His eyes are on me as he gets in bed, watching every move I make as if I'll escape before he can capture me in his arms again.

It's rational to recognize I might not be thinking clearly right now. It's also reasonable to realize that sleeping with him wasn't one of my best ideas, especially if we're to move on in life pretending it was casual sex.

He asks, "Are you coming to bed?"

I'd come so close to climbing under the covers. It would

be so easy to enjoy the time we have left, but what happens after? "I think..."

He sits up, and the covers fall from his toned torso, his strong shoulders displayed as he rests his arms on his knees. "Do you want me to leave, Lauralee?"

The question lies between us as the words race through my brain in search of the answer. I shake my head. "I don't know what I want, but I shouldn't want this like I do."

Without words, he gets out of bed and moves across the room to where he'd left his jeans on the floor. "I'm gonna go."

"Maybe that's best." My insides sure don't believe what I'm saying. I feel closer to being sick.

He stilled when I spoke, but without looking back at me, he gets dressed, grabs his socks and shoes in his hand, and walks into the other room. I make it to the doorway in time to see him grab his keys and unlock the front door. With his hand on the knob, he looks back at me over his shoulder. "I didn't want to complicate your life." He opens the door and steps outside. One last look back not only captures my eyes but also my heart. That's when I know that complicated is all we can be together. "See you around, Shortcake."

I raise a hand, but the words choke in my throat until it's too late to respond. The door is closed, leaving me with a heavy chest that I'm pretty sure is my heart. "See you around," I whisper while locking the door.

Leaning my head against it, I tap my forehead twice, conflicted if I made the right decision by cutting him out before getting hurt, or if I just let one of the best things to happen to me in forever walk out the door.

I lift my head and turn back to the bedroom. Walking through the quiet apartment leaves too much room to second-guess myself. It was a fun weekend fling. *Nothing more.*

"Exactly." I laugh, though it's forced. Throwing my hands up in the air, I try to laugh harder with real intention. "You're being absurd, Lauralee. It's not like Baylor Greene's your soulmate or anything." Even saying it out loud sounds ridiculous to my ears. But then my feet stop just as I reach the bed, and I look back toward the front door again. "I'd know if he were. Right?"

Ignoring how my entire body wants to run to see if he's still here by chance, I lie to myself, and say, "I'd feel it. Right?"

Would it be so bad if I just checked?

I roll my eyes as I head back to the door. Unlocking it, I rationalize once again that I was never supposed to fall for Baylor Greene. So I need to stop acting like I have.

Tugging the door wide open, I stare at the empty lot. Why do I do this to myself? Now all that's left is a stupid buildup of hope dropping to the pit of my stomach. This is good. Pain into power. Now I have the answer I needed.

There's no such thing as soulmates.

CHAPTER 10

Baylor

IT'S NOT the first time I've fucked up.

I can confidently say it's not the tenth or the hundredth either. A thousand times might be pushing it, though. I'm not that bad.

Yet I've successfully fucked up with Lauralee.

Slamming my hands down on the steering wheel, I stare out at the sun rising in the distance over the open road that leads to the ranch. It's a sight to behold and one I miss more often than not these days when I'm in Manhattan. But it can't take the sting away.

Should I turn around and apologize?

Or let it lie like I usually do?

I honestly thought Lauralee and I were on the same page, so I'm not sure why she took offense to me stating the obvious. Maybe it's that simple. It didn't need to be said. So when I did, it messed up what we'd just shared.

Ultimately, isn't this best?

No misunderstandings.

No confusion as to where things stand.

No feelings getting hurt in the aftermath of whatever this is. Well, other than what's already been said.

Crossing the cattleguard reminds me of all the times I used to try to sneak back home in high school. I knew how slow I needed to go to keep from alerting the entire ranch and, more importantly, my parents back then. Now, here I am, a grown man going four miles an hour over the metal grate hoping to keep everyone here less wise to my comings and goings.

I park a little way back from the main house, figuring I might be able to sneak into the house and get a few hours of sleep in my old room at the top of the stairs versus heading down to my sister's place and trying to get past the kids unnoticed.

When I carefully close the rental car's door, I hear, "Creeping around your old haunts?" I spy my best friend coming from the barn with a bucket in his hand. "Or sleeping around with your old hookups?"

"Now, Tagger. Don't be jealous," I say, chuckling as I walk toward him. Tossing my keys in the air, I catch them and stop with a few feet remaining between us. "Not all of us are settled down." I pop the imaginary collar of my T-shirt. "Some of us still have some wild oats to sow."

He chuckles. "Some of us are happier settled. You might want to consider trying the alternative."

"I think I'm good for the time being." Checking the time on my watch, I ask, "It's Sunday. Why are you up and about so early?"

"It's the only way I can make sure Pris gets her rest. Working the ranch is in her blood. She likes to be busy, so if

I can beat her to some of the chores, she's more likely to sleep in."

Although their relationship came with some turmoil, mainly from me, I couldn't have found a better match for my sister. He treats her how she deserves. As for her, she's his perfect match—a partner and spouse. They make an envious team.

That is . . . if I were looking to be in a relationship and all that. I'm not, so it doesn't matter. It's just good they found each other, is all.

Glancing at the house, I say, "I'm going to head in and get some sleep."

"Have a good one."

I start for the house again but stop and turn back when I reach the porch. "Hey, Tagger?"

Turning around, he takes a few steps back from where he was heading. "Yeah?"

"When you and Christine were dating, was the long distance an issue?"

He studies me, then sets down the bucket. Shoving his hands in his pockets, he replies, "It was because of the woman. It wouldn't have bothered me with anyone else I'd dated. With Pris, the distance was brutal. Have you met someone?"

Do I lie to him?

He'll suss out the truth. He knows me too well to fall for my lies. I say, "There's a woman of interest."

Grinning, he rubs his chin. "There's a lot of miles between Peachtree Pass and New York City. Dating long distance isn't something I'd recommend, especially with a job as busy as yours is. But for the right woman . . ." Tagger just picks up his bucket and says, "I'll see you later, man."

"See ya."

Why am I even asking questions that I already know the answer to? Guilt? Lauralee's mad. For now. She'll be fine with her miles-long line of guys who'd kill to date her. I'm probably the last person she wants to be in a relationship with anyway.

I sneak into the house only to be greeted by my dad sitting at the breakfast table with a cup of steaming coffee. "Morning," he says.

"Does anyone sleep around this ranch anymore?"

He laughs, which turns into a cough that he finally clears. "Did you see Chris or Tag out there?"

"Tagger."

"He's been a good addition to the ranch." He sips from the mug. "And to the family."

I shut the door behind me and hang the keys on a hook beside it. "Are we talking about Tagger now?"

Sitting back in the vinyl chair, he slides his mug closer to him across the yellow Formica-topped table with metal trim. Other than a few corners I nicked off growing up, that table will outlast us all.

"We're talking about you, son."

I run my fingers through my hair. "I just want to get some sleep."

"We'll talk later, then."

Oh joy. Should I get it over with now or take his offer? "Yeah, probably best." I walk to the stairs and head up.

When I reach the top, I hear him say, "Sunday is for resting. Get some good sleep, son."

Before I close the door to the bedroom, I reply, "Thanks, Dad."

Time slows here in Texas. It's nice to embrace that effort, even if only for today. My dad seems to get that even if he has other things he wants to discuss on his mind. No use talking when tired. Nothing good will come of it.

Learned that firsthand.

After settling in, I lie in bed with my eyes closed, but my mind stirs too much to rest. I'm taken across the Pass to where I left, remembering how she moved on top of me, her hair falling over her shoulders, those brown eyes locked on mine. The smile that played between the angel and the devil on her lips, her mood tempting her one way or the other with each rock of her body as she got closer to the reward.

I scrub a hand over my face. *She's so fucking sexy.* Lauralee's the kind of sexy that gets noticed in a room the moment she walks in, an unclaimed trait that she seems oblivious to possessing.

Yet she knows how to work when she wants to. I've seen her down at Whiskey's in a good pair of fitted jeans, a halter top showing off that midriff, and even a short skirt a time or two. Lauralee Knot is an anomaly, that's for sure.

Opening my eyes, I stare at the ceiling and the poster I hung when I was sixteen of a hot chick in a pink bikini and heavy makeup wielding a giant wrench. Did I actually believe she was a mechanic? Clearly, I could suspend belief back then when necessary. The woman is hot but not really my type these days.

I close my eyes, this time keeping my mind off the one I want to think about, and try to get some sleep.

"Bay Bay," Daisy says, standing on the picnic bench beside me and resting her head on my shoulder.

"You gonna miss me?"

When she nods, I set my fork down and swallow the

potato salad I just shoveled into my mouth. Wrapping my arm around her, I kiss her chubby cheek. "I'm going to miss you, too."

Beckett finishes chowing his corn on the cob and sets it down. "When can I come visit?"

While Daisy makes herself at home on my lap, I reply, "Anytime, buddy. I heard you still keep in touch with some of your friends from school in the city."

"We play games online together." His upper lip is stained red from Kool-Aid, always a telltale sign of summer on the ranch. His hair is lighter than it's ever been, another sign. But he's looking more like his dad every time I see him.

"Maybe you can see them when you're up there."

He looks at Tagger, who nods his approval. His dad asks, "That'd be fun, right?"

"Yeah. I'd need different clothes, though."

That catches my sister's attention from where she's sitting at the end of the picnic table in a lawn chair. "Why is that, Beck?"

He shrugs. "I like my clothes, but they're not for New York."

I set a wiggly Daisy down, who's quick to run to her mother, and say, "They're for whatever you want them to be for. You be who you are. It will all work out how it's supposed to."

I'm not sure by the indifference on his face that he's convinced, but he at least nods to give me some assurance. "We're starting on the fort when you visit next. Right, Uncle Baylor?"

"You have your design ready, and we'll get the wood next time I'm here."

"I've already started." Popping up, he asks, "Can I be

excused? The team is forming at five. If I'm late, I don't get to play with them."

My dad says, "You did well finishing that meal. I'd say you can run along if it's okay with your folks."

You'd think he was about to pee his pants by how antsy he is when he looks at them. Christine says, "All good. We'll let you know when we bring the cobbler out." He's already running when she adds, "Have fun."

Tagger reaches over and takes Daisy from her mom and situates her on his shoulders as he stands. "You up for a walk, Baylor?"

We don't get much guy time like we used to, so I have to take the offers when they come. "Sure."

I come around the table when he leans down to kiss Christine on the head and whispers something that tickles a grin onto her face.

Following him when he trails toward the fence line, I have a feeling this is more than just hanging out. The moment he sets Daisy down, she beelines right back to her mom, leaving him laughing. "Wherever she ends up in life," he says, "she's going to be running the place. She's the sweetest kid, but she's got fire in her."

"Like her mom."

His laughter comes heartier. "Just like her." We walk farther and eventually round the bend toward the equipment barn. The sun is still high in the late May sky, so there's no relief walking along the gravel road that leads us there.

"This morning—"

"We don't need to rehash anything said before the sun rose."

"How about finishing it?"

How do I talk about who I was with without outing Lauralee? "Get whatever it is off your chest then."

"You're asking me about long-distance relationships like it's a possibility. You and relationships aren't usually a mix. What gives?"

I kick a rock, then scratch the back of my neck to see if something pops into my head that doesn't give everything away. Nothing except the truth appears. "It's not unheard of. It's just not something I had much interest in. You know how much I work."

"I also know how much you play."

Shrugging, I keep my eyes in the distance across the cornfield. The stalks aren't tall enough to block my view of the property just yet. "Things change. People do. I'm thirty-three. Having someone around more often isn't the worst idea." I don't even know what I'm saying, but I might need a shovel to dig myself out of my hole if I keep talking.

"Long distance isn't having someone around more often. It's making the effort to see them. Who is she?"

"No one, Tagger. I was asking. That's it. No motive behind it." The truth. I like Lauralee, but that's it. I'm not moving back to the Pass to be with her like he did for my sister.

He stops and crosses his arms over his chest. Staring at me, he studies my eyes for the lies, then looks out over my shoulder. "There's not a lot of options here. I'm assuming you're not hooking up with Mrs. Smith now that she's widowed."

"She's eighty-three, fucker."

He chuckles. "That only leaves Maple Thornton down at the feed store and Lauralee. Since I know neither of them would give you the time of day, my guess is you're seeing some girl from Dover County you met at Whiskey's." Lowering his arms, he adds, "Am I right?"

I'm not sure how I feel about him assuming that about Maple or Lauralee. Maple hits on me anytime I walk into the store. So I'm not sure where he's getting his information, but I'm the one who won't hook up with her. I'm more curious about why he included Lauralee. What does he know that I don't? "Why wouldn't they give me the time of day?"

"Because they know you."

Still confused, I shake my head. "And?"

He rolls his eyes as he starts back toward the house. "You think Lauralee would hook up with you when she knows your dating history? Or should we call it your dating present?"

"I don't think you know her as well as you think you do."

I'm shoved to the side under another loud laugh. "And I don't think you know her at all. Look, she never claimed to be innocent, but she has her standards."

"Geez, thanks, friend." I'm not actually mad. He's right about her and me, but that doesn't change the fact that I've just spent the past two nights with her. So her standards must not be as high as he thinks . . . wait . . . *Fuck*. Did she lower her standards to sleep with me? Was it a pity fuck?

No. Not possible. She wouldn't do that, and everyone knows I don't need anyone to pity me. I don't like this conversation.

"I was no better. Nothing is tying you down, so no judgment over how you spend your time, but Lauralee is . . ." He seems to search the sky for a reply.

I try for disinterested, but I'm hanging on his unfinished sentence by a thread, ready to shout to get it out of him. "Lauralee is what?"

When he stops, his eyes fix on mine, a stare that hardens without a threat behind it. "I don't even know if Lauralee likes you, so I'm fairly certain she wouldn't sleep with you."

"Fairly is not a no."

"Sure, I can leave a little wiggle room to be wrong, but she's out of your league, brother."

"Want to bet?" What am I saying? I'm so fucking competitive that I'm challenging him over something I won't be able to prove without sharing the details. *No way.*

"I'll take that bet."

"What do you mean you'll take the bet?"

"You threw a bet down, and I'll take it. No way will Lauralee Knot sleep with you."

This would do nothing but muddy the situation. Lauralee and I agreed not just to keep this on the downlow but neither of us had any interest in pursuing things. That's why her reaction wasn't what I expected. I gave her the space she seemed to need to sort through what was on her mind. It felt like the wrong decision at the time and in my gut now. But she still didn't show up today for the meal, making it known how she feels. So our secret is safe. *Why risk it?* "What kind of nonsense is this?"

"You act like it's the first time we've made a bet over a woman." When we reach the corner post, we stop and look toward the house he built down the hill. "Dahlia Stouffer, sophomore year in college. Rita Manning, first year at the investment firm."

This time, I shove him to the side. "Okay, what-the fuck-ever. I get the point, but this is different."

"How so?"

I look at him like he's grown a third head. "This was college and New York shit we pulled. This is different."

"Because you know her?"

"Yeah, exactly that. And when I come home, I don't want to have a mess to clean up or need to avoid Peaches' Sundries when I visit."

"It's okay if you're not up for it."

He goes low, knowing I can't resist a challenge. "Motherfuck." Rolling my eyes, I don't know why I'd ever agree to this other than it would be the easiest bet to ever win. Especially since I've already won. "Fine. What are the terms?"

CHAPTER 11

Baylor

"I didn't expect to see you in today, Greene." I turn away from my Manhattan view to see my boss walking into my office. Robert Goodman, current president of Taylor and Goodman, checks his gold Rolex. "And before two o'clock. No wasting time for you."

He used to impress me when I was in my twenties, trying to climb my way to the executive floor. Now, I see how he flaunts his past achievements boldly on his wrist with no effort to do what made him rich. He just wants us to make him money. Maybe that can be said for the entirety of the corporate world. "No wasting time," I reply, moving around my desk and sitting.

"Good trip?"

Images of Lauralee naked under me come to mind. The way her eyes clenched closed and her mouth opened wide when she came has run through my head a few times since I left. So has her agreeing for me to go. I know it was the right thing to do, but I'm ready for it to feel like it was. Because right or wrong, it still feels like a mistake. I sigh. "Yeah, but it's good to be back." Not a complete lie. Time and distance from what happened this weekend isn't a bad thing for either of us.

He taps my desk. "How's the week look?"

"Two new client meetings and four current clients for their yearly updates. I'll be going over the progress, profits, and projections for the third and fourth quarters."

"I'm sure you can get a few more appointments scheduled." Taking a seat in front of me, he leans back and rests his ankle on his other knee. "What are the asset valuations for the new clients, at least?"

For quick reference, I flip a page in my notepad and scan down toward the bottom. "One is valued at seven-hundred and forty-nine million, and the other is at twenty-three million."

"That sounds like potential." He grins and glances out the window. "You earned this view." When he turns back to me, he says, "I want you to start thinking more long-term with the company."

"I've thought long-term since the day I was hired, Bob."

Slapping his leg, he sits forward. "And that's why you're sitting on the thirty-second floor with the executives." He stands. "Good work, Baylor." With a snap of his fingers, he grins. "The summer company party is at my house in the Hamptons this year over the Fourth of July. We're doing the big fireworks display and cookout thing. A room is reserved for you and a guest. I'm hoping someone significant to mingle with my wife and keep her occupied while the boys smoke cigars."

When he says "significant," I get the unsubtle hint. *Don't bring a fling or a one-night thing as my overnight date.* The only thing is, I don't have someone significant in my life.

"Or you can come alone, but we prefer these events to be family-focused if you get my drift." Other than him just saying he's trying to pawn his wife off on other guests to distract her from what he's doing, he can't be clearer than that.

"Understood."

"That's good."

As he heads for the door, he adds, "And let's try to be in the office before lunch next time. It looks bad to the other employees to see you coming in late."

It's tempting to tell him to fuck off since I left the Pass at three o'clock this morning to make sure I was on the first flight out of Austin, but I like my job and this view quite a bit, so instead, I reply, "Yes, sir."

He points back at me. "You're going places, kid." When he leaves, I continue staring at the empty doorway, unsure what to think about the interaction. He's right. I worked hard to earn this office and every client I serve. I've made my clients millions, and I'm closing in on the one billion mark for career win investments.

But I'm not a kid. That he sees me as a cub among the tigers still trying to earn my stripes is a problem. Eighty-hour weeks isn't enough? Has donating most of my weekends gone unnoticed? All the overnights before a big pitch pointless?

Why the fuck am I doing all this if I'm not getting noticed?

A head pops around the corner, and my assistant makes his way in. "I waited until the coast was clear," Mickey says, crossing the office.

"Clear from Bob? He's generally harmless unless you lose a client's money or, worse, him." Though he's currently on my shitlist. I leave that tidbit out.

In his mid-twenties and barely out of grad school, Mickey doesn't need to be burdened with the reality of working in finance. Yet. He'll learn it on his own soon enough. He sits in the chair that Bob abandoned. "He still insists on calling me Michael because he said Mickey is unprofessional."

"What does he know? So many greats in history are named Mickey. Mickey Mantle. A power switch hitter, the Baseball Hall of Fame, World Series record holder. Damn, he was even a Triple Crown winner." Kicking back, I lodge my feet on top of my desk and lean back with my hands behind my head. "And then there's Mickey Mouse. Look how his career blew up in a major way. Can you imagine if he had been called David or Mark the Mouse? It wouldn't have worked. Mickey was the only way to go."

"Not sure that one's going to convince him." He chuckles, then tugs at the knot of his tie to straighten it. "He's stuck on Michael, but the thing is, my name isn't Michael. It's actually Mickey."

"I can't say much. I was named after the university my parents attended. Go figure."

"Good thing they didn't attend Kalamazoo."

"Ha!" I drop my feet to the floor and start punching on keys to bring my computer to life. "Good fucking thing. Good weekend?" He shifts as if he's hesitant to answer. I look at him, recognizing the sly smile he's trying to hide. "That good, huh?"

"Pretty great."

I remember those nights. I had more of a life when Tagger lived here. When Beck was with his mom, Tag and I were unstoppable. We didn't have to work for attention. We just walked in, and it fell at our feet.

Basketball on Thursdays.

Just fucking around the city with too much money to burn for guys in their twenties.

When he had custody of his son, we'd go to games or watch from one of our apartments, order pizza, and teach the little guy all about football, baseball, or whatever was on.

I had a life.

Now, I have work that's not noticed by anyone. The fun is gone, which means, I need to make some big moves or move on.

Should I live vicariously through him? Probably not, but I need to know someone's having a good time. "Night out with the guys?"

"It started that way." He leans forward, resting his arms on his knees. Lowering his voice, he says, "You know how it is."

"Vaguely," I reply, grinning because I remember the good ole days a little too well when my best friend and I ran this city. Studying my schedule for the rest of the day, I then turn back to him. "Can you make sure conference room four is available for my three o'clock?"

Glancing down at his phone, he ticks off boxes listed on the screen. "I've already reserved it for the Sullivan meeting. I've ordered beverages and a tray of snacks just in case anyone's hungry. It will all be set up before you arrive. Do you want me to have a drink cart brought in?"

"I made them twenty million in the first two quarters of the year. We definitely need the drink cart brought in. How late are you staying tonight?"

"How late do you need me?"

I redirect my attention out the window to mentally work through my past meetings with the Sullivans. I return my gaze to the computer screen and flip to emails. "Don't stay past six."

"Six? That's early."

Do I tell him how he might one day be sitting in this very office, and they'll still think him sacrificing all his spare time was a waste? Nope. But I don't have to be complicit. "Six is good."

He stands and starts for the door. "There are four files with all the reports and bound for them to keep. But I also have the email ready to send with everything electronically."

Mickey's too on top of it. "You're making me look good."

"That's my job, right?"

"No. Your job is to predict the stock market for clients. If you had to name one investment for me to sink a few million into, what is your recommendation?"

"On the spot?"

Crossing my arms over my chest, I chuckle. "Yep."

"I'd go with Westcott Enterprises at the corporate level, but if you're looking to make some real money and aren't afraid of a gamble, I'd niche down to the Westcott Racing division for next season."

My jaw practically hits the desk. "You're telling me to invest in a race car team?"

Holding his hands in the air, he laughs. "I'm not telling you to invest in anything, but I feel confident in research."

I run my fingers into my hair, thinking through his recommendation. "I'm not sure what to say."

"Is that a good thing or bad?"

"Good, I think." I glance at the TVs hung on the wall showing the markets around the world and the ticker banners scrolling across the top just to see if their stock shows up. "I'm impressed with the outside-of-the-box thinking. I'll do some research and get back to you."

"Sure thing."

Just before he walks out, I add, "And Mickey?" He looks back. "Don't let Bob call you Michael since it's not your name. It's good to stand your ground early on. You'll get more respect that way."

"Will do." He shuts the door behind him, leaving me forty minutes to catch up on work before I need to be ready for the meeting.

First things first . . . I pull up Westcott stocks and start researching their profits and margins. I'm always looking for a good investment. Who isn't in this business?

There's a rush of adrenaline when a stock stands out from the masses. I'm getting that gut instinct now. It only takes a few articles to see that Mickey's right. They're on an upward trend, and shockingly, the price is reasonable. It's not ground floor, but I'm thinking we're nowhere near the peak of potential. I need to watch this for a few days and set the alerts.

He may be my assistant for now, but he's a quick learner. If this stock reflects the right trajectory, he'll be managing his own clients soon. If I make the right moves, he'll be enjoying this view soon, and I'll be running my side company full-time.

Is that the goal? It wasn't before this afternoon, though I was making strides for it over the past couple of years. Now, I need to be looking at the big picture for my career since Taylor and Goodman aren't doing it.

Redirecting my attention, I sift through emails for the ones that need immediate replies. The Fourth of July invitation sits at the top marked urgent. I click on it and skim the basics: date, time, attire, and the little details. I didn't have plans for the fourth, but I wasn't bothered by staying in the city for the holiday or even heading back to the ranch to spend it setting off fireworks and barbecuing like old times.

That brings me back to the bet, which has been lingering at the back of my mind since I saw it again. I know the devil won that round, but can I redeem myself to Lauralee by explaining what's on the line if she finds out?

I mean, I'm already an asshole for taking it. And then me leaving her place instead of talking to her just adds another layer of my fuckery. Sure, she wanted me to go, so that shouldn't make me the bad guy because I left.

I just can't stop thinking it could have played out differently between us if I had stayed. Not just for future sex, though I am an asshole for wondering if I still have a chance. But more because I don't want her to regret what we did. Or worse, feel shame for it.

That would fucking suck.

Accepting a bet regarding our sex life isn't going to win me any points. But it can get me that car, a car I've wanted most of my life. It's a car I was warned never to go near, and one of the few things left of my mom's that I could have. So Lauralee can call me an asshole all she wants. My intentions feel justified.

I check the time and gather my stuff. After setting my phone on Do Not Disturb, I head to the conference room, ready to make the Sullivans very happy and secure an extension on their contract. Maybe that will get Bob's attention. Or will it be my resignation that does the trick?

Lots to think about, and now, this damn party date to figure out . . . I can't say I'm happy to be back.

I TWIST the cap off the bottle of beer and fling it to the trash from between my fingers. "Score."

My voice lacks its usual enthusiasm. I'm not surprised. I've been up sixteen hours after traveling and working late again. It's easier to go through the motions than expend the energy.

I drop onto the couch, sit on the edge, and set my beer next to a container of beef and broccoli with noodles. After turning on the TV, I take a long gulp, and dig in. I'm starving, just now realizing I didn't eat anything today except breakfast on the plane at eight this morning.

Clicking through channels, I land on a baseball game. It makes no fucking sense that they're airing the Cardinals vs. Bluejays game instead of the Yankees or even the Mets. I sit back and zone out on it anyway, happy to be back in my own place, eating, and soon to be sleeping in my own bed again. I slept well with Lauralee, but that bed at my dad's house needs replacing. I'm probably bruised where a spring jabbed my back all night.

I shove another big bite in my mouth when my phone lights up. A text from Tagger appears on the screen: *She's a beaut.*

A photo pops up, showing the cover pulled back from the classic car that's been buried in a shed of a barn for more than thirty years. *My mom's dream car.*

She never got to drive it. But I could. I want to fix it and bring it to life again. Whether I win or lose it in this bet, she deserves to be driven again. If for nothing else, in my mom's memory.

Me: *She sure is. You've given me another reason to return.*
Tagger: *Lauralee?*
Grinning at the sight of her name, I shake my head.

She's a reason I could justify, but I type: *The fort for Beckett, and I'm going to start fixing that car.*

Tagger: *Good. I'll take my wife on sunset spins with the top down.*

Quick to correct him, I reply: *I'll let you borrow it sometime, but that baby is all mine.*

Tagger: *First, you have to win the bet.*

Me: *I'll win alright. Don't you worry about that. Just get ready to see a lot more of me.*

Tagger: *My wife and kids will be thrilled.*

I laugh as I respond.

Me: *You don't miss me, Tag?*

Tagger: *I guess I don't mind seeing that ugly mug around the ranch and kicking your ass in basketball.*

Me: *You kicking my ass in basketball isn't a thing. Reverse that, and you've got facts.*

Another message shows up before I can swallow a gulp of beer. *Prove it.*

The fucker is always so fucking competitive. I guess that's why we're such good friends. I text: *Happy to. I'll be back for the festival.*

One last message from him pops up. *See you on the court.*

This is what I miss. I just didn't realize it until I spent time there this past weekend.

I turn up the game, grinning like an idiot, and finish my noodles.

CHAPTER 12

Lauralee

"The Peach Festival is just around the corner," my mom says, coming into the shop like we're continuing a conversation started on her drive over. I laugh to myself as I load fresh scones onto a tray in the display cabinet. She asks, "Do you mind calling Tagger to help get the decorations down from the attic at the house?"

"I can't be calling him all the time. We can't give him a honey-do list like he's my husband." Standing upright, I slide the door to the case closed, then lean on the counter to watch her fiddle with a display of peach-themed tea towels with our logo.

Her eyes meet mine over the top of the metal rack. "Chrissy won't mind."

"I do, though." I keep my voice steady despite how I feel. "I can get the decorations down myself, Mom."

"You're never home anymore."

Calling the apartment my home is tempting, but I'm not

looking to hurt her feelings. What should I call a place that feels more me lately than anywhere else, though?

Why the hell does Baylor come to mind?

I thought I'd shaken him out of my system, yet he manages to invade my thoughts every chance he gets. Figures. I roll my eyes for allowing it to happen, like at night when I'm alone and wanting to replicate the orgasm he gave me. It's been fruitless, literally, but I refuse to be a quitter. Tonight is a new opportunity after all.

Though, admittedly, I couldn't even look Chris in the eyes when she stopped in two days ago. If she knew what I imagined her brother doing to me, she'd disown me.

Lordy, I need professional help. I need to look up some tips and techniques on how to free my mind of intrusive thoughts of one of the most handsome men ever to walk the planet. He arrogantly owns my headspace like he owned my body that night. Goodness, he's made a mess of my mind.

I can't even make strawberry shortcakes anymore without his absence hitting me upside the head. All because of that nickname he seems to have adopted for me. And, secretly, I love it. It makes me feel special. That's how desperate I've become for attention. I don't know whether it's sad or good that someone can make me feel so alive when we're together. Bad. That's what this is. I shouldn't be feeling anything toward Baylor Greene other than casual acquaintance or friendship second removed at most.

He's in New York.

I'm here.

No use dwelling on the fact that it's been two weeks since he was in Peachtree Pass, but I still feel the ghost of him haunting me in my day-to-day. It's not fair to me or him, considering I'm the one who agreed he should go. That was for the best, so why am I mentally dragging him back into my present like he should have stayed all along? *Figuratively, of course.*

"I'll do it tonight after dinner."

My mom comes behind the counter to inspect. She's never critical of the changes I've made to the shop over the years. Just curious and more than happy to give advice. "The paper napkins with peaches on them would be a great upsell near the register for the festival. Have you started cleaning the ice cream cart that will be stationed on the festival grounds?"

The festival is the Super Bowl event for our small town. It's the best time of the year around here. We're busy and making money. But it's also just a good time all around.

Dusting my hands off on my apron, I reply, "Already have the napkins stocked and ready to display. The cart is getting cleaned on Sunday. It's the only time I have this week to do it, but I did hire two girls to run the cart for the festival's duration. They're even making their own schedule. I will be approving the final hours."

"Oh, that's great."

Not sure how she'll take this, so I ease her into the idea while fidgeting with the birthday-candle display on top of the cake counter. "Two of them are looking for regular work. I've been thinking about bringing them on a few afternoons a week and for some weekend shifts."

My mom stills her hands on the register that she had started wiping down and looks at me. "It's a big job to run this place."

"Even bigger these days." I roll a stool over and sit, keeping one foot planted on the floor and the other on the foot bar. "I've turned away three orders in the past few days because I simply do not have the time to add more to my schedule. Lunches, especially, have become more popular. We have two small bistro tables, but we have more regulars from Dover County driving in for lunch lately. I'm out of food by noon and most don't have a place to sit and eat what food they do get."

"The whole area is growing." There's concern in her voice as she looks over the shop as if she'll know what to do after a once-over. "They built a new subdivision up Highway 160. Fifty-two acres with thirty plots." Leaning her hip against the counter after facing me again, she adds, "I like that you're thinking big picture. I was starting to worry you didn't want to continue running Peaches."

I'm not sure what would give her that impression when I spend every day here—baking, cleaning, prepping for each day and the next. "I wouldn't be here if I didn't. You built this place. I grew up here. It's a part of us, but I've grown the shop and café as much as I can on my own. We either need to cut back on what we offer, change around what we do and can offer, or expand into the empty shop next door."

My mom's hair is always impeccably in place. Today is no different, so this is the first time I see her fussing with a curl hanging on her shoulder and rebelling against the flow of the others. I can see her thoughts cloud her eyes before she turns away.

I hate the empty space and the silence between us, but I need to hear what she thinks. As much as I consider this place mine, it's not really when it comes to legality and paperwork.

Her smile is soft, as if bad news is following when she looks at me. "I can't take on more loans for an expansion, and I don't have it in me to make the kind of decisions necessary to run the shop like it needs anymore."

My heart sinks. *What is she saying?* I knew my ideas were long shots, but I didn't expect her not to want any change at all, or worse, to sell it altogether, which is what it's sounding like right now.

She says, "Peaches also have pits."

It's a saying she's always said. The sweet always comes with sour. Hard with soft. The universe has a way of balancing things out. That's been true since my dad left us. I just don't want the pits on the other side of progress to be standing in my way any longer. "I know but—"

"But . . ." She cuts me off with her hand held up between us. "You can and do."

"What does that mean?"

With her eyes set on mine and a gentle slope of a smile on her face, she replies, "It means you're ready to take on those things. The shop has been yours for years, honey. I think we should make it official. Once it's in your name, then it's not up to me. It would be yours to do what you want with it."

So much crosses my mind that I don't know what thought to settle on first. I think she can tell because she comes to me, taking my hands though they still have residual flour on them, and holds each in hers. She's not deterred, and says, "I've been thinking about this for a long time, Lauralee. It's not a snap decision for me. I gave you control years ago, but you didn't own it. Now it's time to change that."

"Are you sure?"

Squeezing my hands, she replies. "Very." When she backs toward the register to pick up dusting it where she left off, she adds, "But I hope you still let me work here and there."

"Of course. Anytime you want."

"And since you mentioned it, I think you should expand,

hire more employees, take a few days off each week, and take this place to the next level."

I rush her, throwing my arms around her. "Thank you, Mom. I'll make you so proud."

When she turns in my arms, she hugs me tight. "You already have."

Stepping back, I'm unsure what to do with myself. Celebrate or start planning? But then I stop, and ask, "What are you going to do?"

"The house and car were paid off years ago, so I'll take some time and figure out my next adventure. Travel?" Flipping her hair over her shoulder, she laughs. "Or maybe I'll become a small-town influencer on social media. I'm seeing a hole in the market."

"I didn't even know you were on social media outside of the 'Book app.'"

"It's addicting." She walks by me, patting me on the arm. "I'm going to grab a sandwich for dinner tonight. I have a feeling you're going to be too busy to come home with the planning you have ahead of you."

I grin, almost unbearably so. Hope soars in ways I haven't felt in years, making the possibilities seem limitless. Yes, the bubble will burst in some ways, but I've been preparing for that my whole life. I'm ready to hold on to this feeling for as long as I can.

I wonder what Baylor will think.

Wait, huh? Why would I share this with him?

Oh.

My.

God.

That man! He's going to haunt me to my deathbed.

Pris will be over the moon. She's wanted this for me

forever. I'll text her as soon as my mom takes off again. I say, "I promise to get the decorations down this weekend."

The shrug is so insignificant that I almost miss it. "Don't rush on my account. This is all yours now." She pushes through the door to the back. When she returns with a paper-wrapped sandwich in her hands, she says, "Put it on my tab."

"Never." I give her one more hug before she leaves. "Thank you."

"It's well-earned. We can start on the paperwork in the next few days." She cuts through the store toward the door but stops, and says, "I almost forgot to tell you. The apartment got rented." My heart stops in my chest. "The reservation came in just before I left."

"For which dates?"

"Prime time. Starting Thursday of the Peach Festival and running for a week in total. That's our peak week. They already prepaid the full amount."

My heart starts beating again, but this is the pit in the peach of being given the shop. The bad with the good. "What's the name?"

"Single traveler out of New York. Mickey something booked it for his boss." She does a little shoulder shake of excitement. "Who knew our little festival would attract fancy New Yorkers. She pushes through the door. "Love you, honey."

"Love you."

I'm happy about the money. That one reservation alone covers a quarter of the costs to build the apartment, so that's a big win. But a New Yorker? How'd they even hear about our annual festival? "Yeah, who knew."

CHAPTER 13

Baylor

I PUSH the signed contract across the table.

The real estate attorney stands and offers his hand. As soon as I shake it, he says, "Congratulations. You just bought half of Main Street."

"I consider it an investment in my hometown's future."

"A noble purchase?" he asks, stacking the papers and tucking them into a file.

"Not noble but needed. I believe it can be brought back to what it once was."

He grins. "I've seen the pics. Was this in your lifetime or a bygone era?"

I glance at my attorney, Mark, who has made no qualms about his dislike for the other guy. His face is still soured by the joke he made about Texans not five minutes before asking me to sign the paperwork. I almost punched the fucker, but he represents the now-former owner of that strip of shops, so I pushed my pride down and focused on the matter at hand.

It's been years since Peachtree Pass has been active outside of the festival time of year. The farm and orchard get plenty of out-of-towners driving in for the day during spring and summer, even for pumpkins in the fall, but otherwise, half that strip center is sitting empty.

I reply, "It's something I've wanted to do for some time. It was a great place to grow up. I want that for other families. That starts with bringing more business to the area."

He comes around the table, heading for the door. "Sounds like you're ready to move back."

Moving back isn't that foreign of an idea. Everyone from my dad to my best friend mentions it regularly. Tagger did a few years back, so of course, it's crossed my mind a time or two. It's a nice reprieve from the city, a slower pace that gives me room to think about stuff other than my clients' portfolios and how the stock market is doing.

As for settling in as a solid plan, I'm not seeing a place for me in the Pass. I own 10 percent of the ranch, but now I'm a guest on the land.

I got the impression from Lauralee that she was making the apartment her own, so finding it listed and ready for reservations is a temporary solution for my next visit. But it's not a viable long-term plan. Or maybe it is. *Fuck.* I don't know what I want anymore. "Not ready to leave New York," I reply just to end this uncomfortable conversation.

Mark walks ahead with the other attorney as they discuss the final details and filings. I follow, stuck in my own mind. As the official owner of that strip, I can get with Lauralee and the other tenant to see what we think the town needs and what would be a good fit in the other three vacant spots. This isn't about me. It's about bringing money into the Pass's economy.

The county was named after my family, but this doesn't

feel like an obligation or a burden on my shoulders to save the town. It feels like an opportunity. I can't wait to share the news with Lauralee and my family. Even though I'm not sure where we stand on things, I know Lauralee will be thrilled that the ownership will be local. Well, I'm in Manhattan, but yeah, no need to complicate this.

Outside the building, the other attorney leaves, but Mark says, "Congratulations. You own a sizable portion of Peachtree Pass." He grins. "It's not every day someone can say they bought a town. And he's not wrong about it being noble. A lot of towns are left to wither as the population ages. I'm sure your family is proud."

A driver slams on the car horn, drawing our attention. When I turn back, I confess, "No one knows. This isn't about getting any glory. I'm handing it off to be managed by a leasing company out of Austin. I'll have some say when they get offers, but I'm not looking to run it day-to-day. I just want to be a part of reviving it." Cocking my eyebrow, I laugh. "Any interest in running a pizzeria in the Texas Hill Country?"

He chuckles. "My born-and-raised Manhattan wife isn't looking to move to the country. But I'll keep it in mind."

"You do that," I continue teasing as we shake hands. When we part ways, my phone vibrates in my pocket. I pull it out to read while heading to the corner to catch a cab. My feet stop as soon as I see it. "Holy shit. Mickey was right." I grin so fucking big seeing the Westcott Enterprises stock take off.

I throw my arm up and hop in the first cab that stops, give them the address, and sit back. *What a fucking day.* I spent a million on a real estate deal after a tense negotiation, but just made back double on the market.

Back at the office, I call Mickey in. "You're not gloating,

are you?" I ask when he comes in and closes the door with a grin so big, he might crack his cheeks wide open.

"Might be."

I stand and hold out my hand. When he shakes, I say, "You made me a lot of money today."

"You bought the stock?"

"Of course, on good advice. I hope you scored a win."

He nods, sitting on the other side of the desk. "I made more money today than my dad made in a year when I was growing up on Staten Island."

"I love a success story. Congratulations." I start typing a reply to an email, but stop to add, "I submitted it in the stocks to watch to Taylor and Goodman. I listed you as the adviser."

He leans forward like we might be overheard even though my door is shut. "I'm not an adviser, though."

"Not yet, but you have talent and deserve the recognition." I angle to face him. "This is how you move up. It only takes one surefire hit, and you'll have your own office soon."

"Thanks. I appreciate you putting it in the ledger."

"You're welcome. Now go find your next rec." I turn back to the email I've started.

"For you or for the company?"

I chuckle. "Both. I'm always up for making money."

"It does have a good taste to it." He stands to leave. "You still leaving tomorrow for Texas?"

"I am. I'll be back on Monday before noon." Just as Bob requested.

"Well, you're booked for the flight, and a short-term rental will be ready. Let me know if you need anything else."

"Thanks, especially for making me money."

He laughs as he leaves. "Anytime."

I finish the day, wrapping up work here so I can get

home and start packing. Tucking my phone in my pocket, I tap the last key to shut down my computer before walking around and turning off the TV screens. Although I can't escape checking in regularly while I'm traveling, I'm more than happy to leave the markets behind for today.

On my way home, I stop at a deli and pick up my favorite Italian sub for dinner. But while I wait for it to be made, I start thinking about Lauralee and the Sundries shop. She has the small café and bakery, which are her pride and joy from what I've seen. I wonder if she's thought about expanding to a full deli or restaurant. I don't know her mom's or her finances, but food is what brings people together and to town. A bar and a few other stores, so even locals wouldn't have to travel to Dover County anymore, would be a good addition.

I get my sandwich and head home with more ideas, though I really need to be hands-off. Ultimately, it's an investment to make money and not a side project I need to take on.

I know a little brunette I wouldn't mind taking on. I just don't know how she will feel about me being back in the Pass tomorrow. Hopefully, she'll be grateful since she's making bank off me on that rental. But we'll see. Lauralee is nothing if not spirited. I'm just hoping some of the energy can be expended in bed like last time.

I will either be welcomed with open arms and kisses or have the door slammed in my face. I shouldn't be looking forward to finding out as much as I am. But I can't wait to see her again.

THE INSTRUCTIONS WERE CLEAR. Go to the counter in the Sundries shop to retrieve the key. I park the rental car out front on Main and check the mirror like a teenager going on his first date. I slam the visor up. "What the fuck am I doing?"

I could pat my face or douse myself in cologne, hoping I don't look as tired as I feel and don't smell like the stuffy air of an airplane, but I don't. A shot of adrenaline is running through me because I'm about to see her again. It's noticeable because I haven't felt like this about someone in a long time. Hoping for the best, I run my hand through my hair and get out.

Opening the door, my gaze travels to the bakery counter first. Disappointment is quick to set in. The bell already alerted my entrance, but I still don't hear a welcome or announcement coming from the back kitchen. I look around and walk to the register. "Hello? Hey Shortcake?"

The kitchen door swings open, and Peaches greets me with a smile. "Baylor Greene is back in town. Welcome home."

"Thanks. It's good to be back." I ask, "How have you been?"

Her grin grows as she stops on the other side of the counter from me. "Fantastic actually."

"I like to hear it. Fantastic looks fantastic on you, Mrs. Knot."

She laughs. "Peaches works." Waving me off, she says, "I'm not going to bore you with old lady stuff. Did I hear a request for shortcake?"

Shit. "Uh, yeah. I crave Lauralee's more than I should when I'm back in New York."

"Hers is the best." She slides the door to the glass case open. "Do you want one or two?"

I haven't heard anything or anyone in the back. No noise is heard at all other than the two of us. "One or two what?"

Her brows pinch together, and she laughs humorlessly. "Strawberry shortcake."

"Oh." I bend to look in the case. "I'll take all eight for the family at the ranch."

"Perfect." She pulls the tray out and says, "I'll box these up in the back." Before the door swings closed behind her, she looks back. "Lauralee's at the apartment waiting for a renter to show up if you want to stop by and say hi. This will take me a few minutes anyway."

"Good idea."

"Cut through the kitchen. It's quicker."

I come around and follow her through the door. She has her back to me when I push out the door under the staircase. With that earlier adrenaline rushing back, I take the steps by two and knock on the door.

When it swings open, her smile falters. Not the welcome I was hoping for, but the door hasn't slammed closed yet. "Hi there," I say, keeping my voice low for no other reason than it feels like the moment calls for it.

She blinks a few times, then smiles. It's not as big as it was, but it's sweet, matching the one I've been dreaming about for almost a month now. Leaning against the door, she tilts her head to touch the wood, and says, "I'm so glad you're here."

"Oh yeah?"

"Yes, I've been wondering . . ." Her gaze drops down between us, a shyness coming over her as her cheeks pinken.

She's better than any memory. Her brown hair shines in the sunlight, and a sparkle allows me to discover the gold flecks and a few greens dotting the comfort of her warm brown eyes. I'm given a teasing peek of her tan stomach when the top rises along her ribs, and her shorts hang lower. She's summertime personified and so beautiful that I'm tempted to skip the pleasantries and kiss her. I don't because she's one of the reasons I was looking forward to this trip, and I'm not going to blow it on the first day back. I ask, "About?"

Straightening her spine, she squares her shoulders. "If you had any good stock tips for me, Mr. Finance Fancy Pants?"

The smirk comes naturally, but resisting those lips doesn't. I do, though. "I have a tip for you."

She tries hard to restrain her own smirk but fails as it tickles its way onto her mouth. "Is it considered insider trading if you share your *tip* with me?"

What is she doing to me? *The tease.* "It will be inside *her,* alright." Rubbing my thumb over my bottom lip, I steady my gaze on her and lean in. "I could be taken to jail over such a risky proposition, though."

Her eyebrows bounce once, and she leans in as well. "Sharing your tip with me might not be worth the risk then."

I cup her face and scrape my lips against hers. Just as her eyes close and her hands hold tight to my biceps, I whisper, "You're always worth the risk."

CHAPTER 14

Lauralee

MY BODY WANTS to melt against him, and my mind still swirls in the swoon, but it's that other part, the part of me that wants this man more than seems feasibly possible, that wins out.

I kiss him, holding his arms as he moves me inside the apartment. He lowers his hands to get a good grasp of my ass, and I squeal as he lifts me from the floor. The thrill of seeing Baylor again, those blue eyes telling me how much he misses and craves me without a word uttered, had me riled for more the moment I opened the door.

His pace is quicker as we get closer to the bedroom. Wrapping my legs around his middle, I shamelessly rub myself against him, needing the friction, which already has me tugging at this pesky shirt. "Take it off," I say through jagged breaths.

He stops, tilts his head, and grins. "You want this shirt off, Shortcake?"

"I want all of it off." My core tingles in anticipation.

Pushing me to the wall, he uses it as leverage to take the shirt off over his head. God, I missed these shoulders so much, the muscles, the divot on the corner, highlighting his hard work. *Just all of him.*

I throw my head back as he kisses across my shoulder. His fingers are deft as the button of my jean shorts pops open, and the zipper is forced halfway down. I start on his neck as he shifts us back into action. Then I come to my senses and throw my arms out wide. The tips of my fingers grip the doorframe, and I breathe, "Stop."

His head straightens on his neck as his eyes latch onto mine. He's breathing as hard as I am when he asks, "What is it?"

"I have a reservation arriving any minute."

When his brows pull together, his eyes briefly dart from my lips to my eyes. I don't have to be a mind reader to know what he'd rather be doing. I'd rather be kissing him, too. "A reservation for what?"

I don't know why that makes me laugh. It's probably this carefree feeling he evokes in me. It's probably him being here and kissing me like it was his top priority upon returning. And I don't mind that one bit. I can't say I haven't thought about how this reunion would be or even go—if he would be mad how we left it or understand the mixed emotions.

"The apartment," I say, lowering my feet back to the floor. "It's rented for the entirety of the festival."

His head shakes as it juts back on his neck. "What are you talking about?"

My smile is wiped away as confusion sets in. "I'm talking about this apartment we're standing in right now. Someone rented it out for top dollar." I grin, as this investment is already starting to pay off. "You need to get out of here before they show up."

"Who?"

"What do you mean who?" I laugh again as I slip out of his arms but flatten my palms to his torso to start working him back toward the door. His skin is warm, his chest hard. I bend to pick up his discarded shirt and toss it to him. "The renter. Mickey something."

His expression morphs from confusion to a rogue grin that makes me want to kiss him again. I don't because if I do, I won't want to stop kissing those lips until I've come. "Baylor, you need to go. We can catch up later."

"Baylor?" *My mom* . . . her footsteps are heard as she treks the staircase. "You still up here?"

"Shit," he whispers, pulling his shirt back on over his head and running a hand through his hair. "What do we do?"

I start to laugh quietly so my mom can't hear, which starts to make Baylor laugh as well. I whisper, "And here I thought we were adults, but Mom shows up, and we're suddenly afraid of getting caught." I fidget with my hair to smooth it down before remembering the button of my jean shorts is still undone. I start to button them back up and silently mouth, "Go. Go. Go."

I hop-step away from him just as my mom reaches the top platform. Her eyes go from him to me and then back to him, and she smiles. Holding out a large box, she says, "Here are your shortcakes. Do you want me to put them on a tab, or would you like to pay now?"

"You didn't have to bring those all the way up here, Mrs —" She scolds him with a glare. I know that look very well. "Peaches," he corrects. "I was just about to come back down."

"Figured you kids were having a nice visit, but didn't want you to forget your order." She glances at me with a proud grin. "I know my Lauralee can be distracting."

"She sure can be."

I shoot him my own glare, but that wry grin sitting satisfactorily on his face tells me he has no regrets whatsoever. He's going to give this away if he's not careful.

Feeling more awkward than ever, I put out my hand to rest on the peninsula but miss the counter and slant sideways. Quick to catch myself, I ask, "Shortcake, you say?"

Catching the amusement on Baylor's face elicits my embarrassment that he caught my major miss as well as my mom. She says, "Everything okay?"

Inwardly rolling my eyes at myself, I try to shake it off and try again. This time looking anything but nonchalant as I use the counter to hold me up. "Fine. Totally fine. Great. Incredible."

Baylor starts shaking his head, looking down under the lightest chuckle. Even he knows I'm struggling, so he says, "Let me take those from you, Peaches."

My mom grins like he's her knight in shining armor. I can't say he doesn't make me feel the same. His mouth on mine made my heart thunder in my chest. There's still a rumbling, though having your parent interrupt like you're two teenagers trying to sneak around and have sex put a slight damper on our momentum. That and the renter. I check my watch. He's late.

She says, "Baylor here was so sweet and bought all the shortcakes for his family."

He takes possession of the box. "Don't want to show up empty-handed when I have the best dessert in the Hill Country to bring them." Glancing at me, he says, "Delicious shortcake."

I could crumble to the floor like the pound cake that plays second fiddle to the fresh strawberries. His words are so devilishly delectable, I eat them right up and am ready for seconds.

I need to get a grip. Not everything has an underlying sexual innuendo, though that absolutely did. "Well," I start to break up this mess of a conversation and walk toward the door to shuffle them out. "We should get out of here before our reservation shows up."

Baylor says, "I'm the reservation, Shortcake." Both of us dart our gazes to my mom to see if she caught the nickname. He holds up the box, and adds, "Shortcakes need to be delivered to the ranch."

But I'm still stuck on the other thing he said. "What do you mean you're the reservation? A Mickey is listed."

"I thought you were joking earlier."

"About?"

He comes closer, but the way he moves so fluidly across the floor makes me wonder if it's the volition of our connection instead of this conversation. "I thought you were just giving me a hard time." He sets the box next to me on the counter. "Mickey is my assistant. He booked it for me. My name should be listed somewhere."

I look from him to my mom. "Did you see Baylor's name listed anywhere?"

"No, I just looked at the bill paid section."

Taking my phone from my purse I'd set on the floor nearby, I pull up the reservation app and read over the details. Baylor chuckles before crossing his arms over his chest. My eyes slide from the screen to him. I'm not sure why relief comes over me, but my shoulders drop the tension and slight panic that had begun to build over this potential error. "Mickey was on the credit card. Baylor Greene is listed in the notes as the guest."

"Happy to be the first guest." His smugness is easily detected, but that smirky smirk says it all.

"If you hadn't been sneaking around to make a reservation, I would have given you a discount."

"I'm happy to pay full fare."

I shrug and set my phone down. "If you say so, money bucks."

He looks at my mom, and says, "I'll come down and pay for the shortcakes."

"I have the bill downstairs when you're . . ." She glances between us once more as if she realizes she might have interrupted something, then walks to the door, throwing her hands up. "When you're ready. No rush on my account."

Oh lordy. I won't hear the end of this unless I come up with a darn good cover story. As soon as she's gone and we hear the last of her steps down the stairs, we still wait until the door to the shop slams closed.

I run into his arms again, our mouths crashing together in a flurry of sexual gratification. But then I rip my mouth and body away again. Wiping the corners of my lips, I say, "We can't do this."

"She's waiting on me to pay."

That sobering thought does the trick. "Right." I take a deep breath and lick my lips. "You rented my place." It's not a question, so I don't know what I'm asking. I'm still just surprised. Pleasantly so.

"Yeah. I'm hoping the landlord stays to keep me company."

I lean against the counter, still facing him with my breath racing like my heartbeats. "I'm not sure how I'll pull that off without her knowing or figuring it out."

He comes to me, taking hold of my hips. "We'll figure that out later." I watch as his tongue seduces his bottom lip and lean against him. When his arms come around me, I feel that same relief I did earlier when I discovered he'd be here for the weekend.

"My family is expecting me. You want to come out and have an early dinner with us?" Tapping the box, he laughs. "And shortcake? I have plenty to go around, though this wasn't the shortcake I'm craving."

"Oh yeah. Tell me more about that."

Bending over me, he kisses my neck. "How about I show you?"

I don't want to stop. I want to feel him showing me everything until I scream his name. But I know that can't happen at the time being. I snuggle into the crook of his neck, breathing him and the woodsy cologne in that makes me go weak in the knees. "I'd like to go if the invitation still stands."

His eyes find mine, and he nods. "The invitation still stands."

"When are they expecting you?"

The grin on his face widens, and those eyes are bluer than a Texas summer day but hold the intensity of a devil at play. "I didn't give a time, but I'm thinking they meant around three or four."

"That's hours from now," I whisper.

"How do you want to pass the time?"

Not ten minutes later, I finish tying an apron around his midsection and give his ass a squeeze before I step back. Coming around to face him, I tap the tip of his nose while grinning like a loon. "Do you know how sexy this would be if you were shirtless?"

"You mean how much sexier this would be?" He tugs at

the apron's waist, but then his eyes lift above my head when the kitchen door swings open. I step back from him, putting the metal worktable between us when my mom walks in. She clasps her hands together in delight. "I see Lauralee has recruited you to make cupcakes for the festival."

"I'm at your daughter's beck and call, so she can do whatever she wants with me." His eyes dart to me. "How can I be of service?"

He's so naughty that I roll my eyes, but when I look at him again, I kind of soften to him. Baylor is trying. He's here for me without any expectations of what we are or what we were when we parted last hanging over our heads. I wouldn't call him perfect, but he's pretty close to it in my book right now.

She says, "Five hundred should cover the first two days."

He looks at me. "How many are made?"

I hold up a big fat zero with my fingers. "I was planning to make them this afternoon."

Not deterred in the least, he says, "Well then, let's get to it."

CHAPTER 15

Baylor

"Ride with me," I say, taking a large cupcake pan out of the oven and setting it on the rack behind me. "To the ranch. I'm staying here anyway. I can bring you back to your car or . . . you can stay."

I peek over at her. She's leveling the batter in the last pan to go into the oven by tapping the metal to the counter several times. Her hair is nested on top of her head, and flour is dusted across her cheek, or maybe it's sugar. I'll need to taste it to verify.

Tasting hasn't been an issue with her cupcakes. I've practically eaten my weight in the small peach cakes. It's still tempting to take another just to check for quality and all that good stuff.

As soon as she turns toward me, she asks, "Sorry for the banging. I didn't hear the last part."

The banging conjures images of her bent over this very worktable or spread across it naked for me. I would lick her nipples free from the powdery mess we made before making her come under some stellar and hit-the-right-spot fucking. I adjust myself over the apron. We were so fucking close to having sex earlier. Hours later, I'm caught in another obligation—heading to Rollingwood to spend time with the fam.

It wouldn't normally be a negative, but I'd much rather act out some fantasies with my sexy little baker than eat potato salad in a hundred-and-three-degree temps.

"Baylor?"

"Yeah?"

She smiles, but the emotion dancing around her irises tells me she knows where I disappeared to. When she crosses the room, I open the oven to set the pan inside, closing it right after. She doesn't rush away. In fact, she comes closer than she's been all afternoon and rubs her hand along my side. "I think you were inviting me to stay with you tonight. Or am I making that up?"

Her mom's voice travels through the crack of the swinging door from the front of the store, where she's been serving customers while we bake. It's a reminder that pushes Lauralee to move away from me.

"Not making it up," I reply in a lowered voice, not wanting her mom to hear us talking. "I want you to stay with me tonight."

Her smile grows, but she still tries to temper it. "How would we do that?"

"Easy. We just come back together, and you stay."

Glancing at the door and then back at me, she leans forward. "No, I mean, what would I tell my mom since she knows it's rented out? That kind of forces me to stay at home."

I lean forward, wanting to kiss her, but whisper, "You tell her you're a twenty-nine-year-old woman, and you're having a sleepover with me tonight."

"Ironic because every time I'm with you, there's no sleep involved."

"You can tell her we're having sex, if you prefer."

She bursts out laughing. "Um, no, thank you. That's not a conversation I'm up for having tonight or any other time, for that matter."

"Look," I say, resting down on my forearms, which puts me almost eye level with her standing. "I want to see you and spend time with you. Whether that's in the bedroom or outside of it, I want that. It's a busy weekend for you, so I understand that you don't have a lot of time to give. But if you find yourself with a few spare minutes or want to stay over, I'll help however I can."

Her eyes glisten under the fluorescents of the kitchen. No tears, but sincerity shadows them as if they weren't already the most beautiful eyes I've ever seen. She leans on her forearms, bringing her so close that our hands touch. "Okay, since you're being all charming and everything, you're going to have to sneak me out, Greene. You up for the task?"

"I'm up for anything that includes time with you." She stands when the door pushes in just the slightest. Looking to make sure the coast is clear, she turns back to me and says, "If I go to the ranch with you, I still need to frost these before ten a.m. Frosting goes quickly, but five hundred is still a lot."

"Like I told your mom," I say, straightening my spine to my full height and swinging my arms out. "Beck and call, baby."

She briefly eyes the oven behind me and comes around, stopping next to me. Looking up, she whispers, "You're quite the surprise, Baylor."

"In a good way?"

"Unfortunately for me, in a terribly charming way." She moves closer to the oven to spy on the cupcakes through the glass window.

"I wouldn't call it unfortunate."

Turning back, she looks at me over her shoulder while slipping oven mitts on her hands. "Me either." *God, I love the way she blushes for me.* "After this batch comes out, I can freshen up, and we can head out."

I nod toward the door. "I can take care of it if you want to go ahead."

She reaches for the bow at the waist of her apron and tugs the tails. "You sure?"

"Yep. I have it handled." Checking the timer, I add, "Six minutes and we're golden."

"Okay. It's going to be a late night, though. I really do have to frost some of the cupcakes, and I'll need to clean this mess."

"We got it covered."

"Thanks." She pushes through the door to the front of the store.

I can hear her and Peaches talking, but it's muffled, so I don't know what they're saying. When she returns, though, she's smiling as she passes through the kitchen to the back door. "My mom is going to close the shop. Give me five minutes, and I'll be ready."

"I'll be here."

As soon as she leaves, the timer goes off. I won't be responsible for ruining a batch, so I'm quick to pull them out of the oven and put them on the cooling rack. The place is a mess, so I try to do what I can, turning off the ovens, dusting the flour off the counters into the trash, and then finding a rag to wet and wipe them down. It's not the best job, and probably not one Lauralee would approve of, but I hope she'll appreciate the effort.

She walks in, her feet stopping so fast that she tips forward a little. "You cleaned?"

I shrug. "I wouldn't say it's clean, but it's a start."

She lunges for me, opening her arms, but then catches herself just before they land around my neck. Patting my chest is a consolation prize. "Thank you, Baylor."

"You're welcome." I take the apron off and toss it in the laundry bag. "You ready to face the family?"

Adjusting her purse on her shoulder, she locks the door and starts for the front with me trailing. "It's not like I'm meeting my boyfriend's family for the first—" The words choke in her throat, and she turns back. "Right?"

I've thought about her a lot since I saw her on my previous visit. I didn't even go on any dates, not feeling it after spending the night with her last time. Who could possibly compare?

Great, now she has me questioning where things stand between us. I shake it off but keep nodding like an idiot. "It's Chris and Tagger, the kids, and my dad. Family you've known your whole life."

"Right," she says, nodding just like me. "They're practically my family as well. Not by blood but by relationships." She pushes through the door and goes right to her mom to hug her. "I'll be back later to clean the kitchen and finish the cupcakes." When she pulls back, she adds, "It's going to be a late night because I also need to frost them, so don't wait up."

And just like that, the groundwork is laid . . .

If we pick up where we left off earlier, it's going to be late alright.

"Have a good one, Peaches."

"You, too. Y'all have fun and say hi to your dad for me."

"I will."

As soon as we're in the rental, Lauralee buckles herself in, but the look we share makes me think this drive is about to get a lot more interesting. As soon as we're on the road, I reach over and rub her thigh. She changed tops, exchanging the crop top for a loose-fitting shirt that hung around her frame, with no midsection on display at all. Hidden. I don't approve. "I do like those shorts on you."

She looks down as if she didn't know she was wearing them. "Thanks. They're just old jeans I cut off."

"You always did know how to wear denim."

Angling toward me, she laughs. "You make it sound like you noticed me when I'm pretty sure you never thought twice about me before the last time I saw you." She rests her head on her hand, a smile working onto her relaxed expression.

"I've thought about you," I say, taking her hand in mine and folding my fingers with hers. "I should have . . ." I put my attention back on the road. "I sure noticed you at my sister's reception."

"Lost opportunity?"

"One I've regretted since."

Her hold on my hand tightens. I don't even know if she purposely gave the subtle hint, but I notice. She asks, "You have?" Her voice is as soft as her gaze.

"Of course. You're a beautiful woman, Shortcake," I reply, trying to play it off a bit. I don't know why this seems like a good time to just stick to the facts and own them, especially with her. She's given me an open forum to be who I am. No games. No fronts or masks, no role to play. Just me with her.

"Quick detour." I pull off on an old dirt farm road. The

property was abandoned before I was born, so it might be private property, but there was no one to enforce it. I stop just past the rickety fence posts and shift the car into Park.

There's not been one ounce of argument from her. She sits there, trusting me. It's a weight that I haven't carried for anyone in years. I'm not that guy in New York, but she's making me think twice back here in Peachtree Pass.

I undo her seat belt and then mine before leaning over the console to run my fingers over her cheek. "I'm going to kiss you."

Her hand covers mine, and she leans in, her breathing deepening. "You don't have to ask or warn me. Just kiss me."

I press my lips to her, so much of this feeling like the first time. Her eyes close in complete trust, her soft mouth molding to mine, and her other hand finding my side and rubbing before trying to pull me closer.

The fucking console keeps me from her, but as our kisses deepen, our tongues begin a slow dance to encourage more. Her hand dips to my lap and rubs over my erection. I push against her and lower my hand to slide over her tits, one and then the other. Lifting myself over the console, I trail kisses toward her ear and whisper, "Put your seat back."

She fumbles beside her, and then it slowly glides back for me. When she's lying as flat as the seat goes, her hand returns to my legs and goes higher. I capture it. "I want you to touch me so badly, but I don't want to come in my pants and then see my family."

I slide my hand over her belly and pop the button on her jeans. "But I want to make you feel so good you'll be thinking about it while we're eating."

A small laugh escapes, and she says, "So you want me to come in my shorts, though?"

"Yes. I do, and I want to smell you on my fingers for the rest of the night."

Her eyes widen as her chest rises before falling again. Breathless, she whispers, "Yes, please. I want that so much."

"You just enjoy, baby, while I make you come so hard." I know I can't fuck her, though she looks at me like she wants nothing less. I can't even get out and eat that sweet pussy of hers because we can still be seen from the road.

I'm kicking myself for not driving farther onto the property, but I didn't know it would escalate like this. A gorgeous woman begging for me to please her? I'll do everything to make that happen.

I focus on her shorts and getting them down past her knees so my hand can fit properly between her legs. Hovering over the console that's digging into my lower stomach, I kiss her while sliding two fingers between her lower lips.

Her hips buck as her mouth leaves mine to grasp for air. I slip down to her entrance and tease her with my fingertip. When her hand covers mine, she pushes as hard as she can. "Please, Baylor." Her eyes roll back in her head as the crown digs into the leather.

The glimpse of the highway behind us sets my desire on fire. I need to feel her pulsing around my fingers. I push one finger into her wet heat, and the slick sides grip and squeeze around me.

Little moans rumble through her, but it's when I push in another finger that sends her ass off the seat. "So good." She licks her lips and begs, "Yes. Yes. Yes."

I pull out and push back in, watching her body come alive before me. Her nipples push against the shirt, and her mouth hangs open. As she starts to fuck my hand, I bend over and bite that tempting nip. "Ah," breaks free from her throat, giving me the opportunity to kiss her. I do and pick up fucking her where she left off.

My fingers continue to pump as I watch her body. Watch that stunning face reaching the peak before she tumbles into her release.

A siren blares, startling me. "Shit."

"No," she says, gripping my hand so hard to hold it in place. "Finish. Finish. Please, Baylor."

I look up to see the deputy getting out of his car. A rock and a hard place. I can't disappoint her now. I fuck her so fast and hard that she screams, "Oh God, yes!"

The car door slams closed, causing me to look up once more. *Fuck. I'm going to end up in jail for this.*

Her hips bounce against my hand and with her last breath exhaled, she sinks to the seat with her eyes still closed. "Hate to cut this short, but you need to pull your pants up fast." I fall to the driver's seat and try to push down my hard dick so it's not so obvious.

She's still catching her breath when she casually raises her seat to the upright position again and then pulls her shorts back up. Just when she buttons the top closed, there's a knock on the window. I ask, "You good?"

She straightens her shirt and takes a deep breath. "So good." When she smiles, her bliss has her eyelids hanging lower and a smile that even the scare of a cop catching us can't wipe clear.

I push the window open and scan his name tag. "Good afternoon, Officer McCall."

CHAPTER 16

Baylor

"It's Deputy McCall." He lowers his sunglasses and looks over the top of them. "I should have known it would be a Greene causing a ruckus."

"No ruckus," I say, biting my tongue before I tell this fucker to back off. "Just stopping to check out the old property."

He looks out at the run-down farmhouse ahead and the junk littering the yard, and then back at me again. Bending down, he smiles when he sees my passenger and takes his sunglasses off . . . as if he wants a better look at her. "Lauralee Knot, what are you doing with this troublemaker?"

"Baylor's not so bad." I look over at her when I hear the syrupy Southern accent that she thickens when speaking to him. Little does he know, she's the troublemaker. "What can we help ya with, Dirk?"

"Listen," he starts, "you can't park on this here property. So unless you're broken down, you need to move along. You hear me?"

"Loud and clear, Deputy." The car is still running, but I fudge with a knob to act like I'm listening to some degree. The wipers slide across the windshield while fluid squirts out, hitting the cop on the side of the face. "Shit, I'm sorry." I make sure the wipers are turned off and steal a glance at Shortcake, who is about to lose it laughing.

She covers her mouth and turns to face away from us.

Lifting from the quick ducking he did, the deputy wipes his face with the back of his hand and hits me with a scowl aimed in my direction. If indecent behavior didn't get me thrown in jail, that wiper fluid assault just might do it. "I'm going to give you the benefit of the doubt and assume you did that on accident."

"It was a pure accident, sir. Sorry about that."

Annoyance purses his lips, but then he bends down once more to smile at Lauralee, which I find fucking annoying. "You headin' out to Rollingwood Ranch?"

"Sure am," she replies with a honeyed smile. The woman knows how to lay it on thick when she wants to.

He adds, "Say hi to Christine for me."

"I will." She waves her fingers at him. "Have a great day, Dirk."

He walks away without acknowledging me again but taps the roof of the car as he works his way back to his own vehicle. I watch in the mirror until he backs out of here. Throwing my gaze toward the beauty next to me, I ask, "How are you doing?"

"Amazing. You?" She's so chipper that I have no reason not to believe her.

"Never better." I shift the car into reverse before turning the rest of the way around. "It was a close call."

"You're telling me. I almost didn't get there." My arm is

punched. "You were going to let me just suffer. I'll remember that."

I stop the car again to look her square in the eyes. "It only would have been a few minutes. I would have made sure to get you there right after. But I also didn't know you were an exhibitionist. I'm intrigued, Ms. Knot."

She's still smiling like she's walking on sunshine. "Depends."

"On?"

Reaching over, she scrapes her nails gently across the back of my neck before resting her arm on my shoulders. "With whom, when, and where I am."

I move to rest my hand on her leg and kiss her. She meets me halfway without question. That seems to be what our relationship is based on. I'm not questioning. Just acting on instinct. But when I lean back, looking into her eyes, I'm starting to think we could be more.

The odds are against us based on distance alone. Thinking about how settled she is here with the shop she's running, I imagine she's not looking to leave her mom alone.

Sliding my hand over her inner thigh, I rub the pad of my thumb on her soft skin. "Peachtree Pass probably isn't the where and when you'd like. We know how it goes here. One whiff of a relationship travels like a live wire through town. But what are your thoughts on New York?"

She rests her head back on the seat and looks ahead at the road when a car passes by. Her eyes remain staring into the distance for a moment, maybe more, but when she turns to me again, her gaze softens. "Are you asking me to visit you in New York, Baylor?"

I gently squeeze her thigh and rest my head back while facing her. "If I were?"

"I don't want 'if I were.' I want you to stand behind your words." She massages the crook of my neck, easing the tension the deputy built up. I lean into it, into her. "I know it's hard when we're just getting to know each other." Tucking hair behind her ear, she briefly lowers her gaze to her lap. "But I need to know if you're asking me to come to New York to see you or just talking about a future kind of thing."

This has escalated in a way I didn't see coming. I don't have a prepared speech or a line like I would typically have on hand to respond in a way to protect myself. But protecting myself from her isn't something I need to do.

There's no hiding anyway when she sees exactly who I am and she's still here beside me, still kisses me like it means more than a fun few hours in bed or even meaningless sex. Shit . . . I like her. *A lot.*

She doesn't take my shit or anyone else's, for that matter. She doesn't need me. If she's here, it's because she wants to be. That's so incredibly sexy. To be chosen by her.

Taking hold of her hand, I bring it to my mouth and kiss the top twice before asking, "Will you come see me in New York, Lauralee?"

Her smile is worth the directness. "So formal, Mr. Greene. What happened to Shortcake?"

I chuckle with a slight shake of my head. "I can't win."

"You're winning. Trust me, you're doing everything right." Her hand squeezes mine, and she adds, "I'd love to come see you in New York, but only on one condition."

"Anything," I reply, kissing her hand once more.

"I can stay with you."

Leaning over the console, I kiss her cheek, and whisper in her ear, "I wouldn't have it any other way, Shortcake."

When I drop back to my side of the car, she's still leaning back against her seat, with a dreamy look in her eyes that usually comes after her release. This time, it's for me. Totally worth putting myself on the line and risking rejection.

She says, "If we stay here much longer, Deputy McCall will have a problem."

I shift into Drive and pull off the property and onto the road again. But I'm not letting her off the hook from my previous curiosity. "As for your earlier suffering." I chuckle, and ask, "How long has it been?" She hums, and her eyes face ahead as if deep in thought. "I may be jumping to a certain conclusion but one that I have no right to judge, but selfishly, I'm hoping twenty-four days."

"Why twenty-four—*ohhh*." She laughs. "That jump's not so off because, sadly, you're right."

"Do you mind me asking why that is?"

"You can ask anything you please."

Since there seems to be no embarrassment attached, I ask, "Why haven't you come?"

She doesn't avoid eye contact, but I only receive it here and there as she keeps redirecting her attention outside the vehicle. "I don't know . . ." She readjusts in her seat and then says, "Truth?"

"Absolute."

"I've been struggling in that area, which I've mentioned before, but I think you've tainted me." A playful shove to my arm is followed by a nervous laugh. "I shouldn't have admitted that."

"It's okay," I say, not laughing at all. "I feel the same about you."

"You do?"

I nod, but then I remember a few times. "Well, almost."

"Almost?" she asks, her voice pitching.

"Don't worry, baby, I haven't been with any other women. But I didn't have trouble getting off to the memory of you and me together."

Her shoulders ease, and she sinks into the chair again. "Really?"

"Really. You give quite the show. I love watching you come." Just when it seems her heart is in my hand, we reach the entrance to the ranch, which puts our time alone on the back burner until later.

Begrudgingly, I slide my hand to my side of the car as we cross through the open gates with large oak trees standing tall on either side. Pretending not to be attracted to her mind and body is becoming harder, making me regret ever agreeing to hiding whatever this is we have going on between us.

I don't know what's come over me. The Texas summer heat, the hottie next to me, or that this place has started to feel more like home again every time I visit. *Probably all three.*

But really, I know the real answer is just one. *Shortcake.*

Stealing one last glance before we must put on the "just friends act," I ask, "You ready?" I park the car outside my dad's house under another oak and crack the windows, hoping to keep the temps inside the car from melting the dash. It's brutal out today.

"As I'll ever be." She pops the door open before I have a chance to even offer.

My sister stands on the front porch, reaching the railing and leaning forward with a huge smile on her face. "Lauralee! I didn't know you were coming."

"Your brother talked me into it."

Christine's eyes dart to me and then to her friend again. "That was nice of him."

"Very nice," she adds, looking over at me. "He drove and all."

"Hey, Bay," my sister says, now smiling at me. "Welcome back."

"It's good to be back." I adjust my jeans now that my hardness has subsided.

Lauralee climbs the few steps up to the porch and gives her a hug. Just like family, she asks, "What can I help with?"

"You're the guest. Make yourself at home, and I'll get you an iced tea. It's too hot to be outside for too long without a drink in hand."

"Baylor?" When I hear my name, I find Tagger coming toward me from the barn. "Come take a look. I moved the car up here. Thought you'd like to see." When he spies Lauralee, he smirks. *The fucking bastard.* "You guys ride out together?" He's going to give it away before I'm ready to explain.

Lauralee laughs. "Hello to you, too, Tagger."

"Sorry," he replies, taking his hat off and holding it over his heart like a true Southern gentleman. "Hello, Lauralee."

She rolls her eyes but then laughs again. "Hi."

He says, "You should come with us."

She skips down the steps like the adventure is too good to pass up. "Where are we going?"

Tagger replies, "Looking at the car that Baylor wants."

When she catches up, we start for the barn, and she asks, "What car are we talking about?"

"It was a gift to my mom." Just inside the open doors, I see the car with the cover on it on the far side. "I'm sure the horses loved that being brought into their territory."

He walks to our largest male and strokes just above the

nose. "Nightfall doesn't mind." Pointing out the open stall door, he adds, "He comes in here a lot of times during the heat of the day to try to keep cool."

"Don't let him near the car."

"Don't worry," Tagger groans, "your precious is safe in here."

Lauralee slides up next to me. Her hand touches my back but then falls to her side again. I move in and peel off the cover just to take another good look at her—the car, that is, though I don't mind one bit seeing Lauralee here with me.

I nod for her to come closer. "My dad bought it as a gift for her but never had the time to fix it up. Running the ranch and farm kept him busy."

"From what I remember," she says, "so did you every Friday night in the fall and baseball in the spring."

It shouldn't surprise me that she knows about that or even remembers since she and my sister were dragged to a lot of my games. But it does feel good in a way that only someone who's known you so long can summon. Sometimes I forget how much a part of my life she's been. Guess it's easy to forget when you weren't paying attention.

I had my eyes set on so many other things back then—playing my best for recruiters, scoring with girls, and getting into too much trouble with Tagger, to name a few.

Coming closer, she bends down to peek through the window. "It's a beautiful car." Standing upright again, she steps back and looks the car over from front to back. "What are you going to do with it?"

The question has me glancing at Tagger, who conveniently and guiltily looks away. At least he feels some shame for making me agree to this bet. "I want to fix her up."

"Can I help?" she asks.

"I didn't know you knew about cars?"

A quick pop of her shoulders leads to her saying, "There's a lot you don't know about me."

Right then, I know what I'm going to do. *Like the car, I'm going to fix that.*

CHAPTER 17

Lauralee

"I shouldn't," I say when Chris offers me another glass of wine. "I'll be drunk soon, and that won't get five hundred cupcakes frosted tonight."

"Five hundred?" She states, "Good lord. Do you want some help?"

"I'll get it done. I always do."

She sets down the bottle. "Here I thought you were still living the high life, hitting Whiskey's on a Thursday night while your old wingwoman was out here in the country growing babies. But frosting all those cupcakes makes me think I have it much easier on the ranch."

I laugh. "I barely have a life these days. I don't even remember the last time I went out, but here you are, a total badass superwoman. You always have been. Anyway, you never drank that much before the babies."

"But I always had fun drinking with you."

I reach across the table and take her hand, giving it a squeeze. "Cheers to that."

Christine glows from happiness even when she's not pregnant. More so when she is. I have nothing but love for my friend, even if I don't get to spend as much time with her anymore.

However, Baylor has been a fun distraction. I glance at the far end of the table, where I find his eyes already on me. He takes a sip of his water and holds it up just enough for me to catch him silently toasting to me.

I try to keep my smile to myself so no one else notices, but when I look up, Chris's eyes are glued to me. She glances down at Baylor and then at her husband. I swear she and Tagger speak a secret language through their eye exchanges that the rest of us aren't privy to.

With a couple of fans positioned a few feet away, the strands that escaped my topknot tickle my face. I tuck them behind my ear and whisper to Daisy, "Come to Leelee."

Daisy toddles to the side of me and raises her arms in the air. I lift her onto my lap and fuss with her adorable curls, hoping to mask the scent of betrayal that my friend is clearly smelling when it comes to her brother.

I look up, and say, "She's so cute I can't stand it. How is a being this perfectly adorable?" Unable to resist the urge, I kiss her cheeks and blow a raspberry.

Her hand pushes against my face as she giggles. "Leelee."

Turning her around on my lap, she rests her back on my chest. Her mom grins with pride at her. "You're looking heated, sweetie."

Their dad had gone inside a while ago. We're all sweating and overheating at this point. Daisy says, "Hot."

When Christine stands from the picnic bench, she says, "I think we're getting too deep into the summer heat for the fans to keep us cool outside. Dinner at my house next time." She pauses with her hand on her belly and takes a breath. "I'm so stuffed. I probably shouldn't have eaten that second strawberry shortcake you brought, Baylor."

He leans forward. Glancing at me, and then at her, he says, "Couldn't let them go to waste."

"They're too delicious for that. It was so good, Laur."

"Thanks."

She presses the back of her hand to her head. "I think I need air-conditioning and some bad reality TV." I hadn't noticed how flushed her cheeks had gotten until she stood.

Tagger comes around and says, "I'll drive you down to the house."

She nods and comes to my side of the table. Giving me a quick side hug, she says, "I'll see you tomorrow at the festival."

I stand to give her a hug with Daisy planted on my hip. "Do you need anything?"

"Rest and to cool off. That's all, but I am trying to talk Tagger into getting a chilling pool."

He laughs. "We have a river less than fifty yards away. That ice water could cool off the Texas sun."

She wobbles her head with an eye roll. "He's not wrong. Maybe I need to go sit in the river for a bit." Rubbing her stomach, she adds, "I think the air-con will do me right tonight. I'll see you tomorrow, though?"

"Yes. Text me when you're heading there."

"I will." She rubs my upper arm. "Thanks for coming out here."

"I always love coming to see all of you."

Tagger takes Daisy into his arms, then looks at Baylor as they head for the utility vehicle. "You hanging out or taking off?"

"I'm going to take off. I'm tired, but you owe me a game of basketball before I fly out again."

"You're on." Glancing at his son, he asks, "You coming with us, Beckett?"

"Can't I stay with Uncle Baylor?"

Baylor leans over to his side, wrapping his arm around his nephew's back. "Hey, buddy, since we have the festival tomorrow, I was thinking we could start on the fort on Sunday before I leave. What do you think?"

"Yesss." He sits straight up on the picnic bench. "Dad gave me a hammer that's all mine."

"Make sure to have it ready."

"I will."

The UTV is started, but Beckett gets up in a hurry. "Bye."

It's so sudden that it makes me laugh. "Bye, Beck?"

He waves before dashing after the vehicle. Tagger stops just in time for him to jump on and sit in the back. As soon as they round the road leading to their house, Baylor turns to me, and asks, "Did you have a good time?"

Now I'm rubbing my belly. "I'm stuffed and glad I came. Thank you for inviting me."

"Anytime." Angling one leg free, he smiles the kind of smile that could make me fall head over heels if I'm not careful. I really don't want to be careful with him. I could blame the wine, but I'm starting to think it's just him. He stands and walks closer to hold his hand out for me. "You ready to go back?"

I take it, and he pulls me to my feet. When I'm pulled against his chest, I whisper, "I'm ready." I want to touch him so badly that I glance slowly to the right to make sure his dad isn't watching. With the coast clear, I rest my hands on his chest. "Ready to pick up where we left off?"

Taking hold of my hands, he waggles his eyebrows. "Where'd we leave off, Shortcake?"

I cock my eyebrow and grin. "Guess you'll have to find out."

"When you said I'll find out, I was thinking you meant upstairs."

"As soon as we finish frosting these last three hundred cupcakes, that's where we're heading." With a frosting bag in my hand, I smirk at him. "I promise to make it worth the detour to finish these."

"I'm going to hold you to that."

He has a way of making me feel too comfortable to share this side of myself. "Good. I was hoping you'd be holding me to several places." I start frosting down the row of twenty-five cakes, but add, "The bed. The wall. Maybe the peninsula." Should I feel some shame? *Nah, it's Baylor.* From everything I've seen, he doesn't judge people like that.

"I'm learning all kinds of interesting things about you." He packs up the previous batch I already frosted and tucks the box in the fridge. "Can't say I don't want to learn more."

I pause with the tip of the piping bag pressed to the next cupcake. I turn around to face him. "I want that, too."

"You want to learn more about me?" The surprise in his tone catches me off guard.

"Of course. Why wouldn't I want that?" Pressing his hands to the worktable between us, he looks at me like. . . I don't know what that look is. *Happiness? Curiosity? Flattered?* And then it occurs to me. It's all those things. "What's happened between us has been fast. I mean, look at you. You obviously don't have trouble getting women, and I'm no exception. But I want you to know that although I see you as a sexy piece of meat—" His mouth falls open, making me laugh. "Kidding. I'm kidding." When our laughter dies down, I say, "You are very handsome, like ridiculously so, but that's not what I like most."

"What do you like most?"

There's such a boyish charm about him in the moment, like he's not some model of a man loose in Manhattan who's given compliments all the time. We both know that's not true. Women trip over themselves to catch his eyes, but I caught them.

I don't feel special because of his attention. I feel special because of how sweet he's been to me. He doesn't hesitate to jump into the mix to make my life easier, to check on me if I'm feeling confused about what's happening, or even willing to keep us secret so I don't have to deal with the aftermath after he leaves.

I come around the table, setting my bag on the table on the way to him. Wrapping my arms around his neck, I confess, "I want to get to know you better. All of you, and who you are as a person, here and in New York City."

His hands cover my hips, and he moves closer. The grin he was wearing flattens as his eyes drop to my lips. When his gaze slides up to mine again, he says, "I want to get to know you better as well."

I'm kissed. My breath is stolen right when I take it, leaving me no choice but to steal it right back. It's not deepened, but the pressure is perfect, wanting and controlled, sweet, but with passion.

When we part, my eyes flutter open to find him staring at me. "I've never known anyone like you, Shortcake, and I've known you my whole life. Seems like I've been wasting a lot of time on other women."

"I wholeheartedly agree," I say, smiling from the inside.

He taps my nose and kisses the tip. "But first, cupcakes."

I groan.

It's not like I usually mind frosting them. It moves fairly fast as a process. I just feel like we could find better ways to spend our limited time together. "But alas, cupcakes."

Though it feels wrong to leave the strength of his fingers digging into my hips, and that expression on his face makes me feel like the most beautiful woman he's ever seen. I'm becoming addicted to the desire. How his pupils widen when I move closer, as if he needs to take more of me in, and that grin that I'm only privy to on occasion, usually followed by a kiss. I slip from his hands and grab the piping bag again, but the smile stays right where he put it on my face.

"We're moving quickly."

"Do what you need to do. I'm in no hurry."

I keep my head down and my hand moving across the cakes, but guilt sets in. I glance back at him. "You must be tired, though. If you'd like to go upstairs, you can."

He comes around the table and rubs my back. His eyes stay on the project in front of us as if he knows I need to focus. I stand back up, though, and wrap my arm around his back. Leaning my head on his arm, I say, "You don't have to wait on me. This is my problem, not yours."

Kissing the top of my head, he says, "I like being here with you. I find it fascinating to watch you do everything with such ease and certainty. You don't question yourself or your abilities. You dive right in and just do it." I look up at him, feeling seen and so cared for under his gaze and swimming in his words.

"Cupcakes are hard to mess up."

"It's not about the cupcakes, Shortcake. It's about how you contribute to everyone around you and step in without being asked. Everything's better because you were a part of it."

"Aw," I hum, feeling my cheeks heat under his sweet compliments. "Thank you. I appreciate that. No one has ever said anything that nice to me before."

His arm tightens around my waist just as I lift to kiss him. It's only a peck, but I'd take a bushel of those from him any day or night because this feels so right. "You deserve to hear it more."

A million things run through my head, making excuses for why he's being so nice, from the time of night to wanting to get laid. But none of those fit just right because his voice is as genuine as his eyes are sincere.

I may not be able to pinpoint the moment things between us changed, or maybe it's been slowly morphing since his last visit, but I'm eating it up. It's not the chemistry between the sheets, though I can't complain. No, it's the silent moments, the choices he makes to accompany me, even when we haven't made any intentions public.

So I stop questioning and get out of my head, deciding to let my heart lead me through this with him. I'd rather hope for the best. If I get hurt, I'll deal with those consequences.

"We should get back to work so we can finish. You're moving fast. Then we can go upstairs together."

My heart wasn't racing before but now it is at the mention of getting to stay with him again and whatever else we want to come with that situation.

When his hands disappear from my body, I sneak a peek at him as he moves around the kitchen, already so comfortable in this element. Before he catches me staring, I turn back and start frosting again.

Just after midnight, I switch off the light after cleaning

for the past hour. Baylor's already holding the door open for me. I take one last look around and lock up before we make our way upstairs.

My feet are dragging, and my arms are kind of sore from doing that same motion for the past few hours. The festival is a huge undertaking physically, but mentally, I feel like I'm already forgetting something. As we enter the apartment, I say, "I have to be up early to get everything ready for the cupcake cart."

"How early?" he asks, closing the door behind him and locking the deadbolt.

"Six, at the latest." I don't turn on the lights as I walk to the bedroom. Enough light creeps in through the cracks of the blinds to guide the way.

"I can drive you home if you need to sleep there."

I'd almost forgotten about my mom knowing he's renting the place. I check my watch. "I'd rather stay here. Anyway, she'll be asleep, and I'll be out the door before she wakes up. I think our secret is safe."

I flip on the bathroom light and reach for my toothbrush. When Baylor comes with his toothbrush in hand, I add the paste so we can brush together. It's hard to focus with him around, though. A giddiness finds me, making me giggle through the white foam. The sudden reaction sends dribbles of paste down my chin.

He grabs a tissue to clean me up before I even spit. As soon as we do and are finished, I say, "It's fun to have you here."

"I'm glad you stayed." He exhales a day's worth of exhaustion as he glances in the mirror and drags his hand over his unruly hair. "I'm so fucking exhausted."

"Let's go to bed."

We wrap up in the bathroom individually, so when he

comes out, I'm already tucked in. I'm not sure what to expect to happen. Will we have sex or go to sleep? I'm open to both because either way, I get to sleep in his arms again.

My body is calm, peace filling the room as he climbs in next to me. He kisses me but doesn't linger. Instead, he pulls my back and body to his chest and wraps me in his arms. "Hey, Shortcake?" he whispers against my hair.

"Yeah?" I don't know why my breath stops in my chest, but my heart stalls along with it.

Although I'm not facing him, the sudden tension between us makes me nervous. He takes a deep breath and slowly exhales before his words float against the back of my neck. "I'm developing feelings for you."

I smile, not obnoxiously so, but the kind that comes from hearing him open up on his own. "What kind of feelings?"

A kiss is placed on my shoulder before he says, "I'm falling for you."

I need to see his eyes, so I turn in his arms. "You are?"

"I am. It's not something I do, but the more time I spend with you, the more I want to be with you." He chuckles lightly. "Does that make any sense?"

I cup his jaw, then run my fingers over his cheek. "I feel the same about you." I kiss him just as his hand slides along my ribs. Tucking my leg between his, I know right then that sleep will have to wait.

CHAPTER 18

Baylor

SLEEP WEARS OFF SLOWLY. In the first conscious moments of the morning, I reach across the bed to pull Lauralee to me.

Cold sheets. Empty. Shit.

I groan, rolling to check my phone, but judging by how bright the bedroom is, I know it's well into the morning. The screen lights up with 9 a.m. flashing right at the top.

Fuck.

She's long gone.

Sitting up, I scrub my hand over my face and roll out of bed. And like every morning shower, I have a plan in place before I'm drying off. I'll check the shop downstairs first, and if she's not there, I'll head out to the festival and help her set up.

By the time I'm dressed, I get a text from Beckett from Tagger's phone number: *Dad said barrel racing at 1 p.m.*

He isn't asking me specifically, but your nephew texts with that much context for only one reason. I reply: *I'll see you at 1.*

The quick emoji wearing a cowboy hat in response leaves me smiling as I slide the door to the apartment open, with sneakers on my feet and my head bereft of a cowboy hat.

Used to be that this town would eat you alive if you showed up to the peach festival without the standard gear, and I forgot to grab them yesterday when I was out there. So I text my sister: *Do you mind bringing my boots and a hat out to the festival for me later?* I stare at the phone for a minute, but when she doesn't reply, I shove it in my back pocket and grab my wallet to get going.

I step out of the apartment to find the parking lot full of vehicles. Not sure what's going on, I decide to walk instead of drive to the front of Peaches Sundries. I'm met with hordes of people lining the sidewalks on both sides of the street, a sea of peach in both directions. "The parade," I grumble to myself.

I'd forgotten about it, though I rode the floats every year in high school. Before that, the kids would chase them and collect the candy they threw. My memories of this event have always been good, but I'm quick to turn on it when it's keeping me from my Shortcake.

I say hi to a few folks I recognize or vice versa while walking to the store. The bell chimes like it always does when I enter, but Lauralee does not greet me. I don't even recognize this kid. "Welcome to Peaches," she says. "Can I get you a peach cupcake or a breakfast sandwich?"

Tempting.

Since I won't be of any use on an empty stomach, I order the sandwich to go and make myself a coffee from the machines by the cola. When I return to the counter, she has it wrapped up, and says, "That will be seven fifty-three with the coffee."

I tap my card and try to act casual with the inquiry. "I'm a friend of Lauralee's."

"Oh," she says, her expression brightening. "Well, you came at the right time. She should be coming by here any minute. You should catch her out front."

Nodding, I take the sandwich and coffee, and say, "Thanks," before heading back outside. I eat, occasionally looking both ways to see if I can spy her coming down the sidewalk, with no luck. It takes most of the sandwich and me finishing my coffee before it occurs to me.

My Shortcake is a beauty queen, a former Miss Peach Festival, to be exact. I'd almost forgotten since I wasn't around back then. But I've seen the photo and remember my mom updating me about what was going on with everyone, including my sister's friend. I shouldn't be surprised she's going to be on a float. She's earned the spot. But she didn't tell me. Wonder why that is?

"Hey, Bay." I turn to see my sister hurrying down the sidewalk, kids in tow. Beck's eyes light up as he races toward me, and I ruffle his hair a bit as he laughs and steps away.

"I didn't know you were coming to the parade," I say, kneeling when Daisy runs in my direction too. It's then I notice the boots in my sister's hand. My boots. Turning my attention back to the little spitfire, I toss her up into the air. "How are you, Daisy girl?"

"Bay Bay." She takes the hat off her own head to put it on mine, pushing down until she covers my eyes. She finds it hysterical. I find her cute as all get-out.

I lift it to smile at her. Those big blue eyes shine, reminding me of my mom's. Daisy favors my sister in appearance over Tagger, but Christine looks so much like my mom that it's hard not to feel a little tightening in the chest when looking at her. My mom would have been an incredible grandmother to these kids. "Is that funny?"

She nods but quickly gets distracted when the band rounds the corner onto Main Street. Beckett stands at my side like always, but my sister says, "I brought you a shirt as well. Figured you could get by in your city jeans, but you need a proper western shirt to go with that hat and boots." She hands me the shirt that had been draped over her arm.

When I examine it, nothing is familiar about it, though I like it. "This isn't from my closet."

"I took it from Tagger's. You guys look about the same size." Glancing back, she says, "If you're quick, you can be back here before the final float turns the corner." I can't tell if she knows something more than she's saying, mainly that Lauralee and I are . . . what are we? Sleeping together, in a relationship, or? I'm not sure, but when I look at her face, I think my sister is warning me, so I don't miss this.

"Thanks. I'll go change."

I go back to the apartment and change into my pearl-button short-sleeved western shirt and boots. Topping my head with my summer cowboy hat, I'm back before I'm even missed. "You should get some candy, Beck."

He looks at my sister, who is quick to say, "Go on. Have some fun. We'll be right here."

When he takes off running, another kid launches from a nearby lawn chair, calling his name. They slap their hands together in a high five, then scramble for candy on the sides of the vehicles together.

I say, "What do you think about him coming out to visit me this summer?"

She looks a little surprised, but then she smiles. "He'd love more time with you, and I know he sometimes misses

New York. He talks about the pizza." She shakes her head in laughter. "He *really* misses the pizza."

Daisy has wrangled both of us to hold her hand, but I know she can't see a damn thing down there. I lift her onto my shoulders so she can view the parade fully.

Christine says, "I'll talk to Tagger, but I think it would be good for him. His mom has been coming to Austin or San Antonio when she flies in from Paris. So he's not been in the past few years."

"Just a few days," I say, "but I think it would be fun to have that one-on-one time with him."

She points in the distance. "Look, Daisy, it's Leelee."

My attention is caught the moment I see her on that giant pink-and-white float. Her hair is down around her shoulders under a sparkling tiara. Wearing an emerald-green fitted gown that almost outsparkles the tiara, she's fucking stunning.

Daisy clasps her hands together and squeals, "Princess Leelee."

"Yeah, she looks just like a princess," Christine says.

"She didn't tell me she was in the parade," I mention as the float gets closer.

"A parade couldn't be put on one year." She looks up at me, and whispers, "The town had no money for it. So they're a year behind. The new Peach Queen is crowned by the ten-year anniversary queen. That's Lauralee this year."

It's the moment her eyes find mine in the crowd, the smile that blooms before my very eyes that has my heart thumping in my chest. I wave to her like the others, and when she winks, I know it's for me. She waves with both hands to Daisy, who bounces in excitement. "Leelee," she shouts.

Christine steps around the front of me after they pass.

Reaching up for Daisy, I lift her and pass her daughter into her arms. "She looked beautiful. Don't you think, Baylor?"

She always does, but I'm not sure what to say that won't put her on the scent of something more going on. So I reply, "Yeah. Sure. Beck said you'll be at the rodeo at one?"

"I want to catch the barrel racing." My sister was the best when she participated. "Do you want to meet us there?"

"I'll be there."

Standing on her tiptoes, she says, "As soon as I find Beckett, we're going back to the ranch. We came out for the parade, but we'll need naps before tackling the activities this afternoon. Dad and Tag are wrapping up duties with a few of the ranch hands before everyone takes the rest of the day off. I also need to make sure they're drinking enough water today. It's a hot one."

"Sure is. Hey, thanks for bringing the hat and gear."

"Anytime." She laughs. "Can't have you looking like a city slicker now, can we?"

"Come here," I say, wrapping her and her growing belly, and Daisy up in my arms to hug them both at once. I kiss both their heads and hold them. Not for long because it's too hot out here for that, but long enough for her to wrap her free arm around me, too. "I love you, Pris."

"That's your one freebie with that name."

I chuckle. "So feisty." When I release them, I'm not released in turn.

Instead, she holds me, tucking her head to my chest, and whispers, "I love you, big brother."

Griffin and I were close in age, and as brothers, we were friends. I never appreciated my sister as much as I should have. The past few years, since my mom's death, her running the ranch and then marrying my best friend have managed to bring us closer. I appreciate the second chance she gave me to make amends for leaving her to pick up the pieces when I couldn't. And Griffin barely made it back to the funeral before he took off again. Same goes for our little sister's wedding.

I don't hear from him nearly enough, but I'm to blame for not reaching out more, either. I want to be here for my family as much as I can.

When she steps back, she takes a deep breath. I swear those are tears forming in the inner corners of her eyes, but she laughs it off and rolls her eyes. "It's always good to have you back." She starts walking backward and away from me down the sidewalk. "Maybe you need to consider staying here for good one day."

"It's always on my mind," I lie. It wasn't until Tagger moved here, I should say. Over the past month, after spending time with Lauralee, I have also had that thought pop in and out a few times. I can't give her hope when it's just not a possibility with my job, and how I'm growing my career. Speaking of . . . "Hey, what do you think about a New York-style pizzeria downtown?"

She laughs. "Beckett and Tagger would eat you out of your profits. But I like the way you're thinking, Bay." She turns to go, cupping her hand to the side of her mouth, and calling, "We're over here, Beckett." He runs to her side, excitedly showing her all the candy he collected.

Having visions of my own kids running to show me how much candy they scored isn't something I expected, but I'm not upset by them. I even start smiling to myself as I walk to the apartment to wait for Shortcake since she'll need to change before leaving again.

When I enter the place, I hang the key on the hook and drop my hat on the counter. Sitting on the couch, I don't need any entertainment. My mind is in overdrive thinking about what Christine said. Is Peachtree Pass somewhere I'd want to settle?

When Tagger and I left for college on a football scholarship, neither of us had any intention of returning to this small town. We wanted the opposite. Excitement. Energy. An office job over working outside. Working a ranch, a farm, and even the orchard is never-ending labor. It's everything we were escaping.

We were never looking back. Until he did. Becoming a dad changed his mind, his views on life, and how he wanted to raise his kid. I'm sure my sister complicated things, like she always does, but the story goes he fell in love the moment they saw each other again.

I'm not a dad, but the rest of the story seems to be aligning with mine and Lauralee's. Coincidence or fate? Are we both doomed or graced with the chance to move back and have another start in this life that could lead to happiness?

The door opens, causing me to stand. When she walks in, she smiles as soon as she sees me. "Hey there, stud."

"Hi." I wipe my hands down the sides of my jeans. Suddenly, I'm having thoughts of being greeted by that smile when I come home in the evenings. I shake my head to clear what's not real and appreciate what's right in front of me. "I think I'm the luckiest guy in Greene County." I slide my hands around her waist and kiss her neck.

"Oh yeah?" I'm not used to laying my emotions out on a platter to be examined, but I will for her so she knows I'm trying. If anyone else had asked, I wouldn't be making the effort.

Lauralee is different.

I haven't been able to pinpoint why I've felt so comfortable and at ease sharing a side of myself that I usually don't.

Now I know. It's not just because we're having sex, though that's fucking fantastic. She holds me accountable for what I'm saying. No bullshit lines will work on her. She wants the truth, and she returns the favor. And I have no doubt the same would go for my actions.

I've gotten away with a lot in my dating life, but know I won't with Lauralee. Why do I find that so appealing? I don't want to disappoint her.

My feet aren't held to the fire, but my heart feels like it is. I'm starting to think I'm past falling and have already fallen. If my mom were here for me to confide in, which I used to be able to do whenever I needed her, she'd tell me the same. Then she'd tell me not to blow it because Lauralee is one of the good ones and worth making the effort.

"What made you say that, Baylor?" she asks because I'm an asshole for keeping her waiting.

"I was so close to saying something about you being a beauty queen, but I don't want to." Raising one hand to caress the side of her neck, I say, "I'm the luckiest guy because I was the one who got to be here when you walked through that door."

No bullshit.

Just the God's honest truth.

CHAPTER 19

Lauralee

He's distracting in such a good way.

I practically fell off the float when I first saw him. Seeing Baylor back in a cowboy uniform has me rethinking why I'm at the festival instead of attacking him in bed. He looks good in his regular clothes, but the man always knew how to look beyond hot back in the day. *He hasn't forgotten.*

His body is broader, and I swear he's taller than yesterday. Impossible, but to me, he's becoming larger than life. Could it be that my feelings for him are growing exponentially? *Probably.* That would be reasonable, but I don't want to be sensible when it comes to us. I want to have a good time, and he's giving me that repeatedly. I need to trust my gut for once. No time like the present.

It's not only his appearance that has drawn me in. I'm a sucker for a guy who has the world at his feet. Strong, intelligent, successful, kind, and confident. He wears his heart on his sleeve only for me to see. Baylor's done a damn fine job of revealing his to me, and it makes me a bit weak in the knees. It's like a secret he's dared to share only with me.

He's still been walking around this festival like the hometown hero he is, soaking in the attention he's been getting. I'm not surprised, though. The Greenes are original to the area, and every generation is more beloved than the previous. He, his brother, and Christine are carrying that torch. They're almost like local celebrities—*good and bad*—everyone knows everything about them. It made it hard to sneak around when we were teens.

As for Baylor, it's another reason we need to keep things on the quieter side. If he wanted to stop seeing me, everyone would know. *God, that would be so humiliating.*

Why even put myself in that position?

My heart starts racing, so I take a few steps away from the cart and the other employee to inhale a deep breath. Slowly, I exhale through my mouth and wipe the sweat from my hairline with the back of my hand.

It's ridiculous that the consequences of a relationship ending gets me worked up and sweating. Will it ever change? *Will I?* I thought I'd worked through these issues. I guess my dad leaving unannounced caused damage that my mom's love wasn't enough to fill despite her best efforts.

But Baylor's not my dad. I can't make him pay for the aftermath. This is an opportunity to change things, and I'm taking it.

I look around, hoping to see him, though I don't expect to. Getting stuck managing the line wasn't in the plan, but I had to do what needed to be done. I wrap up at the cart, collecting the till proceeds for the day before night falls because it's already overflowing. To say this has been good for business would be an understatement. The festival brings in enough money to cover months of rent. Adding the cart has almost doubled that.

I tuck the money in my purse, then loop the strap around my chest, letting it hang across my body as I wander through the fair, looking for Baylor, Christine, and the others. Seeing a friendly face working the hot dog cart, I ask him, "Have you seen the Greenes?"

He replies, "I sold the kids hot dogs by the arena about an hour ago."

"Thanks." I take off toward the rodeo arena, hoping to find them watching the show. I walk around, but it's not crowded enough for me not to spot them quickly. Working my way back out, I cut through the back of the tents and start toward the fairgrounds.

Pulling out my phone, I text him: *Where are you?*

My hips are grabbed, and I'm spun around. "Right here, baby." He kisses me. I forget the noise and the crowds, the fear I was worrying about not ten minutes earlier, and my concerns disappear.

Baylor and me, and our lips connected is all I need.

But reality has a way of sneaking in, and it does this time to ruin the good time. As much as I want to sink into the deeper end of where this is heading, I start worrying about others seeing us.

I lick my lips when we part, my eyes fluttering open to see this handsome devil smiling down at me under the wide brim of his cowboy hat. "That's quite the greeting."

"You're quite the woman."

"Well," I state with a poke to his chest. "You're lucky I realized it was you, or you'd be lying flat on the ground right now from a cross punch to that perfect face of yours."

"Why does that turn me on?"

I burst out laughing. "Because you're utterly incorrigible. That's why."

"No lie detected when it comes to how I feel about you."

Is it in my head, or is he getting more charming by the hour? I glance around, and when I see the coast is clear, I sneak attack a kiss to his incredible mouth. Biting my lower lip, I drop back on my heels and ask, "Where are the others?"

"Ferris wheel." Offering his elbow, he asks, "You want to take a spin?"

I hook my arm with his before I realize how this will look to everyone. Hiding what feels natural is already annoying. I slowly pull away and nod. "Guess we should keep some space between us."

"What impression do you think us walking together will give?"

I shrug. "Not sure, but I don't want to find out either."

"That's fair, but one day, my beauty queen is going to be right where she should be. On the throne of my arm for the whole world to see." As if he hadn't already made me swoon, there he goes again. His expression turns serious, and then he says, "I have something important to talk to you about."

Although we're walking, my feet start to drag. Is this when I wake up from the dream I've been living with him? "What is it?"

"You admitted yourself that my face is perfect—"

"Oh God, here we go." I laugh. "Go on and get it out of your system now so I don't have to listen to it all night."

He's already chuckling. "Hey, it's not every day you hear how attractive someone thinks you are . . . *Oh wait.*"

Shaking my head, I laugh again. "Yeah, exactly." Throwing my hands up in surrender, I add, "I've learned my lesson to never feed Baylor Greene's ego because I know I'm not going to hear the end of it." I eye some pink and blue cotton candy up ahead.

He nudges me with his elbow. "Ah, come on, Shortcake. If it makes you feel better, you're the only woman who I care feels that way about me."

"Sadly, that does make me feel slightly better." I keep teasing, but to know that's what he thinks does make me feel special in a way I didn't before. He likes that I find him attractive the same as I like that he feels that way about me.

What's not to love about a man I'm insanely attracted to finding me sexy, struggles to keep his hands off me, and likes to spend time with me like last night in the kitchen when it's purely innocent. Just the two of us talking and getting a job done. But I need to keep him on his toes, so I joke, "As much as I love talking about your face, your ego, and everything else about you, I might need some cotton candy if this is going to continue."

He veers off to the stand to the left. "Pink or blue?"

"Pink, please."

He looks as proud as a peacock when he presents it to me. "As you wish." He's so cheesy that it's adorable. Does he act this silly in New York?

I have a feeling he doesn't, which makes me treasure him more. "Thank you, sir."

"I like the sound of that."

Opening the bag, I reply, "I bet you do." I hold it out to him. "Want some?"

"It's all yours."

"You would have thought eating three cupcakes for lunch since I was too busy to break away from the cart would deter me from more sugar. Guess not." I laugh, but he doesn't. When I glance at him, he seems to be deep in thought. "What's on your mind, stud?"

A smile breaks free when he looks at me. "Sorry, I was just thinking about you and me."

"I like this topic."

The tips of his fingers graze my wrist. It's barely felt, and I'm sure no one could see, but his touch shoots right through me like electricity. "Me too." He stops, shifting in front of me, his eyes setting on mine again, and asks, "Remember how I mentioned you coming to the city?"

Not sure why I suddenly feel shy, but I whisper for only him to hear, "I remember."

"Would you consider helping me?"

"Is it illegal or illicit?"

Chuckling, he replies, "No."

"Disappointing." I smirk. We come around the corner from the last large tent and start toward the games section. "Try me anyway. What is it?"

He stops in front of the ring toss, and says, "The company I work for is hosting their annual summer event over the Fourth of July weekend. In the Hamptons."

"Say less. The Hamptons? I'm there." I start laughing because I crack myself up sometimes. "Just kidding. I'm not inviting myself to your event." A kid screaming over a dropped ice cream behind him briefly steals my attention.

When I look back at him, he says, "I am."

"You are what?"

"I'm inviting you to the Hamptons. If you have any interest in going as my date."

I rest my hand on his chest. "I was just giving you a hard time. I didn't mean to make you feel guilty."

Covering my hand, he grins. "No guilt. I was going to ask you if that weekend would work for you to visit, and if so, if you wouldn't mind a night suffering through a work event in the Hamptons."

"Sounds like torture—"

"The property is huge, and it's on the water," he's quick to add as if he didn't pick up on my sarcasm. "I think you'll love it."

I lower my hand despite my desire to keep it right over his beating heart. I love that it's beating harder as if his nerves have kicked in. I didn't even know this man got nervous until now. Why is he? "I was just teasing, Baylor. It sounds like a dream. Truly. But on the surface. What are you not telling me? Is there a catch?"

"There is." He reaches for my hand, but then realization dawns in his eyes, and he shoves them in his pockets. "I've been working for a promotion."

"Okay."

"Well, they feel they want their executives to be more established."

We start to stroll again, maneuvering away from the crowds forming at the games, but I glance up at him. "You've done very well, so I can't imagine you haven't already proven yourself." The cowboy hat shades his face, but those blue eyes are still so captivating. All he has to do is look at me, and I'm willing to say yes to anything. Good thing he doesn't know that. *Yet*... I'm not exactly a closed book.

"They value family." I see him shake his head, but I'm not sure I was supposed to notice. With his hand over his heart, he's quick to clarify, "I value family. They only value the image of family since it's no secret in the city that the partners have wandering eyes away from their wives." He laughs, but the humor isn't heard. "Ironic since they're worried that my . . . let's call it bachelorhood. My being single is an impediment to my promotion in the company."

I'm not sure if I should laugh or be mortified. "Your dating life is being used against you?"

"To put it bluntly."

This doesn't help quell my earlier concerns about relationships. I've not been in many even though I can justify it because of lack of options in the country, not finding the right guy, or protecting myself. But deep down, I still wonder if my dad leaving us high and dry plays a part.

Why can't I just enjoy myself for once? Not everything has to be analyzed or overthought to the point of exhaustion. I take a breath. *Just enjoy your time with him, Lauralee.*

Redirecting my energies back to him, I bump into him. "You're a hot bachelor."

"Hot, you say?"

Pointing at him, I narrow my eyes playfully. "Zip it, Greene. As I was saying, you have . . ." I correct myself since I'm not sure where we stand, but his telling me he's falling for me feels like a line in the sand for us. Our relationship changed right then. To what, I'm not entirely sure, but I'm willing to find out. "You *had* every right to date who you like. It's your personal life, and it shouldn't matter if it's not affecting your job. You also said you needed my help." Totally forming my own conclusions, I ask, "Do we get to play 'couple' in the Hamptons?"

"I was hoping you'd agree to be my girlfriend for the weekend."

That sounded a lot like he wanted to ask me for more. And I'd be lying if I didn't acknowledge that I'm over-the-moon flattered by his proposition. "I'll be your girlfriend for the weekend." He thought of me to help him out of this predicament when he has every right to ask someone else. Confessing he's falling for me doesn't mean he's shackled to me forever. Our relationship is finding a stride we're both comfortable with. That's a good thing that I appreciate.

A rogue smile crosses his expression before he rubs the edge of his jawline. "It's a selfless sacrifice, Ms. Knot. I do appreciate it." His kicking in a little country accent wins him some bonus points, even if it's done in jest.

"I'm not totally selfless, Baylor. I get to spend time with you out of the spying eyes of Peachtree Pass." When he looks at me, I waggle my eyebrows because he's not the only one who can flirt.

He smacks my ass, then he raises his hand high in the air to wave. "Hello, Mrs. Marion."

"Good to see ya, Baylor Greene," she replies.

Oh great. Our old Sunday school teacher bore witness to him smacking my ass. We share a look and start laughing, which dispels the embarrassment that tried to take over.

We reach the edge of the Ferris wheel and look up. Christine, Tagger, and the kids are in a car near the top. Beckett waves at us, so we both wave back.

Baylor produces two tickets, almost like he'd planned this all along, and hands them to the operator. The guy says, "You're next. Get up on the platform and stand to the side."

The ride comes to a stop. He unloads the car before welcoming us in and shutting the door. Sitting across from each other to balance it, I'm given full opportunity to stare at him. He takes advantage of the situation by staring at me.

His smile evokes mine.

His laughter tickles mine out of my throat.

But it's when he sits forward and takes my hand that I lose my breath. Rubbing his thumb over my knuckles, he asks, "You ready to get out of here after this?"

"I've been ready since I saw you in that hat."

CHAPTER 20

Baylor

"Do your parents know you're up this early?"

Beckett follows me as we trek to my dad's truck. "Sometimes I think my dad knows everything." He doesn't make that sound like a positive.

"Parents are like that, but they need to be at your age." I pull open the door and climb into the cab of the truck. He climbs in on the opposite side. "Seat belt." I start the engine. "In a few years, you'll be venturing out on your own more, so you don't need to grow up too fast. Let him enjoy being your dad while he can."

"Won't he always be my dad?"

"Good point. Yes, he will be. Just like my dad is mine." I look toward the house to see him rocking on the front porch. "Wave to Grandpa."

We both wave before we start for the feed store. "What's on the list to get, buddy?"

He pulls his paper from his pocket and begins naming what we need to start on the fort. We've had a good conversation during the drive. He's a smart kid, but he's also ready to spread his wings. He can run around the ranch, but I think he has a little up-to-no-good streak in him, just like his dad and his favorite uncle.

"Baylor!"

Damn, I'm literally two steps into the place. I don't know how she had time to spot me. I turn to the left and see her hightailing it toward me. I pull Beckett to my side, and reply, "Hi, Maple. How's it going?"

"So good to see you. I only got a few glimpses of you at the festival yesterday before you'd disappear."

Maple's *okay*. She's always been nice enough, but she doesn't get a hint at all. Or she's ignoring them. I still don't tell her that I caught her following me no less than two times and ducked through the back of vendor tents to throw her off the scent. "Oh, wow. I didn't see you at all. I was with my sister and her family."

"And Lauralee Knot by the ring toss when I saw you last. Are you two a thing?"

Beckett looks up at me now with the same question lingering in his eyes.

"You know she's my sister's best friend?" I ask, playing dumb.

"Sure, everyone knows. It's also Lauralee," she says as if that is all we need to know. She's right. It's all I need. Throwing her arms up, she laughs. "Stranger things have happened. Like your sister and Tagger Grange."

I look at Beckett, annoyed he had to hear that. "It's not so strange. They're great together."

"You know what I mean."

Beckett wiggles out from the arm I had loosely around him, and says, "Don't talk about my parents."

Maple's hand goes to her chest as her mouth hangs open. "I didn't mean to upset the little fellow."

"I'm not so little, and soon, I'll be big."

I do a double take. The first snap comment surprised me. The threat bothers me. "Beck, let it go. This is nothing to get upset about. Maple wasn't calling them bad people. The two of them falling in love just surprised some people, including myself."

"Not me. Grandma taught me all about love, so I knew."

"I think the story is that you knew before they did." I smile, hoping to ease his defensiveness.

"She told me the recipe."

I'm not sure what he's talking about, but I'm glad he's back to himself.

Looking at Maple, I say, "We have a lot of shopping to do."

"Yes," she says, "I'll leave you to it, but let me know if you need my help."

"We won't," Beckett replies as I guide him away.

I glance down at him, realizing he may not be related by blood, but he still takes after me. I've never been prouder. "Damn, kid. We need to get you out on the football field."

"I started last season. Dad finally talked my mom into letting me play. It was just flag football before. Now, we get to tackle."

"I don't envy the player going against you." I'll always be his biggest hype man. We turn down the aisle with the tool belts. "Let's get you fitted."

Supervising makes me feel old, though I enjoy watching Beckett and his friend Macon piece together the wood on the ground like a puzzle. "What do you think about altering the plans to include a deck you walk onto at the base? Just in case it's muddy? It gives us a level floor to work from as well."

They both stop and stare at me, but then Beckett says, "So start with that first?"

"If you do," I reply, "it's something you can work on when I'm gone. If you get it done, we'll be able to move to phase two when I return."

He looks at his friend and shrugs. "What do you think?"

"Sounds like something my dad would suggest."

"So that's good, right?" I ask, hoping to convince them since we're not making much progress with the current plan. I won't take it over, though. Beckett has the final say.

He picks up a two-by-four to drag it to the middle of the trees. Dropping it, he says, "It will last longer if we do it right. That's what my dad always says."

"Mine too," Macon adds. "Measure twice, cut once."

I cross my arms over my chest, entertained by how they work through this.

Beckett finally looks at me. "We'll build the deck. Promise to help me build the first floor when you visit next?"

"I promise."

He turns to Macon. "Want to get snacks and play some video games?"

Macon looks relieved. "Yeah, I'm hungry." They start walking away, chatting about a suit they won in the last round, leaving me behind.

"Wow," I mumble to myself. "Guess we're done here." I'm not serious, so I chuckle as I work my way out of the woods to my dad's truck. We already unloaded all the wood, so I start the engine and cruise up the hill to his house. As soon as I make the curve around the main barn, I smile at the sight of her.

Dress blowing in the wind and hugging one side of her body. Her hair whipping up a storm as well while she visors her eyes from the sunlight shining on her like the angel she is. My dad sits on the edge of the UTV nearby and directs me to park next to him.

I shut off the engine and toss him the keys as I head for Lauralee. "Thanks for letting me borrow it. We got quite a bit of wood brought down to the fort."

"How's it looking after one shift?"

Lauralee's smile shifts to the side, always trying to control the broad one she wants to share. Our eyes meet, and I smile because damn, she's a gorgeous sight to behold. Before I get caught up in her, I turn back to face my dad. "About how you'd expect when herding two nine-year-old boys. Might want to step in as foreman while I'm gone. I'm sure you have some knowledge to share on building a deck."

"I've built a few in my time." He stamps his cane in the dirt.

The scar on the side of his leg is visible but healing. "How's the knee today?"

He waves me off. "Pfft. Stop worrying about me. I'm good. You have enough on your plate like Lauralee waiting on you while you're over here yapping with me."

"I do worry."

"I'm good, son. Soon, I'll be kicking your ass on that basketball court."

"You're sounding like Tagger, and you know how that goes."

He chuckles. "Yeah, well, I can take you both. So let's not make a big deal of this, especially when you have company."

"Okay, Dad. You won this round. But I'll be back soon enough and bugging you again."

"Now go on."

With a grin, I turn around and start walking. Tapping my hat higher on my forehead so I can take in the full view of her, I smile for a different reason. *Her.* I reach my girl in only a few steps but force myself to stop just shy of kissing her. "Hi."

Her hips sway twice, and her cheeks pinken for me. "Hi."

I can tell my dad is still behind us, probably already figuring us out. I'm sure he'll say something later. But right now, man, I wish I could kiss her, hug her, touch her in any way. Time's slipping away from us, and I'm going to miss her come tomorrow. I don't regret spending time with my nephew and keeping my word, but hell, I missed her today. "What brings you by?"

"You." I love that she doesn't bother to lie and just says what she wants. And I'm the lucky bastard who fits the bill. *So fucking sexy.* "I wanted to see you before you leave later tonight."

"Did you really think I'd leave without a proper goodbye?"

"We hadn't made plans, and I knew you were spending time with your family. I wasn't sure if I should even drive out."

"I'm glad you did."

A loud clearing of the throat behind me grabs our attention, and we both look at my dad. He says, "I'm going to go inside so you two can talk privately."

When I turn back to Lauralee, she says, "I think he knows."

"He definitely knows, but since the cat's out of the bag . . ." I swoop in, cupping her face, and kiss her like I wanted to originally. We waste no time with niceties. Instead, our mouths open, and our tongues entwine. There's an urgency that hasn't been there, but with it being Sunday, it's come into play.

When air becomes necessary, our lips part, but our foreheads press together. We both breathe, regulating our breaths with our eyes still closed. "You make me wish I could stay," I whisper. The words came so easily that I question when the emotion was formed that created them.

Last night when we were making love or yesterday when we were making plans? The moment I saw her again, if the truth be told. But how can so much change in the course of a few days?

I lift my head and look at her. *That's my answer.*

She whispers, "I wish you could stay, too. It was just getting good." Her laughter trickles away too quickly. A weighty sigh escapes her, and her smile falls. "I can't even land a joke right now because this feels heavy and too important to goof it up."

Giving her some space to sort through her thoughts, I step back, but only once. My own selfish needs still win out. "You're not goofing anything up. You can say what's on your mind, baby."

"I didn't expect to fall for you, but here I am, just a girl from a small town who's about to have her heart broken when you leave tonight." Her admission is a shot to my heart.

I must get on that plane. My job is on the line if I don't. *There's just no way I can now.*

I won't be the guy to break her heart. Not now. *Not ever.* "I'll stay the night."

CHAPTER 21

Lauralee

I don't know why I'm nervous.

The drive back letting too much time pass?
The anticipation of what's about to happen?
The thought of Baylor leaving?

God, so much is running around my mind that I take a deep breath and focus on the right here and now, so I don't miss it.

We haven't said much since we walked into the apartment, and we moved about like this is how we live every day. Though I'm sure, like me, he's going through the motions as if we don't have this ocean of separation coming our way. At least that's how he's been kissing me since we got here.

Standing at the bedside together, he leans back, but his eyes are still closed, and he licks his lips as if he's still savoring me. No words follow, but they don't need to.

I open my mouth, needing more oxygen to reach my lungs because he gets me so worked up that it's easy to forget simple things, like breathing, until it's direly necessary.

When he opens his eyes, his fingers tighten on my hips. "Ten days, and I'll see you again. I already bought your ticket."

"It's not my ticket I'm worried about." I find myself wanting to hold on to him even tighter, too. "When do you have to leave?"

"No later than one thirty." He brushes my hair back from my neck to caress it with his hand. "You'll be fast asleep and too exhausted to notice."

I grin. "Can you guarantee that?"

"I'll make sure you're taken care of." He kisses me again. The back of my knees hit the bed, and I fall until I'm sitting. I hold one leg up. The hint not subtle. He takes hold of the boot and works it off, then pats his leg. I prop my other foot up to remove that boot as well.

There's no frenzy. No urgency to our kisses.

I take off my socks. He takes off his.

While I unbutton my dress, he's undoing his jeans and pushing them down.

When my dress lands on the floor, his shirt keeps it company.

Reaching behind my back, he unclasps my bra, his gaze adoring my entire body with every new inch exposed. After I slide up to rest my head on a pillow, Baylor climbs over me, kissing my legs as he works himself higher.

In the afternoon sunshine flooding through the bedroom's open blinds, he stops at my ribs and runs a finger over my ribs on the right side. "Tell me about your tattoo," he says, keeping his voice low. "I've seen it so many times, but it was too dark to read what it said until now."

"Choose who chooses you." I reach down and run the

tips of my fingers over it. It's so delicate it's not felt anymore. "I forget about it most days." I rest my arm over my forehead. "Which is strange to think about because it used to always be on my mind when I got it."

"Why did you choose that quote?" It's a simple question that doesn't seem to have such an easy answer. His hand is warm, the heat radiating through my body under the spinning ceiling fan. He slides up next to me, resting his head on the other pillow. "We don't have to talk about it if you're not comfortable."

I turn to look at him. "I've asked you to share your heart and inner thoughts, and you're going to let me off the hook like that?"

Although I'm teasing, he's not when he replies, "Tattoos come with a story. I'll wait until you're ready to share yours."

The trust we've built came quicker than with most people, but so did my feelings for him. I don't want to hide, especially when he's given me a reason not to hide. I say, "My dad left when I was seven. Kissed my mom goodbye, and me on the head as I ate breakfast and then walked right out the door like he was going to work." My throat tightens. "I was eating Lucky Charms. I haven't thought about that in years." I quickly dip my head sideways into the pillow. "Not so lucky, huh?"

Baylor reaches over and caresses my cheek, running his thumb over my temple as his fingers weave into my hair. "I'm not going to spin this to find some bright side to that situation. That was a shitty thing to do to you and your mom."

Even though it's not an event in my life that I focus on, Christine was always there to comfort me over the years. My mom was too, but it was just different. With her, I needed to be cognizant of her pain, and I didn't always have the strength to consume both of our pain. A bucket only holds so much before it tips over.

I'd tip over some days, and my best friend helped right me. So hearing Baylor just lay it out so plainly—not trying to explain how it wasn't my fault and not making up excuses for him to make me feel better—takes off some of that weight of the burden I'm forced to carry.

It is exactly what it looks like on the surface for all the world to see and judge, including me.

My dad chose to leave after raising me for seven years, after vowing to my mother to protect me, after knowing me for seven crucial years of my life. It was hard to realize I needed protecting from him.

He leans over and kisses my forehead. When he falls back to his pillow, he says, "Choose who chooses you."

I nod, not sure anything more needs to be said, and I don't want to spend our last few hours dwelling on the past when I can be here with him instead. I lean forward and kiss him. Just like earlier, it's slow. We take our time to appreciate the feel of each other's lips, the way our tongues find their way together, and our hands hold the other like we fell in love a long time before now.

Is that possible?

Could our souls have known all along?

He hasn't found love, though he's traveled all over. I didn't find it when I stayed here.

I've never been overly romantic, but deep in my heart, I was still hoping to find my soulmate one day. Under the tender embrace of this man, I start to wonder if it's been him all along.

When he dips to kiss my neck, I whisper, "Make love to me, Baylor."

He lifts his head so our gazes connect, revealing the appreciation he has for me. A gentle smile lifts his cheeks, and he ducks to my ear and kisses me. "I'll make love to you, baby."

His hand works its way down my body and slips between my legs. It never takes long with him, but the magic strikes faster this time. When he fills my body with the weight of him on top of me, I'm free to feel everything he's giving. But one of my favorite things is pleasing him. To bring him to his knees is such an aphrodisiac.

We roll over so I can take charge, riding him with his eyes fixed on my body, making me feel sexier than I ever have. And when he starts to lose his grip of control, his hold on me tightens, and his eyes start to roll back in his head. I can tell the moment his release nears—his eyes clench closed, his body tenses, and his movements become erratic under me.

He flips me to the bed, lifting my leg over his shoulder, and fucks me until we both fall apart together. But when we're left lying with the sun beginning to set outside, I hold on tightly to him. I kiss his shoulder, and whisper, "I don't want you to go."

"Me either, Shortcake. Ten days," he says, resting his head next to mine.

His words are a good reminder of the countdown before us, making it easier to keep things in perspective. "Ten days," I add, my body finally running out of air.

He rolls onto his back, letting his right arm flop wide, and exhales loudly. His eyes are closed when I cuddle up to him and drape my arm over his chest. I say, "I wanted to give you something."

"What do you want to give me?"

"I thought it only fair to give you a 10 percent discount

off your reservation since the sex has been so good this weekend."

I can't see him, but his chest vibrates when he bursts out laughing. "Only 10 percent good?"

"Fine." I lift my head to see his smile, anchoring my elbow to the bed. "You drive a hard bargain. Fifteen percent."

He grabs me, tickling my ribs mercilessly until I'm begging for forgiveness. I'm given a reprieve when I agree to 20 percent. But when I get up to use the bathroom, he catches me by the wrist, causing me to turn back. When I do, he says, "I don't need a discount to make love to you." He pulls me onto his lap, wrapping his arms around my waist. Placing a kiss on my shoulder, he looks up at me, his lips lingering on my skin. "I don't want your money."

"What do you want, stud?"

Running his hand on my back, he says, "You. Only you, baby."

Dinner was nothing more than a frozen pizza and fruit I had on hand, but neither of us wanted to leave the apartment.

It's a quieter night. We don't mind as long as we're together. So by the time we're in bed and he's spooning me from behind, he says, "Remember when you wake up tomorrow that I wanted to stay. Will you do that for me?"

I'm not expecting my emotions to overwhelm me, but tears form and escape the corners of my eyes. My heart lumps in my throat, leaving me too choked up to reply. I nod.

He kisses the back of my head as his arm tightens

around me. We lie in silence until the only sound is gentle breaths that lengthen as the night goes on. And then I fall asleep against my best efforts to stay awake.

With a gasp and my heart racing in panic, I sit up, opening my eyes. The room is dark, and the silence deafening. I can't hear him breathing or feel the warmth of his hand on me. The bed isn't dipped behind me, and the covers are made like he never existed at all.

Baylor's gone.

I've never felt lonelier in my life.

One Week Later . . .

"I don't understand." I sit forward on the chair, my heart beating hard in my chest. "Do you mind explaining it to me one more time, Mr. Josten?"

The real estate leasing agent takes his pen from the pocket of his dress shirt, drawing my attention to the sweat circle extending around his armpits, and taps the loan agreement with the tip of it. I wasn't expecting a visit from the new management company based in Austin, which is now in charge of our lease agreement. And if I'm hearing him correctly, I definitely would not have given him a piece of my strawberry cobbler on the house. Or the vanilla, light-on-the-syrup-heavy-on-the-cream specialty coffee I made specially for him.

"What do you do again?" I ask, my thoughts scrambling under the blindside of this situation. He's not much older than I am, but he's talking to me like I'm a child, slowing his speech as if the actual words were the problem. No, it's the new rent increase that's an issue.

"I'm the new five-county rep for the company hired to manage its portfolio."

"And my shop falls under your jurisdiction?"

"Well, that's one way to put it. I'm here to help with whatever you need."

Anger starts bubbling under my cooler demeanor. "By raising my rent so high that it will put me out of business?"

"Well."

"That's a lot of wells, Mr. Josten."

"Well."

"There you go again. I guess I'm wondering when the management changed and why."

"The property was sold recently to a venture capital company. They hired us to acquire new contracts for the change."

"You were told to raise the rent? I'm just surprised that they can increase it in the middle of the lease like this."

"No, we're tasked with pricing real estate accordingly. It's our expertise." Tapping the contract again, he adds, "And we're not increasing it in the middle of the lease. Your lease is up in six months. That's when the increase will kick in." He sits back in the bistro chair, seemingly proud of the job he's doing. "That is, of course, if you renew. If you choose not to, then—"

"I lose my shop." I look through the window to see something that's been a part of me my entire life. I think about my mom and all the hard work she put in through debt and paying off overdue bills, working seven days a week for years until I was old enough to cover a shift.

I feel sick.

As I look around Main Street, it's easy to see that there's not much here. My shop, the clothing store a few stores down, the post office catty-corner to me, and the fourth-generation-owned grocer across the street. There are more empty spaces than filled. Will any of them be able to survive this kind of corporate greed price increase?

My mom entrusted her shop, her other baby, to me. Am I going to lose Peaches Sundries & More the moment I take ownership? "What are my options?"

It's the first bit of humanity I've seen cross his face. He even takes it a step further by showing me empathy in the shape of his mouth before he speaks. "There are only the two. You sign, or you close the shop and move out."

I look down at the contract. Two options. *That's it.*

Wrapping my arms around my stomach, I ask, "Do I have time to think about it?"

"You have one week to renew the lease per your current contract. It states six months. With the recent change in ownership and needing to get the contracts updated, we've added a week to help you out."

"Thanks," I reply, not able to be grateful when I'm ultimately being forced out. "What happens if I vacate the spot?"

"The owner has big plans to revitalize the area with new businesses and bonuses to bring new families to town."

"Bonuses to move here, but nothing for the residents who have lived here for generations?"

He redirects his eyes to a car passing by, not bothering to respond. We both know why. There is no satisfactory answer he can supply.

I stand, taking the paperwork in hand, and say, "It's a long drive back to Austin. Would you like your coffee to go or a water or soda for the road?"

"A cola would be great. Heavy on the ice."

Walking to the door, I reply, "Got it."

I make it just how he requested, the born and raised

Southern hospitality side of me coming out, and push through the door to the sidewalk. He's standing, beads of sweat forming at his hairline. "It's hot today."

"That's Texas for you." I hand him the drink. "That will be four fifty-nine." Call me petty, but I seem to have lost my manners. My registers' gain.

"Oh, okay," he says, digging his wallet out from his back pocket.

When he hands me a five-dollar bill, I ask, "Keep the change?"

"Sure." The annoyance coats his reply while the sweat rolls down his forehead. "One week, Ms. Knot. Have a good day." He walks to his car parked out front, but I stay a moment.

And when he looks back, I wave. "You, too, Mr. Josten." Jerk.

I walk inside. I've heard that bell chime more times than I could ever count, but it never gets old. It's come to symbolize more than a sound. It's my dreams and goals all in harmony.

Glancing down at the paperwork in my hands, I realize it doesn't matter what it says. As he stated, there are only two options. For me, there's only one.

Tomorrow, I'm making a trip to the bank.

CHAPTER 22

Lauralee

It's been so hard to keep my mom in the dark about what's happening with the shop. As I sit here nervously waiting for the loan officer to return, I wish I could lean on her for support. Her advice would mean so much to me, but that would involve me telling her about my trouble.

Not even two weeks into owning the place, and I'm on the verge of losing it.

Shame claws at my insides. I haven't slept well since Mr. Josten showed up with the news. Everything hinges on this loan, making every blink I take feel like a snapshot of Mom's disappointment. The images of us packing up our livelihood haunt me. I can't do this to her.

Through the glass, I see him returning with pronounced steps that echo under the crack of the door. I've been sitting for well over twenty minutes by myself, left to stress without a way to calm my nerves. I sit straighter upon his approach, worried I'll be judged otherwise.

He's already speaking like the conversation started

outside the office. "... interest rate has gone up significantly. The current loan was paid off years ago, so it would be a brand-new loan at today's rates, not yesteryears." He sits down behind his desk and taps the papers on the top.

"Which is?" I ask, feeling the need to hold my breath right after.

Looking over his wire-rimmed glasses, he replies, "The monthly payment would be detrimental to a business without substantial resources. As much as we appreciate the original loan being paid in such a timely manner, it's been years since the shop has earned credit."

"What about my personal credit? I pay my credit card and car payment on time every month."

"I ran your credit as part of the initial analysis. It's good, but there's not enough history for us to take on that risk financially." It figures that not being in debt would be considered a bad thing. I want to roll my eyes but restrain myself as he continues, "The rate for the shop, including the income for the apartment, isn't something I'd advise, Ms. Knot." He leans forward and whispers, "I've known your mom a long time, since grade school. I can't in good conscience recommend continuing this process. It will bury you in debt that I know, based on the numbers you submitted, would have the bank owning your shop in less than two years."

The disappointment that chokes my throat cuts off any air of rationale that I would have had under different circumstances. I move to the edge of my seat, placing my hands on the desk to hold on to something solid. "Please help me. What can I do? The apartment can be used as collateral, if needed."

"I'm sorry. It doesn't work like that. The bank has made its decision." He sits back, managing to clasp his thick fingers together and rest his hands on his belly. "If you were married or your mom was willing to be a cosigner and use her house as collateral, that would change things. With good-to-great credit, the rate would be points lower and more in line with what you can afford on a monthly basis. Banks want their money back. It's that simple."

"Simple . . ." I sigh as I stand. There's no use wasting more of his time or mine. I need to come up with an alternative plan, and I only have ten days left to sign the new leasing agreement, or I'll lose the chance to save it altogether. "Thank you."

As I walk out his door, he says, "I wish I could do more for you. Good luck, and say hi to Peaches for me."

I would, but then she'd know I was here begging for money. Perhaps it's time to tell her. Would she cosign for me? Would it make a difference since she's retired? She doesn't have a large savings account or money on hand, and I don't like the way he went straight for her house like a tiger spotting his prey. No. There is no way I'm risking losing that as well.

Walking out into the bright sunshine of the afternoon, I cup my hand over my eyes and look down the street. The bank isn't far from the shop, though it's not attached to the same building. I begin to walk back despite the ninety-eight-degree heat. Sweating is the least of my concerns right now.

A car passes, the horn blaring. Startled, I grab my heart as I watch it slow down. "Lauralee Knot," Mrs. Marion calls through her open window as she comes to a stop.

I detour from the sidewalk and go to her car. "Hi, Mrs. Marion. How are you?"

"Well, there's something I've been needing help with."

"Sure, how can I help?" She waves me closer, then looks in both directions. There's no one else even close to us and not even another car driving by, but I'll play this game. I move closer and bend forward. "What is it?" I whisper co-conspiratorially.

"You and that Baylor Greene aren't a thing, are you?"

Oh gosh, I should have known... I'm not one to lie, but I'm happy to beat around the bush with her. "What's wrong with Baylor Greene?"

"You've always been such a sweet girl, and he's ... well," she whispers, "a playboy. You don't want to be tangled up in that mess. You need a good, sturdy husband to get you a plot of land and start a family."

There are so many offenses to what she said that I'm not sure where to begin or how to even unpack it. I'm going to take a breath and try to give her the benefit of the doubt that she has my best interests in mind. But I'm still me and always need to poke back. "First, I don't need a husband. If I meet someone I want to marry, I'm all for that fairy-tale ending. If I don't, I'll write my own." Straightening my back, I look down at her, sympathy for her starting to run through me. She's alone. *Lonely.* Gossiping in town will probably be the highlight of her day. "Second, you should know better than to judge someone from rumors. Even if it were true, can he not change?"

"You're dating?"

"I just don't think it's right to hold stuff against people, especially when it never affected you personally." Good lord, I'm glad she doesn't know about some of my extracurricular activities when Chris and I would go to Whiskey's on Thursday nights to party. I wasn't shy about picking up a guy for the night, and there's no shame if we're both into it, which we were.

More than a month ago, I would have still believed the same about him. But as I've gotten to know him in and out of the bedroom, I think he's just really good at playing the role that everyone wants to see him in. Oscar-worthy actually.

He's not that guy. Well, he is *that* guy, *or was* . . . I think he's changed, and her gossip isn't going to deter me from trusting him.

She stares through her windshield when she sits back in her seat again. Glancing at me, she says, "You deserve someone who will love you to the ends of the earth, dear. You have a good day now, you hear?"

"I hear." I step away from the car. "Bye."

She doesn't peel out, but I could sense her discomfort to get away because I didn't give her what she came for: gossip and confirmation. I don't owe her either and refuse to sustain that small-town feeding frenzy.

I cross Main, then hop onto the covered sidewalk that will lead me back to the shop. Thinking of Baylor has me grinning wildly to myself. I might even be blushing. He does that to me with no effort. His swoony words and handsome face are enough to make my heart start racing. How will this help my predicament, though? It won't, but he sure is a nice distraction, especially at night when we've been texting.

Just a few exchanges have been enough to keep my hopes high for this trip to NYC. It will be the first time we can live normally instead of hiding or sneaking around and just breathe.

Can I really?

There's no way I'll be able to enjoy the long weekend with this hanging over my head. What do I do?

I enter the shop and see my mom near the coffee machine. "Hi, Mom."

"Hi, honey, did you get your errands done?"

"Yeah. Thanks for working."

"My pleasure." She comes to the front of the counter just as I slip behind it. "You sound down. What's wrong?"

"Nothing. I'm fine. I just have a lot on my mind." I set my purse on the back table, and when I return, I catch her straightening the pens because she even likes those to look a certain way.

"This weekend should be the pick-me-up you need." Oh . . . and then lied to her. As if I couldn't feel worse. "It's been a while since you've gotten out of town for a few days. Austin with friends sounds like good fun."

Telling her I'm flying to New York to spend time with Baylor isn't something I'm ready to share. The long talk that would come with it is worth avoiding.

I'm making a mess of my life one lie and omission at a time. Is this really who I've become? The sex is fantastic. *Oh God, I'm pathetic.*

I've mostly been looking forward to spending time with him in a way we've not had the chance to when he's here in Peachtree Pass. That doesn't ease the guilt of lying to my mom about the trip or what's going on with the shop. And don't even get me started on looking my best friend in the eyes the other day and telling her I wasn't interested in anyone to protect Baylor's and my secret. It reminds me of when she was sneaking around with her husband. The parallels grow greater by the day.

"I'm looking forward to it." That is something I don't have to lie about.

"I can close the shop today. I'm here anyway. Why don't you go pack and take a few hours off?" She already has a rag in hand to start her next task.

I don't want to ruin her fun. "Thank you. I'll take you up on that offer." Maybe a long bath will help me sort through my problem and come up with some solutions. I jump at the opportunity and hurry upstairs.

The water is filling the tub, I'm pouring a glass of wine even though it's only four fifteen in the afternoon, and I put on some light jazz to try to relax. Panicking won't get me to come up with clear answers to this issue.

I sink into the hot water and lean my head against the tiled wall. Closing my eyes, I let my mind drift before tackling the larger problems. The white wine is crisp and cool, a nice counter to the heat of the water.

My phone buzzes on the edge, and when I lift it, I smile. Answering after the second ring, I say, "I miss you." If he can put himself on the line for me, I can do the same.

"Glad to hear I'm not the only one," Baylor says. By his tone, I can imagine the grin on his face. The city is loud in the background. The sound of cars and a rush of wind fill the space behind him, setting the scene. "I can't wait to see you again, Shortcake."

I sink a little lower in the tub to cover my chest while holding the phone to my ear, not wanting to miss anything he says. I even hear him breathing and find comfort in the sound, knowing I'll be back in his arms again. "Two days."

"Two days."

I sit up, almost knocking my wineglass off the side of the tub. The water splashes around as an idea begins to form.

Oh my God . . .

No, I can't.

We can't.

Can we?

I can't risk my mom losing her house because of greedy venture capitalists in Austin. So that only leaves one other way to punch myself out of this corner. *Marriage.*

Desperate times call for desperate measures.

CHAPTER 23

Baylor

Pushing through the door, the bell above my head reminds me of Peaches Sundries, leaving me smiling as I start down the sidewalk with the bouquet in my hand.

She should have reached the city by now, so I pick up my pace, not wanting to be late. I round the first block and start to jog to reach the next, cut the corner, and head for the entrance to my building.

"Evening, sir."

"Evening, Paul," I reply, entering through the door he's opened for me. "Good Thursday?"

His arms go wide, and a big smile splits his cheeks. "Always the best here in the city. You?"

I start for the elevator but turn back with a stupid grin. "Good. I have tomorrow off for the holiday, and it's about to get a whole lot better than that."

"Ah! Your guest is arriving today. I have it noted. I look forward to meeting Ms. Knot."

"You're going to love her. Have a good one." The doors

open, and I step onto the elevator and punch the button for my floor. With no time to waste, I rush to my door and slip inside.

The place is clean, everything tidy and where it belongs, but I still have some nerves for her arrival. I hope she likes my place, and damn, I hope she likes me as much as she does in The Pass.

I look down at my work clothes, then set the flowers on the counter and rush to the bedroom, where I enter the closet. What can I wear? Jeans. Okay . . . fuck. I know she likes me in cowboy wear, but I don't have that here. I pull on a T-shirt and jeans, deciding to keep it casual rather than being in a suit to greet her.

Rushing to brush my teeth and put on fresh cologne, I fuss with my hair before putting on sneakers, grabbing the flowers, and going back downstairs to wait for her. When I enter the lobby, Paul grins, knowing exactly what I'm up to. "She must be special, Mr. Greene."

He's no stranger to seeing a few women come and go over the years, but he's never judged or made any snide remarks.

"She is." More than special, Lauralee is different. I've never missed anyone like I have her the past ten days.

A black SUV pulls up to the curb out front. Paul goes to open the door, but I'm right behind him and walking through it. The driver opens the back door and there she is. Her smile is the balm I needed to soothe the part of my heart that's been missing her so much.

Pretty dress. Hair hanging over her shoulders with more curls than usual, charting their own path down the strands. Her eyes brighten when she sees me.

Breathtaking.

She swings her legs out and hops to the ground. She

looks short among the skyscrapers but no less beautiful. In fact, she's more gorgeous than ever. "Hey there, stud," she says, coming to meet me as I close the distance.

I wrap my arms around her and kiss her, needing this connection to her more than I realized. I was so busy with work that I barely gave myself time to breathe, much less dwell on her absence from my life. Because if I did for too long, I wouldn't get any shit done. My mood shifted, and it was hard to focus.

The luggage bumps into my leg, causing me to pull back from her and eye the driver. He says, "You're all set, Ms. Knot."

"Thank you," she says, scrambling for her purse. "Wait, I need to give you a tip."

"No." I place my hand on hers. "I'll tip through the app."

She laughs. "That's fancy."

When her eyes slip to the flowers, I hand them to her. "I saw these and thought of you."

She immediately dips her nose to smell the soft pink roses, the vibrant pink peonies, and the daisies dotting the bouquet. "They're so pretty and thoughtful." She lifts to give me a kiss, and says, "Thank you, Baylor." Her cheeks blush in the same shade, reminding me how she can't hide her sweetness from me.

"You're welcome." Taking the handle of her suitcase in one hand, I hold her hand with the other, and we start walking. "I'm glad you're here."

"Me, too," she says with a little hop-skip in her walk.

Paul opens the brass and glass door for us when we return, and I say, "This is Paul. Paul, this is my Shor— Lauralee Knot."

Tipping his head, he replies, "Nice to meet you, Ms.

Knot. Please let me know if I can be of any assistance during your visit."

"Thank you. I appreciate that, and it's so nice to meet you, too." She reaches out to shake his hand. It's not common practice, it seems, according to his reaction, but he happily accepts the offer. "Have a good day." When we cross through the lobby, she looks around and then at me, her hand tightening on mine, and smiles. "He was nice."

"He's a good guy." We step onto the elevator, and I punch the button for the twelfth floor. "It's weird that you're here. In a good way, but different."

She stands beside me when the doors close, bumping her hip against mine. I wrap my arm around her, bringing her in again, and kiss her. When our mouths part, she licks her lips. "I know what you mean. This feels . . . real, official in a way."

The doors open. I let her walk out and follow her with the suitcase. After unlocking the apartment, I hold the door and trail in after her. "I want to talk to you about that."

Glancing back over her shoulder, she asks, "About what?" She redirects her eyes forward and walks straight to the windows to look down.

"Us."

She turns around as if I've hit the jackpot. "Same. I'm glad you brought it up." Looking at the kitchen, she works her way back to set the flowers down. "Your apartment is really nice. It's sophisticated, like you."

"That's not something I can say I've been called before."

"Well, you've grown in ways that some of us never had the chance. Experiences and new cities have changed you. You fit in this surrounding. Vase?"

I want to take offense at what she's saying. Saying I don't fit in Peachtree Pass feels a lot like rejection. I reach for a vase stored in a cabinet above the fridge. It's not something I've ever used, but I was told to always have one on hand just in case.

Taking it to the sink, I start filling it with water. "How should I take that?"

"It's in a good way. It's different, like you said earlier, but it's nice to see this part of your life and you in it." She comes to me and leans against my chest, wrapping her arms around me. "You're sexy in both settings."

"Now you're just charming me, Ms. Knot."

"Is that all it takes? A compliment."

I kiss her cheek, then return to staring into those pretty eyes of my brown-eyed girl. "It's a great start."

"Good," she says, taking a step back and grabbing a knife from the block. "Now that I have you buttered up, I need to talk to you about something important." After cutting the twine wrapped around the flowers, she starts trimming the stems one by one.

"Okay. Shoot."

"Maybe you should sit down or have a beer."

"I need to be drinking to hear what you need to say? Should I be worried?"

"No. Not at all." Her words are beginning to rush from her mouth, "And remember, you can always say no. There's no pressure from me because I know this is not only out of left field but also a huge life decision."

I'm staring at her, more concerned than before, feeling blindsided. At least if it came from left field, I would see it coming before it hit. Leaning against the counter, I watch as she trims like her life depends on it. I reach over and cover her hand. "Look at me, Shortcake." When she does, I ask, "Just say it."

"Will you marry me?"

before following, leaving her eyes still glistening with trust in me. I'm the one who betrayed her, and she's come to me for help. God, I'm a fucking asshole who's about to lose the best thing that's happened to me when I didn't even know this was going on behind the scenes. *Unacceptable.*

I need to fix this. *Whatever it takes.*

"He said I need to be married to get the loan . . ." It only takes a few minutes for her to work through the remaining details of the leasing agent's surprise visit and then her trip to the bank. "I begged," she says. *Begged* . . . she had to fucking beg because of me. "I can't afford that on my own, but the bank won't approve me for the loan. I've just taken over as owner, and I'm going to lose the shop. It's a staple in the town. It's . . . you know. There's not much else. What will I do? Move away?"

"You're not moving," I say with a ferocity that comes from my gut.

"You can't guarantee that, Baylor."

"I will." I hadn't shared that I bought the building, not with anyone back home, and now is probably not the time. It wasn't a big deal I was actively focusing on. I just put the pieces in place to manage it, and now I'm watching her world fall apart because of my actions. "You can put stock in my word."

I'm now left with two concerns of my own forming.

One. Why the fuck did that real estate management company raise the rent? At no point did I direct that to be done. I wouldn't have. It's the opposite of the purpose I had in buying it. I wanted to support the community. *Not make it go under.*

Two. The impact of my part hits deeper than anyone's aware. If she finds out, we're done standing on the cusp of being great together. *Fuck!* I don't want to lose her.

Looking down at how trusting she is, her hand still resting on my leg, I scratch the back of my neck as guilt starts to consume me.

Her energy shifts, and a sweet smile I missed seeing so damn much appears on her lips. "But here's the kicker," she says as I sit in silence, kicking my own ass for creating this nightmare for her. "Getting married will benefit you as well."

I dart my gaze to her, trying not to look as thrown off as I am. I'm usually well-rehearsed in controlling my reactions. I must be in my business dealing with clients, but leave it to Lauralee to figure out how to throw me off my game. "I can't wait to hear this," I say, "but I'm fucking starving. Are you hungry? We can talk over a meal, or I can order in?"

She wraps her arms around her waist. "I'm starving, and you're right. I didn't even get a tour of the place before I launched into this whole mess." She pushes up and straightens the skirt of her dress. "Is this okay?"

I stand, needing to touch her, hold her, kiss her so all-consumingly that the craving becomes unbearable. I take her in my arms and do just that. Kissing her feels like the perfect spring day back in Texas, tastes like the strawberries we're both so fond of, and her body fits against mine like we were made for each other.

When our lips part, I say, "It's perfect, like you." I brush her hair over her shoulder on one side and then dip to kiss the exposed skin. "You don't have to be anyone different for me or anyone else for that matter. I love you for who you are."

"You do?" Her shoulders soften as everything seems to weigh on this answer by how her eyes still glisten.

I was coming into this weekend wanting to see if she wanted to truly commit to making this work with me. I didn't have a plan. I just know how I feel about her. "Yeah. I think you're an incredible woman, Lauralee."

She rests her head on my chest, holding me like I'm holding her. Tilting her chin up, she says, "I think you're amazing, Baylor." With a laugh, she adds, "Maybe all this isn't so far-fetched after all."

I take her hand and start for the door. "It's far-fetched, alright, but maybe not as far out in left field as we thought."

"Does that mean you're considering it?"

No.

Maybe?

After opening the door, I lean against it for her to cross my path. "I'm going to need more details." This is not how I saw our relationship progressing. Jumping five steps ahead wasn't in my plan, but she's intrigued me more than anything. And although I could make a call to end raising the rent, I want to know how she will spin this to my benefit. Good entertainment or am I open to following through with it? I need another beer and food before hefty decisions are made. "What are you hungry for?"

"New York–style pizza. Ever since you talked about opening a pizzeria in town, I can't stop craving the real thing."

Getting a good grab of her ass, I say, "I've been craving the real thing as well." So fucking much. Even with marriage being tossed about, I'm not deterred from the need I have to be inside her again.

She taps my chin. "Pizza first."

"I know just the place."

CHAPTER 24

Lauralee

NEW YORK IS LARGER than life. The buildings disappear into the clouds, and the sidewalks hold more people than I've ever seen in my life. The pace is fast. Everything stands in stark contrast to Peachtree Pass.

As I sit on a barstool at the tiny window counter of a hole-in-the-wall pizza joint two blocks down from his apartment, my shoulder still tingles from almost being taken off by some man who refused to change his path on the way here.

The place can't hold more than ten people, but it gets the job done and serves a great slice as big as my head. I still managed to devour it. Swiveling, I bump my knees into Baylor's, catching a smile sneaking onto his face, and ask, "Is this the kind of pizza you want to bring to Peachtree Pass?" I sneak another peek at the bustling street. I've never seen so many people in one place. If only the shop had this kind of foot traffic. "Because I'm going to be dreaming about it when I'm back in Texas."

"I think a pizzeria." He glances around the place, his eyes sharpening on the details before he turns back to me. "A full sit-down restaurant with some counter stools for a quick lunch would be a good addition. What do you think would work to draw in more visitors and business to the downtown area?"

"I've been looking to expand the café portion of the shop." With my elbow rested on the counter, I tilt my head onto my hand. "More light fare—salads, more sandwiches, quiche, that kind of thing—since it's mainly me doing all the cooking and preparing."

"You want to expand?"

"Business is steady." I shrug, but I don't know why. I'm usually proud of what my mom and I have accomplished. But I was never in the situation of begging for money before either. "My mom established the shop years before I took ownership."

"But you've grown it. I don't remember it being such a destination when I was younger."

"From ice cream and peach-themed ceramics to a small café and full gift shop. We even have a fruit and veggie stand from your family's farm on the sidewalk out front on the fourth weekend of the month all summer and fall." Reaching over, I rub his leg because I want to be as close and touching him as I can, and I can do it openly without anyone here caring or even noticing. "Everyone loves peaches."

His hand covers my hip and leans forward to give me a kiss. "Not me. I prefer shortcake." A thrill zips up my spine like it does every time he's near. Reaching down, he takes hold of the metal stool and pulls me closer, not giving a damn about the screech it makes against the floor. Lifting one side of his lips, he smirks. "It's my favorite flavor."

I lift my hand to run across the back of his neck. I don't have anything clever or sexy to say in return. I just like how freeing this feels to be here with him. I still give a lame shot. "Luckily, I brought you some."

"Can't wait for dessert later."

It's tempting to talk him into returning to the apartment, specifically to the bedroom, but we haven't continued our conversation from earlier, and it's still weighing on me until we get it settled, one way or the other. I set my crumpled napkin on the pizza plate when a commotion on the other side of the window grabs our attention. I glance at Baylor, who rubs my lower back in reassurance. "Nothing to worry about." He's right regarding the argument, and they move along.

But my heart is still burdened. "Can we talk?"

"Always, Shortcake."

I honestly didn't know what he thought about me asking him to marry him earlier, so I breathe a sigh of relief hearing him so open to the conversation. "The leasing agent said the new owners will be offering bonuses to new tenants." I swivel on the barstool to face the window again, wanting to drop my head in my hands in frustration as my blood begins to boil. I turn my gaze outside and start traveling the height of the building across the street instead of seeing him study my expression as I work through the part that stings most. "Such an insult to me and Cathy down at the clothing outlet."

The tip of his finger presses under my chin, angling me to face him. When I do, the warmth of his palm caresses my cheek. It's not a showy gesture, but it's intimate, comforting, his eyes engaging as I stare into them. The bond that started back home in Texas feels stronger than ever. Even if he turns me down, I feel less alone in this battle.

"Forget him," he says. There's a ribbon of anger in his tone that I'm not used to but I appreciate. "He'll get what's coming. Focus on the shop. Peaches Sundries & More is the anchor of our downtown area. It's what has kept Peachtree Pass alive all these years. Nothing is going to happen to it. I'll make sure of it." I'm not sure how he can help other than the way already presented, but hearing his strength when I feel weak gives me hope, not only for the business but for us. He's standing with me, beside me, and giving me the support I need. No questions asked.

I'm loved. Even though the words haven't crossed his lips, I can see it in his eyes when he looks into mine. It makes me feel bad for peddling marriage like it's one of those conning street games. It's a big deal and a bigger commitment. It's supposed to be between soulmates, between people who love each other endlessly. Our relationship is just starting, and though I feel closer to him than anyone else, are we ready to take on that responsibility?

It's a business arrangement. *That's it.* If I forget the purpose or fail to focus, I will lose everything. My shoulders soften when I look at him, though. My feelings for him are deeper than I'm used to, new in unfamiliar ways, but what I had always thought love would feel like. So would it really be a purely professional arrangement if we got married? My heart knows the truth.

He says, "Let's get out of here. I want to take you to this park about ten minutes from here."

We toss our trash and hit the pavement. I'm still blown away by the level of noise—from people in every direction to the cars jamming together on the streets. My head feels like the stool, swiveling on my neck to take in everything I can. And though it's already seven, we're no closer to sunset despite the street being shaded by the skyscrapers. I always love the longer summer days.

Baylor takes my hand, keeping his eyes ahead as his thoughts seem to hoard his attention. The silence stretching between us hasn't made it uncomfortable, but I'm starting to miss the sound of his voice. I grin at the ridiculousness of that. We were just talking not five minutes ago at the pizza place. I think I would be officially classified as an addict to this man.

I squeeze his hand, needing a fix, which brings his gaze back to me. He grins that same one I was greeted with upon arrival, like the world can start spinning again, making me fall even harder for him.

He asks, "Do you want to talk about it?"

I've been too nervous to broach the idea again even though it's mine to begin with. Getting food in my stomach has helped. My thoughts feel clearer, and I don't know, less worried about how this will end. He's giving me that comfort to speak freely. "I'd like to."

"You don't need to be worried. Whatever is decided, things will work out. You're not losing the shop."

I stop walking. He stops and turns to look back with our arms stretched between us. "How can you be so sure?"

"Because I won't let you lose it." I'm granted a smile that tries to reach his eyes but fails just shy of its target. "I have money, Lauralee."

I know he has money, and if the rumors are right, a lot of it. Would he give me a loan with interest . . . better interest than the bank, so I can actually afford the rent? I have no doubt. Should I accept it? "I can't take your money. There's no way I'd ever feel right about that, especially on such a risky investment." I step closer, resting my hand on his chest. "This arrangement needs to benefit both of us."

The warmth of his smile keeps me calm, knowing I've got an ally. "Since I know you, I'm assuming you already have a plan. You want to lay it out for me?"

I laugh because he really does know me well. "So," I start, happy to get into the details. "We leave for the Hamptons on Saturday. Since I was already playing the lead role of the lady in your life, I was thinking . . . Well, you said your bosses have this family values image they want to uphold."

"I think *project* works better knowing their history of philandering."

I cringe. "Yikes."

"Yikes is right. That's why the suggestion that my being single doesn't look good for the company is preposterous."

I can't say this makes me want to meet them now. But a free vacay to the Hamptons is worth it because I'll be with Baylor. "What if I come as your wife?" I stare at his eyes as his gaze shifts to the left of me, his thoughts darkening the blues. I continue by saying, "I know this is an off-the-wall plan. It doesn't have to stick, but I'd be remiss if I didn't mention it as an option to help both of us out of our predicaments. You can get your promotion. I get my shop. Life is perfect again."

Angling his head, he asks, "You've really thought about this, haven't you?"

I'm not sure if it's rhetorical, though, as he processes the plan. "Day and night. I can barely sleep."

"It's a different approach." He pauses as if expecting me to interrupt. For once, we're on the same page, so I stay quiet. "Is getting married what you really *want*?"

His emphasis on want isn't lost on me. I shift my weight and my gaze for a moment but decide that won't do. Standing straight up, I lock my eyes on his, which temper on contact. "I don't have many options, Baylor. It's just a wedding. It's worth it to save the shop." Holding out my free hand, I try to express myself better. "And if you can benefit, it feels like a win-win."

"It's not just about the day. You'd be married to me. *Legally*," he stresses the ending. "Wouldn't it just be easier to take my money?"

The thing is, being legally bound to him doesn't scare me. Maybe it should, but I won't hesitate to marry him if we both get what we want. "I've come to terms with the sacrifice we'll be making. I'll be taking away both of our firsts—wedding, marriage, and—"

"Honeymoon?"

That sure perked him up. "I hadn't gotten that far in the plan, but sure," I say, with a laugh and pop of my shoulders. "If you'd like that, I'm always up for a vacation." We start walking again. Considering how fast New Yorkers hustle, we're probably clocking more of a snail's pace, but I don't mind. I like holding hands with him in public.

As we cover another block, I've overlooked something important. *His input*. This isn't just for me, though I feel like a used car salesperson trying to close a deal. What he thinks matters to me. "I don't know if you're genuinely considering it, but if you are, how do you think we handle it?"

"I'm thinking tropical. The fewer clothes required for you, the better."

I snort and elbow him playfully. "Should have known that's where your mind would go. Not the honeymoon, though I'm noting that down just in case for the future."

I'm still giggling when he adds, "I think that's for you to decide. The bank would know we're married if you're using my financials. Would we tell everyone else? How? By announcement? A party? Show up with rings on our fingers?" He briefly closes his eyes as he pinches the bridge of his nose.

"Truthfully, I don't know. I hadn't thought about that aspect, but you're right. If the bank knows, everyone knows. Our families would be upset to find out after the fact, especially my mom. I already feel awful for even contemplating getting married without her knowledge."

"I'm not closing this down, but maybe that's the answer. One decision could lead to more problems than we started with."

I fear that if I allow myself to acknowledge that I'll back out altogether, and that means choosing to lose the shop instead of fighting for it.

An opening between the buildings comes into view. People are meandering and filming themselves in the center of a rose-filled garden. The sea of pink makes me stop in my tracks to stare, a small gasp escaping simultaneously. I look up at Baylor, and ask, "Is this where you were bringing me?"

His chin lowers as a shy smile takes hold. "I thought you'd like it."

"It's like the flowers you bought me." I knock into him, tipping my head to his arm as love fills my heart like a balloon. "So beautiful."

We take our own selfie at the edge to capture as many flowers behind us as we can.

"They change out the flowers every couple of months. Tulips in April. Roses are for June. We're catching the last of the flowers in bloom."

It's even quieter here, a smaller crowd than the one on the streets. Some people are reading on the surrounding benches, but most are appreciating the sight of this colorful magic in the middle of the gray city. "This is the most lovely thing I think I've ever seen."

"I don't know. The peach orchard in bloom is quite the magnificent sight." We stroll the small path, and his arm comes around my shoulders. When he kisses the top of my head, I'm reminded that we can do this here. We can be a couple out in the open, kiss and hold hands without worrying about gossip traveling the grapevine.

But my heart still clenches when he mentions home, making me wonder if he ever thinks about returning. I reply, "Blooming peach trees are stunning. It's weird how you take things for granted when you've seen them your whole life." Staring at the pink petals of an especially showy rose in front of me, I think about my mom and dad and their relationship. Is that what happened with them? They stopped seeing what was right in front of them? I'm pretty sure I'm never going to get that answer. I'm not even sure my mom knows why he left. Wouldn't she have told me by now? "Do you think that happens in marriage?"

"I don't think it has to. I always found comfort in my parents' relationship. It wasn't exciting in obvious ways, like flashy jewelry or fancy dinners out, but their love was quiet, steady, and reliable. It's something I've come to appreciate in stark contrast to dating in New York." He looks at me, and says, "I used to catch them exchanging glances and small smiles when they thought we weren't looking. I took that for granted. Now it's a fond memory."

"I'm sorry."

"Don't be." He laughs to himself, shoving his free hand in his pocket. "I hadn't thought about that in so long. Years. It's nice when those memories return." Pulling me in front of him, he adds, "I'm glad you're here."

"I am, too." I hug him, closing my eyes and soaking in as much of him as I can to take home with me.

"You've presented a good argument, Shortcake. Clever

including the benefits for me," he says, bringing us back to the topic without me prodding, which I appreciate.

Laughing, I reply, "Guess I'm not as sneaky as I thought."

"If we did this, how would it work? We could get married here." There's no tension in his body that I can feel or in his face when I look at him. I kind of expected him to shut this conversation down. Yet here he is, leaving the door wide open for consideration. "But there's a waiting period."

My heart starts beating so loudly that it fills my ears, making me think everyone within twenty yards of us can hear, especially him. "Are you really considering this?"

"I can see the value."

"The value?" I laugh when I remember I'm in his element and that's finances and the corporate world, a long damn way from the Hill Country.

Chuckling, he says, "Maybe not the best way to phrase it, but I see the upside to the proposition."

"Sounds tawdry."

He raises his eyebrow. "Isn't it?"

"It's impressive how you manage to make everything sound like an invitation to bed."

With the most casual shrug I've seen him give, he says, "It's a gift."

"That apparently keeps giving."

We work our way from the park to the water's edge, sitting on a large stone wall. He looks at me. "I have a client who's a judge. I've made him a lot of money in the market. I'm sure he could pull some strings for us and get us in tomorrow."

I sit up, my body tensing while the wind whips through my hair. "Tomorrow?" The shock of it hits, but I remind myself that this is an arrangement. *My scheme even.* I guess I thought this would feel more victorious, spontaneously romantic, and less sacrificial to the dreams I've carried outside of my career. Guess we can't all have what Christine and Tagger have. I need to take what I'm being offered. "That's sooner than I expected, which makes no sense since we go to the Hamptons on Saturday."

Anyway, I'm to blame. I presented it like a deal he couldn't pass up. I finally sell him on it, and now reality hits.

What did I expect? Hearts and roses, or we'd be marrying for love? We've just started dating, technically. The expectation of this being anything more than financially beneficial for either of us might be the most absurd hope I've had. So I kiss finding a soulmate away, and heartstrings and Cupid's arrow goodbye. This is nothing more than a promotion for him and me keeping my shop for as long as I can. *Nothing more.*

He replies, "Otherwise, it would have to be next week, but you're leaving on Sunday." He stands in front of me, perched high on the wall. He rests his hands on the curve of my knees, and the sincerity in his eyes makes my heart race. Sweet, caring. He's considerate. He'd do this for me. I hold on to that. "My schedule is double-booked next week." His voice is lower, and guilt coats his words. "I can't cancel the appointments, or I would."

"And the following week is too late. It's past the deadline." Baylor's doing this for me. Sure, there are perks for him, but I could be his girlfriend, and he'd have the same outcome. But for me, I need to be married to make this as straightforward as possible. "Tomorrow, huh?" This feels so fast, much quicker than I could have imagined.

I hold out my hands. When he takes them, I hop off the wall to my feet. "It's not how I imagined things going, but yes."

"Yes?"

"I'll marry you, Shortcake." His mouth lifts on the right side, but it's not smirky like usual. It's a smile that grows and spreads like wildfire across his handsome face.

"Really?" I bounce in front of him.

"But on one condition."

I plant my feet on the concrete, having no idea what he could want from me to seal this deal. "Which is?"

"I get to buy you a ring."

Swaying back and forth, I breathe a huge sigh of relief. I hadn't thought of a ring. I just wanted to be married to him. "You don't have to do that."

"I want my wife to have a ring."

My wife . . . I'm dead. I could roll right into that water after hearing that. Sink to the bottom, never taking another breath, and I'd be happy. Just like that, he makes my heart race again and my head wonderfully spin from swooning. I hold him, grounding myself in him so I don't melt into a puddle in front of all of Manhattan. I'm marrying Baylor Greene and want to be alive and well for the big event.

Oh. My. God.

We're getting married.

CHAPTER 25

Baylor

MARRIAGE IS A BIGGER deal than we're pretending. As a guy who never thought about marriage much, my shoulders are surprisingly relaxed, my jaw isn't clenched, and I'm not sweating. Weirdly, I'm okay. Happy even. Can't say I would be with any other woman, but Lauralee's different.

I love her.

The admission, even silently to myself, practically knocks me on my ass. Love isn't something I saw coming. I wasn't even looking for it. It found me in the time away from her after the festival. The quick calls we'd share at night and the occasional texts were nice reprieves from the chaos of the stock market. *But not enough.*

I don't want to be without her. Ironically, I'll still be without her most of the time. How will we make this work? I want to be married and go to bed with her every night. Not make a call to say good night to my wife. When I say I do, I'll mean it. When she says it, it's temporary. *Fuck.*

The shower turning off alerts me to adjust my pillows

against the walnut headboard before sitting up and situating myself. After sending some texts, I set my phone on the nightstand and clock the curtains still open with dots of light speckling the darkness outside. I don't think about the city watching me anymore, but she'll be exposed. I hit the remote to close the curtains and give us privacy.

We still have a lot to talk about, but setting that aside, I want to enjoy our time together and lie in bed with her. *And other things . . .*

"We don't have to stay married," she says, coming out of the bathroom with a towel wrapped around her torso. Freshly showered with her hair piled on her head, she's tan against the bright white of the material, and her skin glistens with a few drops on her shoulders that she missed. I'll be happy to take care of those for her with my tongue. "There have been shorter Hollywood marriages than two weeks, so we wouldn't be the first to change our minds. Well . . ." Her hair bobbles on top of her head when she shakes it. Sitting on the edge of the mattress, she rests back on one hand. "Not that we're changing our minds. More gaming the system to work in our favor. Two weeks tops and then you're free again."

"But what if we did?" The way she views this as a merger more than a marriage doesn't bother me. It's only come about because of a business agreement. So that makes sense. I can't fault her when I haven't been forthcoming with my feelings.

I can talk about myself all day at work, talk shit on the basketball court, and have never minded bragging about myself to other women. She doesn't want that from me. She wants what's in my head but also my heart. It's a big ask. But I'm giving her both without admitting the truth—I'd marry her if she had asked simply because she loves me. I know a good thing when I see it.

"What if we did?" Her eyes widen. "Stay married?"

"Yes." We're a new relationship to her with training wheels still attached. I'm already riding without holding the handlebars. I know we're meant to be together. She just doesn't see it yet.

"Baylor? Aw. That's so sweet, but I know you aren't looking for marriage."

We agreed to keep it a secret, not to hurt her mom or my family, but to include them when we're ready to reveal it. If we do. As I listen to her now, there might not be a need.

"Why do you say that?"

She aims her gaze at the pillow next to me and then back at me. "I don't know why I thought that. Believing that you prefer dating over commitment? When was your last relationship?"

"When was yours?" I snap back.

Offense shapes her expression, dragging her lips to part. Very distracting. "That's not fair. I don't have the same options back in the Pass as you do here."

I stare at her for a moment. I've done this to myself, and her best friend probably didn't do me any favors over the years. Do I blame my sister? *Nah.* She didn't have all the facts, but she also probably wasn't far off from the truth, and she has my best friend who witnessed plenty of bad behavior. I'm sure he leaves himself out of some of those details, though. I won't spill our secrets. But I do say, "Neither one of us is particularly walking around with our head in the clouds. That's a luxury never afforded us. We're products of hardworking ranching families or seeing things through a different lens. Who knows. But I want to be clear on marriage. It means something to me."

She crawls across the mattress to situate herself next to me. With a mischievous grin, she whispers, "It does?"

"Yes. I know this is about money for us, but I could write you a check if that's all it was about, or make sure you have free rent for life—"

"How would you do that?"

Shit.

This hole keeps getting deeper. Eventually, I need to put the shovel down. Not tonight, though. I'm going into this with my eyes wide open because it feels real to me, as real as she is before me now. *When should I let her in on that secret?*

I'm starting to think that the perfect time is after the I dos, which makes me a horrible fucking person for taking advantage of the situation. Looking at her here in bed with me, she fits into my life in the city like this is every day for us. *It could be.*

Though I shouldn't trick myself into believing she'd move here because I know she won't or can't. *Both.* So I enjoy her presence and the way she looks so at home while I can.

"I've made plenty of money."

"Oh," she says, looking down at the folded towel on her thigh. She's already shaking her head before looking back up. When those beautiful browns hit me, she smiles. "I can't take it, like I said before." Moving closer, she lowers her eyes to my mouth as her hand slides over the cotton restraining my erection.

My breathing deepens as she awakens my entire body with her touch. "C'mere." Climbing onto my lap, she straddles me. Bringing her face closer, I whisper into her ear, "What if we want to stay married?" I kiss her cheek and under her jaw.

She sits back with that mouth open again, reminding me

how stunning those lips are wrapped around my dick. "Do you want a contingency plan?"

What do I want her to say? That this isn't just about finances? My phone vibrates on the nightstand, causing me to look over at it. "It's from the judge."

I reach for it. His text reads: *I'll fit you in at two p.m. Have the license stamped by the clerk. I've left your name and instructions for my assistant.*

Flashing the screen so she can see it, I say, "Seems we're getting married tomorrow."

"Shouldn't I be nervous?"

That's my girl. I knew I wasn't alone. Hoping, at least. Holding her hips, I push the towel up on one side to see my favorite strawberries. As I run my fingers over the tattoo, I reply, "I'm not either."

She leans forward just enough to wrap her arms around my neck. "People have rushed into marriage quicker."

"We don't have to justify it. If it feels right, it is." I start to unwrap my pretty package, untucking the corner of the towel and discarding it on the floor. Pulling her closer, I tongue her pink buds and then kiss the space between her breasts, imagining how they would feel wrapped around my erection. Shaking myself from the thought, I know I'd rather be inside her right now.

Sitting back, I watch as her chest rises with each deep breath she takes and lowers on the exhale. She rocks her hips slowly back and forth, seeking her own pleasure as her lids flutter closed.

The damn phone buzzes across the wood nightstand again as an unwelcome distraction. Her eyes slide to the screen and then to me. "Busy guy. Do you need to check that?" she asks through panted breaths.

"It can wait, but I can't." I flip her to the mattress,

wedging myself between her legs. Her laughter fills my ears, and the way she looks at me like I've hung the moon makes me feel whole again. "I'm so fucking glad you're here."

As soon as I pay for the license, we're good to go until this afternoon. I hold her hand while we cut across the courtroom and out the doors. "I want to take you somewhere."

"Where?"

I turn back. She stopped two steps higher than where I landed. The happiness that seemed to come from the inside when we were filing for the marriage license is wiped clean from her face. "What's wrong?"

"This is happening really fast." She takes one step down, bringing us closer, and basically eye level. "I know I wanted it, but it's like I didn't take time to acclimate to the idea, and now we're here in a hurry from place to place to get stuff done, and I don't know what I'm supposed to be doing."

"You're not supposed to. It's not every day we get married." Running my hands along her waist, I try to give her comfort. "You're not alone in this. As for the errands, I want you to get a dress that you love, one that will make you feel as beautiful as you are to me when you look back at the photos. Not one you just happened to pack."

"I didn't even think about photos. I haven't had time to think about any of it, and it's all hitting at the same time now."

"Hey, don't stress. We have four hours until we need to be back, and I have you covered." I start walking down the steps with her, and say, "All you need to do is go back to my apartment."

The tension has eased from her face, and I've earned a smile from her. "What's at your apartment?"

"Everything you need. Dresses, hair, makeup. Lunch because I don't want you starving when you say I do."

When we reach the sidewalk, she stops again. "How'd you do all that on short notice?"

"It's New York, baby. This city never sleeps. I also have a lot of connections. Might as well use them." I see the black car I hired pull up to the curb and guide her to it. I open the door, and she slips inside. I lean down but don't get in. "I'll see you back here at one forty-five, okay?"

"Wait." Stopping me from closing the door, she asks, "You're not coming with me?"

"I have a few errands of my own. I'll be right here at this very spot waiting for you, though. I promise." Dipping down, I steal a kiss. "Call me if you need anything. Oh, it's all covered so don't worry about money. They're taken care of."

Her palm is still pressed to the door when tears flood her eyes. Threatening to tip over her lower lids, she tilts her head back. She takes a breath, then looks back at me. "Thank you."

I nod and shut the door. Rubbing my chest, I try to loosen the knot that's formed. Weddings are supposed to be emotional, but I didn't expect it to hit so hard. I twist my wrist to check the time. I throw my arm in the air to hail a cab. As soon as one pulls over, I hop in and say, "The Diamond District."

An engine and four tires just got delivered. You sure are fucking confident.

I read the text from Tagger again and chuckle as I reply: *It's in the bag.*

I look at the rings again before telling the salesperson, "I'll take them." I have no idea what kind of rings Lauralee would want, so I went with something that reminded me of her. Dropping my credit card on the counter, I'm buying all three—her engagement ring, the wedding band, and mine. I'm showing up prepared.

I turn back to my phone when the screen lights up again.

Tagger: *Pris hasn't said a thing, so I find it hard to believe anything is in the bag. Also, Lauralee is out of town partying. She probably met some guy in Austin.*

Me: *I'm not afraid of competition. Never have been. Remember in tenth grade when Sara Kinsey—*

Tagger: *Stop right there. Sara Kinsey played you, dude, so don't go dragging her into this.*

Me: *Truth hurts sometimes.*

Tagger: *You're the one who will be hurting when I'm driving that car. Thanks for buying the new engine and tires.*

I know him. It doesn't matter if I win or lose this bet, he'd make sure I got the car. But he sure does like to fuck with me. Touché.

I take the ring boxes and tuck them in my pockets. No need to advertise that I just spent a shitload of money when walking in this part of town. I catch a cab and head to the next stop to get my suit that I sent out to get pressed while we were at the courthouse earlier.

After changing at my office, I grab a bagel to eat on the way back to meet her. I want to be standing there when the car arrives to deliver her. I made her a promise I intend to keep, knowing I'm about to make another I will always honor.

I stand on the sidewalk for a few minutes, getting stares from passersby. One woman even asked for my number. "I'm taken." That was the easiest phrase I've uttered recently.

Spying the car coming from around the corner, I straighten my stance and wait. The car stops, and I don't wait for the driver. I pull the door open myself, too anxious to stand by.

She comes from the shadow of the back seat, her feet landing on the pavement as she takes my hand. When I see her, my whole world stops.

Her hair is down with shiny, soft waves framing her face, the depth of colors on display. The light makeup accentuates her natural beauty instead of detracting from it. The dress fits her ribs and chest but flares out from there, and when the wind blows, the skirt flutters. It's her, all of it. Knowing she didn't change who she is at heart makes me love her even more.

With a smile, she rests her hands on my shoulders. "You clean up real nice, stud."

I slide my arms around her waist, unable to say much except, "You're breathtaking." Holding her hand, I take a step back. "Let me look at you."

Her cheeks blush, and she giggles, giving me a little twirl. "You like what you see?"

"Fucking love it."

"Oh." She turns away and dips back into the back seat to grab something. "I almost forgot." She pulls out the bouquet I gave her yesterday. "I tied a white ribbon around them. Aren't they perfect for the occasion?"

I never could have guessed the flowers I bought on a whim because they reminded me of her would end up being her bridal bouquet. "Meant to be." Nodding behind me, I ask, "Want to get married?"

She laughs. "We got all dressed up, so we might as well."

A cool breeze reaches us at the top of the steps. I'm drawn to stop and take it in, closing my eyes to feel it against my face. A sense of peace runs through my body, and when I open my eyes, she says, "I think your mom is with us."

"I think so, too." Lauralee is on my left, and comfort walks beside me on my right.

We aren't kept waiting long and are led down a hallway to the judge's office. When he joins us, our witness walks in with him. Mickey comes to shake my hand but gives that up to meet Lauralee.

"Thanks for coming," I say after quick introductions to both. "Figured since you'd find out tomorrow anyway, it would be good to have you here."

"It was not a text I was expecting."

Lauralee laughs . . . a little too hard. "I'm sure."

I say, "People can change. I'm standing here ready to marry this beautiful woman."

The judge says, "Are we ready to get married?"

My girl steps up next to me, and says, "We are."

"Let's get started then." It's then I notice the photographer tiptoeing in behind us.

The judge reads the usual vows, though he veers sometimes into a modern version that I appreciate.

When Lauralee and I are facing each other, I slip the rings on her finger, which causes her to take a staggering breath. I think I did good, judging by that reaction. Still holding the rings on her finger, I say, "I choose you, Lauralee Knot. Today. Tomorrow. Forever. I do."

Tears fill her eyes, but the smile contradicts any sadness. She even laughs to herself, which lightens the mood for all of us. Taking my hand in hers, she slides the ring I bought in platinum to match hers on my hand. Looking me in the eyes, she says, "I choose you, Baylor Greene. Today. Tomorrow. And forever. I do."

"I now pronounce you husband and wife." The judge grins. "Go on and kiss her. Let's make this official."

I caress her jaw, holding this stunning human in my hands, and take a moment to look into her eyes. "I love you, Lauralee. With all my heart." The words feel natural, like they've been on the tip of my tongue waiting for this moment.

"I love you, too, Baylor. So much."

And when I kiss my wife, my heart confirms that when I said forever, I meant it.

CHAPTER 26

Lauralee

Cloud nine exists on the steps of the courthouse in New York City. It must be because I'm floating on air with him. "My handsome husband." Romantic. Charming. Sweep-me-off-my-feet husband. He lifts me from my feet, twirling me around for everyone to see. I throw my arms wide, soaking this in, and kiss him.

Life is a dream with Baylor.

I'm set down, but he still holds me close and whispers against the corner of my mouth, "My gorgeous bride, I'm so in love with you." Dipping me in the middle of the steps, he kisses me again.

With my hair hanging down and my weight secured in his arms, I reply, "You sure know how to make a girl feel special."

"That's how you make me feel."

I'm not sure how to handle all this romance. Every word he says is more swoony than the last. "How will I ever return to our normal every day when you're spoiling me like this. I'm going to be rotten to the core after all this sweetness."

He chuckles as a section of his hair falls over his forehead. I like his hair ruffled. I like a little stubble coating his jaw and when his shirts have a few wrinkles. It's life taking hold. But I won't complain about how he looks today. My jaw dropped wide open when the car came around the corner and I saw him standing there, waiting for me. Looking that good should be a crime, and I'm just the gal to take him into custody. But do I deserve all this like it's a real wedding?

I imagined something low-key. We'd just go to the courthouse and get this taken care of. Instead, I have a cushion-cut diamond the size of a small blueberry on my finger and a band wrapped in platinum with diamonds all the way around. I think my car cost less. Actually, I know it did. I've never seen something this expensive, much less worn it on my finger.

I'm just a country girl who grew up with a single mom barely making ends meet. Baylor has handed me the keys to his kingdom, making me feel like a princess.

When I'm righted, I spot a photographer taking our picture like we're celebrities. "Someone's taking photos of us."

He looks back over his shoulder and then at me again. "It's the photographer I hired to capture our special day." My mouth opens and closes again, my thoughts jumbling from one surprise to the next. When I glance at the photographer again, he waves at me. I wave back before returning my gaze to Baylor, who says, "You only get married once."

The photographer is forgotten as my mind stumbles through the "only get married once" response. Maybe it was a slip of the tongue, but I find myself holding on to it like a life preserver. Otherwise, I'll start to question what we're doing. And that's the last thing I want to do when I've not felt this happy in forever.

I want to live out this fantasy to the fullest before reality sinks in again. Standing next to him, I lean my head on his shoulder as we face the photographer. Our hands are clasped with the bouquet hanging down at my side in the other. "You really did think of everything."

Letting new love and the joy of the day win, we pose all over—walking down the sidewalk, me laying my head on his lap when we sit on a park bench and vice versa, and strolling through the nearest park with blooming flowers. I was so embarrassed at first, but these are fun for us, so I release my inhibitions and enjoy the process.

I even laugh so hard while eating a hot dog that I almost choke. And then that makes me laugh even harder.

Does cloud ten exist? Nine will never capture this feeling adequately.

When we return to his apartment, he swoops me into his arms and even carries me over the threshold. "I don't think you've missed a detail," I say, protected and safe in his arms.

He kicks the door closed and kisses my cheek as soon as my feet land on the ground. Embracing him, I'm not ready to be apart and lean toward leading him into the bedroom to end the day wrapped up in each other. "Did you have a good day?" His voice doesn't hold the familiar confidence he carries in life. It's not boisterous like it is when he's hanging out with Tagger. It's not even laid-back like he sounds with his family.

There's a shyness to it, an uncertainty in his tone. He's quieter and more reserved. I can see both the boy I knew growing up and the man he is now, needing me to reassure him. I slide my hands over his shoulders and around his neck. My heels are high but still not high enough to reach his lips without a lift. I kiss him and then again. Soft and slow. Gentle and caring, hoping I can give him what he's coveting most. *Love.* "It's been the best day of my life."

His arms are so strong when he holds me to him. There's no escaping that I'm the life preserver he needs. "Mine, too."

Taking his hand, I lead him into the living room and dip the bouquet back into the vase. "What do we do now?" I ask, open to the possibilities ahead to decide on my own. "We can make love." He smirks in response. "Or eat something?" That smirk gets smirkier as expected. "Watch a movie and cuddle together on the couch, or something super New Yorky and sneak up to the rooftop to stare at the stars."

He rubs his chin as if this is a life-and-death decision. I'm thinking we'll be doing all of them at some point in the night, so why decide? "Do you have a frontrunner?"

"All of it sounds magical if it involves you."

"Listen to my wife laying on the charm."

A girlhood dream comes back to me, one I had pushed down so far that I'd forgotten until now. "I don't think there's much I can contribute to make this wedding day any more perfect than it already is, but if I had one more wish, it would be to have a first dance with my husband."

With his eyes locked on mine, he shakes off his jacket and loosens his tie. He means business of the sex appeal kind. I don't typically have a suit fetish, but I'm finding it hard to hide how attracted I am to this man. A heaving chest and a stare that tells him to take me straight to the bedroom might be a dead giveaway. He challenges my telltale signs with one of his own—lowering his chin, his bright blues are shadowed by seduction. Under that gaze, I'd let him do anything to me. And if he rolls up those sleeves, I'm done for. *Died and gone to heaven.*

He leaves me practically panting for more, *the jerk,* and turns to pick up a remote from a wooden bowl on the coffee table. Music filters through the space from invisible speakers in just a few clicks. The music sets a mood for romance, making me wonder if he always has this playlist queued or if he set this up for us as well. He remembered everything else, so I feel he also prepared for this aspect.

Taking me into his arms, he asks, "May I have this dance, Mrs. Greene?"

I'm glad he's holding on to my waist, or I'd be mush at his feet. Greene is not a name I ever thought I'd be despite feeling so a part of their family. But to hear it from his lips with the title hooked on the front, I get overwhelmed with emotion.

I lean against him, listening to his heartbeat and hoping he didn't see me lose it over the enormity of being his, a Greene by all intents and purposes, and married to him. It's so much all at once to take in.

Baylor rubs my back and whispers into my hair, "I didn't mean to upset you."

"You didn't," I say, keeping my cheek against his chest. "It's been an amazing day, perfect in every way possible. Thank you." I know that probably won't placate him. He's starting to know me too well for that, but how do I protect myself? I love him—solid, real, and in all senses—but I don't want my heart to get broken. Which is where this is destined to lead. We didn't get married for love, but we've landed in the middle of it. "This feels real, Baylor."

I'm starting to hate how much I love the feel of his hand on my shoulder and the way his touch shoots through my entire body. I have no control when it comes to him. He holds all the cards and the winning hand when it comes to me. Closing my eyes, I try to pacify my concerns.

He leans in and kisses the curve of my neck, whispering against my skin, "It's whatever we want it to be."

I tilt my neck, opening for him. "I don't want this to end, but that's not why we agreed to get married."

His mouth stills, and then he looks back at me. "Nothing must be defined tonight. We can have one night."

He's not wrong. One night of living the fantasy won't do any harm. It's tonight, and then we're back to our normal lives. *Heart intact.* "One night."

Remember that, Lauralee, I silently warn myself.

And then I remember we have the Hamptons tomorrow. Okay, so it's a few nights, but I deserve this. I deserve this man and the way he looks at me like he's starving and I'm the main course.

We've been pure chemistry and sexual attraction since the night of the storm. It's so easy to fall back on the familiarity of our physical connection, to distract from other matters and beating organs that demand to be heard when my heart is on the line. I kiss him.

He lifts me off my feet with our mouths still attached. Maybe the physical is where he finds comfort as well because he starts down the hall to his bedroom. When he sets me down, we stand face-to-face as husband and wife. The sounds of the city become a distant memory. All I hear is our breathing as time slows for us to catch up.

I almost hate to take this dress off. It's so pretty and makes me feel even more so, but I turn around, dropping my head, and ask, "Will you unzip me?"

His hand drags down my spine until he reaches the fabric. I close my eyes when his lips press to my back, followed by the sound of the zipper reaching my ears. My ribs fully expand again, and I take a deep breath as the fabric falls open.

He says, "Bend over the bed, baby."

I thought we'd make love, looking into each other's eyes, so I'm disappointed by the request. Moving to the mattress, I lean down and rest the weight of my body on my forearms.

Baylor stands behind me, dipping to remove one shoe and then the other before sliding his hands under the skirt of my dress and up the side of my thighs. He asks, "What did you wear for me on our wedding night?" His tone has an edge to it, more jagged with each word spoken. He flips my skirt over my back, and the cool air breezes over my exposed ass. "Beautiful."

The thong doesn't have much fabric to it, but I knew he'd approve when he saw it. Just a strip of white lace that he slides his finger under, angling them through my lower lips. He doesn't need to tease or taunt. I'm already wet for him.

Keeping my eyes closed, I rest my head on the bed. The anticipation twists in my belly as the feel of hands on me and the sound of him moving closer already has me so worked up that I could come. He bites my ass, not enough to hurt or break skin but to let me know he's here. "Do you know how incredible you look like this, Lauralee?" He leans over my back and trails kisses between my shoulder blades and up, before reaching the shell of my ear and licking the curve of it. His fingers dip into my entrance. "I'm going to fuck you so hard, baby. But first, I'm going to make you come."

"God yes," I beg on an exhaled breath.

He toys with my clit and slips back to my entrance. "How does that feel?"

"I want . . . Ah—" He buries his digits deep inside me, causing my body to react by moving against him.

"What do you want? Tell me."

"I want to come, and then I want you to come inside me."

His breath covers my ear, and when I crack my eyes open, a smile crosses his face. "I want that, too." He picks up his pace, fucking me with his fingers and teasing my clit. My body submits, crashing down onto the bed and falling apart for him.

I try to catch my breath as he slides my panties down my legs and starts to undress. When he's naked, I push myself up, standing before him, and let my dress slide down my arms and puddle on the floor.

My breath is still uneven, but I know one thing. This time, I want to see him. I move to the side of the bed and then climb to the middle to position myself and fully embrace whatever he wants to give.

The bed dips but stops before climbing on, looking me over once and then again. His swallow is harsh, his Adam's apple bobbing as if I've left him breathless. When he finally covers me, I butterfly my legs, welcoming him into my fold.

Pushing into me, he doesn't stop until he's seated deeply within. Our eyes stare into each other's, our breathing mingling, and our body bonded. But it's the emotional connection I have with him that intensifies. Not because we've had sex but because I love him, and he loves me. That changes everything.

I'll greet the heartbreak with open arms if I can just hold on to this feeling a little while longer. A deal with the devil is struck, and he leans down to kiss me. A groan of pleasure rumbles from his chest to exchange through our breath as he moves, slow at first but then faster and harder.

I hold him, turning my head to rest above his shoulder, which taps my chin every time he pushes in again. We become a blur of bodies and breath, moans, and whispered adorations from his lips to my ear. It's all so much all at once —the heart, the mind, the beats, the breaths, and coil springing free when he hits just the right spot again and again.

My mind goes blank, my body moving on instinct. And when I call out his name as I tip over the edge into my own release, he follows. Gritting his teeth, he pumps into me erratically, my name a swear on his lips. "Lauralee. *Fuck.*"

We still as much as our breathing allows. My mind is calm, and my body is at peace. I wrap my arms around him as much as I can and lift my head to place a kiss on his neck. "Guess what?" I whisper.

He lifts like it's a struggle, but I can see the start of the smile that wants to reveal itself. "What?"

I can't hide mine, though. "We tied the knot."

With a nod, he kisses me. "It's official." He rolls from on top of me to the side, dropping his arm wide in invitation. I slide and snuggle against him. "You're all mine, Shortcake."

I've always been fiercely independent. I had to be from a young age. But those four words make me feel like I'm a part of the family. *I'm his.* And he's all mine.

CHAPTER 27

Lauralee

"Are we almost there?" I ask, whining to playfully taunt him.

Baylor shoots me a look, his eyes dancing before a laugh bursts out. "I stopped and got you beef jerky, strawberry candies, and a large blue raspberry ICEE that's stained your lips." I flip down the visor in the car he rented to see if my lips really are stained blue. I playfully punch him in the arm because they aren't, but my tongue sure is. "We've stopped twice for bathroom breaks, and you polished off a six-piece chicken nugget meal. What can I do to make this drive less painful for you?"

"Ice cream sounds good."

His head bounces forward on his neck. "I don't know where you put it."

I pop my shoulders. "I've been burning calories like nobody's business because of you." I grin, twisting my lips to one side. Last night was exhilarating and exhausting in the best of ways. My muscles ached from the deliciousness of him taking me twice and then returning the favor once more for good luck. That's a thing, right? Sex for good luck.

"Fair point. We did make the most of our wedding night." His eyes return to the road, and he says, "Next stop I see that has ice cream, you got it, baby."

I hold up the convenience store bag stored at my feet. "For the record, I've only snacked on the candies. I haven't even opened the jerky yet. I got it just in case."

"Just in case of what?"

"We get stranded and have to survive in the woods for days before being rescued."

Chuckling, he says, "I don't think it's possible to get lost or stranded in the woods between Manhattan and the Hamptons."

"We were raised in Texas. We come prepared. Have you been gone so long that you forgot your roots, Baylor?"

The silence draws my gaze to him as a myriad of emotions plays through his eyes as he glares ahead. Now I feel bad. He must feel me staring because he looks over and asks, "What?"

"I didn't mean to hurt your feelings."

"My feelings are fine." His words are curt, and though it's invisible, I see that mask I thought he left far behind our relationship slip back on.

"Sounds like it," I snark even when I know better. I reach over and rub his leg. "I really didn't mean anything by it. It just came out."

"It came out because you believe that. You believe that I'm more New York now than Peachtree Pass."

"Isn't that what you wanted? You left and never came back. I would think you would be proud of the direction of your life. Maybe I'm wrong for jumping to conclusions." Just as I pull my hand away, he captures it and brings it back to his lap.

"You're not wrong. It's no secret that Tagger and I had big plans, and those plans panned out." He glances at me. "That doesn't mean that our hometown didn't shape who I am as a man or isn't still part of me."

Leaning my head back and angling my body, I face him. "You glide seamlessly between the two worlds, but eventually, you'll have to choose one."

"Why?"

"I'm there, Baylor." I don't know why I say it. The thing that I tried so hard to repress, to never pressure him into deciding. Lifting my head, I stare down at the rings on my finger. I foolishly forgot that this isn't real. We aren't. We said one night, and I'm dragging it into the next day. I'm only supposed to play the part in the Hamptons. Pretending to be in love with him when I really am. I face forward again, and add, "Forget I said that."

"Lauralee, don't do that. Don't close down on me."

And as timing would have it . . .

I'm already closed off. "Don't miss the stop," I say, pointing at the small gas station coming up on my side of the road.

He pulls over and drives across the gravel parking lot to a spot in the front. As soon as he shifts into park, he says, "I know you're there. I think about it every fucking day of my life, wishing you were here or I was there so we would be together. I don't have an answer that will feel satisfactory to you when you already think I'm doing this on purpose."

"I don't. I don't think you don't want to be with me. I think you feel caught between your career and . . ." I don't want to say it. It sounds childish, though it's true. "I won't make demands of you." A humorless laugh escapes me. "I can't anyway. You don't work that way. Neither do I. It's one of the few things we have in common."

"We have more than that in common."

"Like?"

His pause only reaffirms my statement.

But then he says, "We both love strawberries, and Texas sunrises rival the sunsets for best in show, but we'd choose the early morning spectacular every time." I catch my breath, afraid to make a noise in fear the mask that has slipped again will work its way back around his heart. "When I look at you from the long side of the picnic bench, I see how much you care about me. I care about you more than you can imagine. You're not alone in feeling you've found something special, something most people will never experience."

Is it fair to make him continue like this? Probably not, but I gobble it up heart and soul and swallow it down, savoring every word he says. "Which is?"

He pauses, his fingers still wrapped around the steering wheel and his knuckles whitening. As if it pains him to admit, he replies, "True love."

"Well," I start, the growing anxiety vanishing in an instant. "I have no comeback because I can't argue with that." I stretch forward. "Does anyone else know what a romantic you are?"

"No. I've worked hard to conceal it, but you just bring it out in me." When he grins, the world feels right again. I do just from seeing it.

Laying down my emotional weapons, I say, "I'm thinking one of those chocolate-dipped ice cream pops sounds good."

He nods in silent understanding. I like that we both

know when the war is over and peace is restored. "You want to go in with me or wait here?"

"I'll wait here."

"I'll be quick." Opening the door, he steps out, but before he closes the door, he makes sure to lock it. Protected and safe. Always with him.

Watching him walk away is quite the view, too. He gives fantastic backside, even better when he's naked. My insides shiver in giddiness that he's mine. Even if only for the time being.

I sit back, adjusting the seat belt from scraping my neck when Baylor's phone lights up on the console. Tagger texts: *Four rims and a new steering wheel showed up today. You can order all the parts you want. You're still losing this bet, fucker.*

Having no idea what he's talking about, I glance up to see Baylor at the register inside. He waves the ice cream like he struck gold. Laughing, I wave back.

Another text pops up, causing my gaze to deviate back to the lighted screen: *Pris said she thinks Lauralee is seeing someone. Is it you? Did you finally score to win the bet?*

I read that again.

And then once more until Baylor exits the store and walks to the driver's side of the vehicle. Bending down, he taps the glass and then points at the lock, which is fastened.

My gaze moves back to his phone just before the screen goes dark again. "*Did you finally score to win the bet?*" loops in my head.

A tap on the glass brings me back to him . . . *Am I just a bet?* He did this for a car? I know what car he wagered, too. The only one that would be worth sacrificing me for in return—the 911. *His mom's car.*

God, I'm such a fool for falling for him.

I feel sick.

"Open the door, Lauralee. The ice cream is melting."

Glancing over, I say, "I don't want it."

His brows buckle together in the middle. "Why not?"

Wrapping my arms over my stomach, I try to keep myself from vomiting. He gets the hint I wasn't intending and walks to the trash can outside the door to toss it. I push the button to unlock the door and then angle away from him toward my window.

When he gets in, he rubs my shoulder. "Feeling carsick?"

"Yeah," I reply, deciding it's easier to go with that until I can process what I've discovered. A bet. Just thinking about it brings me closer to tears.

"Do you want to sit here a bit longer or go for a short walk to get fresh air? We're not far from the house. Less than an hour if you want me to drive to get there sooner. Tell me what you want to do."

His voice is distancing as I fade into my thoughts. I summon the strength to reply, "Just drive."

"Sorry you're not feeling well."

I roll my eyes, and snap, "I bet."

"What?"

I don't bother repeating myself. I need to figure out my next step. Trapped in the Hamptons at his boss's house isn't ideal, but neither is paying for a car to take me back to the city. *Five hours* . . . that would be a month's worth of rent. I sigh, realizing I'm going to be stuck, so I need to make a plan to get through the weekend. Anger is going to be my best ally.

MEETING his boss and his wife wasn't as painful as I expected, and they were over the moon to find out we got married. With those formalities out of the way, we settle in upstairs in one of the eight bedrooms they chose for us.

It's beautiful in buttery yellow and white with pale blue accents. More formal than I'm used to. This would get so dirty back home after a long day out on those dusty roads and ranches.

I finish touching up my makeup and brushing my hair in the bathroom, which I locked him out of so I could be alone. I manage to zip up the white dress I chose for the party to go along with the Fourth of July theme, and because when I saw it yesterday as a wedding option, I knew it was better suited for today. And since he was paying . . . I just wish I had known about this bet then. I would have kept everything.

When I come out, he's lying on the bed fully dressed and waiting. He catcalls me. "Turn for me." Funny how I found that so charming yesterday, and today, it makes me want to light a fire to burn the place down.

"We should go." I pull the door open and start down the hall.

His heavy footsteps echo behind me. "Hey, Shortcake?"

I keep walking, reaching the top of the staircase. As soon as I take hold of the railing, I'm stopped by his stupid giant wall of a body standing in my way. I shift to the right, but he shifts with me. I go left, and he's still there blocking me. "What's going on? Why are you mad?"

"Oh god," I say, throwing my arm up. "Where do I start?"

"The beginning is good."

I wonder if he means the beginning, when two grown-ass men made a bet for him to sleep with me? I'll assume he thinks he's slyer than that. "Ha! I bet." I attempt to maneuver around him, but I know it's wasted energy, and I'm not willing to risk my life in these heels to outrun him. "Can you move, please?"

He tries to take hold of my hand, but I tuck it into the pocket of the dress. That was one of the features that sold me on it. It's coming in handy. "You're not talking to me?"

"Not if I can help it."

His eyes harden. He grabs the railing and stands taller. "What the fuck is going on, Lauralee?"

We're at an impasse. I'm in no mood to talk to him at all about anything, and that's all he wants to do. I exhale, my shoulders falling from the mental exhaustion. "Can we just go to the party? Please."

Our eyes stay fixed as seconds pass, but then he steps to the side and out of my way. "So much for the happy newlyweds."

"You don't have to worry, Baylor," I say, taking the steps slowly so I don't trip down the spiral. "I'll play my part as I promised. You'll be heralded as the family man they're looking to promote and then we can go our separate ways. The bank can send the paperwork to you." Yeah, I'm not letting him off the hook.

Stopping at the marble-tiled floor of the foyer, as Mrs. Goodman called it because she's rich and fancy like that, he waits for me. He holds his elbow out for me when I reach the bottom step. I debate if I need to take it or if I want to walk beside him instead. I take hold with my hand and lift my chin, ready to make our entrance.

I FEEL bad for being so bored.

Sure, everyone is nice enough and all the ladies have been fawning all over me as a newlywed, more than happy to impart advice, and coo over my rings. But I never want to hear another thing regarding fashion in Capri. Who cares?

They do. Apparently, a lot. No matter the season, they have the perfect outfits ready to go. "Do you get to Europe much, Lauralee?" Mrs. Goodman asks as she sips her watermelon spritzer. I've already downed three. They're light on the alcohol, so I asked for a double last round to get me through the rest of this event.

"I've never been." The audible gasps startle me. With all the ladies staring, I don't know where to go with this, so I lie to spare myself the humiliation, "In fall."

The four women take a collective sigh of relief. One even had her hand over her heart in concern. She lowers it, so I think I'm in the clear. Mrs. Goodman rubs my wrist. "You should see Paris in the fall. It's stunning."

"I'll have to make it a point to visit during the season."

I keep eyeing Baylor, the anger I felt earlier subsiding with the passing hours. Should I have said something and given him a chance to explain? Am I the bad guy for being hurt in the first place? No. But my pain has morphed into disappointment in myself for falling for a playboy. Of course he'd treat dating like a sport. It's what Baylor Greene has always done. So the bet shouldn't come as a surprise. He's doing what he does best—winning. Whether it be on the football field or in the bedroom, he's been spoiled with choice. That's not something I want to be a part of. Anymore.

Spotting the buffet, I say, "If you'll excuse me," and slip away from the group. I should have done that an hour ago. I get a plate and walk the length of the table, adding everything from a slider to potato salad, a scoop of mac and cheese, and a cookie because I need to eat my feels.

I take my plate and head to the edge of the lawn that

leads to a beach and the ocean. I've never seen a house this big, and the lawn with the pool, the guesthouse, and landscaping are something I always imagined celebrities having.

The mac and cheese is good, so I take another bite, staring ahead at the water.

"I like to see a woman who eats." Baylor's boss slides up next to me, facing the ocean.

Nothing like being shamed when I'm holding a damn appetizer plate. I lose my appetite and struggle to swallow down the last bite I took. I lower the plate, wishing I could dump it now.

He says, "My wife and her friends eat like birds to keep their figure, but they're much older than you." I'm not sure why he's still speaking to me when I've given him no indication of interest. But he keeps going. "Baylor's going places." That has me glancing his way. He's grinning like we're old friends and sharing secrets. He's older than expected. He has at least ten years on my mom. With white and gray hair combed to the side, he's smaller in stature standing in opposition to his arrogance, which befits a tall male model, basically Baylor if I'm being honest. "We're happy he brought you into the Taylor and Goodman family. We'll be seeing lots of each other. That will be nice. You and I spending more time together. I can take you out on my yacht. Have you ever been on a yacht before?"

It's not a question, but it sure does sound like a threat of him insinuating more than business acquaintances. "You're crossing a line you don't want to, Mr. Goodman."

"I've crossed many lines." He rocks on the heels of his loafers with his hands tucked in his pockets. I can hear the jangle of change or keys, which grates on my last nerve. "It always works out well for me."

Squaring my shoulders to face him, I reply, "Not this time."

"You're very pretty."

"I'm also married and have no intention of cheating on my husband."

His hands go up in front of him. "Who said anything about cheating?"

"Bob?" Hearing his wife standing behind me stiffens my spine.

I release a heavy sigh. He's good, making it look like I was the one coming onto him. *Asshole.*

I could bother to tell her the truth, but when I look back over my shoulder, there's no anger nor jealousy scribed in her expression. Disillusionment might describe it better by the lack of fight in her eyes. She probably accepted this fate years before I entered the picture, trading the lifestyle for happiness.

She puts on a smile that can't be more fake, and says, "It's time for the toast, dear."

He walks by me, hitting me with ire in his eyes when he passes.

If this is what it means to be rich, I choose my life with all the struggles that come with it any day.

I'm still unsure what to do about the bet and the betrayal of Baylor, but a plan finally comes to mind. I cross the lawn, tossing my plate in the trash, and go to him.

He walks to meet me halfway, his smile holding the uncertainty of someone who cares and is worried about me, not someone who would make a lame bet to sleep with me. He extends his arm, then I walk into the offer, and he brings me to his side. He's still so comforting, like my favorite blanket that keeps me warm on stormy nights.

It's more difficult to stay mad when I still see him as my

friend and feel him as my husband. Yesterday wasn't that long ago. The impact it made still lingers and thrives in my heart.

He kisses the side of my head, then asks, "You excited to see the fireworks?" There's such innocence and hope in the question.

It's not ideal, but I'd rather lose everything than sacrifice my soul. Even him, if it comes to that. "I'm leaving, Baylor."

CHAPTER 28

Baylor

"Why are you leaving?"

Lauralee wrangles away from me and looks around as if checking to make sure no one is listening. Setting her eyes on me again, she whispers, "I played my part. Now I'm leaving."

"Three hours? That's it?"

"That's it." She walks away like I won't follow her.

I'm right on her heels, willing to follow her off a cliff if that's where she's headed. "You're not going to talk to me about it?"

"What's there to say?"

I catch up to her, matching her pace while trying not to look like I'm fighting with my bride at a company party the day after we got married. "Telling me what's wrong would help. What did I do, Shortcake?"

She stops, tilts her head to the side, and hits me with a glare so hard it about knocks me backward. "Don't call me that. You've lost your privileges."

I balk. "My privileges?"

"Yes. You've lost them as my husband and my friend. You can call me Lauralee or Ms. Knot. That's it."

"I prefer Mrs. Greene."

She scoffs with an exaggerated eye roll. "I bet."

A clue to what's fucking going on would be nice, but it doesn't seem like I'll get that luxury. "Why are you always saying that? You've said it three times today."

I swear that steam shoots from her ears. "This is why I can't talk to you. You do stuff like that and expect me to just fall over like a domino at your whim. Not this time." She starts for the house again, giving the partygoers surrounding the pool a wide berth.

I know better than to push this too far in the middle of the party. We go inside. I give her some space to get ahead of me again, sensing she needs it. And though I have plenty to say, I wordlessly follow her to the bedroom. As soon as I close the door, I keep my tone lowered and say, "Please talk to me."

She'd already launched her suitcase onto the bed, but her hands stop after she unzips it. With her back to me, I can tell the debate she's having with herself by the way she shakes her head before looking down, clenching her eyes closed. She finally turns around, tears streaking her cheeks, but she holds her head high. "Tagger texted earlier when you were in the store. I'm not sure if you got it."

"What did he text us about?" I'm already pulling my phone from my back pocket, but dread is kicking in. My heart starts thundering in my chest when I touch the screen to see a missed call from a client, which I knew about, but beneath is a buried message chain.

"It wasn't to us. It was to you. You left your phone in the car when you got the ice cream."

Fuck. Fuck. Fuck. Fuck. Fuck. *Fucking hell.*

She sits on the bed, her body leaning on the suitcase as if she needs the support. "I can explain," I start as I tap on his name.

"I'm sure you can, Baylor," she replies with no argument, but it doesn't sound like there's room for the truth either. "Or should I say I bet?"

I read both of his messages and then look back at her. My feet want to move, but I hold myself back, thinking that this is about respecting her space and not me right now. When a tear dangles from her chin, I whisper, "I'm sorry."

She nods and pushes herself up like this is the last of her energy left. Flipping open the suitcase, she whispers, "I bet."

Fuck me.

"I know you're hurt, Lauralee." I take a step closer, not wanting to creep up on her, but I can't stand the distance.

Turning around, she huffs. "You know because you're the one who hurt me."

"I did."

"Knowingly." She drops her head into her hands and starts crying, her sobs muffled, but the ache is heard. It's fucking torture to see her in pain, but especially because I caused it. Did I really think this would end any other way? I'm so fucking stupid. When she lifts her head, her brown eyes shine with gold and those beautiful flecks of green in the evening sun streaming through the window. "I fell in love, but I was nothing more than a bet to you."

"I love you. That is real. When you said it felt real last night. It feels fucking real to me, too. I didn't even know I had a soul until you came along."

"But you decided mine wasn't worth the vows you spoke." Putting her hands on her hips, she looks down at the carpeted floor and shakes her head again. When she looks up, she says, "I don't know how to get a divorce since this is new to me." She laughs without humor in it. "Twenty-four hours. Must be some kind of record."

"We don't have to make any rash decisions. Nothing has to be decided right this second. Please. Let's—"

"The worst part is that I don't even know if I can afford a divorce, but let me make one thing clear. You and I are through."

The words are sharp, cutting right into my chest and severing my heart. Like my soul, it didn't come to life until I fell in love with her. That confession won't help, and other words don't come, the ones that would make this right as she hurries to pack and abandon my life. Losing her is the last thing I want. I can't.

She grabs three dresses from the closet, pulling them from the hanger. "I was naive. I didn't know what I was getting into. That's what I get for following my heart instead of my head." Throwing the dresses in the suitcase and fisting her hands at her sides, she yells, "I married you because I loved you. If I didn't . . ." She sucks in a harsh breath. "This wouldn't—" She shuts her mouth abruptly, grabs a small bag from the nightstand, and tosses it on top of her clothes.

I brace myself for the response before daring to ask the question. "This wouldn't what, Lauralee?"

"This wouldn't hurt so much." She sinks onto the bed, her feet barely reaching the floor. "I trusted you had changed. You haven't."

I walk to the far side of the bed and sit. I've never felt worse in my life. "If I could change this—"

"You can't. It's done, and we're over."

With our backs to each other, I tell her the truth because

I may never get another chance to. "I made the bet because I had already won it."

That sits in the air between us like a dark cloud keeping us apart. I look down at the wedding ring on my finger. Nothing ever felt right until I was wearing it.

The bed shifts from her side, causing me to look back over my shoulder. My eyes meet hers, and she asks, "How?"

None of this is going to help my case, but I can't lie to her now that it's out in the open. "Tagger was catching onto me being gone and coming home early. He was digging for information, figuring I was seeing someone." I blow out a breath but keep going. "We had already had sex but agreed we weren't ready to share our relationship. That's when he bet me my mom's car that someone as incredible as you would never give me the time of day. But Lauralee, we had already had sex. I knew I'd win, but the win wasn't going to come out until we decided to go public."

She studies my eyes before her gaze lowers to the bed.

So I hurry to finish. "Was it stupid to make the bet in the first place? Yes. Immature. Absolutely. I regret it so fucking much. I'm sorry. You didn't deserve to be part of something that two fuckups didn't think through."

Reaching for a loose thread on the comforter, she looks back at me. "And you will win your mom's car? That's the prize?"

"You are the prize. That car isn't mine unless you're in my life, not because of a damn bet, but because if you never wanted us to go public, I'd gladly lose the car if I have you."

With a sigh, anger escapes her. "I'm trying to piece this together to give you the benefit of the doubt. The car isn't yours because Christine owns the majority share of the ranch, which also means Tagger does. This is because you and Griffin gave most of your shares to her for running it?"

"Yes." It doesn't surprise me that she knows the details. She's my sister's best friend. And it was a big deal, a gift we gave our sister since she had more than earned the ranch and farmland. "My ass of a best friend knew exactly what he was doing by including the car."

"He dangled it in front of you, and you grabbed the chance you were given to own it." Sliding her knee on the bed, she angles more of her body to face me. I hope that's trust I spy reentering her eyes. It sure looks like it. "Does that sound right on target?"

"Bull's-eye." That she's even granted me the benefit of the doubt has hope returning that we can work this out.

She leans back on the stack of pillows lining the padded headboard as if she's not in such a rush and holds her hand with the rings up in front of her. "It's really crappy to find out about this, especially through his text. I understand the reasoning. I know your mom's car is important to you." Sitting up again as if she can't sit still, she twists the wedding band around her finger. "You could have just told me about it. I would have made sure you won without throwing our relationship under the bus." She throws her hand out. "Marriage aside, we were dating, Baylor. We were in a relationship, even if we hadn't defined it. I was supposed to be your partner, someone you can tell anything to and would be on your side, but this..."

Just when forgiveness is within reach, it slips through my fingers again. "Please give me a second chance. I love you." The words cause my heart to ache and my throat to tighten. "We're real, baby."

She turns her back on me again when she drops her feet to the carpet. I can plead all night, but I can tell she's decided. Pushing off the bed, she comes around and stands in front of me. I wedge my legs apart so she can get closer.

"This marriage may have been created out of necessity," she says, resting her hands on my shoulders, "but I still deserve respect."

"You do. I'm so sorry for doing something so stupid. I'm even more sorry that you got hurt because of my choices." Reaching forward, I hold her by the waist. "Will you forgive me?"

Her expression softens, her tears have dried, and a sympathetic smile creases the corners of her lips. She sits on my lap, wrapping her arm around my neck. "The road to hell is paved with good intentions. I believe you didn't hurt me on purpose. I've been worked up all day thinking about that text, and then your boss said weird stuff to me, and I lost my appetite. I didn't even get to eat my cookie. All day, I had to grin and pretend I'm a happy newlywed when I couldn't stop thinking about the bet."

My soul feels whole, holding her again, her laughter the balm it needed. I could lose her. The reality of that sinks in deep. "I'll buy you however many you want. You want to own Levain Bakery, it's yours."

"I'd be happy with Peaches." With the prettiest smile I thought I'd never get to see again, she looks up at me and asks, "Can we go back to the city?"

"We can leave right now if that's what you want."

"I don't want to be here anymore. I'd rather spend my last night only with you."

I lift her to her feet when I stand, but I don't let go. I almost had this taken away from me, so I wrap her in my arms and kiss her head. "Thank you."

When her arms come around me, she tucks her face against my chest while rubbing my back. "It's going to be okay."

Through her own pain and the embarrassment I caused, *she* comforts me. "I don't deserve you—"

"No, you don't." She laughs as she leans back, trusting me to keep her from falling. "This wasn't so bad that it couldn't be fixed with honesty from the beginning." *Honesty.* That's all she wants.

I need to come clean about owning the building back home and soon. Why do I get the feeling that isn't going to smooth over the way that this did? Especially since we're now married.

"We all screw up," she says. "It's how we handle it after that matters." With a look I'm not as familiar with coming over her face, she says, "You know what this means, right?"

"No. What does it mean?"

"We're getting Tagger back."

I don't know if I should support this idea or be very afraid. Doesn't matter. I'm Team Lauralee all the way.

WE REACH the bottom of the staircase to find Mrs. Goodman coming from the living room. Her eyes are set on Lauralee when she says, "I want to apologize for what happened."

Shock ripples through Lauralee's expression. "Why would you do that?" Disgust coats her words, and she glances at me. I have no fucking clue what's going on, but I think there's more to the story of why we're leaving based on the interaction between them. "He'll never change. Why would you stay?"

"Because not everything is black and white." She clasps her hands in front of her and puts on a smile. "You're young and in love. One day, things could change."

"Don't pass your failed blessing onto me. We're nothing

like you or your husband." Lauralee turns so fast that her hair flies over her shoulders. Her heels clack against the marble, and she pulls the large door open.

I don't know what I'm supposed to say, feeling caught in the middle of who knows what. I glance at Mrs. Goodman, who doesn't seem fazed or bothered by the harsh words. There seems to be acceptance instead.

She's my boss's wife, though, so walking out seems ominous for my future at the company. But my wife matters more to me. So I walk to the door but stop when Lauralee turns back again, and says, "I once heard that when you marry for money, you will earn every dime. That's the difference between us. You married for security. I married for love. Enjoy your money."

I want to ask what happened between them, but I'll wait until we're in the car and away from the house. I open the door for her, then load the suitcases into the trunk of the rental. When I slide into the driver's side, I close the door and look at my wife. "What was that about?"

"Nothing." Her voice is so casual like nothing just fucking happened inside.

I start the engine. "That wasn't nothing. I'll defend you to the ends of the earth, Shortcake, but can you fill me in since I'm going to be facing her husband on Monday?" I stare at her as she chews the inside of her cheek. When she peeks over at me, I can tell she actually thought this would be dropped. It won't. "I'd like to have the story straight so I know what I'm walking into."

She reaches over and touches my cheek so lovingly with a smile to match on her face. "It was handled, so there's no need to worry about it."

"I'm worried." I'm not really, but I am intrigued.

"You sure you want to know?" Her hand returns to her

lap, the sweet smile disappearing with it. "It's going to upset you, and I don't want you upset."

"Well, now you have to tell me."

She reaches the gearshift in front of the console and shifts it in reverse. "I'll tell you back in Manhattan."

My foot doesn't leave the brake. "Tell me now, Lauralee." The effort she's making to keep this from me has me gripping the steering wheel tighter.

"Mrs. Goodman's husband propositioned me."

I shoot my gaze ahead, staring at the brick wall in front of us. I hope this steering wheel is made of steel under this plastic coating. If not, it's about to be destroyed. When I look back at her, her brown eyes are fixed on mine. Those same eyes that usually calm me have concern riddling through them. She reaches over and rests her hand on my forearm as if to reassure me. "I handled it, Baylor. So we can leave and pretend this day never happened." Her expression softens, and she says, "We'll make love all night and—"

"When you say Mrs. Goodman's husband, you mean Bob, my boss, right?" She murmurs something, but I can't hear her. "What was that?"

"Yes." Throwing her arms up, she sinks against the seat, giving up. "Yes, it was Bob. I told him that he crossed a line, and I'm married. That didn't stop him." That. Didn't. Stop. Him. *What the fuck?* "He's the kind of asshole who thinks his money impresses me, so he invited me out on his yacht. When I said I'm married—"

Anger rushes through my veins. I shove the car door open, reaching the house before I hear her calling my name. "Baylor, don't. Stop."

The conversation with Mrs. Goodman makes a lot more damn sense now. Cutting through the house, I swing the back doors open and rush onto the back lawn, searching for him. My arm is caught. When I look to my right, Lauralee says, "You don't need to do this. Come with me. We're leaving. Together, remember. Just the two of us."

"Just the two of us."

"Yeah." She smiles.

I don't respond because I see that wife-fucker at three o'clock. I charge forth, not giving a shit. I've put up with enough for too fucking long anyway.

He sees me coming, his hands coming out as if it's possible to stop a charging bull. "Women lie, Baylor. She's lying. Are you really going to throw away your career for a woman who came on to me?"

"Don't you ever fucking talk about my wife, or I'll make sure you can't utter a fucking word again." I stand in front of him, this frail little man whose ego is bigger than he is. I know the damage I could do to him and the repercussions that would follow. Jail. Charges filed against me. Losing my reputation. Destroying my hard-earned career.

Lauralee stands just behind me, and says, "He's not worth it. I promise you." As much as I want to believe her, I also want to obliterate him. "I love you, Baylor." Hearing those words from the voice of an angel calms me down.

I take a breath, knowing this is not who I want to be with her. "I quit."

"You quit?" He laughs. "I was just about to announce your promotion to the entire party."

"No, you weren't. Fuck you. You're just an asshole who hit on my wife, and when she turned you down, you tried to save your ass."

I turn and take hold of my wife's hand.

He shouts, "You're done, Greene."

"You're right. I'm so fucking done." I walk away, not regretting a damn thing. I feel the opposite of how I expected. I feel free for the first time in years. It's not only because I'm free from a company I've come to despise but also because of the woman at my side. My partner in crime. My wife. I glance down at Lauralee and smile. "Ready to head back to the city?"

"So ready." We don't make it two minutes from the house before she says, "I'm so proud of you. Do you know how sexy that was to watch you take control of the situation?"

"I'm going to need you to tell me."

"I'll do you one better." She raises her brow. "How about I show you?"

She showed me alright. We're lucky I didn't wreck on the way back. And when we get back to the apartment at one in the morning, I show her just how lucky I am to have her in my life. *Twice.*

CHAPTER 29

Baylor

I'M surprised Mr. Goodman didn't demand rain since he banned me from the building. He'd love to know I was stuck out here drenched and probably begging for cover. Though he should know me better than that.

It's sunny despite him because I'm fucking winning.

Approaching the doors to Taylor and Goodman, I stop myself from going in and wait farther away. Since I'm not allowed in the office, it's good to have friends on the inside. This side of the street is doused in sunlight, like a spotlight showcasing me. I doubt Goodman could miss it even if he tried. Good. Fuck him.

I put on my sunglasses and text: *I'm here.*

Since last week and over the weekend, my checklist got longer. I experienced the best high of my life, and then some lows that I'll get over in time. I've fallen behind in getting messages sent. Prioritizing my list, I send an email to my attorney, Mark, to get the paperwork ready by the time I land in Austin on Thursday. I'm not showing up empty-handed. Especially after how the bet was received. Not well.

Honesty. That's her only request of me.

That's what I'll give her. I'll face any consequences and fight for our relationship.

Then there's the matter of this Josten guy at the property management company. He still hasn't replied to my email asking why he went rogue and jacked up the prices on the strip of shops I purchased. Going rogue for your own kicks, then hoping to get praise is not how things are done.

Mickey backs through the door and looks both ways before seeing me. "I tried to get all of your personal belongings. I'm going to do another sweep when I go back up, though, just in case I missed anything."

"I appreciate that."

He laughs. "Your name plaque has already been removed. If it's any consolation, it ripped off the plaster."

"I appreciate that level of pettiness." He hands me the box. "This is it, huh? My career didn't amount to much."

"Your career is sitting in bank accounts. This is just a box of knickknacks that didn't make the mantel at home."

It's a good perspective. With more money than I thought possible for one person to have, I never need to work another day in my life. That's not the path I'm interested in taking, but I'm financially comfortable to do what I want.

Which is? I have no fucking clue.

I'm not even in my mid-thirties. That's too young not to be productive, not to transition my career to a new company, work toward a new dream, or figure something else out. But what?

Looking up at the skyscraper, most of my career has been spent here. I had stability and growth in this building. It's incredible that one event changed everything.

Do I have regrets in the aftermath? *One.* I didn't hit him. That would have felt good. Though my reward on the car ride home felt better. Guess it's good I controlled my urges.

Shifting the box under my arm to shake his hand, I say, "I won't keep you."

"You're not. I started putting out my résumé last night. I don't think this is the company for me either."

"Wherever you land, they'll be lucky to have you. You have a rare talent in this industry. Good instincts. You have to follow no rules, only laws in our business. You can always go out on your own. You don't have to work for someone else."

Mickey squints when a reflection off the mirrored window hits his eyes. Maneuvering closer to the building, he says, "I've been considering it. I learned a lot from you. I know you'll end up where you're supposed to be, but I enjoyed working with you, Baylor."

"Same. If you need anything, just text."

"Same. And I'll let you know if I find anything else before they clear it out."

"Thanks. I'll be seeing ya." I'm not entirely sure that's true, but he's a good guy. Maybe we'll grab a beer one day when I return to the city. I start down the sidewalk, walking straight into the sunlight and letting it cover me. This feels like I'm taking steps in the right direction. Shortcake would probably call it destiny. I'll let her win that argument.

"Hey, congrats again on the marriage."

When I turn back, I see him shielding his eyes as he looks in my direction. I reply, "Thanks. Best thing I ever did." Every step away from this building and company is lighter and easier to take. It's time for a new start.

Without much time to take this box back to the apartment, I order a car to the airport. I don't want to be late. It also gives me time to call my girl. Unfortunately, it goes to voicemail. "I love you." That message feels like it sums up everything I wanted to say nicely.

"We got hot dogs like we used to when I was little," Beckett tells his dad. "And Uncle Baylor said we can meet my friends at the park tomorrow. But he didn't get the ice cream. He said he forgot."

I chuckle. "Is it that bad, Beck?"

He puts Tagger on speakerphone. "Can't believe you forgot the ice cream." I can hear him laughing.

"I'm ordering it now." There are a few things I want to discuss with Tagger regarding the bet and how it played out, but I think it's best to do so in person when I fly back with his son on Thursday. "How's my car doing?"

"Sitting on rotting rubber in the garage where we left her. You aren't expecting me to work on it, were you? That's all you, man."

"Like the fort," Beck adds, calling me out.

I look up from my phone after ordering his favorite New York ice cream to be delivered. "I see you talk crap like your father."

Beck laughs. "He always says I get it from you."

Figures, the fucker. "I'm sure he does." I laugh as I sit on the couch to watch the game even though it's on mute. I used to sit here and watch with my best friend. Now I have my buddy here to keep me company. It's only a few days, but the timing was good, so it worked out to fly him here. I've broken a few promises. I don't want to break my word again, or I'll have nothing left to give.

They wrap up their conversation, leading Beck to join

me in the living room. I ask, "Do you watch much baseball at home?"

"No. More football in the fall season."

"How's tackle going?"

"Rough."

He doesn't laugh, but I do. "Yeah, it's like that until you build a tolerance to being hit. You know what I was taught growing up?"

Slumping in the leather chair, he glides his eyes to mine. "What?"

"If you're the fastest one on the field, you don't have to worry about getting tackled." His grin reminds me of Tagger's—devil in the detailed corners, genuine when it expands.

"That's good advice, right?"

"Yeah. I'm getting faster, but not fast enough not to get tackled." The tips of his toes reach for the edge of the coffee table. He's always been a part of our adult lives, so sometimes I forget how young he really is.

"Practice. That's always the key to being the best."

"That's what Grandpa Grange says."

Memories come back of us boys out at Tagger's or the ranch racing each other. Competition is in our nature, but we've taken it too far more recently. It's all fun and games until someone gets hurt. Hurting Shortcake is now something I have to live with and make sure I never do again.

Beck's asleep in the chair before the ice cream arrives. I put it in the freezer before I tuck him into bed in the extra bedroom where I have my home office. I pause at the door for one last look back at him.

The only time I ever thought about kids was when I was trying to prevent it from happening. Would it be so bad to have a few of my own? Before I get ahead of myself, I'm reminded that Beck has always been an easy kid to be around. Never fussy, though the sass is coming out as he gets closer to those teen years.

I'm pretty sure any offspring of mine will come with a big dose of hellion inside. Maybe Lauralee's genes can balance them out. I close the door and walk down the hall to the living room, scratching the back of my neck. I'm starting to not recognize myself.

I jumped feet first right into marriage, and now I'm thinking about kids . . . as in having them? All it took was the right woman to come along. Now that she's in my life, I'll give her the universe.

A text is waiting on my phone when I return to the couch. Three black-and-white photos from our wedding day accompany the message: *A preview of the big day.*

My lungs scream for air, making me realize I hadn't been breathing. I never considered myself a sentimental man, but seeing these photos of Lauralee looking at me like I can do no wrong reaffirms my commitment to love this woman with all that I am.

The flash flares in her eyes, highlighting the glistening tears when we exchanged our vows. Her entire body is filled with too much happiness to hide on the courthouse stairs as we run down them together. The smile that holds no limits to joy, the way it reaches her eyes, and the swing of her arm. She's carefree, how it should be.

I look damn good in my suit. It's always been a favorite, but I only wear it on special occasions. On short notice, it worked out great.

But it's the last image that stole my breath when I first saw it, just like she did the night we spent together in her apartment in May. So much has changed since then, but I'm beginning to believe most of it's been inside me. She's rocked my world and flipped it upside down. The view isn't so bad from this new angle. I actually quite like it.

Most people would gravitate to the other photos full of laughter and movement. Not me. This is my favorite. Simple. Classic. Two people in love. No showy grins or knowing exchanges. We stood on the steps with her head resting on me, holding hands, and the flowers lowered on her other side. It feels real, subtle, and intimate, a photo only taken for us to enjoy.

I reply to the photographer's text: *Incredible. Can't wait to see the rest. It's last minute, but I'd love to give my wife a copy of that third photo. Any way to rush a print and bring it over by end of day Wednesday?*

She replies: *If you don't mind the rush fees, I'll hand deliver it myself.*

Me: *I'll cover the charges. Thanks.*

I send the photographer my address, instructing her to leave it with the doorman. Lauralee will love seeing this. I can't wait to give it to her. And kiss her. God, I miss those lips and everything else about her.

With my baseball team in the lead going into extra innings, I decide to turn off the game and get some sleep. Beck will be up early because I promised him pancakes at his favorite breakfast joint before we go to the park. He's a pancake monster I'm happy to feed.

By the time I'm in bed, I don't text my girl, I call.

"Hey there, stranger," she answers, sounding like a smile is set on her face. It is on mine just from hearing her voice.

"Gone for twenty-four hours, and I'm already a stranger?"

Laughter travels the distance to my ear. "Any hours away are too long. I miss you."

"I miss you, too." I'm a sentimental fucker for her, that's for sure.

"You picked up Beckett today?"

"I did. He walks around like he never forgot where he came from. The kid feels comfortable in the city."

"Best of both worlds, I suppose. Speaking of where you came from, are you still coming back on Thursday?"

Reaching over, I click off the lamp. "Yes. I want to see you." Staring into the nighttime cityscape, I study the way the windows with lights shine like stars dotting the building. The reflection of the moon bounces off the metal trimmings at varying heights. I'll never see anything like this in Peachtree, but I don't need to. Living among the buildings has been nice, but I'm ready for fields and trees and no neighbors to bug me.

"That's good," she replies as if she feels relieved.

"Did you think I would cancel?"

"You're busy. And now with no job, I know you have a lot to do."

"It can wait a few days for me to come see you." I close the curtains since I'm no longer a working man with obligations before the sun rises. "Beck said he's made progress on the fort. He's ready for the muscle to come in, so I'll be out there on Friday while you work."

"And the car? I ordered a book that came in so I can assist you." She doesn't bring up the bet, which I'm grateful for. Her ability to forgive and move forward, even though she won't forget, is something I admire. She's genuine in everything she does, even in loving me with the flaws that come along with that.

"I find it so stinkin' adorable that you ordered a book."

"Look, buster, I know you talk all big and stuff. You've worked on trucks and a few vehicles growing up, but this isn't just any car." Her passion is palpable. If I were there, I'd be fucking her while she reads the manual to me. So fucking hot. "It's a classic, and we can't screw it up."

I chuckle, rolling to my side. The bed beside me is empty without her. My soul relates. I reach over, resting my hand where she lay just yesterday. And when I close my eyes, I can still catch the faintest scent of her sweetness in the air. Strawberries.

"We can't," I mumble, a yawn catching me by surprise.

"Get some rest and have fun with Beck tomorrow."

I find myself holding the phone tighter to my ear not wanting to miss a word she says. "I will. Love you, baby."

"I love you, too. Good night."

I lie awake a few minutes more, thinking about what my head is telling me to do and what my heart is guiding me toward. They're not as far apart as they used to be.

"Baylor?" I look up from my phone to see a woman standing a few feet away from the park bench where I'm seated. "It's Katie." Her hand goes to her chest as her smile broadens. I'm drawing a blank. "Katie Wilson," she says as if we know each other.

"Hi," I play along. "How are you?" I've never seen her in my life, but apparently, she's seen me.

Her eyes roll, and her smile morphs into knowing. "You don't remember me. It's okay. I knew what I was getting into that night with you."

"Night?"

"Yeah," she says, sitting on the other side of the bench from me. Perched on the edge, her eyes are set on the kids on the playground. When she glances at me, her smile softens. She's pretty but nothing about her triggers a memory. "We met at a work party probably like . . ." She squints as she works through the riddle. "Seven years or so ago. Your company hosted a client event. My boss at the time brought me as his assistant. We had sex in your office."

"Ah." That didn't happen any other time but once. Her hair is blond when it used to be brown, just below her ears when it was long back then. "You changed your hair."

"I did." Her shoulders curve forward as she tracks a little girl coming down the slide. "The one in the pink coat is mine."

I glance at Beck as if he's my own, checking to make sure he's good, safe, and having fun. That feeling of wanting kids has started to grow without me even feeding it. "My nephew is playing tag with his friend by the jungle gym."

"That's nice. Is he eight or nine?"

"Nine. Yours?"

"She's six." There's a pause between us, but then she laughs. "Don't worry, she's not yours."

I wasn't worried because I never had sex without a condom other than with Lauralee this weekend. *Maybe a little worried.* I've started embracing the idea of a family with my wife, not a surprise I didn't plan on. I wouldn't walk away from any child who's part of me, but I'm glad she clarified.

She adds, "Her father and I are still together. I met him six months after the office incident." Standing, she keeps her body angled toward her daughter, and then back at me. "Are you doing well? I see you got married?"

"A lot has changed over the years. My priorities shifted in a good way. I'm happy. How about you?"

Her smile returns. "I like that for you. I'm good. Really good."

"I'm happy for you, Katie."

She signals to her daughter. "I need to go. Good seeing you again."

"You, too. Take care."

Resting my arms on my knees, I send my gaze to where Beck and his friend are still playing, having a blast by the look and sounds of it. When I sit back again, I look at the photo on my phone. The universe can't be sending a clearer message to me. It's time I listen to it.

CHAPTER 30

Baylor

"Do you need me to call 911, Uncle Baylor?"

Bent over with one hand on my knee, I gasp for air, gripping the chain-link fence to hold myself up with the other. "Funny, kid."

Dribbling the ball around me in circles doesn't help, but it does make me feel old as fuck. I'm only aging from here and barely surviving now. What am I going to be like when I finally have kids of my own? I pull myself upright, still trying to catch my breath, when I eye Beckett, ready to impart some wisdom and buy myself some recovery time. "This is the court your dad and I used to play on every Thursday after work. We'd join a pickup game."

"Do you still play?" Wonder if it was the sweating buckets looking like I'm ready to pass out or me losing the ability to breathe in air that gave it away.

Yesterday, we were all over the city visiting his old school, meeting up with his friends, and spoiling him by taking him shopping at FAO Schwartz. His parents are going to kill me if this basketball game doesn't do the job first.

Riffling through my memories, I can't remember the last time I came out here. "Not much anymore except when we play basketball out at the ranch." I know I must have had more energy, though. This kid refuels with food and is ready to go again when I need time to digest like an old man.

"We play, too. He likes free throws."

I hold my hands out for him to pass to me. When I catch the ball, I ask, "What do you like?"

"Slam-dunking."

Damn. *Unexpected.* "You can slam-dunk?" I dribble the ball in place.

"With help from Dad."

I tuck the ball under my arm and wipe the sweat off my forehead with my T-shirt. "You're going to be slam-dunking on your own one day."

"You think so?"

"I know so." I toss him the ball again and watch as he runs across the half-court to shoot. He scores, making me feel like a proud papa. What impresses me most though is his ability to transition from the city to the country and back again for this short visit with such ease. Kids are so adaptable.

His journey has been the opposite of mine. I went from the country to the city. Could I settle back into a slower way of life as easily? I'm starting to believe I can.

I join him for some more hoops, and he wears me out again. Unlike how exhausting my job is, this is only physical. Like Beck, I'm energized by all the possibilities ahead.

Paul hands me the delivery as soon as he opens the door for us. "This just came an hour ago."

"Perfect. Thanks." I open it as soon as we get into the apartment. I could have this in life on the daily. Is that what the choice is? New York or the love of my life? There's no decision to be made. I made it when I said I do. Seeing the photo only affirms what I already knew.

"Why are you and Aunt Lauralee dressed like you're married?"

Shit. What do I say? I shift my body to block little eyes, tucking the photo under the package, then look behind to find Beckett standing there. "We were pretending." Fuck me, the lies never end.

"Looks real."

Like the adult I am, I go for the distraction tactic. "What do you want for dinner?"

He stares at me like he doesn't believe a word I've said about the photo, then says, "Lasagna."

"A man after my own heart. I'll order in."

I take my first bite of breakfast on the plane while making my move on a travel-size game of checkers on the center table between Beckett and me. I already set him up to win, and he takes the bait, making a move to claim one of my checker pieces.

He says, "I've been thinking about the photo."

I choke down the food I had in my mouth, coughing to clear my throat. After a big gulp of water, I look at him with a face of indifference despite a nine-year-old making me panic inside. I thought he was going to brag about taking my piece. Guess I wasn't as smooth as I thought the other day, though. Man, kids are perceptive. Moving the eggs around with the tines of my fork, I ask, "What have you been thinking about it?"

"I think you love her." *Boom!* He just lays it out like it is. I both respect and fear this kid. He's going to be top-notch at anything he chooses to do with his life. I stare at him, unsure what to say to that. He says, "I saw my dad go through the same thing with Christine. He changed. I saw it before he did."

"How did he change?" Am I really asking this kid for life advice to see if it pertains to me? Why yes. *Yes, I am.*

He shrugs. "My mom says I get all wound up when I have too much sugar. You're different than that. I don't know the word. Christine loves the evenings on the front porch. She says it's peaceful. That's the only way I know how to describe it. Peaceful."

He sees right through me. It makes me wonder if everyone back home will and if our marriage is a secret I can keep much longer. "Is the photo real, Uncle Baylor?"

It's not even eight in the morning, too early to have such a deep conversation about my life. But since we're here, I ask, "Can you keep a secret?"

CHAPTER 31

Lauralee

THE DIAMOND CATCHES THE LIGHT, sending tiny rainbow caustics scattering across the walls of my bedroom. I only get to wear my rings when I'm alone, so I put them on as soon as I walk in the door.

Admiring the pretty on my finger, I don't know how metal and stone manage to make me feel closer to Baylor, but they do. That's the upside to wearing them every day in private, but what about outside the house? Do I dare? I can't. Not yet.

The secret remains hidden from the outside world, but we need to decide when to go public. Something to add to the growing list of things to discuss while he's visiting.

Visiting . . . I hate that his stays are only temporary. I won't pressure him to choose me or Peachtree Pass, but I still hold out hope that he will during this transition. Though I have no right since his work is in the city and I'm sure he has job offers piling up because he's so successful and now a free agent. Call me selfish, I suppose, for wanting him living here instead of only visiting me. Maybe this transition in his career can lead back to me.

A girl can dream.

I check the time before rushing to the bathroom to touch up my makeup, brush my teeth, and try to unknot my hair before he arrives. It's tempting to pour a glass of wine to calm my nervous energy. It's only been five days since I've seen him, but my excitement has me ready to burst.

I'm not sure if I want to kiss him, seduce him, or cuddle. All of it and more, like feed him. The urge I have inside to take care of this man is off the charts. And it seemed to hit out of nowhere. But my gut tells me it started the moment he said I do. I was done for—heart and soul—wild about him.

A knock has me running to the door. As soon as I pull it open, I'm captured in his arms, my lips pressed to his, and he kicks the door closed. Before I know it, we're moving toward the bedroom. Guess the decision has been made.

He drops me on the bed, his gaze traveling from mine to my chest, and then lower as he unbuttons his shirt. I lie there grinning up at him. Letting my gaze dip to his midsection, I meet his eyes again, and ask, "Happy to see me, stud?"

"You could say that." Tugging his jeans down, he asks, "Are you going to get undressed, or want me to do it?"

"I was hoping—" Another knock on the door starts me upright.

Baylor pulls his jeans back up, buttoning the top when he whispers, "Who is that?"

"I don't know," I whisper, moving to the bedroom doorway. "Hello?"

"Honey, it's me, Mom."

My mouth drops open as I turn back to him. He scrambles to scoop up his clothes as I wave him to hide in the bathroom. "Be right there, Mom." I look back at him, and silently plead, "Please tell me you locked the door."

"Nope." He hustles into the bathroom as I move to answer my mom.

Running my hands over my cheeks, I clear any flyaways, then pull the door open. "Hi, what brings you by?"

She looks so happy to see me standing on the patio that I feel bad for not offering to let her in. "I was heading over to Margaret's and decided to bring by the mail that collected at the house while you were gone in Austin." She hands me the stack, and then asks, "Not letting me in? I was hoping to use the bathroom."

I keep the door solid in my hand, not budging a millimeter. "Oh gosh," I start, my mind going blank. And then the worst idea naturally comes to mind. "My stomach was really upset when I got in from work. You don't want to go in there."

"Oh no." Her head tilts as her eyebrows peak in despair. "I can make you some soup if you'd like. It will just take me a quick trip to the grocery store."

I laugh. "Nothing is quick out here in the middle of nowhere."

"True, but I'm happy to do it for you." She peers over my shoulder, and for a brief second in time, I imagine she sees Baylor.

I shift my weight to the other foot to block her view. When her eyes return to me, I say, "No. No. It's fine. I feel better already."

Raising the back of her hand to my forehead, she says, "You're a little warm and your cheeks are flushed." If she only knew why. "Keep an eye on your temperature and call me if you need anything."

Throwing an arm wide, I squeak, "Good as new, and you

know I will." *That's not obvious.* I'm the worst actress ever. I rest my cheek against the edge of the door and smile for her, though it comes naturally. "Thank you. And there's always the bathroom downstairs in the shop."

"Yes. I'll stop in before I leave." Just when I think it's all settled, she sighs softly, and lowers her voice. "If you ever want to talk to me, I'm always here for you."

Not sure where this came from, but I feel exposed under her gentle gaze, like she can see right through me. I give her a hug. "I know, Mom." When I step back inside, I say, "Thanks for bringing the mail, too. Saved me a trip."

"Seems you're living here now when it's not rented out, and it was on the way." She starts down the stairs and adds, "Love you."

"Love you." I close the door and lock it behind me, inhaling deep relief into my lungs. Exhaling, I call out, "Coast is clear."

Baylor comes out of the bathroom not disappointing me one bit that his shirt never seemed to make it on over his muscular torso. I want to lick those abs and bite his shoulder. Is that normal? Probably not, but I don't care. He makes me want to do all kinds of things I never saw myself doing, like secretly getting married. Though I always throw the caveat of the loan in there to make excuses to myself. Deep down, it may have been the driving force, but my "I do" was for me.

Walking over to the peninsula, I drop the mail on the counter. "We need to figure out what we're doing when it comes to others knowing about us."

Suddenly looking sheepish, he says, "I do need to confess something."

"Do I need to sit down for this?"

"I hope not. I told someone about our secret."

I grip the counter for support. "Our secret that we're married?"

Baylor comes to me, taking me by the waist and swaying me back and forth. So innocent, but I know his game is to butter me up. "He knew. I could have lied, but I think he'll keep the secret. He promised me he would."

"Who's he?" I point my finger at him and poke him in the chest. "If you tell me Tagger—"

"Beckett."

"Beckett?" I lower my hand, hooking my finger into his belt loop. "What do you mean, he knew?"

His shoulders hang high before he drops them back into place. "I don't know. The kid saw right through me with his super senses. He asked me point blank on the plane this morning. I could have lied, but I really think he already knew."

My heart kind of melts. I love Beckett and his intuition. It makes me wonder what he saw in Baylor that tipped him off. I might never know the answer to that, so I ask, "What did he say when you told him?"

"He said he was happy that we're happy together."

"That's so sweet." I huff and then hug him. "It's hard to be mad about that. I just hope he keeps the secret until we're ready to share."

"Which is?"

I giggle under his ticklish kisses. "Something else we need to talk about before you leave again."

His spine straightens, and he grins. "Hold that thought. I need to get something from the car. I think it's going to make you very happy. I pray to fuck it does."

"I'm conflicted on the praying to fuck. Is that a good thing?"

Walking to the door, he says, "Yes. It's a good thing. I'll be right back. I have something for you."

I lean against the counter and watch him head out. "I love presents. Hey, you going shirtless?"

"I'm giving anyone spying on us a show."

He's ridiculous. His heavy steps rattle the staircase outside as he rushes down to the parking lot. I turn to the mail to sort through it, but stop on the third letter. "Way to ruin my day." The property management company's return address is bolded in the corner and the envelope is stamped with the word reminder, as if I needed one. It's what I worry about most of my day.

I rip it and open the letter inside just to further irritate myself. Scanning over it, I see it's the same thing I already know. Decision due. Ludicrous rent increase. Sign here. The same as all the emails that Josten guy has sent. Though admittedly, I haven't received one this week, which is odd, considering how frequently he was emailing prior.

Does he really think I'm going to just sign this? He's a fool. This isn't even the full agreement. I'm sure some buried clauses won't benefit me in there, and he just wants me to sign my rights away without a care. I scowl when I see his signature and the management company bolded under his name again. But then I catch a phrase I overlooked the first time. *Representing Greene Ventures.*

The print under it is small, but it's legible. I wrap my arm around my waist and take a deep breath as I study it closer.

Greene Ventures.

Everything from the county to the family to my new last name is spelled the same. I'm used to seeing and hearing it all the time in Peachtree Pass, but that's an odd coincidence.

New York, New York.

There are millions of companies in that city. It's huge. This doesn't confirm anything. It also doesn't deny it.

The phone number listed.

I can't excuse that away when I know it by heart. Baylor. Why would Baylor's number be listed as the contact number? Unless it is.

Dropping the paper on the counter, I jump when Baylor returns. "I have two surprises . . ." he says, but I don't hear the rest.

My gaze lowers to the letter again. Does he own . . .? No. He wouldn't do that. Why would he trick me into marrying him? That makes no sense. It was my plan. He was just going along with it.

"Shortcake?" My gaze lifts, and I turn around with my hands gripping the edge of the counter. He says, "I have something for you."

My gaze travels to the manila envelope he's holding up, but my mind is still on the letter behind me. Shooting him a glare, I stand tall, and ask, "Do you own this shopping center?"

CHAPTER 32

Baylor

"Why do you ask that?" Feigning innocence was never a strong suit. Although it feels justified since I walked out of the sunshine and right into the dark of a situation. I'm going to need some guidance to find my way out.

With her arms crossed over her chest, Lauralee's fingers dig into her skin, whitening the tips. This isn't looking good for me. "Baylor, what have you done?"

I foolishly glance at the door like I entered the wrong apartment. "I was gone for two minutes. What did I miss?"

She reaches for a letter on the stack of mail behind her and rattles it in the air. "Please tell me you aren't Greene Ventures." Her voice is steady but too controlled, as if it could go off the rails at any moment.

Fuck.

Keeping my voice as composed as I can, I set the manila envelope on the coffee table, and reply, "I can't tell you that, but I can say that—"

"You raised my rent?" Beelining to the other side of the room, she smashes the paper to my chest when she passes, putting as much distance as she can between us. Five feet wasn't enough, I guess. "You were behind this all along."

Taking the paper, I glance down, but then tell her, "I was cleaning up a mess I didn't intend to happen—"

"Everything is always good intentions with you, isn't it? Yet I'm always on the negative receiving end of it."

"It seems that way, but it's not plan—"

"My God, Baylor. Where does it end?" she shouts, the words cutting like a razor.

I take a breath, but it doesn't calm my heart thudding in my chest, knowing I'm in trouble here. "It was ending today. I promise. That's what I was trying to tell you." I point at the envelope on the table between us. "That's what this is. The end of it."

She takes a deep breath, but no exhale follows. Instead, her shoulders rattle with a sob that breaks my heart as much as I've broken hers. "Please, Lauralee. I promise—"

"Your promises no longer mean anything. You dole them out like candy and still expect me to believe you after breaking every one of them."

When she turns her back to me, I worry there's no changing her mind about anything other than what she's already convinced herself. But I won't give up. Not on her. *Not ever.* In my fool's heart, I still believe we can find a way back to happiness.

"I'm telling you the truth. I took my eye off the ball, thinking the company would manage the building and not make decisions they were never given permission to do. I know you don't want to hear explanations from me, but please, I beg you to give me the chance to clear this up."

She turns back abruptly, hitting me with a glare that could melt ice. "I'm not one of your clients, Baylor, or some woman you've picked up for the night." Her tongue is sharp and poised to deepen the wound, causing me to brace for what's coming next. Though I deserve to hear it. I deserve to feel the cuts. I want them if she doesn't have to go through it. She crosses her arms over her chest again as if she needs something to hold. "Your bullshit doesn't fly with me."

The accusation breaks the dam. Pointing at the floor, I grit, "I don't bullshit my clients, and no other woman interests me. Only you. It's only been you since the first time I walked through that door."

Throwing her arms up, she rolls her eyes. "Oh my god, it doesn't matter. Those women don't, but I thought I did. I'm your wife who stood with you and said I do. I betrayed myself for believing I was different." Her tears spill over the levee of her lower lids as her voice cracks. "You still chose to lie to me like I wasn't."

"I didn't lie about the rent."

"You lied about the building. You lied about the bet. If lying is your love language, I want no part of it." Her anger wanes, curling her shoulders forward as if the weight is unbearable. "I thought you cared about me."

My insides are shredded, but seeing her in so much pain rips my heart out. "I do. I care about you more than anything."

"Your actions show otherwise." Her tone turns self-righteous as she raises her chin, removing the privilege of her gaze. "What am I supposed to believe? Your words or your actions because they don't align." She starts for the bedroom, but I cut her off. I'm not going to fight with her with a door between us.

"Don't walk away with this unresolved."

"It's resolved. You made sure of it." She turns away from me, her gaze darting to the door like she's going to outmaneuver a former quarterback. But then she says, "Please move, Baylor."

Reasoning doesn't work, and the spiraling drags us further apart in this argument. I'm not leaving until we've said all there is to say. "No. I'm not letting you walk away this time."

That glare strikes like wildfire, ready to burn me to the ground. "Let me?" Her hand plants on her hip, a sign that I really fucked up this time. "Married or not, you don't get to decide what I do or don't. I don't need your permission to leave. I can walk away anytime I please."

She doesn't move. Despite the threat, she holds her ground, not showing an ounce of weakness. She's stunning in her independence, making me wonder if she'll ever let me back in. "Don't you see? That's what you do. You walk away when you feel the slightest discomfort."

"Discomfort?" She scoffs at me.

Not deterred, I say, "You leave—"

"To save myself the pain of being abandoned by you. We both know it will happen sooner or later, so I protect myself from . . ." She closes her mouth just before crossing a line we both know might be a step too far to come back from.

It doesn't need to be said out loud. Although I already know the ending, that doesn't lessen the damage done. "From me?"

The fire in her eyes doesn't burn as bright as it did, and another emotion gets its footing. It's not as harsh, but it's still not forgiving. I don't recognize who she is, and I'm starting to believe that I may not be able to save us. If we can't talk, we have nothing left to give.

Because I need to hear it, I place the final nail for her to hammer home, and ask again, "Are you protecting yourself from me, Lauralee?"

Her hand falls to her side as the other fidgets with the hem of her shirt. Shifting her weight, her eyes stay focused on the floor between us. She whispers, "I'm protecting myself from everyone." She finally looks at me. "If I leave first, I can't blame anyone else. It makes it a lot easier to sleep at night knowing I broke my own heart instead of placing the blame elsewhere."

"Who hurt you?"

"Please." Stifling a sob, she rubs her brow in a sudden motion. I think it's to hide her eyes so I don't see the tears, though I can hear them in her voice. "It's not important."

"It is to me."

"I don't want to talk about my father," she replies, raising her voice again. "You know he left me!"

"And I'm right here because I'm not him."

"You're right. He had the courtesy of walking out without a word instead of lying to me."

"You can push me away, but I'll be here through the highs and the lows. I'll be here when you finally realize I married you for love. Not a damn rental agreement or loan. I married you, Lauralee, because I'm so fucking in love with you that I can't live life without you in it." Shock overwhelms her, widening her eyes and causing her head to jut back on her neck. "And here's the kicker, Shortcake." I lean down, making sure our eyes are padlocked together, and say, "I know that's why you married me, too. Though you do a much better job of lying to yourself than you accuse me of doing." I step aside, giving her the room to make her own decision and go where she pleases, even if that means putting a door between us.

Tears saturate her pretty browns before she looks at the bedroom door like it's her savior. Her feet stay in place, though her breath staggers as she looks back at me with conflict in the lines of her forehead.

I wish I wasn't a debate to her, but I've lost her trust. I can only work to earn it back from here. *If she gives me the chance.*

I say, "I'm not going anywhere. You can push me away all you want, but I'll still be here waiting for you to return. Hoping you do one day."

Her lips part just enough to take in a bigger breath, but then she shakes her head. "What if it takes a lifetime?"

"I'll wait."

I can't handle the silence she finds comfort in. Each passing second is a painful reminder of my misdeeds and how I ruined everything. Maybe that's the point. Maybe I need to feel what I've done to make sure it never happens again. "I'm sorry." The ache is astounding, my hand covering my chest as it splits wide open. "I was doing what I thought was right. I was making an effort to correct my mistakes. I'm sorry you have to suffer because of it, because of me. I'm sorry for not talking to you sooner." I glance at the large envelope on the coffee table again. "I swear it's all in there."

Her eyes chase mine, but when they return, it's not anger I see despite it streaming through her tone earlier. It's disappointment, which makes it worse. This cycle is too vicious to break. I'm losing her. *I can feel it.*

With nowhere left to go and my own tears clouding my vision, I drop to my knees in front of her. "I don't want to lose you. I swear on my life I was fixing this mess from the moment I found out."

"Lowering the rent would have been a lot simpler because fixing one problem doesn't negate the anguish you've put me through." Impatience quickens her response, "It also doesn't explain why you married me either."

"For love," I reply, still holding on to hope like a lifeline to save us both from drowning in the pain.

"I wasn't asking for love. I was asking for a marriage to help with a loan to save my business." *Like a spear to the heart* . . . But her breathing picks up, and she struggles to control the upset in her tone. "So much damage has been done that could have been avoided. Mistakes—"

"We weren't a mistake."

Turning off her emotions as fast as a faucet, her expression turns indifferent. "I'm asking for time because I'm too tired to fight with you anymore." She releases a heavy sigh. "Please. I need time. I'm sorry if that hurts you, but I need to sort through this without the pressure of you wanting everything to be normal again. If you give me nothing else, will you give me that?"

Every fiber of my being screams to fight harder, but her own mask is fully intact and nothing I say will remove it. I'll only cause her more pain. I'm not giving up, but it's no longer about me. I need to do what's best for her. So I'll give her the time requested because *she* needs it.

There's no talking her out of the decision and I shouldn't anyway. It won't serve either of us in the end. I bow my head in defeat and move back into the bathroom to put on my shirt. Carrying my shoes and socks in hand, I return to the living room, stopping just shy of the door. I'm so tempted to look back once more, to take her in and lock the image in my memories. I don't because I also need to believe I'll see her again.

Opening the door, the sun has dipped below the tree line on the far side of the parking lot. I stand in the shadows of the tall cypress and oaks, and say, "I'll always be here for you, Shortcake."

I shut the door behind me, a barrier now between us until she removes it. Our lives and love are now in her hands. I can only pray that we find our way back together again.

CHAPTER 33

Lauralee

I sweep up the pieces of my shattered heart and toss them back into my chest, hoping somehow, someday, I can glue them back together. Until then, I sit on the couch, not sure what to do or think. I don't know how to feel anything other than numb or pain. Both are excruciating right now.

The manila envelope whispers my name, calling me to open it. But I know better than to fall for this trick. Whatever is in there will only blur the lines, and I'm already confused enough. As much as Baylor wants me to forgive him, I can't. Not yet. Not without sorting through the information of what I know and what I feel.

Maybe it's selfish, but I don't want to consider his side of the story before figuring out what's best for me. I was denied that right with my dad. I can't allow the cycle to repeat.

As the last of the day disappears, the room darkens around me. Music can't help, and the TV will only distract me. I need to lie in my feels. I tuck my hands under my cheek, but the ring scrapes across the skin. Holding up my hand, I realize even night can't break the shine it brings. I'm mad that I love these rings as much as I do.

I don't know how much they cost, the carat size, or how to insure them. I just know how they make me feel. Loved because he chose them for me. "What am I going to do?" Divorce him? Make him wait forever? Give him one more chance to make this right and promise he'll never hide anything from me again? Can he? Or is he lying to himself as well?

I want to believe him so badly that my heart aches that he might be suffering. Even when rationale tells me he should. I don't need revenge. I need him to trust me enough to share everything. That's what partners do, but he keeps me in the dark until outside light shines in, exposing another lie . . . an omission. Whatever we want to call it. They hurt the same.

Despite what happened earlier, I haven't closed the door on him yet. I can still feel him in the air around me like he's near. I don't dare check to see if the car is here, but I wouldn't be surprised if it were.

My eyes grow heavy from the exhaustion of fighting a losing battle. I give in, hoping tomorrow brings me the answers I need to map a new course, whether that be with him or traveling solo.

The sound of rain against the window drags me from sleep. I'm slow to open my eyes. I don't know the time, but my body doesn't feel like morning is on the horizon. God, I hope not. I'll be dragging all day if it is.

Lying here, I roll onto my back. Do I fight for more sleep or accept my fate that I'm wide awake? I wonder if Baylor's having more luck. I roll my eyes. He's probably sleeping like a baby without a care in the world. Irritation clusters in my chest, although my gut doesn't believe a word I say.

Deep down, I know he would never hurt me. I can't remain the consequence of the poor decisions he's making. I need to be a consideration from the start. Can he do that? Is it even possible? He's been a bachelor for so long that he's never had to consider anyone else or their feelings. I know he's trying. For me, he is. So am I expecting too much change too fast?

I put my feet down on the floor to sit up. Rubbing the corners of my eyes and wiping the sleep away, I start to wonder what part of my life I've given up for him.

He's never once asked me to give up anything and stepped in without asking when he thought I needed help. He visits more often because he knows I can't leave the shop unattended, making it harder on his schedule. He doesn't ask me to sacrifice anything for us to be together, carrying it all on his shoulders to make us work.

Dammit. Now I feel bad.

What if he was being honest? What if he didn't know about the rent increase? Or . . . I pause, not sure I'm ready to accept this truth. I say it anyway. "What if he married me for love?" What if he married me without strings attached? Would he have truly stood in the courthouse to exchange I dos with no other intentions but to love me forever?

Time is making me feel worse instead of better.

I get up and get a glass of water. Standing at the sink, I drink, hoping it keeps the headache I'm getting at bay. When I lower the glass, my gaze goes to the coffee table and that large envelope he left behind, which has the answers he said I'm looking for.

I take another sip, debating if I even want to open that can of worms. What if it just upsets me more? Setting the glass down, I take a chance, praying I won't be more disappointed.

Grabbing the envelope, I switch on the small lamp next to the TV, then slide down the wall between the door and the TV stand. With my butt planted firmly on the floor, I bend the brads and lift the flap. I dig my hand inside and pull out one of the papers. A photo.

A sob escapes the moment I turn it over and see us from our wedding day. The image blurs through the watery tears as they collect on my eyelashes. I blink to clear them, but they decide to fall down my cheeks instead. Staring at the photo, I'm left without words, and any lingering anger dissipates.

This is the moment I felt closest to him. Not during the vows, though those will always hold a special place in my heart. Not when we kissed. Not even the world of possibilities I felt when we were running down the courthouse steps.

It was at this moment that I knew he was my soulmate.

The good.

The bad.

The ugly.

The beautiful.

All of it tied in a neat package of heart and flowers, love and commitment. I knew standing next to him that no matter what life threw at us, he'd love me through it. And I'd love him no matter what.

I'm not asking for more than he can give, but I won't accept less.

I set the photo on top of the envelope beside my legs and reach up. Turning the knob, I send him falling flat on his back next to me when the door releases. "Ow!"

Rain sprays from his soaked body. Rushing to my knees, I bend over him, a breath away, inspecting for any damage. "Are you okay?"

He rubs the back of his head. "Not sure. Am I still in hell?"

I smile before remembering I'm supposed to be mad at him. "Not sure but you're out of the doghouse. For now. Why are you still out there when it's pouring rain? Trying to get sick and leave me widowed?"

He grins, resting his head on the floor and staring at me. "Truth?"

Sitting back on my knees, I warn him with a raised brow. "It better be."

Smart enough to take me seriously, he replies, "I fell asleep leaning against the door. The rain woke me up about forty-five minutes ago."

"But you stayed instead of getting in your car or driving to the ranch?" I start to stand, picking up the papers and photo so they don't get ruined, and set them back on the coffee table. Turning back to him, I offer him a hand up.

"I told you I'd wait." He takes hold of my hand, and for a split second, I think he's going to pull me to him. He doesn't, and though I'm relieved since I don't want to be soaked by the water puddling around him or his wet hair and clothes, a bit of disappointment also shoots through my veins. "I wasn't going to break that promise after everything else."

When he stands, my heartbeat quickens just like it always does for him. He asks, "How did you know I was outside the door?"

"I didn't. But I felt like you might be, so I took a chance." Distracted by the way his wet shirt clings to the muscles in his chest and wraps around his biceps, I say, "I'll get you a towel."

I get two and take two seconds to catch my breath. Am I ready to forgive him? Or am I only open to hearing him out? I feel caught between the two, so I head back out instead of standing in the bathroom, overanalyzing the situation. "Here you go," I say, handing him one while I bend to dry the floor.

"Thanks."

I leave the towel down to absorb any rain I missed, then return to the kitchen for another sip of water as cover to shamelessly ogle him from the darker recesses of the apartment like a total creeper. But shame doesn't infiltrate my body. I have a right to appreciate my husband all I want.

It's not giving in if I want this to work. And as much as I am madly attracted to this man, his actions will win my heart back. "I saw the photo."

"It's great, right?" His smile is heartfelt, giving me the comfort I felt standing next to him when the picture was taken.

"It is. I love it."

"Me, too," he adds quietly.

"I—"

"I—"

We both start but laugh easily about it. I say, "You go first."

"No, it's okay. You can go first."

Leaning my hips against the counter, I look at him, wanting to see the worst in him, but I can't find it. "I can't take any more lies, not even by omission. So if you have something else hidden from me or other secrets, fess up now."

"There's nothing else." He stands there looking at me with that handsome face and his heart on his sleeve. "Except—"

"Oh God." I squeeze the glass in my hand, bracing myself. "What now?"

"I was going to tell you tonight."

Setting the glass down, I throw out my arms in defeat. "Now's as good a time as ever."

"I was going to surprise you, but I think it's best if I don't." I wait eagerly but try to act casual like I'm unshakable at this point. "There's a piece of property, the one we stopped at that time when Deputy McCall pulled up behind us."

Crossing my arms over my chest, I ask, "Have you already purchased it?"

"No. I wanted your thoughts on it first since it would be yours as well."

I want to hate him, but I can't. "What do you mean as well?"

"You're my wife," he says, his voice low and quieter as if I'm sentencing him to a hard judgment. Life sentence might work better. Till death do us part. We didn't say those vows, but it was in my heart. I'm not giving up on him either. "I want to know where you'd be happiest. Any house you want, I'll build on the land. If you don't like that property—"

"I love that property. It's beautiful. Peaceful. It's closer to the ranch and not far from the shop."

"Less than five miles from Peaches." He looks shy under the confession. "I checked it the last time I was in town."

How? Why? "You did that before we were married?"

"Before you came to New York."

My heart isn't a traitor when it starts racing for him. It knows where it belongs. "You were planning our future together before we even knew we had one." I've been so blind to the lengths he's been taking for us, placing the pieces carefully down before each step we take. And here I was just enjoying the incredible sex.

"I knew, Shortcake. I knew all along. I was just waiting for you to catch up."

My throat thickens when I tear up. I laugh, wiping at the corner of my eye, almost embarrassed. "I'm surprised I have any tears left."

"Are they sad?" The worry in his tone has me coming around the counter.

"No." I need to be close to him. If not in his arms, in his personal space. Reaching forward, his hand meets mine in the middle. "They're happy." Why am I wasting time when I know how I want this to end? *Screw it.* I throw my arms around his middle and embrace him with all that I am. Resting my cheek on his chest, hearing his heart beating just for me, I'm grateful to have this chance. I'm not going to lose it.

His arms are strong, holding me like he was never going to have the opportunity again. Placing a kiss on my head, he whispers, "I'm sorry. I'll never hurt you again."

The pain that was raw, the wounds that I had, start healing from those simple words. Tilting up to look into his eyes, I say, "I forgive you on three conditions."

"Three? Give 'em to me."

"No more secrets. No more surprises." I rest my hand on his chest, and add, "What's mine is yours—"

"And everything I have is yours to own, including my heart, baby. I'll never let you down again."

Looking into those blue eyes I adore, I believe him.

"Wait," I say, "I have one more condition."

"Anything."

"No more hiding we're together."

His right cheek pops into a smirk, and he rubs his thumb over his bottom lip and then mine. "I've been waiting my whole life for this."

I laugh again, the feeling inspiring easier breathing and my body to relax. "And by whole life, you mean last Friday?"

"No, I mean since my mom showed me the photo of you as Miss Peach Festival. You were the most beautiful woman I'd ever seen. And I'd been to college, so that's saying something." His eyes light up as if he has too much to tell me and not enough time.

I can't restrain my own grin from growing. "That sure is saying something. I guess we can say that your mom knew all along."

"She sure did. It just took me a few years to catch on, but when I did, I knew you were the one."

Glancing over from the driver's seat, he asks, "What made you change your mind and open that door?"

I waggle my eyebrows and giggle. "Being shirtless didn't hurt your case."

"I'll remember that."

"Truth?" I ask, mimicking him from earlier.

"It better be." See? He remembers as well. I love that we can turn this around from something negative to enjoy in our own special way.

Leaning my head back on the seat, I soften my smile as I get emotional over it. Though tears don't come this time, it hits the same. "It was the photo. The photo of us at the courthouse. I saw it and realized you were right. When we stood together last Friday in the judge's office, we were there because we loved each other. I couldn't deny that I would have married you even if there were no inconveniences pushing us to do it." I reach over and rest my hand on his leg. His hand finds my lap but travels over, slipping between my thighs to land. If we weren't already pulling into my mom's driveway . . . the things I would do to this man.

"I love you, Baylor."

"I love you, too." He leans over and kisses me. Sitting back, he asks, "You ready to do this?" I nod, still so unsure how to break the news to her. "I'm going to let you lead."

I burst out laughing as I pop the door open. "Are you scared of my mom?"

"Not usually, but I also hadn't married her daughter without prior knowledge either."

"That's fair." We shut the doors and walk to the front of the house together. "I'll lead."

I knock before opening the door as if I don't still technically live here. "Mom?" We scoot inside, and he shuts the door behind us.

"In the kitchen, honey."

I glance back at Baylor, who cringes, which makes me giggle. "It's going to be fine," I whisper. "Come on."

We walk into the living room to find her cooking at the stove. "Will you be eating here—Baylor?" She smiles when she sees us. "I didn't know you were bringing company. I didn't know you were coming over at all." She wipes her hands on her apron. "I can make more for the three of us?"

"No, it's okay, Mom. We're not staying long."

"Heading to the ranch?"

Baylor replies, "It's our next stop. You should come out sometime. I know my dad would love to see you again."

"That would be nice. I can bring strawberry shortcake since you said they love them so much."

I see Baylor trying his hardest not to laugh. No way does Mom ever need to know that inside joke. Tapping his foot with mine, he gets the message.

Looking between us, she asks, "What brings you by?"

My mind goes blank. How do I start this without her ending up hurt for not being invited. Baylor rubs my shoulder, which is not lost on my mom. "I think what Sh— Lauralee is trying to say is—"

"You eloped and got married?" With a knowing smile, she says, "I knew you were in New York."

"How?" I ask, resting my forearms on the tall bar between us.

"Because one of the friends you were supposedly staying with in Austin came home for the weekend to visit her folks in the next town over. She was buying some cobbler to surprise them with."

"Ah. Well, I guess I'm not so sneaky."

She rests her hands on the edge of the counter, and says, "You weren't in high school either."

"Wow, way to call me out like that."

Baylor chuckles. At least he thinks it's funny.

But then my mom says, "I also saw the rings on your finger when I stopped by earlier. It's hard to miss that many diamonds sparkling on your hand." I didn't even think about hiding them when she came by. They're just a part of who I am now. Looking at Baylor, she smiles. "You did really well."

"Thank you, Peaches. We also got married on the spur of the moment. We would have had you there if it were planned."

"Does your family know?"

"No, we wanted to stop by here first."

Coming around the counter, she holds her arms out for me. "I appreciate that." She hugs me. I close my eyes, appreciating everything she's done for me to get me to this point in life. I know how things will change for all of us. I know it will be for the better, but it's still kind of sad to be leaving your childhood behind, even at twenty-nine. "I'm also happy for you both." She turns to Baylor, and they embrace. "I figured you two haven't been together long, but I could see the change in my daughter. The joy you've brought her."

"I love you, Mom." I give her another quick hug before adding, "We need to go break the news to the others."

"I love you, honey." Pointing at Baylor, she fake scowls. "Take care of my girl."

He slips his hand around mine, bringing it to his chest to hold over his heart. "It will be my greatest honor."

My phone vibrates in my back pocket, surprising me. I reach for it just as Baylor reaches for his. When I look at the text from Christine, it reads: I'm having my baby.

"Oh my God—"

"My sister's gone into labor." His eyes fasten to mine. "Detour to the hospital?"

CHAPTER 34

Baylor

I MISSED my niece's birth. I'm not missing this one.

Niece or nephew, I don't care. Healthy and safe are all that matters. Same for my sister. I'm glad I can be here. When we walk in, my dad stands at the edge of the waiting room holding hands with Daisy while Beckett sits nearby playing on his gaming device.

Lauralee and I had held hands until we came around the corner in sight of the entrance. We agreed now was not the time to break our news. We'd rather the family focus on Christine and the baby. "Hey, Dad, how are they?" I ask on approach.

"Last I heard, good heart rates for both, and she was going to start pushing." He checks his watch. "That was about fifteen minutes ago."

Daisy raises her hands in the air. "Bay Bay."

I lift her, settling her on my side, before I kiss her chubby little cheek. "How are you, Daisy girl?"

She giggles and starts blowing raspberries in the air.

I say, "Hey, Beck, you doing okay?"

"Bored," he replies, not looking up from his game.

My dad says, "If it gets too late, I'll take them home and get them to bed."

Lauralee tucks strands of hair behind her ear, and says, "I can do that, so the family can be together." She brushes against my side as she moves closer to huddle in. "I've sat with them many times. I know their bedtime routine."

"Thanks. I'd like to be here when my next grandkid is born. Tagger's folks are on their way." My dad adds, "I wish Griffin could be here. It'd be nice to have the family together again."

Lauralee takes Daisy from me, anchoring our niece on her hip and tickling her tummy. I move closer to my dad, lowering my voice to ask, "Have you heard from him lately?"

"A month or so ago. He's hard to pinpoint on a map, but said he'd be back in Texas soon to visit."

Crossing my arms over my chest, I think about my brother and what drove him away. Same as me, I suppose. Feeling like Peachtree Pass wasn't home once my mom passed. That took me years and talking to my sister to get over. Now, I'm ready to return for good. My gaze tracks over to my wife, who's found a book to read to Daisy.

She's a natural caregiver. Lord knows she takes care of me and keeps me on my toes. I'm pretty sure she would say I do that last part to her as well. We still have plenty to talk about and more details to work through, but I can't wait to start life with her.

I say, "If we can get him to stay longer than a few hours, we might be able to talk some sense into him."

"He once told me he has a traveler's soul." My dad eyes me. "I'm not sure what that means. Sounds spiritual, and you know I've lost my way with the new paths the younger folks follow these days."

I chuckle. "I don't think it's that deep, Dad." I look down the hall when I hear a commotion. Nurses are whispering, so I'm glad to see smiles on their faces, rather than the opposite. When I turn back, I say, "Griff just likes to travel, and since he no longer plays baseball, he's free to do what he wants. He's choosing to enjoy life. Nothing wrong with that when you have the money to support it. I'll text him tomorrow to let him know he has a new niece or nephew and see what he says."

"See if you can get an answer about coming home for Christmas. He told me he can't commit this far out. That was in June, around the time of the festival, when I asked." My dad worries about my brother more than he should have to. We all do to some extent. None of us hear from him as much as we'd like, but he's a grown man who can make his own choices.

"I'll try my best. I think this will take a while. Let's grab a seat."

He grips my shoulder, giving it a squeeze. Thomas Greene is an old cowboy who still hides most of his emotions, but every so often, he lets you know how he feels in quieter ways. I glance over and spot a proud dad grin on his face. More reserved, but that's just him.

His hand falls back to his side, and his gaze travels back to a TV we can't hear from where we're standing. "You got your smarts from your mama, Baylor. All you kids did. She'd be proud of how well you've done, son."

I would have reacted differently to that statement a few years back. The grief from her death would have consumed me for days, and I probably would have taken it out on everyone else around me.

Now I grieve because she'll never get to meet her grandkids. She'll never get to hold the kids I'll have one day. I find relief that she met my wife, even if she didn't know back then, though I'm not fully convinced she didn't.

Parts of me will never heal, but when I set aside some of the anger from her being stolen away from us, I know she's with me. Rediscovering the car makes me feel closer to her again. I can only imagine how driving it will be. The breeze that comforted me on the courthouse steps affirmed I was making the right decision. After all these years, I realized that Mom made me take notice of Lauralee Knot. It wasn't a grand production or anything. Just taking a moment when we were in the living room alone to show me the photo now feels like a sign I never picked up on prior. I didn't need signs back then. I had her.

Now I have Lauralee in my life, and as my wife, and I know my mom is probably thrilled that her subtle matchmaking played out the way it was planned.

My dad is no slouch despite the old jeans and scuffed-up boots. He can fix anything, except apparently that bum knee of his. But there are doctors for that. "How's the knee healing?"

He looks down as if he'd forgotten about it. "I'm almost as good as new."

I'm not taking his word for it quite yet since he's been known to hide his weaknesses, a mask of sorts, the same way we were raised. Lauralee knew what she was doing when she expected more from me. I'll consider it growth that we can talk about anything, including our feelings. That's definitely not how I was raised. "That's good. You've been standing around long enough, though. Let's grab a seat."

We settle in for the long haul just as Tagger's parents arrive. "Did we miss anything?"

"Just on time," I reply, hugging his mom.

Two hours later, Daisy has fallen asleep on my dad's shoulder and Beckett hasn't said two words to me, though he's been talking Lauralee's ear off. I catch some keywords like caterpillar, excavator, and tractor. I'm sensing a theme. Even though the conversation involves large equipment, Lauralee looks fully invested.

Another hour passes before she comes to sit next to me. "I think I should consider taking the kids home. I was going to see if the nurses can update us first."

"I'll go with you."

We walk together out of the waiting room to the nurses' station. The urge to hold her hand is strong, but I refrain, starting to let annoyance get the better of me. We finally make the decision to share the amazing news and are sidelined. For a good reason, but I still want to get it out in the open so I can hold my wife's hand. When I glance at her, she says, "I know. Soon."

At the station, I ask, "Are there any updates for Christine Grange? She's in labor."

The nurse adjusts her glasses and types on her keyboard. "Let me check for you." When she looks back up, she smiles. "Looks like the baby has been delivered. The baby is doing well. The doctor will be out shortly."

"How's my sister?"

"She's doing well and is in recovery."

"That's good. Thank you."

Rubbing my back, Lauralee looks up at me. "We have a new baby in the family," she says, her joy overflowing through the words. I don't think she's even aware of her hand being on me, but I'm not going to tell her either. It comes so naturally for us to touch and connect when we want to, and I fucking need it.

"It's an exciting time." While we return to the waiting area, I say, "I think we should keep the kids here. Chris and Tag will want them to meet the baby."

"I agree. I'll try to keep Beckett up, though we lost Daisy to sleep hours ago."

Just as we reach the family, I hear, "It's a girl." Lauralee and I turn around to see Tagger coming toward us with an impossibly big grin on his face. "We have another little girl."

"Aw. That's such wonderful news," Lauralee says, hugging him. "Congratulations."

He works his way over to us, where we do the handshake we've done since we were preteens, but I tug him in for a good pat on the back as well. "Congrats, brother."

"Thanks. Your sister did amazing." Turning to my dad, he says, "Pris and the baby are doing great. Healthy and happy."

My dad stands to shake his hand. Lauralee takes Daisy to sit with her so she can keep sleeping. Embracing his son-in-law, my dad gives Tagger the old back pat like I did, and says, "Congrats. I can't wait to meet my new granddaughter. Do you have a name?"

"Yeah. It's perfect for her, but I'll let your daughter share the news. I know she'll want to be a part of it."

Since we're sticking around to meet the new baby, Dad and Beckett get snacks and drinks for everyone from the vending machines. It's needed since I know Lauralee and I missed dinner.

But Tagger came and collected the kids as soon as they got back. My dad went in shortly after, and when he left, redder in the face than when he entered—his emotions getting the best of him, Tagger's parents were taken in.

The kids and my dad go home since it's the middle of the night. The hospital is quieter, and I'm not upset about spending time alone with my wife. I just wish it were at the apartment so I could appreciate her properly, and all over, inch by beautiful inch.

Lauralee finishes the last Funyon from the small bag, then shoots me a hard glare.

Cocking a brow since I have no idea how I screwed up this time, I ask, "What?"

"Why'd you let me eat that? Now I feel guilty."

"Why wouldn't I let you eat that?" I lean and lower my voice. "Also, wasn't it you who told me I don't have a say in what you do and don't do?"

With an irritation wrapped in her eye roll, she replies, "That was when it pertained to you. This is about me and devouring a bag of chips like I've not eaten in—"

"In ten hours? You probably haven't." I gently nudge her elbow resting on the arm of the chair. "I know you don't take enough time to eat like you should when working. We missed dinner, so you don't need to feel guilty."

She sits back and sighs before sipping on a bottle of water. "My stomach has been upset."

"That's not good. Can I get you something to help it feel better?"

Reaching over, she strokes the back of my head and trails her nails down my neck. "No. It's fine. It'll pass." She pulls her hand back to her lap, then looks down the hall and back at me. "I have a feeling you'll get to meet the baby soon anyway."

"You will, too. You were family to her even before we got married."

"You don't think she'll be upset?"

"Christine will be upset that it was kept from her. I don't

think we can blame her for that, but otherwise, I know she'll be thrilled that you're officially a Greene." It's tempting to kiss her. I hate that I can't.

Tagger appears in the hall and nods us over. "Ready?" he asks, the smile permanently plastered on his face.

Lauralee is giddy. "So ready."

I say, "You keep grinning like that, and it's going to stick."

He chuckles. "I'm okay with that." Leading us down the corridor, he stops outside the door and holds it open. "Go on in."

Christine looks over from where her eyes had been on the baby in the hospital bassinet and smiles when she sees us. Her lids hang lower, and her hair is pulled back in a knot on her head.

Lauralee rushes to her, and they embrace with gentleness. "I'm already crying," Lauralee says, and briefly peeks over at the baby. "How are you feeling? Can I get you anything to make you more comfortable?"

"I'm good."

I come around, brushing against Lauralee's side, and poke my sister's leg. "You doing alright, sis?"

She laughs. "Yes, big brother." She looks at the baby, and says, "Go meet your new niece."

I walk around, already smiling. The proud dad moves to the other side of the baby and rubs his wife's shoulder. Pink and tiny and so perfect, she's bundled tight in a blanket. I ask, "What's her name?" and then bend to read the card attached to the front of the clear bed. It hits quick . . . Leaning down, I drop my head and rub my eyes since something's gotten in them.

"Are you crying, Baylor?" My sister's voice is barely above a whisper as she rubs my shoulder.

I clear my throat and then stand back up. "No, just got a

frog in my throat," I lie through my teeth, but no one falls for it. They're kind enough not to mention it either.

Lauralee is still on the other side of the bed when she says, "It's okay, Baylor."

Catching the others looking between us, I ask, "Can I hold her?"

Tagger reaches down to pick up his baby girl. He kisses her forehead and then comes around to hand her to me. "She's so tiny," I say, taking her into my hands because she's not much bigger. I adjust her in my arms, already loving this girl so much. "Welcome to the world, Julie Ann."

"Julie Ann?" Lauralee says, in a quieter excitement fitting the room as she comes around behind me and peeks at the baby. "Aw, I love that you named her after your mom. What a treasure."

I felt signs of moving toward the notion of having kids, but it's holding this little one while my wife is leaning against me that seals the deal. I want this. I want this with her so badly. I can wait for her to decide, but I hope we're on the same page.

She asks, "May I hold her?"

"Of course," Tagger replies.

I shift to place little Julie Ann in the cradle of her arms, caught by the tightening in my chest when her eyes shine with so much love for this baby. She's always been beautiful, but she's stealing my breath at this moment. When she glances up at me, her smile filled to the brim with overwhelming happiness as tears fill the corners, words aren't shared. They aren't needed. She and I are family now. That *I do* wasn't just a connection between the two of us. It was a vow for the family we'll create together.

.

CHAPTER 35

Lauralee

"I'm exhausted." After dragging myself into the apartment at 2 a.m., I hang the key on the hook and set my purse on the kitchen counter. "I can't wait to go to bed."

"Is that code for I don't want to have sex?"

I shoot Baylor a look, but I can't hold it for more than a second without laughing. "Of course not."

"That's my girl." He kicks off his shoes and strips out of his clothes while entering the bedroom.

Connecting physically becomes the foreplay to lying together afterward. It's my favorite part. When he has his arms around me, I don't mind letting the hours tick slowly by. Despite thinking I'd fall asleep the moment my head hit the pillow, I find contentment in listening to his steady breathing. He's comfort to my soul wrapped in a big, sexy package.

But I am thirsty, so I sneak out of bed and into the kitchen. Standing in front of the sink after filling my glass with water, I look at this tiny apartment and think about the purpose in which I built it. It was supposed to be rented out, but I've only had one reservation come of it—Baylor's. I've taken over, craving a freedom I didn't realize I was so desperately needing.

Spying the photo, I pick it up off the coffee table and study it again. Though I'll never forget that day or the feeling I had when it was taken, it needs to be framed. I want to see it every day when I wake up and one last time before bed.

I set it back down, eyeing the envelope that I never opened after discovering the photo. Sitting on the edge of the couch, I pull the papers out of it. I don't know what to make of this thick stack of legal documents. Baylor never said what it was. He only said he was fixing this mess. It had to do something with the lease or the management company, but what mess exactly? There were a few...

Since it's too dark to read the fine print, I switch on the small lamp by the TV and sit on the floor nearby so the light hits the paperwork.

As requested by the client... blah, blah, blah.

Change of ownership . . . I flip the page. Greene Ventures. Lauralee Knot. I read the line again, not following the legal jargon in the bulk of the paragraph. Transfer of titles. Blah blah. My name is listed among four others, with the owner listed beside it. Owner of what?

I keep scanning until I find the address listed, not of my shop, but of the entire building, which comprises four commercial spaces, including the fifth, listed as the apartment above it. No... he didn't do that. *Did he?*

Jumping to my feet, I hurry back into the bedroom and climb into bed, facing him. "Baylor?" *No response.* "Are you awake, Baylor?" I ask, gently rocking him by the arm. He groans, but I can tell he's still asleep. "Baylor, wake up," I say in a voice higher than normal.

His eyes fly open. "What is it?" I think he's still caught between sleep and being awake.

When his eyelids begin to dip again, I hold up the papers. "What have you done?"

Popping his eyes open again, his expression is dragged down. "Fuck, what have I done now?"

"This." I rattle the papers in the air above his head. "Did you already do this, or it's not a done deal yet?"

He turns to look up, but confusion wrangles the neutral expression he had been wearing. "This being? Want to fill me in?"

"This contract transferring ownership of the building and shop, even this apartment, to me?"

"*Ah*." He rolls back to his side as understanding seeps back in. Closing his eyes, he says, "I had that drawn up for you. You'll never have to worry about rent again because you'll own it."

"With a mortgage, right?" God, how am I going to pay that?

He lifts his lids again, but I can see he's struggling to stay awake. "I bought the building outright. Even the delinquent taxes were paid in full as well. The unpaid taxes helped in the negotiation." His lips curl up at the sides even though his blink has kept his lids closed longer than they should.

My heart is jumping so hard in my chest that I can barely contain it. "Baylor?" When he opens his eyes again, I ask, "For real? This is real? This is what you were going to give me? The entire building?"

Reaching over, he runs the back of his fingers over my cheek and down the side of my neck. "Yeah, baby. It's all yours if you want it." His grin is dreamy and as sweet as this gift he's given me, enticing me to want to make love again. "I already signed it. All you have to do is sign it, too."

"I can't."

Fully awake now, he adjusts his shoulder, angling his head slightly away as he looks at me out of the corner of his eye. "Why not?" he asks, as if he can safeguard himself from bad news.

"Because there's one major mistake."

"Which is?"

"My last name isn't going to be Knot anymore. It's Greene."

I'm dragged by my hips under his body so fast that I squeak and burst into giggles. With one of his knees spreading mine as he pins my wrist to the mattress on the sides of my head, he kisses me once, but only as a tease of what's to come. "Lauralee Greene. Sounds perfect together. Like it was meant to be all along."

Wrapping my arms around his neck, I pull him closer, and whisper, "Destiny."

Lounging in the hammock, I point at the fort. "I think there should be a window on the back to see the river and on this side so they don't have to open the door to look out toward the house." I pop another piece of popcorn in my mouth and then take a sip of my water.

Baylor pokes his head out the opening where you enter the tree house. "Would you like to come up here and help build it?" He's gotten a little snippy since the beginning of August is hotter than Hades in Texas. Four days in and they've built the main hangout, but since they want a fort, the plans call for an expansion deck elevated on the roof.

Beckett and Macon are playing in the river not too far away, but Baylor is determined to finish this in the next two days so he can work on the car again. After only a few evenings with a spotlight aimed under the hood, he's not gotten more than the engine attached. It's not running in any capacity, though.

Tagger hasn't said a word about him working on it either. *Yet.* We know the bet will eventually need to be addressed. I'm thinking sooner than later.

"I'd be happy to, but I know there's not enough room for me and your ego to work inside that small space." Entertaining myself, I smirk.

"You know what, Shortcake?"

"What, stud?"

"You're looking fine enough to take for a dip in the river."

My hand stops just before tossing another piece into my mouth. Is he serious? "Is that a threat?" I chomp down again.

"It's a promise, baby." He hurries out, starting down the ladder.

Popcorn goes flying as I spin to work my way out of the captivity of the hammock. "Oh no, you don't." I finally land on my feet just as he jumps to the ground, and I start running for Christine's house. "No, Baylor!"

I don't stand a chance, and when I look back at his sexy hunk of a man all shirtless and sweaty—to die for gorgeous—my steps slow. I'm scooped into his arms and tossed over his shoulder over fake protests. "*Oh no.*" I emphasize each word and slap his ass. "What are you going to do to me?"

Swinging me around into his arms, he's already laughing. "You're a bad girl, Mrs. Greene."

I lift to bite his bottom lip and then lick it. "You take me back to that new truck of yours, and I'll show you how bad I can be." About-facing, he starts in the right direction. As much as I'd love to mess around with him in the air-conditioning of that big truck, my responsible side comes out. "We can't leave the boys at the river."

That same bottom lip is now sticking out. I kiss it just before he claims, "That's a shot of reality. Maybe I don't want kids after all if I can't fuck you anytime I please."

"Aw, we can do it later when they get bored and leave you to finish the fort yourself."

He sets me on my feet and wipes the sweat from his brow. "Remind me again why I agreed to build this."

I purposely bump into him as we head back to the building site. "Because you're a great uncle."

"Fine." He rolls his eyes. "I'll finish it."

It took three days, but Christine held a ribbon cutting for the big day. Tagger says, "It's impressive, guys." Patting Beckett's back, he asks, "Did your uncle help at all?"

Beckett eyes Baylor and grins. "He helped some."

We laugh. All of us have been out here at different times to watch and help. I pat Baylor's shoulder. "You did good."

Leaving the boys to play, we walk back with Chris and Tagger. He's carrying Daisy on his shoulders while Christine holds the baby strapped to her chest. Walking beside her, I ask, "Getting any sleep these days?"

"Some." She rubs the baby's back over the padded carrier. "It's good to have my brother back for an extended time."

I glance over at him and Tagger a few feet behind us. "Yeah, he's grown on me."

"I can tell by how much you two are hanging out lately."

This time, I keep my eyes aimed ahead as we reach the field from the woods. "Not much else to do in this town."

"So might as well do each other." She bursts out laughing.

I don't know whether to laugh or fess up. "Did you really just say that?"

She's still laughing when she replies, "I get it. There aren't many people to hang around with our age." When we reach the steps of her front porch, she stops. "We're having a summer soiree kind of dinner on Friday night."

"Fancy."

Holding the railing, she plants a foot on the bottom step. "Not that fancy and very last minute. I thought it would be a nice time to wear a pretty dress. I'll take Daisy to pick flowers we can put in our hair. Candles on the table with wildflower bouquets. The guys can clean up and look presentable again. We can invite your mom out as well. Just a big family kind of get-together."

I can already visualize it. Her front porch with a long table, cloth tails flowing in the breeze and candles lining the length of the table. So romantic. "Sounds beautiful. What can I bring?"

"Dessert as usual, if you don't mind. Maybe some that you have left at the end of the day. We'll be happy to take them off your hands so they don't go to waste."

"Friday is cheddar biscuit day, too."

Pointing a finger at me, she narrows her eyes in warning. "Don't show up without my favorite food in the world."

I laugh. "I would never."

"It's settled. How's seven thirty? It's really too hot before then."

Five o'clock in the evening really is unbearable. Using my hand, I fan myself as drips of sweat roll down my back. "That works for me. I'll invite Mom."

"No worries. I'll send her a text with the details." She

starts up the steps. "I'm going in before Julie Ann and I get overheated. Is Baylor giving you a ride home, or do you need Tagger to?"

"I'm sure Baylor will be happy to." In fact, I know he'll be happy to give me a ride. I keep that gem to myself because she and the baby don't need to hear my naughty thoughts on her brother. "See you Friday." I turn to the guys, who seem to be deep in conversation, and hold out my hands. "I'll wait in the truck. Keys?"

Baylor tosses me the key fob.

Just as I get in the truck and close the door, I punch the button and turn up the air-conditioning full blast on my face. The other door opens, and Beckett climbs in. "Hey there, where are you boys going?" Through the windshield, I spot his friend running inside the house.

"Macon's getting us lemonade, so I thought I'd wait with you." *Unexpected.*

I sit back, glancing at Baylor through the windshield as I try to cool off. "It's hot."

"Yeah." He turns to me and says, "I've kept your secret like my uncle asked me to."

I still feel like I've been exposed somehow, but it's him, and I know his heart is gold. He's also only nine. What's he going to do, extort us for a new video game to keep it a little longer? Maybe I'll just buy him one as a thank-you gift. "We both appreciate it very much. I know it's a big one to keep." We had decided to let the baby own the limelight like she deserves. It felt like it would be odd to be celebrating her birth and then instantly steal the attention away. It's been a few weeks, though, so I do think it's okay to share the news soon. I've been dying to, and the cloak-and-dagger sneaking around and pretending we're only friends is tiring.

He says, "You know you're Uncle Baylor's secret ingredient? That's what he told me."

"I don't know what that means, Beck. What's the secret ingredient?"

"It's the magic that makes something work. Grandma Grange told me it's the love put into things, like her succotash or the fort. When you care about something, it shows in everything you do."

I'm in sweetness overload and smiling ear to ear. "How did you know I'm his secret ingredient?"

There's such innocence in the way he shrugs. "He was different when I visited. Happier. Not that he wasn't, but—"

"I know what you mean."

"He had a picture of you guys. When he looked at it, Christine would call it smitten kitten, but I don't really know what she means when she says it." His brows pull together in confusion. "She called me a smitten kitten when I showed her a picture of Amy in the yearbook."

"You're not getting married, are you?" I playfully tease.

He could shake his head right off his neck if he's not careful. "No, but I'm glad you and my uncle did."

"Me, too." I reach over and wrap my arm around him in a side hug. This kid has a knack for getting right to the meat and potatoes in life, even when the adults can't. "Thank you for sharing with me."

Macon walks down the steps, spilling lemonade over the edge of the glasses. "Yeah." He shrugs again and hops out of the truck. Now that I've cooled down, I hop out too, and move to the passenger seat just as Baylor cuts in front of the truck.

When he gets situated in the driver's seat, I say, "I want to tell everyone we're married on Friday night."

His grin kind of says it all, but when he reaches over to hold my hand, he says, "Friday night it is."

CHAPTER 36

Baylor

I slip my ring on, then flex my fingers. It's weird how different it feels wearing the metal band than not. I've felt the absence of it for the past few weeks. This feels right. Though seeing the rings sparkling on my wife's hand feels amazing.

She spins in front of me with her arms out, her wedding dress as pretty as the day she got out of that car. "What do you think?"

"As gorgeous as the first time you wore it."

"I'm glad I have another opportunity to wear it. I think it's perfect for tonight. From what Christine told me, she's gone all out. She wants the setting picture perfect, *Southern Living* magazine cover ready." Coming to me, she says, "I want to enjoy the dinner, but seeing you back dressed to impress in those boots with your buckle and starched cowboy shirt is making me reconsider my plans."

I walk to the hook on the wall by the door in the bedroom and take my finest cowboy hat. Silverbelly is an odd name for a color but that's what Stetson called it when I ordered. "Wait until you see me with the hat."

As soon as I set it on my head, her eyebrows shoot up and those pretty lips of hers part. "Be still my beating heart." She throws her arms up. "Forget it. We're staying home."

Home.

It's nothing ever formally stated because it was never a place once my mom passed. It was a memory of what used to be my childhood. I didn't know what I was missing in New York until Lauralee came along. Now I feel it. I feel her in my soul because she's my home. Wherever she goes, I go.

The apartment is temporary. One day, we'll have our own homestead and family, and a house that keeps us warm in winter and cool in the summertime. For now, we'll make strides to build that future together. Tonight, we'll start with the announcement of our marriage.

Her arms are around me, and her lips brush against mine. But when she tells me she loves me, I feel whole. With a quick lick of my lips after hers leave mine, I ask, "Ready to go, Mrs. Greene?"

She hooks her arm with mine, smiling like she's the lucky one in this deal we've made. She's fooling herself. Everyone else and I know full well that I'm the one who scored in this relationship. "More than ready."

"SOMETHING TELLS ME THEY ALREADY KNOW," she says, glancing over at me when I park the truck at the house.

My family and hers are all on the porch steps waving at us. Big smiles, dressed up, and a caterer nearby. "Yeah. I'm getting the same feeling." I get out and go around to help her down from the truck. Holding her by the waist, I add, "Do you think Beckett told them?"

"No. He wouldn't." She lands on her feet, and whispers, "She said it would be nice. So maybe it's not about us at all."

"Maybe, but this feels like a setup."

There's a skip to her step as she starts toward the house. "You've outdone yourself, Chris," she says. "This is beautiful."

"The guests of honor have finally arrived," my sister says, beaming from the inside. "We didn't get to attend the wedding, but there was no way we weren't celebrating the newlyweds with a reception." She starts clapping, and everyone is quick to join in. "Congratulations, Mr. and Mrs. Greene."

My girl's cheeks are as red as tomatoes, but that smile... I hold my hand to my heart. It knocks me out. I take hold of her hand like I've been itching to in public since I got back to the Pass. Since they know, there's no use hiding it. "You were right. We weren't hiding it as well as we thought we were."

"I don't know if I was hiding at all anymore."

We're surrounded by everyone hugging and congratulating us while laughter fills the air. Beckett comes to my side and wraps his arm around me. I do the same. "Hey, buddy."

"I didn't tell anyone."

Making me grin, I say, "I knew you wouldn't. That's why I shared with you. Do you know how they figured it out?"

"Christine said she knows Lauralee too well. My dad told her that he saw you guys looking at each other all funny last week." He ducks out of the crowd before I can ask more questions. Smart kid.

My sister squeezes through to embrace me. "Aw, big

brother. I'm so happy for you. Congratulations. You couldn't have picked a better match."

"You're telling me. I'm just glad she asked me."

She steps back, shock strikes her features, widening her eyes. "She *asked* you?"

Shortcake's going to kill me for sharing that nugget of information. "It's a little more complicated than that. A story for another time, and probably her telling it is best."

That makes her laugh like it does me. Anyway, I don't want my wife kicking my ass for sharing without her here to add her own spin on the situation. "That's what sneaking around will do to ya. I know firsthand."

"Ha! You sure do."

Whacking me in the chest, she says, "Good job on the rings, by the way. Wow. They're stunning."

"Glad you approve." When she turns to Tagger, my dad sneaks in. "Hi, Dad. You mad?"

"Mad at you getting married and not telling me?" He shoos an imaginary fly away. "Nah. It's not our business, but I sensed something was different the night at the hospital. I almost asked if things had changed between you two. From friends to . . . you know, more. Seemed there was enough to keep our minds busy, though." Bringing me in for one of his famous back pats, he says, "I just know your mom is celebrating this union. She used to say you two would make a good couple. Something about opposites balancing each other out like she and I did." I didn't expect to get choked up, but sometimes we're not in control of these things. "She wasn't wrong. She made a match alright."

"She sure did."

I steal a peek of my wife kneeling in front of Daisy, who's placing a halo of flowers on her head. Daisy smiles and then shows off the one on her head. "Like Lee Lee's."

Lauralee helps her put hers back on, then gives her a hug.

A punch to my shoulder staggers me, and I shove Tagger back before he pulls me in. "Haven't you hugged me enough lately, fucker?" I joke. We step back and do the ole handshake before chuckling. It never gets old—unlike us. Though my wingman and I are still looking good as married old men.

"It was a bet, not a threat. No one said you had to get married to get the car."

I look down at the new boots he just scuffed with the tip of his. It happens. The first just hurts the most. "That's weird. I swore you said I had to marry her to win the car back."

Panic filters into his eyes. "No way."

Chuckling, I shake my head. "Dude, I didn't marry her to win a bet or the car. I married her because I love her. But I'm also taking full ownership of the vehicle."

"As you should. You went above and beyond. It's going to be hard to top this bet."

"Doesn't matter. I'm out of the betting arena. No more for me. I've learned my lesson. I'm happy, and I'm not fucking this up."

Raising his hands, he's finally giving up. "Understood. Want a beer?"

"Thought you'd have one ready for me."

"Coming right up."

I give Peaches a hug before we all sit down for dinner. It was nice to have her support from the start.

Herbs and flowers mixed in Mason jars. Twinkly lights trapped in smaller ones give a nice glow as the sun begins to set. Mom's nice dishes set the table. I haven't seen these in so long. I'm glad they're finding new use.

With wine and beer flowing, toasts are given. Even Beckett raises a glass of sweet tea and tells us he's ready for us to have a boy cousin for him to play with. I catch Lauralee's eyes when kids are mentioned throughout the evening. She even nudges at one point when she's holding Julie Ann for a bit. "How do you feel about starting a family soon, stud?"

I wrap my arm around her and kiss her temple. "No time like the present."

From across the table, my sister asks, "So I take it you're staying for good this time?"

Holding Lauralee's hand on my leg under the table, I glance at her, and reply, "Can't get rid of me now."

Chris raises a glass of water, and says, "To the happy couple. Welcome home to Peachtree Pass."

EPILOGUE

Baylor

No more masks.

No more hiding behind my past misdeeds.

I own it all, and who I used to be, and Lauralee Greene still chose to love me, flaws and all. I'm smart enough to never keep anything from her again though, not through a lie or omission. Those were the hardest lessons learned, but we found our happily ever after in the end.

I slide up her slick body and kiss her on the mouth. She purrs for me, enticing me to do it again. When our mouths part and eyes open, she pushes my sweaty hair back from my forehead, the look of love engrained in her eyes like I'm the reward instead of the sex. I love this woman more than words could ever capture. She says, "I love when you do that."

Always open to feedback, especially of the good kind, I ask, "When I do that thing with my tongue?"

"That, yes," she says, squirming as if her body remembers how fucking good it was and can't stop itself. "And when you kiss down there like you would my mouth. *Gah!* Incredible. Magical."

"Don't be shy. Go on."

"Earth-shattering..."

"Earth-shattering? I think I've outdone myself." Her laughter is my favorite sound in the world, that and hearing my name on the edge of her release. I've heard both in the past five minutes. *It's a good fucking day.*

I kiss her again because if I could spend my life doing this, I'd make it my full-time job. Since I still don't currently have one, I don't bother fighting against my fate and lean into it, deepening the kiss this time. I swallow one of her moans, savoring every part of her, and then dip my hand between her legs. "How your body reacts to me is such a fucking turn-on. Why is our sex so good, baby?"

"Because it's the first time you've ever involved your heart, my love."

There was no hesitation in her response—like she knew all along—but it hits me like a ton of bricks. And now I see it so clearly. She's right.

Lifting just enough to adjust, I position myself and then slowly push into her. Her warmth welcomes me, causing my head to dip in reaction. I force it up enough for our gazes to latch and watch as her body responds by parting her lips as her legs butterfly open and her breath catches when I thrust deeper.

Our lips brush in need before fastening together, our tongues tangling as we find our rhythm. When her heat becomes too much, I take a breath to slow things down, not wanting to rush the ending. Like a prayer, I whisper, "Lead me *knot* into temptation."

"I see what you did there." Holding on tight to me, her smile is serene, but the words lift the heavy that was building. I like the balance we've struck in our relationship. Humor has gotten us through a few messes. Our love has given us strength. "I think Greene suits me better." Tilting her head to the side to see my eyes, she asks, "What do you think?"

"I love it so fucking much." I thrust in again, sending her head back into the pillow and exposing her neck. I trail kisses down the soft column, wanting to appreciate every inch of her before the day forces us out of bed to face it.

Running her hands over my shoulders, she holds tight with a fire lit in her eyes. "Show me how much you love it."

"I'll do you one better and show you how much I love *you.*"

I show her fast like how we fell in love, and then a second time, slower how our love will endure. There was never any denying our attraction. We worked on the rest to get where we are today. Our unbreakable bond is something I'll always protect.

"I'M THINKING the house should go back there," she says, pointing at an opening among a grouping of trees. The wind is wild here in the clearing. Pulling her hair back with one hand, the skirt of her dress is whipped to one side of her body. She shadows her eyes with the other hand when she looks back at me. "That way, no one can see us from the main, but the house isn't buried too far back on the property. What do you think?"

While she was admiring the land, I was appreciating her. Who knew something so small and feisty could shift my axis upside down? So glad she did. "I'm happy if you are."

Cutting through the tall grass, she lifts on her sneakered

toes and kisses my chin. "I'm happy. Blissfully because of you. You?"

I turn her around to hold her from behind and pull her against me. Rubbing her shoulders and then lowering my arms around her waist, I never expected to find this kind of peace. "I'm happy I broke into your apartment that night."

She bursts out laughing and turns around in my arms. Receiving a poke to the chest, I catch that finger just as she says, "I knew it all along."

I kiss her finger and give her all the credit she wants. She likes to win. We're a lot alike that way, though I never mind losing to her. Even if it comes to our story and how we got re-introduced, as she likes to call it. I know the truth. She was never supposed to be there, but that little mix-up changed everything. I should probably send a thank-you gift to my sister for telling me to stay there. If I hadn't, look at the beautiful life I'd be missing.

I look down the road as two trucks carry the old house away from its original home to its new plot in Dover County. Shortcake donated it to a good cause, creating a home for people who don't have one until they land on their feet again. She even launched a program partnering with local ranches for job placement. We've joined together to reinvigorate Peachtree Pass into a bustling town again. As her husband, I'm lucky enough to watch this woman chasing her goals and making a difference in other people's lives like she did mine. I couldn't be prouder of her.

"We should go," she says, "my mom said she wants to eat at seven."

We start back to the car, but I'm dragging my feet, not really wanting to do this tonight. "I never thought I'd be going on a double date with my dad."

"I think it's sweet."

Stopping on either side of the car, I tilt my head and lean on the top edge of the windshield. "I'm telling you now, if they start kissing, I'm out. No one wants to see that."

She pulls her door open and laughs. "Let them have a little fun, Baylor."

When she tucks herself into the car, I mumble, "Yuck."

One thing that's not yuck is this sexy-as-fuck car. I take a moment to admire it in its glory—sun shining down on the fresh silver paint job, the matte black stripe down the middle, the sweet-as-hell rims, and the cherry on top is that she runs like a dream.

Though she'll never let me live it down that she sat in that barn for months reading the instructions from books she ordered so I didn't fuck it up. My words. Not hers. We made a good team all around and got the job done.

I run my fingertips along the side of the car, inspecting it like I do every time I see it. I never needed to own the ranch. Still, holding a 10 percent share is a great perk of being born a Greene. Who doesn't love making money? But this car was the one thing I always wanted, and even more so after my mom died. And every time we drive with the top down, I can imagine how much she would have loved it. I'll love it for the both of us now.

I fold myself into the driver's seat and start the car. With the fall sun hanging low in the sky, I flip my visor down to keep it out of my eyes. "Have you seen my sunglasses?"

Lauralee looks around. "No. Did you put them in the glovebox?"

"No."

"Wanna bet?"

"This is the weirdest conversation." Not sure what's gotten into her. "Want me to reach over and check?"

"Yes."

I'm confused if she's having fun by making me work for this or if she wants me between her legs. I'm hoping for the latter, giving us an excuse to miss this dinner. The bonus, I'm between her legs again. I run my hand down her thigh and drag the skirt higher until her soft skin is revealed.

My hand is smacked just before getting to the good part. "You're so easily distracted, Baylor. If we're not careful, we're going to be late." I think she's taking this a little too seriously. It's grilled chicken with the folks, not visiting dignitaries.

"Fine," I groan, popping the glovebox open to find my sunglasses that I know I didn't put in there. I never do. As soon as I pull them out, I pause with my eyes locked on a white stick in the dark space. Sunglasses are now the least of my concerns. I flop back and look to her for answers to the question posed in the silent exchange.

It's the littlest of shrugs raising her shoulders, and when they drop again, the sweetest smile shapes her lips. "We weren't careful," she says, this conversation now making a lot more sense.

I reach over to hold her hand, resting it on her lap. "We weren't trying to be."

Her gaze sharpens on mine with assurance housed inside, and a soft laugh escapes her. "No, we weren't."

Pivoting my gaze to the property where we'll be raising our children, I realize one day is sooner than I thought. It's arrived. I drop my head forward and try to wipe the moisture collecting in the corners of my eyes.

Lauralee rubs my back, and whispers, "Are you okay?"

Who am I kidding? She sees through the act. I choke down the emotions that want to overwhelm me and reach over to cup her face, kissing her and holding her to me.

When we sit back, I take her hand and briefly eye the test in the glovebox again. "You're pregnant?"

"Seems the hometown hero knocked me up." As tears that shine with happiness glisten in her eyes, she laughs. "The whole town's going to be gossiping when they find out."

Chuckling, I reply, "Let 'em. I got the girl, the life, and the dream come true. I even got the car. They could only be so fortunate." I lean over and kiss her forehead, lingering there a moment as my heart settles.

Before I can return to my side of the car, she captures my face in her hands and kisses me again. It feels needy and gentle at the same time. I can relate. When our lips part and her lashes flutter open, she looks at me the same as she did when we spoke our vows to each other, and whispers, "Thank you for choosing me."

As if there was ever a choice in the matter . . . I never stood a chance. From the moment she knocked me sideways with that pillow, I knew she was different, and the one I was supposed to be with. I used to pretend the concussion didn't play a part in that decision. But I couldn't rule it out. Now I can. I was a goner for Lauralee from that night onward.

We were always meant to be, and being together is something I'll never take for granted. "It was always only you, baby." We both sit back, a wave of peaceful relief rolling through me. When I glance over at her, she's wearing the ridiculous grin I can't wipe off my face.

"It's going to be a whole new era for us, Baylor. You ready for it?"

"I'm ready." That keeps the smile where it's supposed to be, right on that pretty face of hers.

"Want to bet?"

"Sorry, I'm not a betting man, Shortcake." Running my

fingers through the back of her hair, I smirk. "But if I were, I'd bet my life on it."

Want More? You got it!

Grab your bonus Baylor & Lauralee chapter for this story on my website: www.slscottauthor.com, Click the Bonus Tab at the top, and then use the dropdown menu to go to Bonus - Lead Me Knot

---

Small Town Frenzy is the next book in the Peachtree Pass Series.

YOU MIGHT ALSO ENJOY

Recommendations - These are books you'll enjoy reading after *Lead Me Knot in addition to other Peachtree Pass series books*. These books will grab your heart and have you falling in love along with the characters.

Read in Kindle Unlimited and Listen in Audio

Long Time Coming (if you haven't read book 1 in the Peachtree Pass series) - You met Tagger and Christine in Lead Me Knot. Now read the captivating and joyous journey as they find their way in this small town, big ranch, single dad love story. Free in Kindle Unlimited.

Read in Kindle Unlimited and Listen in Audio

Head Over Feels - Friends to lovers at its finest. The banter, the wit, the teasing, the sneaking around is so fun in this New York City love story where Bachelor of the Year is brought to his knees over the girl next door friend he's crushed on since college. Free in Kindle Unlimited.

Read in Kindle Unlimited and Listen in Audio

When I Had You - A grumpy formula race car driver meets his match in an up and coming, sunshine actress who just so happens to own a share of the racing team. Her older brothers own the other shares. This is a fun sports, single dad romance where the main characters hide their relationship not only from the paparazzi but also from their families for as long as they can... and then everything changes. Free in Kindle Unlimited.

ACKNOWLEDGMENTS

Thank you so much to this incredible team:

Kenna Rey, Content Editor
Jenny Sims, Copy Editing, Editing4Indies
Kristen Johnson, Proofreader
Andrea Johnston, Beta Reading
Cover Design: S.L. Scott
Audio Producer: Erin Spencer, One Night Stand Studios.
Narrators: Willa Jaymes & Nelson Hobbs

Thank you to my amazing Super Stars and my awesome SL Scott Books Facebook members. To those who are not only peers but also friends. I adore our friendship, support, and you!

To my husband & sons, I love you more than the universe! Thank you for your forever support and love. Love you always. XOXOX

ABOUT THE AUTHOR

Suzie loves a great view of the ocean, spicy margaritas, and spending her free time with her family and sweet dog, Ollie.

New York Times and *USA Today* Bestselling Author, S.L. Scott, writes character driven, heart-racing, and swoony romances that will leave you glued to the page. With stories ranging from witty beach reads to heart wrenching and heart healing, her stories are highly regarded as emotional, relatable, and captivating.

Her books are more than escapes for the voracious readers of today. They are journeys of the heart that always come with a happily ever after reward at the end.

Find her at: www.slscottauthor.com

Printed in Dunstable, United Kingdom